THE MAZEMASTER'S MAP

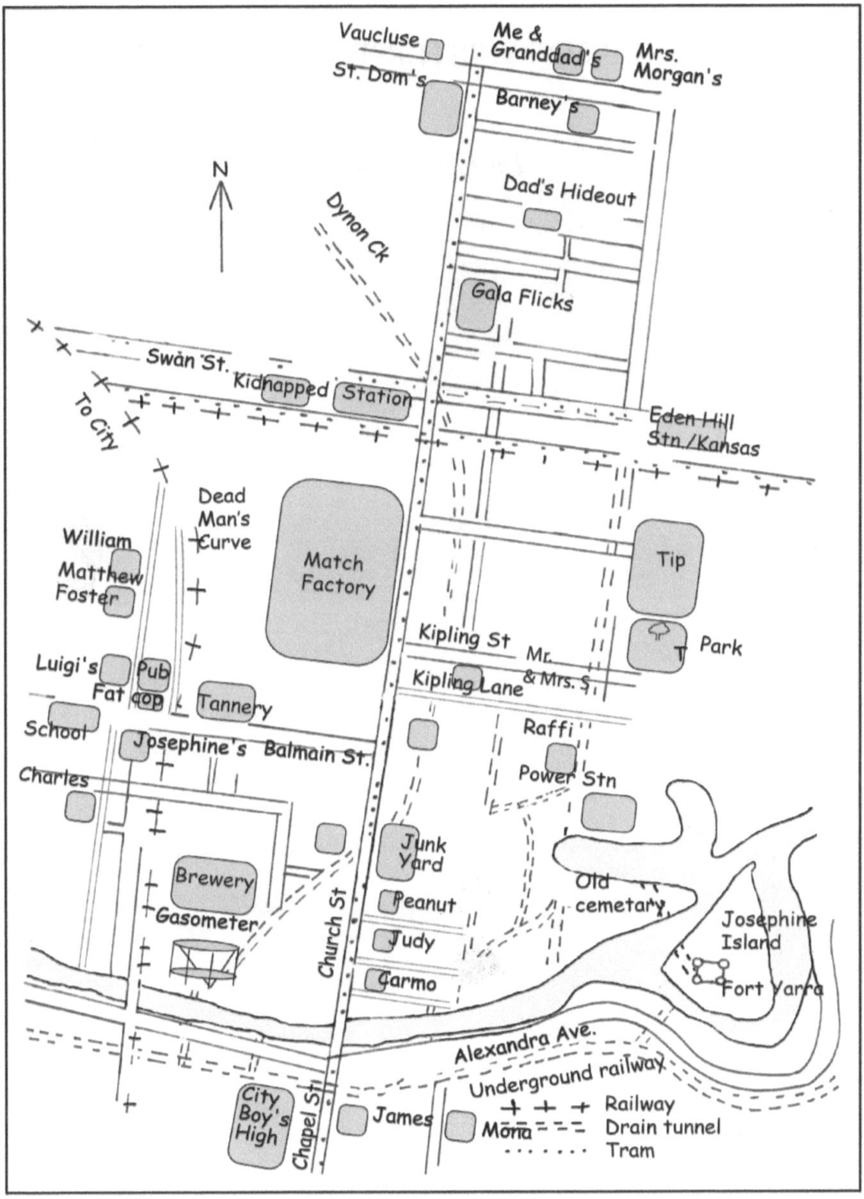

Vaucluse

Me &
Granddad's

Mrs.
Morgan's

St. Dom's

Barney's

N

Dynon Ck

Dad's Hideout

Gala Flicks

Swan St.

Kidnapped Station

Eden Hill
Stn./Kansas

To City

Dead
Man's
Curve

William

Matthew
Foster

Match
Factory

Tip

Kipling St

Mr.
& Mrs. S

Park

Luigi's

Pub

Kipling Lane

Fat cop

Tannery

Raffi

School

Josephine's Balmain St.

Power Stn

Charles

Junk
Yard

Brewery

Peanut

Old
cemetery

Gasometer

Judy

Josephine
Island

Church St

Garmo

Fort Yarra

Alexandra Ave.

Underground railway

City
Boy's
High

James

Morra

Chapel St

+ + + + Railway
= = = Drain tunnel
· · · · · · Tram

ALSO BY PETER TWOHIG

The Cartographer
The Torch

Praise for Peter Twohig

'hilariously on the money ... disarmingly poignant story ... whose vivid descriptions, original, engaging voice and surprising hero in the rough draw the reader into a labyrinth of danger and discovery'
Sunday Age

'a treat: exuberant, intelligent, fun and memorable, especially for the complex, sympathetic portrayal of its youthful hero'
The Australian

'a fresh and rollicking take on the Boys' Own Adventure'
Weekend Australian

'you'll be struck by the charm of the writing, its easy wit and the rich descriptions ... Twohig has a wonderful gift for characterisation'
Canberra Times

'original and delightfully entertaining ... a rollicking ride through a distinctly Australian urban landscape ... with just the right measures of sentiment and plenty of thrills along the way ... will leave you smiling with satisfaction'
Good Reading

'like no other adventure ... A rich cast of shady characters ... plus a quirky plot make for an interesting read'
Launceston Examiner

Peter Twohig was born in Melbourne in 1948 and grew up in Richmond and Dandenong. He survived a Catholic education, and worked in the Australian Public Service until 1992. He then moved to Sydney to become a naturopath and homoeopath. He has degrees in sociology, philosophy and complementary medicine.

Peter's first novel, *The Cartographer*, received the Ned Kelly Award for Best First Fiction in 2012 and was long-listed for the Commonwealth Book Prize in 2013. His second novel *The Torch*, was a sequel, while *The Mazemaster* completes the trilogy.

petertwohig.com

THE
MAZEMASTER

PETER TWOHIG

Warburton Press

Warburton Press

The Mazemaster
First published in Australia in 2021

© Peter J Twohig 2021

Literary Agent: Lyn Tranter
Australian Literary Management
2A Booth St, BALMAIN NSW 2041

Warburton Press
PO Box 9305
Wyoming NSW 2250 Australia

ISBN 978-1-922470-08-9

A catalogue record for this book is available from the National Library of Australia

Cover design & illustration and The Mazemaster's Map by: Kate Twohig

Visit PeterTwohig.com

To Lois

Contents

Childhood is a tricky business. Usually, something goes wrong.

Maurice Sendak

1 Taking the Mick

My brother Michael was kidnapped at eleven o'clock in the morning on Saturday, the 6th of August, 1960. He was two weeks old. That morning I was doing the worst thing a boy can possibly do, bar kissing a girl he doesn't like (or a boy, but I have to tell you right now that there was a very good reason for that), which is to go shopping with his mother, to buy ladies stuff. Normally, this kind of expedition would be carried out with the daughter of the family, at least that's what I have observed from hanging around with James Palmer, who had a beautiful sister (who made me think of what his mum must have looked like when *she* was a kid), and from hanging around my girlfriend, Mona De Coney, who had about five hundred female relatives, all of whom were keen on buying curtains and so on.

You would think that Mum would be content to just visit one shop then, owing to a severe case of exhaustion, call it a day and go home for a frosty or two. That's what Dad would have done. But no, she would have to visit an assortment of shops where it seemed to be less important what you bought than who you bumped into. Basically, if she didn't bump into someone it was not much of a day out, as far as I could see. I suppose I could put up with one of these trips as long as we didn't run into any of my aunts, all of whom had a tendency to kiss first and ask questions later. To make matters worse some of them had moustaches.

On top of all that we were having a visitor after lunch, an old wartime friend of Mum's from Wodonga called Daphne Honeysett – Mum's nickname for her was Daffy (and mine too, just on the quiet) – who was also the aunty of Keith Kavanagh, alias Flame Boy, former child resident of South Richmond, and the same truly disturbed young man who burnt our house down last Christmas. Only Granddad, Mum, and Mr and Mrs Sanderson down in Kipling Street, knew that he had shot through with his mum to Wodonga (a fate worse than death, according to Nanna) to live out his days at his Aunty Daphne's place, where he was completely unknown, and would not even be suspected of starting the odd grass fire if one did happen, which is always on the cards from what I hear.

So while Mum was looking forward to seeing Daffy again she was very nervous, because she was going to have to make something for afternoon tea, and that was like asking Helen Keller to whip up an oil painting.

What I am leading up to is that this shopping business is a stressful and noisy experience at the best of times, but is definitely ten times worse on a Saturday morning, when you're with an angry mother, and you've got better things to do, but you're in charge of pushing a pram while the female half of the outfit is looking at material. I mean to say, a young man can't be expected to be looking everywhere at once.

It was: 'Do you think Aunty Daphne would like some of this?' or: 'Look at this – what do you think?', Mum would ask, unrolling a length of some horrible green stuff. 'That would look good in your room, don't you think?' Mum's brain treated material the same way it treated food. I never knew what to say. Father Hagen was always telling us altar boys to tell the truth, and the brothers at school were always telling us to be kind to our parents, so these sorts of questions practically gave me a nervous breakdown every time they turned up.

On this particular day, we must have gone to just about every shop in Swan Street that sold stuff that only ladies would be interested in, and it was hours before I realised that the real reason we were out and about had less to do with curtain material and foodstuffs than with wheeling Mick out for all and sundry to see.

It was warmish in Dimmeys as we went back for our second visit, Mum having decided that she would definitely buy the horrible green stuff. The wooden floor made rude *pock pock* sounds as hundreds of high-heeled shoes hurried over it. I gave Mick a look to see if he still had his dummy, and he looked at me as if to say that I should have warned him about this place, as about twenty-seven women had stuck their fizzogs into his pram and made baby noises at him. God knows what they were expecting – it was embarrassing. Mrs Powell even said to Mum, with a half a nod towards me: 'This must make it more bearable, dear, *you* know,' meaning the loss of my identical twin brother, Tom the year before last.

Whenever anyone spoke of this they nodded in my direction, as if it had all been my fault, whereas the truth was that if there was any magical way I could make Tom reappear, including human sacrifice, I would have thought of it and done it a long time ago. But there was nothing. I saw him die, I was there, I tried and failed, and there it was. A part of me died with him, a big part, a half. He had been my live mirror; all I had left was the mirror in the bathroom – just like everyone else – which turned everything round the wrong way.

My thoughts were interrupted by Mum half turning to ask me what I thought of something that looked like it needed to be stuffed. Suddenly I was all ears – that is the way to behave on one of these torture trips, otherwise you'll be forced to go on another one the following Saturday as a punishment. But Mum wasn't speaking. She was frozen, with a look on her face as if she was back in Java or wherever it was fighting the Japs. It was one of those looks that you could describe as strained, because I could suddenly see stringy things under the skin on her face I had not noticed before.

'Where's Michael?'

I looked into the pram. No Mick.

'I thought you had him.' This was not true. I only said it to give my brain time to think of something better, something other than the truth, which I was not going to say on pain of being burnt at the stake.

Mum ignored me. 'Did you take him out of the pram?'

'Nuh.' I started looking around the floor like mad, in case Mick had fallen out of the pram. So did Mum, even though the chances of Mick getting up and walking were about the same as Hawthorn's chances of winning the premiership this year. But the difference was that, whereas I was prepared to search every inch of that floor, Mum was not, and was instantly looking at the people around us, all of whom were ladies of some shape or other. Mum only glanced around and had instantly summed up the situation.

'Someone stole my baby,' she yelled at the top of her voice, freezing the blood in my shoulders, back and guts, and the blood of everyone in the shop, and it was a big shop.

Everyone stopped dead. It was like the eleventh hour of the eleventh day of the eleventh month. Mum yelled it again, just in case they had turned to stone for some entirely different reason. This time they all began to look at each other, and at what they were holding, being women. Women who had babies clutched them tightly in case vigilante groups began forming.

4

I ran for the door, pushing my way past terrified ladies clutching all kinds of strange things to themselves, as if possession of a bolt of calico could prove that they were not the baby-napper. The door was open, and I stepped out into Swan Street, actually expecting to see a woman wearing sixteen dresses and a big head scarf making off with the kid, but no. Everything looked normal.

A kidnapping had taken place only seconds before, and Richmond was taking it in its stride, which wouldn't surprise you if you lived in the place. Inside, Mum was screaming commands left right and centre. She was Lieutenant Taggerty again, back in the War, and she wasn't going to put up with any nonsense. I ran across to the road to a pair of coppers who were being overpaid to do stuff all.

'A baby's been stolen from its mother in Dimmeys. Come on, quick.' I don't know why I was doing all this, as I felt like a complete bloody nong for losing the little bugger, and I knew well that the police weren't going to be any help. Stealing a baby in a crowd like that one would have been easy. And I'd lived in Richmond long enough to know that the town was full of all kinds of sick bastards. I didn't tell the cops it was my baby brother, because I knew they'd think I was having them on – I could see how a kid might do that if he thought he could get away with it. The cops ran across the road after me and pushed their way into Dimmeys. Mum was still yelling orders to all and sundry, and was now standing at the front door to prevent the calico-laden mass from escaping. It was a hell of a mess. And to make matters worse, Mum was not only angry, which was normal for her, but scared, and I had never seen her like that before. In fact, I wondered if anyone had.

One of the coppers got on the blower, and pretty soon Swan Street turned into a madhouse, with the whole street from Church

Street to Punt Road being searched for the kid, and everyone with a pram being stopped, and all the trams, to boot. Mum didn't speak to me at all, and didn't look at me. I had the feeling that she was just an inch away from killing me on the spot if I opened my mouth, because I had been right beside the pram when Mick had been snatched.

The police took us home, which was just a short distance up the hill, and took us inside. Granddad was out and about, and wouldn't know what had happened until he came back. Throughout the whole disaster, Mum kept up a steady stream of orders and impolite suggestions to the police, who were convinced that it was the work of a gang, as they called them, when it was plain as day that some nutty mother had done it, because it was just the sort of thing a nutty mother *would* do, and Richmond was chockers with them.

We sat in our living room and waited until a detective inspector called Passmore turned up and asked more stupid questions than I've ever heard asked by someone who was not a nun, and Mum tried to keep her temper, which was not her strong suit.

'Mum,' I said as soon as I thought she'd listen. 'I'm going to tell Mr Sanderson.'

She looked at me without speaking; she had already ceased to love me. But that look was as good as a green light. Mr Sanderson was an old friend of hers from the War, who now lived in an enormous house down in Kipling Street, and had, with his wife, practically adopted me when the rest of the family gave me the heave-ho following Tom's accident, though neither me or anyone else I know had the faintest idea what they saw in me. Mr Sanderson was a heavy in some kind of secret cop organisation that could do pretty much as it pleased, and Mum knew it. Despite a complete absence of reaction from Mum, I got up to go. Passmore did not like any of this a bit, and grabbed me by the arm.

'Just a minute, son, where d'ya think you're goin'?'

We all froze, even Mum. Clearly, I was what Dick Tracy would have called a person of interest.

It was at that moment that Mum saw an envelope on the mantle piece, and leapt at it. I was right by her elbow when she opened it and pulled out a note that said: *I just want you to know how easily I can hurt you.*

'Jesus,' said Mum, wildly. 'They were in here.'

'Do you recognise the handwriting?' asked the copper.

Mum looked at it very carefully. I had never seen her look at anything that way before. It was as if a new person had come into the room.

'No. I want a xerox of this note.'

'Sorry: evidence. I'll take it.'

'It's all right, Mum. I'll tell Mr Sanderson about it.'

'And who is this Sanderson bloke?' asked the copper.

'Friend of the family,' said Mum, her old anger getting into a nice position on the rail. 'Works for COMPOL.'

'This is a matter for the local police.'

'We'll see about that,' said Mum. 'Now please leave before my father comes home. He would take a dim view of the police contaminating the house.'

'And who is your father?' asked Passmore, taking his notebook out again.

'Archie Taggerty.'

The cop put his notebook back without writing in it. 'I see.'

Granddad was no ordinary Richmond citizen. He was Archbold Patrick Taggerty, twice former Australian Bantamweight

Champion, war hero, and extremely dodgy person. There wasn't a thing that happened in Richmond that he didn't know about. He was owed favours by all kinds of people, from bookmakers to police. Petty criminals got away with murder because it suited him. Big crims gave him a wide berth or better still, stayed out of Richmond altogether if they knew what was good for them. He himself had been in Pentridge for carving up a copper, so the story goes – I couldn't get Granddad or anyone else to give me the full story – and had killed one of his opponents in the ring, another bit of information I couldn't get clarification on, only that if the subject came within even a mile of it, Mum chucked a mental, so I knew this was solid gold family history. Even his off-sider and business assistant, Barney Flanagan, wouldn't tell me about it, and Barney and me were mates.

Granddad never drove a car, though he was worth a bob or two, and Mr Sanderson once said he happened to know that Granddad could have a Roller if he wanted one. But Granddad reckoned that he was a man of the people. It was well known in our family that he had helped out more people around the town than he'd had hot dinners without asking for anything in return.

He made his money by lending a quid to other blokes when they were a bit short. These blokes were expected to pay the money back, or they got a little visit from Barney, who was as nice a feller as you'd ever hope to meet, and a semi-retired burglar, so he was someone who liked a bit of peace and quiet. He carried a big knife in a leather sheath under one of his trouser legs and was fond of reminding geezers it was there, so they always found a way of coughing up in the end. Sometimes, blokes just paid him money when they didn't even owe him any in the first place. How lucky can you be?

Sometimes Granddad would get his name in the paper, when he would be referred to as a 'colourful racing identity'. But whenever this happened he'd make a phone call, and the next day the newspaper would say they had made a mistake and were sorry. This only happened a couple of times. I once heard Arthur Minto – that's Granddad's brief – say that he wouldn't mind if it happened more often.

So you can see how the last thing anyone in Richmond (or any other town in Australia, and probably a few nearby countries) would want was to get on the wrong side of him, and I think you could call kidnapping his grandson getting on his wrong side. I thought that the best thing that could possibly happen to the kidnapper would be if Detective Inspector Passmore found him before Granddad and Barney did. To Granddad, Richmond was like one of those rusty tins you find in the back yard that only has to be turned upside down and shaken for a few creepy-crawlies to fall out.

After the police left, Mum pulled herself together like nobody's business, and started organising everyone, which she was as good at as the Queen was at waving. When Granddad walked in, the first thing she did was sit him down on the couch as if she was going to tell him that his dog had just died (because that's what she did to me when Biscuit carked it). Granddad listened carefully while the history of events was told to him by Mum.

'Dad, that wasn't the first note.' She dug into her pocket and handed Granddad a bunch of folded papers.

He read them and gave them back. Then he was up and grabbing his hat.

'Dad, what're you doin'? Daphne'll be here in a few hours.'

'Then I'll be back in two hours. I've got to see a bloke – you know, put the word out – find out what's goin' on.' He grabbed his hat, and left, lucky bugger; I could hardly wait to be old. I grabbed my own hat, which was also a bloke's hat like Dad's and Granddad's, except I found it in a lane. When I went back to Mum, she took one look at the hat and started barking orders, a bit like *The Sarge*.

'And you can take that stupid hat off for a start. I want you to clean your room – it's a bloody mess – in case Daphne wants a lie down. Then come and have some lunch. That means now!'

I completed these tasks in record time and grabbed a sandwich to take with me. The fact that Mum had not forbidden me to tell Mr Sanderson told me a lot. Mum knew that he was in a position to find things out, just like Granddad, and also that I would brief him accurately, because she knew me inside and out.

'And don't forget –'

'I know, Aunty Daphne's coming over and be home in two hours.'

'Don't be smart. I was going to say one hour.'

'Okeydokey, Mum. See ya.'

'Don't I get a kiss?'

Normally Mum was not your kissing type of mother, but I knew she was still in shock from what happened to Mick, so I gave her a kiss. At the door I stopped to ask a question I had already gotten an answer to, but which I had to be absolutely sure about, because I was worried.

'Mum, I just wanted to check that nothing had changed about Aunty Daphne.'

'What do you mean? She's six months older, if that's what you mean. And we're bound to have a visit from your Uncle Seamus – I don't see how that can be avoided.'

'No, I mean, she's not bringing Keith, is she?'

'Off course she's not bringing Keith. That boy will never return to Melbourne. And listen, I hope you haven't breathed a word about him being up at Wodonga. Daphne says he's gone off lighting fires, she thinks for good, so as far as anyone else is concerned we haven't got a clue what happened to him. All right?'

'Ten-four, Mum. See ya in the soup.'

I bunged my bloke's hat back on, to show that I meant business, which usually meant whenever I wasn't hanging around my mates or their mothers (for whom I had a standard kids issue baseball cap, for cuteness), grabbed my bike, and headed off down Church Street.

All the way down I felt like I'd been kicked in the guts, because of what I'd let happen. It just was just like Tom all over again; I had stood by and watched as he had died, powerless to stop it, and I always got that feeling whenever I thought of it. Then that Kavanagh kid had burst on the scene with his loveable way of burning down people's houses. I had done my best to protect him from the law, hiding him here and there, but it wasn't for him that I did it (though I let everyone – except Granddad – think it was), it was a way of trying to get rid of that feeling in the guts. Hell, I even went to Confession to get rid of it, but the priest basically told me to go and get stuffed – he'd keep.

Even though Blind Nellie could see I was going to get elbowed wide at the turn by Mick, that was fine by me. A kid has to do what he can to get ahead, and Mick was helpless, apart from his good looks and his way of getting attention, which sounded like an air-raid siren.

But Mick turning up didn't fix one thing that was definitely wrong. For the last few months Dad had been back at home, after shooting through to his girlfriend, Mrs Bentley's, down at Elm Grove. His return had been Granddad's idea. Barney told me on the q.t. that Granddad, who could be pretty persuasive and had been a very dangerous fighter in his day, told Dad to pull his socks up and give Mrs Bentley the flick, so he did. Granddad, who had more money than he knew what to do with, also gave Dad a car, a brand new blue and white FB Holden, as he did not want to see his grandchild getting around on the back of a Triumph Super Speed motorbike. This car was the most beautiful thing I had ever seen that did not have Josephine Thompson's face on it, and I made a solemn vow to myself that I would devote my life to learning how to drive it. I knew that neither Dad nor Mrs Bentley were overjoyed at this arrangement, and I was glad I was not within a hundred yards of her house when Dad gave her the good news. But Granddad was only thinking of his little girl, I suppose, or maybe Mick. Who knows what goes on in the minds of the elderly?

All I know is that I got a bad feeling from seeing the way Dad let Granddad push him around, because Dad had just been after a bit of peace and quiet and a win over God, who can be a bit of a prick when it suits him. After all, it was him who took my brother Tom away.

These were the things I was thinking about as I rode down to Kipling Street, opposite Bryant & May's Match Factory. I was on my way to see the dodgiest crowd in Richmond who were not related to me.

2 The Sandersons

I rolled up to the Sandersons' door and jumped off, glad to be at a friendly house, as the weather had gotten lousy again. I was definitely not looking forward to riding home, and was wondering if they would let me come back after Aunty Daphne had gone, and stay the night, as it was Saturday afternoon. These days I was practically one of the family, and had even made the spare bedroom my own. I carried my bike up onto the veranda and propped it, because it had begun to rain.

The Sandersons thought I was the bee's knees despite knowing full well that I was a scallywag in the making and needed to be watched closely. For some reason they had practically adopted me on the spot about a year back, and now acted as if they had sworn some sort of secret oath to protect me and give me free advice (mostly about things I should not do) and food and shelter. In short, I was welcome at their place day or night, rain or shine, and did not need to knock.

After our house burnt down at the end of last year they took me, our cat Abbotsford, and my dog Zac, in for a while. They kept Abbotsford because he seemed to take a shine to Mr S, which is one of the strange things cats do, and because Mum never wanted him in the first place. Personally I can take cats or leave them, as I am more your dog kind of kid. Zac was a black Labrador, and one of those dogs who I think had a vicious streak in him that he kept under control at all times, which gave the impression that he was everybody's friend. He also took to the Sandersons, and in fact decided to live at their place half of the time, as all my friends still lived down that way, and it made it easier for me to get around by bike and still visit him.

'Oo-oo,' I yelled in the special way you do with oldies, so they won't have a heart attack.

'Hello,' yelled Mrs Sanderson back, from inside.

The front door was opened by Mr S, wearing a pair of tartan slippers and a big old hand-knitted jumper that had Mrs S written all over it. His face was particularly pale, as if he'd been attacked by a vampire, and he had his little glasses on, which always made him look like a harmless old codger, when he was in fact a very clever cop that could push ordinary cops around like nobody's business. In fact, Granddad had told me that he was a special kind of half spy-half cop, and that both he and Mum had known him during the War, though for completely different reasons. It makes you wonder. But I could go on wondering all day and all night where these parties were concerned – they weren't going to spill any more beans than that.

'Ah, Jack Sterling, as I live and breathe.'

I had used that name – it's actually my secret spy name – when I first met Mr Sanderson last September, and he had asked my name. At the time I was taking a short cut through his property from Kipling Lane to Kipling Street, the sort of thing that is frowned on by strangers – every kid knows that you never give your real name when it looks like trouble. Now he used it freely, knowing it was embarrassing, but also meaning me no harm. Tom would have liked Mr S even more than I did, I think, because he was the cheekier of the two of us and liked a good joke, even if he was on the receiving end.

'H'lo, Mr Sanderson.'

'What brings you down here in this kind of weather,' said Mr S, who could read me like a form guide.

'Well, you know my new brother?'

'Michael, yes. How is he?'

'He was ten out of ten until this morning: someone kidnapped him out of his pram –'

'My God, so that was Michael. We heard about it on the news.'

'But how did they find out so fast?'

'Apparently it happened in Dimmeys, in front of a big crowd.'

I nodded and groaned.

'What is it, dear? Are you all right?' asked Mrs S.

'It was all my fault. I was right there, and I wasn't watching him.'

'But they said on the news that the police already had a few suspects, and were confident of an early arrest.'

'That was a load of bull, Mrs Sanderson. I was there. They haven't got a clue.'

'Who's the policeman in charge?' said Mr Sanderson.

Bloke called Passmore. I don't think Mum likes him. I don't think he knows what day it is.'

'So what did the note say?'

'How did you know?' See? No flies on Mr S. I don't know what a bloke like him sees in Hawthorn. 'You're right, there was a note. It said: *I just want you to know how easily I can hurt you.*' It was written in block letters, with a pencil, and on writing pad paper. And it turned out that Mum had received some notes before this, though I don't know what they said. It means the kidnappers've got something else planned, doesn't it?'

Mrs S looked at Mr S. 'He'll be home again in no time, you'll see. Now you just stop thinking like that – you don't want to make yourself sick,' said Mrs S. But we all knew that there was fat chance of that happening, as I was probably the nosiest kid in Australia who wasn't a girl. Also, I was born to predict trouble; I was famous for it.

'I can't help it. So much rotten stuff has already happened to us.'

Mr Sanderson stared at me, and made the duck mouth. 'Yes, it has, hasn't it? A lot of very bad things have happened to you and to your family.'

I knew what he was thinking: I was twelve, not dumb. 'Well, there was Tom's death. Then I started having those, um, seizures.' I had to say it, because Granddad told me if I called a spade a spade I'd be able to get over them faster. 'Then our house was burnt down by Keith Kavanagh. Everyone knows that. And besides, he told me.'

'Did he tell you? Think.'

I thought. 'Well, no, I don't think he did. But he wanted to. And he burnt down his own house, didn't he? And what about the lumber yard, and the pub?' Flame Boy, as I called him, was a living legend around Richmond, like Batman. But this was the first time the Sandersons had suggested that it might have been someone else who burnt our house down. 'He wasn't the full quid, you know. And he was staying right there, in our house. He had both motive and opportunity.' I had been waiting all my life to say that.

Mr Sanderson did not argue; it was true. And then I remembered something Mrs Foster had told me months before, when Flame Boy was running round loose at the height of his superpowers. She said he had told her that it was not him who had torched our house, and that she believed him. At the time I thought she'd gone nuts, which happens to adults all the time, especially housewives. Now I wasn't so sure.

'What is it?' asked Mr S, who must have seen the look on my face. I could have kicked myself, because I had broken Granddad's number one rule of being out and about: *Don't let the punters see what you're thinking*. But I decided to give him that round.

'He told Matthew Foster's mother he didn't do it, and she believed him.'

'I see. And in all this time, it didn't once occur to you that someone else might have done it? Or that it might have been an accident?'

'Nuh. Who would do that?'

'Mrs Kavanagh was staying with your mother, and both of them smoke. You said Mrs Kavanagh was blind, didn't you?'

'That does it for me,' said Mrs S, offering me another bikky and a cup of hot chocolate. 'Case closed.' I could hardly believe my ears; I did not know she watched that much television.

But Mr S just kept staring at me, not rudely but as if his mind was somewhere else. I picked up the hot chocky and took a sip. Mrs S was just trying to put me off the scent, and Mr S wouldn't tell me what he was thinking if I paid him.

So they thought this was all a big series of coincidences and accidents, did they? I thought that was a load of bull. And that was when I began to wonder if someone had it in for Mum.

Mum was not one of those people who are born with an old person's brain; she was born with a brain that was as sharp as a cheese grater, and only needed the rest of her to catch up for it to do what it did best, which was rub people the wrong way. I knew it, Granddad knew it, and the rest of the family knew it. Even people on the same tram as her, who had never met her in their life, knew it; you could tell by the strain they were under just being there. That is why Mum was a shift manager in the manufacturing section of the Match Factory: when you're making matches you don't want a lot of ladies wandering about bumping into each other, or lighting up their cancer sticks on the factory floor. So you hire someone like Mum, who was a cross between Adolf Hitler and Bette Davis, to keep them in line. She was as popular as castor oil, but she got the job done.

Also she had been a lieutenant during the War, and had done something that Mr S and Granddad knew all about, but kept to themselves. Aunty Betty said she had more medals than General Blamey. I never got to see them, but I knew from Nanna that she got one of them for rescuing Aunty Daffy and some other people from the Japs.

On top of that, Aunty Queenie told me that she had worked in some hush-hush outfit in Melbourne, and had once caught a traitor, who ended up in Pentridge. It worked in my favour that Aunty Queenie wasn't exactly sober at the time, which is often the case with adults who have too many deadly secrets to hold them all in. It was a mystery, like most of the things that had happened to my family, except for the things that involved the grog, women, and, well, that's it: grog and women. I understood some of that. It was the family weakness, and that was because we were Irish, like most of the people in Richmond who didn't just get off the boat.

The point is that I was pretty sure that Mum hadn't just been upsetting people since Tom and me came along; she probably started when she was just a kid. The mark of the gifted person is natural talent. I decided that the suspect would be a woman, living in Melbourne, who had met Mum. I felt very pleased with myself. I had narrowed the list down to a few thousand.

'Penny for your thoughts,' said Mrs Sanderson.

'I was just thinking about Mum. I don't know much about what she did in the War, or much about what she does at the Match Factory, but I bet she's upset a lot of people in her time, mostly ladies, I reckon. That's who we should be looking at for the kidnapping: ladies.'

Mrs Sanderson made a face like she had just smelled Brussels sprouts. 'I'm sure your mother is not the kind of person who –'

'Let's see: If a lady upsets one new lady every week, and there are fifty-two weeks in a year, and she has been doing this for (call it) fifteen years, how many ladies has this lady upset?'

'Now, your mother couldn't possibly –'

'Mm, let's see … carry the three … I make it seven hundred and eighty. Not a bad sort of a number.'

'I'm sure no one has ever upset seven hundred –'

'Call it a round eight hundred, in case she had a particularly bad week.'

'Nobody has ever upset that many people.'

'What about Bob Menzies?' I said that because everyone in Richmond hated Menzies' guts like they hated polio, and that was a lot more than eight hundred people. Also, Granddad had given me the whisper that these two, while nice enough people in their own way, were odds-on to be Liberal voters – and possibly the only ones in the area, which would make them a very rare species indeed, something like the Tasmanian tiger.

'Everyone knows that a politician can never please everyone all the time.'

'And then there was Hitler –'

'Another politician.'

'Was he? I didn't know that.'

'And anyway, your mum's a woman, isn't she? Women don't upset people.'

I could see that she was beginning to weaken. It's all part of the Blayney Interrogation Technique, which I learnt from watching Ron Randall in *O.S.S.*

19

'I can see you haven't met my Aunty Betty, Mrs Sanderson. Tom and me had a theory that it was her who started World War II. Course, it turned out that Hitler started it – I'm just saying.'

'Yes, well, every family has an Aunty Betty, doesn't it, Russell?'

'Indeed they do, even ours – no names, no pack drill. Even so, eight hundred. I think you may have overestimated the number of people your mother could possibly have upset.'

'Still, I think I'm onto something.'

Mr Sanderson weighed in. 'So I'm guessing you haven't discussed this theory of yours with your mother.'

'Correct, Mr Sanderson. I'm waiting for when I feel like getting a thick ear.' Mrs Sanderson had that look on her face as if she was about to throw in the towel, so I decided to change the subject, as I prefer not to humiliate ladies while they are in the process of feeding me.

'And speaking of the Kavanaghs, Keith's Aunty Daphne is coming over to visit this arvo. I think she wanted to see Mick.'

'How is she getting along with her sister and nephew?' said Mrs Sanderson, this being the type of stuff ladies are always interested in. Fair dinkum, talking about babies in front of women is like tickling trout, and ought to be banned.

'Like a house on fire, Mrs Sanderson.'

'I See.'

I immediately felt embarrassed, as I hadn't meant to make a joke. 'Apparently, young Keith has lost interest in fire lighting, which looks like becoming a lost art, like cake decorating.'

'I assure you young man that cake decorating is far from being a lost art, and I will prove it to you on your birthday.'

I took a sip of my hot chocolate. I could hardly believe how easy that was.

After a few more bikkies, and after running out of hot chocolate, I went to say hello to Zac for a while, then went back inside. The truth is, I didn't want to go home.

'I promised Mum I'd get back within an hour. I just wanted you to know what happened, and about my revenge theory. You know, when I told Mum I was coming down here, she didn't stop me – just thought I'd mention that. Also, Granddad was very unhappy about the whole thing. I have a feeling he's asking questions around town. I thought I'd mention that, in case you were thinking of trying to beat him to the crim, as he's got a few hours head start.'

Mr Sanderson sighed and got up to see me out, looking like some old codger who'd lost his marbles. 'I'm sure the police will not require any help to return your brother home safely, and put the people who did this behind bars.'

Mr Sanderson was doing his adult thing; I understood. I just nodded, as that's what you're supposed to do.

'You know you're welcome to come back, if your mother says it's okay, though she'll probably want you to stay with the family. Just thought I'd mention it, to save you ringing up.'

'Thanks, Mr Sanderson. You must have read my mind. But I don't think anyone will want me at home. In fact, I think it would be okay with Mum if I committed hari-kari.'

When I got home, I made an amazing discovery. Mum had made a cake and was just putting it in the oven. In our family this was the same as Snow White building a motorbike from scratch. I tasted the left-over cake mix, and it was okay. I then ate the rest of it, as kids do. The fact is that over the last two years, Mum's cooking had gone down the drain, and Dad and me – and now Granddad – were having a hard time getting by without a stomach pump. But Mum, having fought the Japs, was used to roughing it.

So I was pleasantly surprised, and knew that the visiting Daffy would be surprised as hell too.

Mum didn't have time to cook for lunch, but she let Dad and me cook some eggs and bacon, which you can't go wrong with. Dad even went nuts and chucked a few bangers in, so we were living the high life for a little while, despite it being against the rules to show that you enjoyed it. Granddad came home in the middle of all this and pulled up a chair. I happened to know that when Mum was at work he had been having the odd feed next door with Mrs Morgan, who was his second best friend and someone he had known since he had first moved into his house when he was youngish. I knew because that was the only time they could get together and relax, and because I sometimes joined them. Mum had never liked Mrs Morgan; in fact she hated all of Granddad's lady friends like the Asian flu. But today he was happy to get some real tucker for lunch, because Saturday night dinners were always a bit of a lucky dip, but with an 'un-' in front. Mum was still moving, and I could tell she was forcing herself to get ready for Daffy. I don't know how she did it, but I'd seen this before, her way of turning into a kind of robot when something terrible happened. I gave a hello kiss, but she didn't care.

I decided to give all those present and accounted for a run-down on what the Sandersons had said. 'I told the Sandersons what happened.'

'You didn't tell him about the note, did you?' said Granddad.

'Sorry, Granddad, but he'd already worked it out. But he said the police could handle it.'

'Bloody coppers,' said Dad. 'They couldn't organise a piss-up in a brewery.' I thought that just about summed things up.

In the lounge room I listened to the beginning of the Collingwood versus South Melbourne match on the wireless – it sounded ugly – and Dad and me were glad when Aunty Daphne turned up and saved us from hearing the rest of it. But she was not alone.

When Mum came back from the front door she was equipped not only with one Aunty Daphne, slightly older but otherwise in good working order, but also with one Uncle Seamus, both of whom were looking at each other in some kind of ecstatic state, like the Children of Lourdes beholding Our Lady.

Aunty Daffy was tall, and had hair that looked like steel wool. She wore a molten lava red dress that I had seen before and I guessed was the one she wore on her trips to the big city. Before she even said hello I knew she was going to say it loud enough to make Aunty Vera next door jump. Mum told me once that she was a quiet type of girl before the Japs got her. Those Japs have a lot to answer for, in my opinion. Aunty Daffy had also been a lieutenant during the War, and had been captured by a bunch of Japs, who soon wished they'd just concentrated on capturing ladies who were short, shy and puny that day, and taken no notice of her. For the way she treated her captors, who thanked God when peace was declared, she was given a medal. In short, she was the last person you'd think would fall in love with any kind of man, let alone a nutso Irish poet. But she took one look at Uncle Seamus, and it was like watching an airship get strafed by a Sopwith Camel.

Uncle Seamus was one of those uncles that neither side of the family would claim, being what polite people call 'eccentric' (that's what Aunty Dell says) and what rude people call stark, raving mad (everyone else). The known facts are: that, while fighting in North Africa he frightened the life out of Rommel, who ended up shooting himself; that he was a personal friend of Archbishop Mannix, who employed him as a gardener; that he was Irish; that

23

he was a poet who was forever scribbling poems on newspapers; and that women could not take their eyes off him.

Aunty Daffy had first clapped eyes on Uncle Seamus last summer when she had visited us from Wodonga for the purpose of rescuing both her sister Molly Kavanagh from the Royal Victorian Institute for the Blind, where she had ended up after her son Keith burnt their house down, and (reluctantly) the actual director, producer and star of this event, Keith alias Flame Boy, who was wanted by an assortment of authorities. She had instantly fallen in love with him, and vice versa. It was like one of those TV shows, and just about made you want to barf or kill yourself laughing.

And Uncle Seamus was no different. Whenever he was with her he looked like some evil torturer had attached electrodes to his eyes and pulled the lever.

This was the couple who came into the living room, and began kissing everything that wasn't nailed down. They knew what had happened – that would be Seamus's doing – and immediately sat down and began discussing it in a way that no other family in Richmond – make that the world – would have: they were working stuff out as if the police didn't exist, listing people Granddad might have upset – I couldn't see the point, really – and staring hard at each other the whole time when, in any other family – I was thinking of the Espositos – everyone would have been going nuts and tearing their hair out (except Mr E, who looked like he had torn all his out a long time ago).

For an hour I listened as they talked, swapped news, and drank beer, taking not much notice of me at all, and ate Mum's cake, to be polite. As I sat and watched, it hit me that the kidnapper was probably sitting somewhere safe with her feet up – it would have to be a lady, because no man would be caught dead in Dimmeys

– sipping a sherbet and having a good old chortle. I looked at Granddad and saw him look at me for a few seconds, and realised that we were both thinking about the same thing, probably because Granddad was a bit of mind reader. I gave him a little smile, and he gave me one back. That's the way it is with him and me.

After a while Daffy and Seamus announced that they were going to get some Chinese food for tea, so Mum could rest, and I judged that I would not be required to remain in captivity.

'Can I go back to the Sandersons' for the night, Mum? They invited me, and I could visit Raffi.'

Raffi was a kid I had become good friends with at the start of the year and who was one of the strangest kids in the universe, and this was because he was a dead ringer for me (or I was a dead ringer for him, one of the two), for a very good reason that had a lot to do with Dad and Mrs Radion and the old days – I don't think I should say any more. His hair stuck out like dry grass and his skin was like Luigi Esposito's. And I was the same. In fact, at school some of the kids called me Dago (though usually just the once). Dad told me it was because we were Black Irish, which was fair enough.

Raffi's mother, who was very nice and looked a lot like Mum, and who was actually very pretty for a mother, already knew Dad, as I said, but didn't seem to like him, at least that was the impression I got – kids can usually tell when adults don't like things, because they think we are too dumb to spot it.

As for looking like Raffi, it took months for the penny to drop, and when it did the first thing I did was tell Granddad (because I tell him everything). All he did was tell me not to mention it to Raffi, and to let him work it out for himself. But he only did that last week, and was just at surprised as I had been. Meanwhile

Mum had stopped hating Raffi's guts and accepted that he was my friend, and that was that. The fact is, I had come to think of Raffi as a kind of relative, and felt very warm every time I saw him. Mrs Radion could tell about the warmth thing, because mums can do that, and sometimes she smiled at me, and when she did I smiled back. She seemed to like that.

In the past six months I had been around to Raffi's place about ten thousand times, and always felt good about it, one of the reasons being that, while I knew Raffi's mum had an idea about my colourful street identity, and could see through me like a busted string bag, she accepted my arrivals as inevitable, like bad weather, especially because Raffi and me got on like Noah's ark.

I looked at Aunty Daffy when I asked, because the last time she was down Mum had not been able to hide her terrific hatred for my friend Raffi, but I saw that she wasn't surprised at Mum's change of heart, and realised that she and Mum had probably been writing to each other for the last six months. I have noticed that ladies like writing very much. I think it has a lot to do with the blabbing thing. Whereas blokes are pretty awful at blabbing, and wouldn't even know how to put a stamp on an envelope, ladies can blab many different ways, and most of them could probably blab underwater, or on a rocket sled, or in the middle of an avalanche, if they had some news to pass on.

'Yes, go,' she said, making it sound like: *Don't come back.* 'And take a few clothes; Aunty Daphne will be staying for a few days. You can organise your school clothes later. I'll call the Sandersons and explain everything.' Mum was using her Match Factory boss's voice, but I didn't mind. It was better than nothing. And besides, I didn't feel that I deserved to live with them anymore. I reckoned I was bad luck.

3 Raffi Radion

After tea with the Sandersons I went upstairs to work on my Map of Mystery, which was a huge map of Richmond I had made, showing all my adventures as a variety of superheroes, but mainly as the Cartographer, in the last year. It showed all the shenanigans I had got up to, and their locations, including the underground drains and tunnels I had been in, as that was my special secret world. When I was finished I sat back and looked at it. I realised that somewhere in the maze of streets and lanes in front of me the kidnapper was hiding, like in a puzzle. And in my world, solving puzzles was kid stuff. Larry Kent, Detective, would have been proud of me. I know bad bastards, having met quite a few in my long life, and most of them without setting foot outside Richmond, and two things I had noticed about them were: that they never travelled far from the scene of the crime and also that they always gave themselves away in the end. I was thinking of naming these ideas Blayney's Laws of Gravity, you know, like that scientist bloke. *Whoever does evil has to turn up sooner or later*, you could say. I wrote it on the map. Suddenly I realised that the map had something magical about it, namely that it could double as a kidnapper-finder. The map would make me invincible. At eight-thirty I knocked off for the night and went down to watch *Have Gun Will Travel*. Normally I'd be singing along with the opening music, but that night, as soon as I opened my mouth I began crying, and I don't mean politely. The Sandersons both had to come over and keep me company on the couch, but I didn't care. The crying just fell out like rice bubbles.

Next morning, I got a brilliant idea, and went round the edges of the map, making little walls across the roads that led out of Richmond. Inside was my quarry, if that's the word. I marked Dimmeys and our house in red. In that moment I swore that I would find the bastard who took Mick from me – I'm sorry, I hate to say that about a lady, but I meant it. And if I couldn't outsmart her with my detective and spy skills I had the Secret Weapon of the Blayneys: we are born sneaky. At that moment, if I'd had a cigarette I would have lit it, and there would have been saxophone music.

When I was finished I deliberately left the map in the study on the first floor, so that Mr S could secretly take a peek while I was at Mass, in the hope that he might come up with some ideas of his own. All the way down to St Felix's I felt as sick as a seal, and halfway through Mass I went out the vestry back door and threw up like mad, being careful not to get chuck on my vestments, or Father would have killed me for sure. But I felt sorry – for everything, and everybody; I just had no one to tell. So I cried and vomited at the same time, which it turns out is not that hard.

When I got back I grabbed Zac and shot through to Raffi's place. As usual, I went around the back way, which was shorter, and bowled in without waiting for Mrs Radion to ask me for the password. I found Mrs R in the kitchen making something that smelt pretty good, and made a mental note to eat some of it before the day was out.

'Hello, here's trouble,' said Mrs R.

These days, Mrs Radion was generally keen to see the young feller, though there had been a time when she was not, owing to the many times the police had visited her house, based on my description. But forgive and forget, I always say.

'I just want you to know: someone kidnapped Mick out of his pram while Mum and me were in Dimmeys yesterday.'

Mrs R didn't react. The *Herald* had a lot to answer for, wrecking my story like that.

'So that was your family. My God, poor Jean. Have they any idea who might have done it?'

'Nuh. The police are investigating – and so am I'.

'Well, I'm not sure that Jean would approve of me saying this, but I'll keep my ear to the ground at the factory. When they find her it'll turn out to be some deranged person, you'll see. Now, shouldn't you be home?'

'I'm only in the way there. I'm staying with the Sandersons, around the corner, for a few days.'

'I see. So, what's on the agenda for today?'

'Secret meeting of the Cobras,' said Raffi.

'In this weather?'

'Mario's mum's makin' a cake.' He looked at me. 'Could be tiramisu.'

'Don't you mean Tina's mum?' She gave me a wink. I think another reason Mrs Radion had taken a shine to me was because Raffi had seizures too, only he'd been having them all his life.

Raffi wasn't biting. 'Mum, it's the same mum.'

'Mm, that reminds me, I haven't seen Gabbie for ages.'

'Oh no, Mum it's a Cobras meeting!'

'Okay. I won't spoil your visit to Tina's – I mean Mario's – but I wouldn't mind a piece of Gabbie's cake.'

'I'll see what I can do, but it's a long way home; what if we get hungry?' Raffi liked to have a lend of his mum. I wouldn't have got any change out my mum at all.

'It's a hundred yards away.'

'Oh … yeah.'

Outside, we put on our raincoats, just in case the spitting rain turned to drizzle, or worse, and headed out the back gate into Dress Circle Lane.

'Why would anyone steal a baby?' said Raffi. 'Don't they cry all the time?'

'They sure do, at least this one does. But probably they didn't realise that when they made their plan. They probably regret it already. I wouldn't be surprised if they brought him back. But they'll have a hard time if they try it again.'

'Why would they do that?'

'Because they left a note. It said: *We can do this any time we like*, or something like that.'

'Jeez! What're you gunna do?' Raffi knew I was the type of kid who swings into action.

'I'm gunna make a plan. I've already narrowed the list of suspects down to about eight hundred, mostly women.'

'Shouldn't take long.'

We were always talking big.

Raffi turned left, automatically, but I grabbed his sleeve.

'Where're we going?'

'To Peanut's. I want to get him into the Cobras.'

'Why?'

'Well, his mum won't let him join the Olympians, because I'm in it, but she doesn't know the Cobras even exist. I thought he could keep his ear to the ground, you know for kidnapper clues.'

'Ye-ah. Good thinking, Jack Sterling.'

What I had said to Raffi about the Olympians was true. Mrs Hobson wouldn't let Peanut join my old club, the Commandos, either. Ever since the unfortunate matter of Mr Bogart's rotary hoe, she has this idea that boys' clubs and gangs are criminal organisations, like the Mafia. Mums are always overreacting. I think God's elbow must have bumped against something when he was pouring the getting-shirty stuff into the original mum mix. But whereas Peanut's mum drew the line at kids' gangs, she always let him hang around with me, because she's Mum's best friend. Also, now that there's just the one of me, she has been a lot nicer.

'So we'll tell her we're going over to Mario's place to watch TV.'

'Good one. Old Peanut will love that.' Raffi had known Peanut Hobson for years, as they had both gone to the local state school, but they hadn't been friends until I took Peanut around to Raffi's place one day. Peanut told me later that he had always thought Raffi reminded him of someone, but he could never put his finger on it, and now he knew. Peanut is not the brightest penny in the till.

Most people – especially ones whose hats had badges on the front – took one look at Raffi and thought: *Hello!* It was the story of Raffi's life, a story I had not been aware of until this year. It was the reason Mrs Radion had nearly chucked a seven when she had first come home and found me playing records with him. But once she got to know me she got over the shock of seeing me all the time and wondering when the police were going to show up.

Peanut came to the door with his mum, who could sense whenever I was within half a mile of her house, like radar. She had known Tom and me since we were taddies, because we were born in the same hospital, the Queen Vic, on the same day as Peanut, and were taken home to houses on the opposite sides of the same street to live. The neighbours were thrilled.

As soon as Peanut was old enough to walk he toddled across to my place and latched on to a biscuit, and he hasn't stopped. This was good for his mum, who always knew where he was, and got a bit of time to put her feet up and do whatever ladies do when they put their feet up (I've never seen Mum do it, though she has feet and we have places to put them). You'd think it would be bad for my mum, always having another kid hanging around waiting for something to drop off the table, but she didn't seem to mind, I suppose because it kept Tom and me out of her hair. And anyway, Peanut wasn't a big eater – in fact, he wasn't a big anything, hence his nickname.

'Hello, Mrs Hobson. Hey Peanut, d'ya want to come with us over to Camponi's place?'

'You bet.' He comes out and heads for his rain coat and boots, which are on the porch. His mother stays at the door and watches Raffi and me with a look that I am used to. She is doing what the cops call a stake-out: you know, in case one of us lets slip our secret plan for getting up to mischief. I think I would be good at being a mum, as I know all their tricks. But I notice that she does not ask me about Mick, though she must have heard by now, and I realise that she would have rung Mum. While all this is going on, Peanut is talking his head off about what has been running though his mind all morning, because now he has someone to tell.

'Hey, I've got this fantastic idea. You know how that fire at the tip never goes out? Well, I was wondering if some bloke goes over there every night and puts something on it to stop it going out, you know: petrol or something. Did you know there's a derro who lives under the railway bridge who was in *Ben-Hur*? – true dinks. My cousin Addison – fair dinkum, that's his name: Addison – is going

32

for a trip to Antarctica on the *Kista Dan* – it's an ice-breaker. He's going to measure the ice or something; he can keep that. But we'll be going down to see him off. You blokes can come too, if there's room; I'll ask Dad.' And much more of the same, until his mother could stand no more, and faded back into the gloom, closing the door on us.

It always sounds very exciting the way Peanut tells it, because he is a bit of a wag, and is known far and wide as one of those kids who will take a dead boring situation and turn it into some sort of entertainment. Also, no matter what type of adventure you're having you can bet your bike that he has probably turned up with his head chock-full of brilliant ways to upset people and generally have a chuckle at someone else's expense, which is what being twelve is all about. In fact, when Peanut and me get together it's a bit like matches getting together with crackers.

Mrs Hobson also has this idea that it's me who is the cause of all of Peanut's problems, when Blind Freddie can see that Peanut was born to get into strife. But I have noticed that mothers tend to turn a blind eye where their own little angels are concerned (unless, like my mum, they have no blind eyes to turn). You can also bet that, no matter how dangerous or daring the plan is, Peanut will be in it, for two reasons, which go together like corn beef and pickles: first, he does not know the meaning of fear, and second, he has not got one of those brains that will end up in a jar in the museum.

So the first thing we do is turn towards Brighton Street and cross over toward my old house, which is now a blackened heap, and smells like piddle (I swear) because it has been raining. As we get to Judy Pickle's place who should we see but Judy Pickle herself, standing on the front porch and giving us the big hello. I know that Peanut is very keen on the Pickle (because he has no self-respect at all) and so normally I would steer him over to the fence so they could say hello. But when it comes to the Pickle, Peanut clams up like a beauty whenever she is around, and turns into the complete opposite of his usual old self; it's enough to make you laugh yourself silly.

The Pickle, on the other hand, has her eye on me. I am her oldest friend who is not a girl, and the only boy as far as I know that she has ever kissed, though that was not my idea, and she always has to catch me unawares, as everyone knows. Judy Pickle was not what I would call pretty, though, and looked less like her mother than her father (and he was no oil painting), whom she liked to help build model aeroplanes. And unlike normal girls her bedroom was not pink and filled with dolls, but with pictures of fighters and bombers. I would be willing to give eight to five that the Pickle will one day be the first lady named after a vegetable to fly around the world. Judy does not clam up when she sees me, like Peanut. Instead, she revs up her talking like a nun who feels a sneeze coming on.

'Where're you off to?'

'Never you mind,' says Raffi, who does not take well to sudden interrogations by girls.

'I think I should come along too,' says JP.

'Oh yeah? Why?' asks Raffi, getting into the swing of things.

'Because he needs someone to take care of him,' says JP, giving me one of those looks you give your pet Shetland pony. The horrible fact is that, being my old next door neighbour, Judy has seen me have a couple of turns, and now regards me as her patient, with her as my nurse. I don't think Mona De Coney would like that too much, if she knew.

'Well, that's what *we're* for,' says Peanut, who is very fierce when it comes to friendship, and once told Mr Purvis, the father of his over the back fence friend Shane, that if he ever tortured Shane again – that was the time his old man poured boiling water on his legs – he would tell the police, which he did anyway, and was told by them to bugger off. Basically, if Peanut even got a sniff of something bad being done to some kid he was all over it like a horse blanket. But he says this to Judy in a soft kind of way, because he wants her to see him not as an argumentative kind of kid, like her, but as a caring kind of kid, like a kind of male nurse, which Mum says really do exist. Judy immediately softens a little, and nods and sighs at the same time, which girls are probably born doing. I think it is definitely lucky that Judy does not know that Raffi has turns too, or she'd probably duck inside and change into her nurse's uniform.

I can see that we are not going to get rid of the Green Vegetable, and we have urgent club business to get stuck into, so I go inside her front garden and up onto the porch, and say to her, quietly: 'Judy,' – Granddad's First Rule of Conversation: *Say their name* – 'we are taking Peanut to a secret club meeting at Mario Camponi's place. If we bring a girl, I will be expelled from the club. How about I drop in on the way back, and you can make me some hot chocolate or something?'

This hits the spot with the Pickle, who puts her lips up against my face and speaks quietly as follows: 'All right, dearest.'

After we leave I cannot help noticing that the other two have very evil looks on their faces, though they do not have the nerve to say anything to the Blayney kid. I walk along feeling very worried about what Mona will say if she ever finds out about this conversation. But why should she? She does not know JP. She does not even live in Richmond, but in South Yarra.

When we get to Mario Camponi's place, who should we meet in the living room, talking to Tina and her mum, but Mona De Coney.

I was just thinking that this was not my day, when Mrs Camponi grabbed me and gave me a friendly bear hug and kissed me on both cheeks, and I saw that she was in tears. Then she patted the lounge beside her, and said to me, 'Please. Sit down,' and I noticed that the family was very quiet, which was for me a first. 'Mr Camponi and me, we heard about your baby brother, Michael –'

'Isn't it wonderful?' said Mona.

Mrs C frowned like a flat tyre. It was one of those Italian looks that I hadn't learnt yet. 'We heard what happened to him.' She looked at her husband, who had a very serious look on his face, and had been nodding at me as he puffed on his pipe.

'You don't worry – I will make enquiries,' he said.

Mrs C went to speak again, but Mr C gave *her* the Italian look, and she clammed up. What I wouldn't give to be able to do that.

'You tell your parents I will make enquiries.'

I was confused. 'They didn't mention our family's name on the news. How, um …?'

'Your grandfather ask my cousin Tony to help.' He gave a little nod to Mario, to let him know that he could proceed with Cobra Club business.

We ended up going with Mario over to the old gasometer, which is where we held our secret meetings and after taking the oath Peanut was made a Cobra and given his secret snake name, Tiger. Then I made a little speech.

'Yesterday, my baby brother was kidnapped out of his pram while we were in Dimmeys. I need to find the kidnapper, before he – or she – *strikes* again' – it was practically a club rule to use snake words if you could – 'and I wondered if anyone had any ideas.'

'But Python, you live up on the Hill and we all live down here.'

'But the people who did it might not live up there. Or you might hear something that will help us. Just report anything different or suspicious, and I'll do the rest.'

'Is your grandfather going to kill them?' This was the voice of Sol Rogers, whose father knew a lot of dodgy people and was, according to Dad, in some vague way connected to the casino over the fish and chip shop in Church Street. I wondered what Granddad would say to this.

'No, but *I* might.'

Another Cobra spoke. It was Darko Stepanovic, snake name Brownie, a kid who looked very snaky and evil, and knew how to play soccer. 'My father will find this person, and when he does, he will blow him up.' He said this in a serious but friendly way that made me think his father would fit right in around here.

'Whoa, Brownie. My family have plans of their own, and they won't be able to carry them out if this guy is spread out all over Richmond.'

'Okay, but when my father hands him over, he might he missing a few fingers and toes.'

This was followed by a much longer silence that is normal in club conversation, which tended to run more to what was on at the pictures that coming Saturday.

'Okay, but not fingers, just toes.' I was thinking that the kidnapper had written some notes, and Granddad might need whoever Mr Stepanovic caught to write something, to compare the handwriting – that's what you always do.

Darko thought this was reasonable. 'I'll tell Dad.'

4 La famiglia makes enquiries

My conversation with Darko had frightened me, mainly because of how seriously he took the matter. I realised in that moment that I would do anything to get Mick back, and I wasn't ashamed. I knew that a lot of people all over town were working on it, and would all be talking to each other like mad, but they were never going to let me in on the act, and would take a dim view of me doing anything myself. So whatever I did I would be doing alone. Besides, I had to believe that the next target of these rotten bastards – they had become a gang – could be me, as they had said that they might strike again. And if they caught me as well, we were both sunk.

And I wasn't the only one who was worried about how things were going. Mario didn't say much on the way back from the gasometer, just kicked a tin along in front of him. I reckoned that, being Italian, he would be upset about us losing Mick, as he was really a gentle kid, despite being the Captain of the Cobras, and was probably thinking about what Darko had said; but I knew he wouldn't blab. He and his family had been kind to me when things were getting me down. Also, their TV came from Granddad (he sometimes found TVs still in their packing boxes just lying around, and when he did, he always passed them on to those less fortunate).

Peanut hardly spoke all the way back to his place, and walked along with his fists clenched, and frowning. I knew what he was thinking, of course, because the old Peanut was as easy to read as a *John and Betty* book. Raffi and I looked at each other, but didn't say anything. When we dropped Peanut off at his front gate, we said: 'See ya, Tiger', which made him smile for the first time, then walked down to Raffi's place. There, we organised a spot at the dining room table, and looked at each other.

'Will Darko's old man really cut off the kidnapper's toes, d'ya think?' asked Raffi.

'Not if we find him first.'

'What can *we* do?'

I saw the problem: Raffi was a good kid, but unlike me hadn't been around, and didn't know anything about the bad side of Richmond. However, I'd worked out that he was one of those cluey types.

'Raffi my son, you know a lot more about stuff than I do, because of all those books of yours. Believe me, that's bound to come in handy. In fact, I've decided to change the name of our club to the Detectives, and make you a detective sergeant.'

Though Raffi had been one of the club's more recent recruits, he had straightaway impressed all present and correct with his powers of bullshit, which left me standing at the starting gate. That, plus having a brain that was always brimful of ideas, would come in handy.

'Ye-ah. Thanks.'

'Now, get your detective notebook, and we'll make a plan.'

We made three headings: *The Detectives*, *Contacts*, and *Clues*.

We reckoned that the Detectives would be useless at finding kidnappers, but would not be useless at eavesdropping on their or anyone else's oldies. We made a list under the first heading, as follows:

1. Jack Sterling (Capt)

2. Raffi Radion (Det. Sgt)

3. Charles Dixon. Charles was one of my best and oldest friends, who lived over in Dover Street. His mother was a manager at Darrods, and was also the stand-in Darrods Girl on the Big Wheel segment of *In Melbourne Tonight*. She was also extremely beautiful. Apart from smelling ten out ten all the time, his house was definitely a good place to hang out.

4. James Palmer. James was my newest friend, and the only club member who lived across the river in South Yarra. He was a terrific kid who I'd only known since last summer, and who liked the same things as me. He had a very beautiful but mysterious mother called Leslie, who I thought might have powers and abilities far beyond those of mortal women – my secret name for her was Wonder Woman (also, her bathers were midnight blue, which makes you think, doesn't it?). Also, James's sister Veronica looked like Wonder Woman must have looked like when she was twelve.

4. Johnno Johnson

5. Douggie Quirk. Johnno and Douggie lived down in Prince Patrick Street. Their parents and homes were more or less interchangeable. Douggie's big sister Maureen had had a baby, which practically made her famous. Johnno's sister had yet to do anything like that. But Johnno Johnson was the kid tipped most likely to win the next New Year's Eve Brighton Street Dog Race, with his new bitzer, Bluey, providing he wasn't nobbled, because nobbling was an even more popular sport than actual racing, owing to a rather tempting book that was traditionally made by the 'Mayor of Brighton Street', Mo Giorgi.

6. Luigi Esposito. Luigi was the only member of the club who was from overseas, being from Italy. He had about two thousand brothers and sisters, and a mother who could cook so well you wanted to desert from the Blayney Platoon and go over to the Esposito Battalion. You only needed to know a few words of Italian and you'd blend in there for ever.

7. *Lettuce Gettis.* Lettuce (not his real name) was our latest member, and was by far the most mysterious, as he had one ear missing. We were very lucky to get him, as there was a big demand for mysterious kids among the secret clubs of South Richmond.

Under the heading *Contacts* Raffi listed the Cobras. It was Raffi who got me into their club, and he himself got in because his girlfriend Tina was the sister of the club captain, Mario Camponi. The other Cobras weren't really friends of mine, but you never know your luck in a big city, Granddad always says. And of course there was Darko.

Then I added Barney Flanagan, Granddad's mate. Raffi had met him once or twice and didn't know what to make of him, pretty much like all the other honest people in Richmond, though the villains (and the police) knew different. I could tell that Barney liked Raffi though, and I came to realise that he had always known who he was. But when it came to keeping secrets he was an expert. When I added his name Raffi raised his eyebrows and did the big eyes.

'He's my secret agent, only he doesn't know it.'

'Doesn't he work for your granddad?'

'Yep, but he drinks like a fish, and might let something slip – never know your luck.'

'Ye-ah.'

'So, Raff, you got any contacts?' I asked, to be polite. He thought for a long time, then shook his head sadly.

My number two resource was my knowledge of the City of Richmond, especially the streets and the drains below them. You could say that I had not had a wasted childhood. I had walked along every main storm water drain in South Richmond, and even had a hideout in one of them and, as it was close to Raffi's house, I was now sharing it with him. A few years before some bloke had kidnapped the Harrigan kid and hidden him in that same spot, which was marked on my *Map of Mystery*. So I wrote in the *Clues* column: *The Map*. Then I turned to Raffi again.

'So Raff, got anything for the *Clues* column?'

'Mm, the kidnapping was in Dimmeys, so I'll bet it was a lady who did it.'

'Yeah, that's —'

'And she got clean away in just a few minutes, so I reckon she had help.'

'Yeah, a gang —'

'Probably a bloke with a car.'

'That's what I was —'

'A Holden.'

'Why?'

'Cos no one would notice it.'

'Anything else?'

'She probably looked like an ordinary mother, I mean, not a loony or anything.'

I was astonished at all this thinking, as I had never seen what Raffi could do when he strained his brain, and straightaway got a terrific idea of my own.

'I'm impressed, Raff. In fact, I've decided to promote you to Lieutenant in Charge of Clues.' I shook his hand. 'Congratulations, Lieutenant.'

'Thanks, Jack, I mean Sir. You know, the doctor at the hospital told Mum I had an abnormal brain.'

'Oh yeah, I forgot about that. Just don't strain it too hard. Ten-four?'

'Ten-four.'

Next day at school a funny thing happened. Matthew Foster, a kid no one could stand the sight of, but who was probably the friendliest kid in Australia, came up to our group in the playground with another kid in tow. We'd seen this kid around, but he always kept to himself.

'G'day fellers. This is Eddie. He's my new next-door neighbour.'

Eddie had a look that said something like: *I need all the friends I can get – I'll take anything – hence Matthew Foster.*

'Eddie who?' I said, just to show him who was boss.

'Williams. Foster said he'd introduce me to his friends.'

I wanted to tell this Eddie kid that this time his parents had *really* landed him in it, but I was too polite to say so. Soon enough he would work out for himself what a pain in the arse God had issued him with for a next-door neighbour and he would with a bit of luck throttle Matthew Foster and report for duty a much relieved kid.

'So where did you live before?' asked Johnno Johnson, with a touch of his tough voice, which is what you do with kids you just met.

'North Richmond.'

'So why'd you move to *South* Richmond?' Johnno again, though we all wanted to know what could possibly drive a family to do such a weird thing.

Eddie shrugged in kind of lopsided way, but kept looking at Johnno. He did not feel like a kid, but more like someone who has

44

been let out hospital too early, and I couldn't help wondering what was wrong with him.

'Eddie's dad's a *test pilot*,' said Matthew Foster, going off like a bomb.

Now, I didn't come down in the last shower, and I know just as well as any other kid in the universe that you only say your dad is a test pilot if a) you're talking to a girl and there's no one else around, and she will never be able to prove you wrong in about two thousand years, or b) there are no other boys within cooee, or c) you are in Tasmania. As none of these things were happening, I thought this was highly concentrated bull of the kind you wouldn't want to step in.

'Oh yeah?' said Douggie Quirk, taking over from Johnno, 'So what's he testing at the moment?'

'Canberra bombers. He works at the Government Aircraft Factory, over in Fisherman's Bend.'

I was just about to call his bluff, when Matthew chipped in: 'I've seen his flight suit and helmet.' This was the kind of information you hardly ever got from a bull artist (unless that bull artist was Raffi Radion, who was full of the stuff and would probably end up in the *Encyclopaedia Britannica* one day), and put a different complexion on things. Matthew Bloody Foster might have been a lot of things, but he was not a liar. 'You know, Dad said that if he had not decided to be a food taster he would probably have been a test pilot himself. After all, they're really the same thing, when you think about it.'

But I was thinking that the Detectives had to snap this kid up before one of the local clubs did, as there was practically an epidemic of them and they were always on the lookout for mysterious or at least interesting kids, which is why we recruited the one-eared Lettuce Gettis. The problem was that we had told

MBF that our club – in those days it was the Commandos – had broken up (because he was in it), and had secretly reformed it as the Olympians. I know it was a white lie, but Barney says that's always okay when it's in a good cause, or when you're telling it to the authorities. So: how to recruit Eddie without taking MBF at the same time?

But then Matthew himself came up with the solution. 'Hey, me and Eddie are thinking of starting our own club. What d'ya reckon?'

'What would it be called?'

'It would be called – wait for it –' said Matthew, being his pesty worst, 'the Rockets!' And he said this last word as if it was the most important word ever uttered by any living creature, including aliens on Venus.

It was then that the sneaky side of me swung into action. 'How about you guys form a club for the kids in Cremorne, and I form a club for our side of Church Street, and the two clubs form a special secret partnership, like the United Nations?'

So that took care of that. The next thing I did was to secretly organise a meeting of our club straight after school, before we all shot through, and make a few announcements.

On Wednesday after school Mona's Aunty Lucky picked the two of us up in her MG, and took us to Coco's in Carlton for coffee and cake, which is something she had done on many occasions. Apart from driving a sports car Aunty Lucky was no ordinary aunty, as she was a comic collector, probably the only girl one in the Solar System, and was my main source of comics. But the main thing about her – her real name was Luca Theresa Maria Helena Martello – was that she was the most beautiful grown up I had ever seen, even more beautiful than Charles's mother, who had been

46

on TV heaps of times. These drives of Lucky's were heavenly, as I always sat in the front with Mona sitting on top of me with her arm around my neck, which was definitely the closest to her that I ever got.

Mona didn't say a word to me when she came over to the car, but looked extremely worried, like a girl in a movie who has just discovered that her pet racehorse has developed a nasty cough and won't be able to take part in the Big Steeplechase, while Lucky looked like the star of a different movie, an Italian one about racing cars and spies.

'Hello, young man,' said Lucky. 'I know your family must be going out of their minds with worry, so I thought you might like a little break before going home.'

'Hello, Lucky.' She had told me I didn't have to call her Aunty, which felt very weird, like calling Father Hagen Paddy, which is probably what his mates back in Ireland call him. 'Thanks. I'm actually staying with the Sandersons down in Kipling Street for the time being, because Mum's friend Daphne is staying with us.'

'I'm sorry,' said Mona. 'I didn't realise yesterday what had happened to Michael.'

'That's okay. My family's not telling people it was Mick who was kidnapped.'

'But they told Uncle Vinnie.'

'They must have thought he was special.'

Mona nodded, seriously.

At Coco's, Mona ordered, as usual. This was the only time I was ever able to get hold of some real coffee, and it was like having a sherbet bomb go off, not in your mouth but all over your body. I made a mental note to devote my whole life to drinking the stuff. I would be a saxophone-playing, coffee-drinking spy, or detective – or both. But there would be coffee.

47

'So,' said Lucky, when Mona had toddled off to talk to Mr Coco about cake, 'what can you tell me?'

Now let me tell you that this Lucky character, in addition to being the sharpest lady on the planet, probably able to leap tall buildings at a single bound, and work out how to install atomic reactors into sewing machines, would already have known all the details of this crime, just like everyone in Melbourne with a wireless. And also, she seemed to know a lot of people. But a bloke like me, who has Granddad for a grandfather, knows when he's talking to a fellow villain, not that I'm saying I'm a villain or anything – it's just that I've learned to read the signs. And for Lucky, just being as beautiful as her was a sign. I had noticed, for example, that she was always showing off her, um, figure in some way when she was talking to me about the price of fish, and this was something that made me feel like telling her my whole life story from start to finish in one big blab.

'Well, I s'pose you know most of it. I don't really know anything new, because I've been staying with the Sandersons. I don't think they want me at home until they get Mick back. Mum blames me, I think.' I hadn't meant to say it out loud. Now that I had, it had the ring of truth.

Lucky spoke softly. 'There was a note, wasn't there?'

'Yeah, it said they were going to strike again, something like that.' I was so busy being cool, and looking at Lucky's, um, figure, that I fell right into her delicious trap. Granddad would have killed me if he'd been there. She'd been fishing, and not with a fishing rod but with gelignite. She must have seen the look on my dial because she put her hand on mine.

'Don't feel bad, Mr Blayney' – she was always calling me that – 'You're a hard man to trick, but I couldn't resist trying. I've heard all about you and your exploits – Mona tells me everything. Don't worry, whatever you tell me stays with me. But in this case, I might know someone who can help. I just have one request, please don't tell your Grandfather what I said. It's family business, and they wouldn't approve. I'm going to ask my friend to make enquiries because we're practically family. *Capisci?*'

'*Capisco.*'

'Hey, *il tuo italiano suona piuttosto bene,*' said Mona, suddenly appearing and speaking loudly.

'*Grazie.*'

'Lucky, he says it like an Italian – *grazie.*' She rolled the r.

'I think Mr Blayney will soon be able to pass for one of us,' said Lucky. '*Che ne dici?*'

'Mm, *un giorno.*'

'Aunty Lucky, he understood!'

'Where did you learn all that Italian?' said Lucky. 'Not from the Camponis, surely?'

'No, from the Espositos. Luigi Esposito is one of my best friends. Whenever I'm around there we all speak *italiano. E' fantastico.*'

'Then you must keep it up, and we will help, won't we Mona? One day we will make a linguist of you.'

I knew that Lucky could speak about eighty-seven languages and probably play the ukulele at the same time, but I still didn't know what she did for a crust. 'Is that what you do?' I buried my face in my coffee as if I didn't care, but really I was busting to know, because I already knew that Granddad didn't entirely trust her, just because of who her uncle was, not that I'd ever heard of him. It was clumsy, I know, but she had fished me with dynamite, so I thought I'd try the same thing on her. Mona, meanwhile, was busy looking at the cake display cabinet, on the off-chance that Lucky might shout her another.

'No, Mr Blayney, though my job demands that I do a lot of travelling, mostly in Europe. So having a few extra languages is necessary. If you must know I also speak French and German, and bits and pieces of a few other languages. How's the coffee?'

'*E' fantastico, grazie.* Best coffee I've ever had.'

'I'll bet Mr Coco's is the *only* real espresso coffee you've ever had. Am I right?'

'*Giusto.*'

She clapped her hands, and I wondered what she'd be like to kiss, then straightaway hated myself.

'What's right?' asked Mona, who had been watching for Mr Coco's return.

'You're boyfriend, that's what. You must hang on to this one, Mona. I like him.'

I blushed. I was not used to girls talking about me while I am right there, unless it's to tell each other what an idiot I am – boys are used to that.

'I'll think about it, Aunty Lucky, but only if he behaves himself. Some of the girls at school think he's okay, you know.'

'That doesn't surprise me. Now don't forget what I said, Mr Blayney. It's our little secret.'

I hadn't forgotten. And I hadn't forgotten something else she'd said: that she would make enquiries. That is what Mr Camponi had said: *enquiries.* It must be something Italian's say. I decided that I would make a few of those myself.

5 The Merri Express

On Saturday morning I had brekky with the Sandersons, then went down to Raffi's place to see what was what. As I watched Raffi munching away on his toast and jam, I thought about what had happened to him a few weeks before, when the truth had dawned on him about him and Dad. Mum and Dad had taken Mick over to Mrs Carruthers' place to show him off, and had let Raffi have a hold, but when Raffi and Dad looked at each other, that's when the penny dropped. Raffi had not looked at me the same way since, even though I had smiled at him, to let him know it was okay. He'd twigged, but I realised that it was up to him to say something – only he didn't. But I could tell he'd been shaken up inside – connections will do that to a kid every time. Now, over brekky, he finally piped up.

'Penny for 'em, Raff.'

'I was just thinking about, you know, your Dad, and … everything … I think, I think …'

'I know what you mean, Raff. I've been thinking about it too – a lot.'

'What does it mean? Do you think Mum knows?' I turned this question around in my mind and had a good look at it – nothing happened. I looked at Raffi, and he was looking at me, and frowning. 'I mean, what am I supposed to say to her?'

'Nothing, Raff, I think she already knows … everything.'

'Yeah.' He shrugged and made the big eyes. I thought that just about summed it up.

What he needed that day – both of us, really – was a bit of cheering up. What we needed was: *The Secret Railway!*

'Look, I've been thinking. How about instead of spending the morning getting bored to tears trying to do jigsaw puzzle number two hundred and fifty-seven, which will probably turn out to have a piece missing, we have a little adventure – of the *railway* kind, if you see what I mean.'

'Nuh.'

'I mean, I think it's time we took the *Cannonball Express* to Kew.' That got a smile out of the old Raff – call it a gift.

I was talking about something we had done back in May. I had taken Raffi over to the island in the Yarra – I had renamed it Josephine Island after Josephine Thompson, but always called it Blood Island when I went over there with James – and shown him the greatest secret that any kid ever had since the beginning of the universe: the entrance to an underground railway tunnel built during the war, to carry ammo and stuff around Melbourne and which, according to Mr Sanderson (who banned me from ever going down there again or telling anyone, unless I wanted to go to prison for about twenty years) were then turned into emergency escape tunnels for when the Russians start dropping atom bombs on Melbourne.

In fact as soon as Mr Sanderson found out I had been down there, he arranged for new padlocks to be put on the gates and doors to the place. But they had missed the one on Josephine Island, which was just a trapdoor in the basement of the old anti-aircraft gun emplacement. Just getting there was as scary as hell, because the only way to get onto the island is to go over to the power station pool, climb down a steep cliff, and go through a tunnel made to carry a power cable under the river and over to the island, where the towers start.

Once there, you have to get into the fort through a little window, go down to the basement, open the trapdoor, and follow the railway tunnel under the river. But once you're underground it's like being in Heaven. I took Raffi all the way to the underground railway yard under Alexandra Avenue near City Boys High, showed him the three little green trains all parked in a row with their little electric locos on the front, and swore him to secrecy. I thought it was okay for Raffi to know about it, because he was not the same as other boys, though I wasn't sure that even Mr Sanderson would understand.

We had found the tunnel lights on, and taken one of the trains west to Kew, which, according to a wall map down there was where it came out. After going through a series of lonely little stations with names like Riversdale, Scotch, and Swinburne, we came to a station called Merri, where our way was barred by a metal gate. Raffi was terrified, which did not surprise me, but I should have felt calm and relaxed, like any superhero who steals underground trains for a living, like: *Railwayman!* in fact. But all I could think of was that the Harrigan kid, a little kid who was kidnapped a few years before, was taken down to a place like this by a local loony, who did very bad things to him. I thought of Mick, and wondered.

At Merri there was a lovely steel door in one of the walls, and I was immediately keen on opening it, but the old Raff was at his wit's end, and chickened out in a very big way. So it was back to the old homestead for us. Still, that door wasn't going anywhere.

So here we were again, down in the strange-smelling railway tunnel and finding the little trains parked just as we had left them.

This time I showed Raffi how to drive the train and switch everything on, and soon we were gliding down a tiled tunnel in terror, but without making a sound, until we arrived once more at Merri Station.

We had plans for that steel door in the wall, and quickly got it open. Inside we found a staircase which led up to another steel door. We opened it, and found ourselves in a concrete room and at the bottom of a set of concrete steps; but this door had to be held open.

'Wait here a sec and hold the door while I have a look,' I said.

I pushed on, and at the top was another door which opened to the outside, where there was a small yard full of heavy electrical things surrounded by a high fence with barbed wire on top. It was an electrical sub-station. It looked as though no one had been there for a long time, as there were weeds everywhere.

On the other side of the fence, in a big paddock, was a smallish green circus tent and all over the place were caravans towed by big, flash cars, formed up in two big circles, like wagon trains. And everywhere there were people, and there was music. They were having a good time. On the left side of the paddock was a winding line of trees that I knew ran beside the Yarra. I stuck my head around the door and read a large sign on it: *DANGER. HIGH VOLTAGE.* I saw that the door was actually in the side of a low cliff that had once been a quarry.

Then I looked back to the fence, to where there were a few bushes, and saw a girl about my age having a pee. She watched me with a cheeky look on her face, as if she was daring me to look, though I would have had more chance of not looking at a train wreck. I felt my face glow hot. She was beautiful like a film star and had dark, laughing eyes and deeply suntanned skin. There was a huge red scarf wrapped around her forehead, and she wore a long flowing dress that seemed to be every colour at once. When she left my heart stopped pounding and my breathing came back a little and I and pulled my head back in.

I went back down to Raffi and took over holding the door. 'Go and have a look, but just open the door wide enough to take a peek, and don't go out. It's a power station. But there's more – you'll see.'

'Cool!'

When Raffi came back we went back to the train, while Raffi chattered like a five year-old.

'D'ja see it? A circus, what a bewdy.'

'I'm not sure it *was* a circus.'

'It had a circus tent.'

'But it wasn't coloured.'

'And what about the animals?'

'I didn't see any.'

'That's funny, I didn't either. Maybe it's a carnival.'

'There weren't any rides.'

'I don't get it,' said Raffi.

'Me neither.' But I'd heard stories, mainly from Mrs Hutchinson, about caravan people like these, and wondered if they might be gypsies, and then I wondered if they were the kind of gypsies who kidnapped babies. But I kept quiet, in case Raffi thought I was dumb. One thing I did know was that I was going to go back to that park if it killed me.

When we emerged into what was left of the daylight on Josephine Island, I turned to Raffi, spat on my hand, and shoved it out. Raffi had been a boy long enough to know what was happening, and spat on his hand and grabbed mine.

'I swear to keep the Secret of the Lost Railway.'

'I swear to keep the Secret of the Lost Railway.'

It was one of those moments when you feel that nothing more needs to be said or done. But something felt horribly wrong, and I felt fear, as if I had just swallowed poison and nothing had happened yet.

'What's wrong?' said Raffi, as we walked back to the power cable tunnel through the tall fennel.

'I don't know. Maybe we shouldn't have taken the train.' I said that because I still felt worried by the thought I had about the Harrigan kid, and about Mick.

'But we got away with it, didn't we?'

'Yes, but I feel that we started something, like when you start an avalanche just by hiccupping.'

'Are you going to, you know, chuck a wobbly?'

I could see that I had thrown a scare into the old Raff, and that this was pretty unfair of me.

'Wobbly! I'll give you wobbly in a minute, my boy.' I pushed him into a bush.

'Well okay then. So what's wrong?'

'I'm scared Mick's going to die.'

Raffi just looked at me. No one had said that word, not one person. And I wanted to see what would happen if I did it first.

'Maybe they'll bring him back when they realise whose kid he is.'

'Yeah, but it won't make any difference. They've bitten off more than they can chew this time.'

I could tell that Raffi was scared at the way I had suddenly stopped being an explorer and started being a really worried kid, because we both knew that was how a seizure sometimes started, and it was one of our deadliest secrets. He grabbed me gently by the sleeve and began leading me back through the tunnel under the river to the secret entrance at the back of the old cemetery, and

I let him, because it seemed like a good way to practise, in case he had to do it for real. Every now and then he looked at me to see if I was okay, and I was.

When we got back to his place we flopped on the lounge, and stared at the blank TV screen.

'How do you feel?' asked Raffi again, almost whispering.

'I'm okay. But something happened to me. I saw something.' I was thinking of the girl with the suntanned face, and how she watched me over her bunched up dress. 'It's not a wobbly, it's a message; I get them all the time.'

'Who's it from? Hey, maybe it's a message from Mick, telling you where he is.'

This was something I hadn't thought of, but which I straightaway realised might be right. I couldn't think of any reply to this, and I could tell that Raffi hadn't meant to upset me.

He ploughed on, to make me feel better. 'Or maybe from Tom?'

'Actually, I think it is. He's telling me … he's telling me: *Raffi's … a … prawn.* Oh no, wait: *Raffi … loves … Tina.*'

I said that to put a stop to the talk about the sudden feeling, because it really did feel as if there was a message, just one that hadn't had words, and that didn't make sense. A part of me knew that all I had to do was keep my eyes and ears open and it would come to me, just not today. I couldn't tell Raffi any of this, because it didn't sound like kid's stuff, but more like something Nanna or Mrs Bira came out with when they were tipsy, or reading the tea leaves, or both. So we wrestled instead, which is what you do when you're hungry and tea's not ready.

I was glad that I'd found a way to take Raffi's mind off him and Dad, but I knew that all I'd done was put off something that wasn't going to wait long.

Now I was back in the warmth of Raffi's house, and munching on some chocolate crackles Mrs R had whipped up while we were gone. It's a strange thing, but I was prepared to share everything with Raffi, and I think his mother sensed this; she accepted me into her home as if I belonged there. I often worried, however, what would happen if Mr Radion came home from the Snowy and found Raffi and me hanging out together, so I decided to ask. I left Raffi sorting his alleys out for the Great Big Alley Comp we were going in that week and at which we were going to clean up, and found Mrs R in the kitchen. I smelled scones.

'Mrs Radion?'

'Mm?'

'About Mr Radion.'

'And it was such a nice day, too. What about him?'

'Raffi said he's up the Snowy.'

'I certainly hope so.'

'When d'ya reckon he'll be back?'

'Never.'

'But he lives here doesn't he?'

'No. He and I didn't see eye to eye, so we went our separate ways.'

'Good. I mean, that's good, isn't it?'

'Works for Raffi and me.'

'He's not really Raffi's dad, is he?'

'No.' She dropped her head as if the invisible string holding her head up had snapped, but then was suddenly retied. 'Your father is Raffi's dad. You and Raffi are half-brothers. But you worked that out a long time ago, didn't you?'

'Yes, but Granddad said not to tell Raffi, just to let him work it out for himself.'

'And he has, don't you think?'

'Yes, he has, but he still hasn't said much about it.'

She called Raffi from his room. 'Raf-fi!'

'Ye-es!'

'Come here, please.' She rinsed her hands, and we all went into the lounge room and plonked on the sofa in front of the heater.

'Raffi, it's time we talked about a few family things, just the three of us.'

Raffi looked at me as if I was going to bite him. His mum put her arms around both of our necks.

'You know what I'm going to tell you, don't you, darling.'

'Yeah, we're related.'

'That's putting it mildly. You two are half-brothers. You both have the same father, Bill Blayney. It happened a long time ago, obviously, and no one wants to talk about it, but there it is. It's the reason you two are dead ringers for each other. And it's why you love each other so much – don't worry, I've noticed, and I'm very happy that you have each other. And I just want you to know' – she turned to me – 'that you will always be welcome in this house as if you were my own son. I think that deep down Jean would want that for you, though I don't think you should tell her I said that.' She gave us both a squeeze, and kissed Raffi. 'Well, have I said too much? No? Well, do either of you have any questions?'

'Mum, is that why we both have epilepsy?'

A part of me wished that Raffi had asked her something entirely different – like if that was why we both liked Lonnie Donegan – anything but that.

'Yes, I think so, though I'm not clear about that. I mean, Raffi you've always had it.' She turned to me. 'And you've only had it since your brother Tom died, haven't you?'

'That's right, since just after it happened. But I don't like talking about it, because that frightens me a bit. Sorry, Mrs Radion.'

'That's all right, we don't have to talk about it today. Maybe we can talk about it when you feel like it.'

I relaxed, because that wasn't going to happen in the next two hundred years.

'Now, has there been any news about Michael?'

'Nuh. Anyway, no one talks about it when I'm around.'

'They don't want to worry you, that's all. They know how much you love him.'

'Yes, I do. I just hope the lady who's got him's taking care of him. He's not used to' – I didn't know how to say it – 'baby food, you know.'

'Yes, I know. And I'm sure she will. And if I know your mother, she won't be sitting around doing nothing, either.'

I thought out loud: 'Neither will Granddad.'

'Yes, well that's what I meant, I suppose, though I don't know him personally.'

'He's terrific, Mrs Radion. He'll catch 'em, and then –' I'd said too much.

I think Mrs R realised that, because she suddenly changed the subject, which a lot of people do when Archbold Taggerty's name comes up.

She jumped up. 'Hey, let's get those scones out of the oven.'

After scones and jam, Raffi and I went for a walk across to the old ghost cemetery called *Bethstone*, near the electricity station, where we had turned the old caretaker's hut into our new, above-ground hideout.

As we walked through the long grass and the tombstones, I noticed that the undersides of the leaves of the knobbly and dense peppercorn trees were hung thick with dark, glassy beans. Raffi saw them too.

'What are they?'

'Chrysalids. They turn into black butterflies.'

'When?'

'Soon. If we come back at the end of winter, we'll see them escape.'

'Black butterflies.'

'Judy Pickle's dad calls 'em crows; they've got one of these trees in their back yard.'

Raffi shivered. 'Let's get inside and get the fire going.'

This was what we did when we went to our headquarters, as it had a stone fireplace, and we made sure there was always a stock of paper and firewood. Soon we had a fire going, which we both tried to hog, then propped on the old bunk and put our feet up, and hopped into a few scones and jam we'd brought along.

'Hey, you know that plan of yours to catch the kidnappers?'

'I'm still working on it.'

'How long do you think it'll take to find 'em?'

'Not long. I've already got Darko investigating.'

'He's all talk.'

'And then there's the Detectives.'

'I don't reckon they could investigate their way out of a wet paper bag.'

'Charles might: he's pretty cluey.'

Raffi nodded seriously; he knew that Charles and me were like that.

'I just know I have to do *something* – he's my brother.'

'*Our* brother.'

When Raffi said that the strangest thing happened. It was like one of my fits, only in the chest, and it made me start crying like a girl whose golliwog has just been run over by a beer truck. I mean I was howling like a cheap puppy. Raffi put his arms around my neck and hugged me, not the way a mum would (I guess) but in his own way, which was better. His face was against mine, and I could feel his tears on my face, and hear his crying mixing with mine like two Buddy Holly records being played at the same time – I was thinking: 'That'll Be The Day' and 'Not Fade Away'. Raffi wouldn't have known it, but he was really hearing Tom's voice. Then I was just crying for Raffi and me, and feeling him fill the space in my chest that had been swollen but empty for a long time. I didn't have to know what Raffi was crying for, but our hearts were only an inch apart, so pretty much the same thing, I guess – Richmond kids can always guess.

Raffi gave my arm a punch. 'Hey, what d'ya say we go for another underground trip to Merri next week, and explore that electrical place at the end of it? Come on, you know ya wanna.'

'I say we don't, because first of all, there are people who would eventually find out, Mr Sanderson being the main one, and I don't want to break my promise to him again, and second, you could easily get fried in one of those places, and I'm too young to fry – get it?'

'*Too young to fry.*' He punched me again.

But Raffi had my number. I *did* want to get down under the ground again: it's what Railwayman likes best. Also, I had noticed that whenever I am down there, smelling the mustiness and the loneliness, the Dread that keeps springing up inside me like a daymare can't get a decent grip on me.

'I love exploring those tunnels,' said Raffi.

'Don't rave, Radion, you were crappin' yer dacks down there.'

'That's true, but I still loved it.'

I knew what he meant. That's what life was all about: packing death and loving it. But he had a point, and I decided to start planning a new adventure under the city where I knew the pickings were good and Mr Sanderson had no idea of them.

'Well, leave the planning to me and I'll see what I can do. In the meantime I thought you should know, just between the two of us, that now that I live up on the Hill I'm going to find out if there are any clubs up there and see if they can help me find Mick.'

'What if there's no clubs up there?'

'Oh, they're there, all right young Raffi. I know because half the kids at school are in clubs and most of those kids live in other parts of Richmond. Take it from me, there's heaps of juicy and unsuspecting clubs up there, just waiting to be infiltrated by … *the Octopus!*

'What —?'

'Yes, the Octopus who, with his trusted offsider from Fawkner Street, the Squid' — that's you — *'spreads his Tentacles of Doom all over Richmond's Streets and lanes, creeping into unsuspecting clubs and gangs, collecting clues about his baby brother's cruel kidnapping, and striking fear into hearts of bullies and crims.'*

I demonstrated the Tentacles of Doom on Raffi.

'Did you say *the Squid?*'

'Like it?'

'No, not much. Why the Squid? Why not the Barracuda?'

'Okay, Barracuda it is. I just thought you looked more the squid type.'

'I'll give you squid type in a minute.'

'Oh yeah, you and what army?' He grabbed me in a headlock.

It always ended up like this.

We didn't go home for a long time. We sat watching the lousy weather get even lousier, and feeling cold and shivery; we stayed together like wombats in a burrow. We didn't talk, but we held on to each other and sometimes we held hands. And when Raffi started to sing 'Cathy's Clown' I joined in. Next was 'Running Bear', with me doing the *ooga-oogas*, because Raffi knew all the words, and 'Only The Lonely' – we left Roy Orbison for dead. There were tons of other songs, and Raffi knew a lot more words than me.

'Hey, how come you know all the words? I could never remember them all.'

'Probably because you had a brother to muck around with, but I just listened to the wireless all the time.' Actually, I thought that sounded like a pretty good way to have fun. 'Anyway, Mum didn't like me going out much – I don't know why.'

'Maybe it's because you look like me.'

'Yeah, that would explain all the visits from the police.'

'Yeah, s'pose ... sorry.'

'But it's true, isn't it: you've been in strife a fair bit?'

'Yeah. Raff, remember before, when you asked me if Mick might be sending me messages?'

'Yeah.'

'Well, I've been thinking. Mrs Bira, who lives up near our old house, knows about that stuff – she's from Russia you know – and people go to see her to find out all kinds of things; I know Mum used to.'

'She was at Mrs Carruthers' place, that day I met Mick.'

'Yeah. Let's go and visit her on the way home.'

Mrs Bira was happy as Larry to see us, because she had known me since I was born.

'Well, hello, this is a pleasant surprise. And Raffi, isn't it?'

This Mrs Bira knew perfectly well, as she was sharp as vinegar.

'Hello Mrs Bira. We were wondering if you could help us, you know, see if Michael might be trying to tell us where he was.'

Mrs Bira didn't say anything, but opened the door for us, and led us down to her living room, which had a fire going, which we headed straight for.

'Did your mother send you?'

'No, she'd probably kill me if she knew.' I thought it best to be truthful. Raffi nodded, to back me up.

'Well, I'll tell you something, and if Jean asks me, I'll tell her the same thing: I've already asked, but the board' – she turned to Raffi – 'that's the spirit board – *he* knows what I mean – told me something that didn't make sense. They often do that, the spirits. Oh well, I'm sorry boys. Would you like some cheese blintzes with raspberry jam?'

'Would we what, Mrs Bira? Um, what did the spirits –?'

'Never mind. I shouldn't have said anything.'

When we got home, we took off our wet shoes and went inside with our arms around each other's necks, like little kids, and stared at Mrs Radion while she watched Gerry Gee saying something laughable about the Richmond footy team, who were on the bottom of the ladder, and tried to look interested. She tore herself away, and looked at us for a while – we must have looked different – and I saw her eyes go red and watery. At home, it's at times like that I usually run like hell, in case Mum's next move is to go troppo, but here there was no need. I just watched her eyes go slowly redder and waterier, and wondered if it was good or bad.

6 The Hanged Man

I had thought that I'd be going home that weekend, but the Sandersons told me that Mum and Dad had asked them to keep me for another week, which was all right for me, though it meant that Mick still hadn't been found. The next day was a Sunday and I, being an altar boy over at St Felix's church in Cremorne, was rostered on for the eleven o'clock Mass, a Mass that had its plusses. For one, you didn't have to get up at sparrow fart, when it was extra freezing, as I would have to the following week for the seven o'clock. Second, you got to have brekky, as long as you scoffed it before the three hour fasting period, which meant that you could stuff yourself stupid. Mrs S knew all about the fasting rule, and had made sure that I had an early feed. But Raffi had told me that he wanted to go too, so I went over after breakfast to pick him up.

'Well, now that we're all together, there's something I wanted to share with you, Raff. One of the reasons I don't mind you going to Mass, is that you're a Catholic too, at least Mr Radion was, and I am: we just never practised, but you were baptised right here in St Felix's church. Don't worry: we'll sort it out somehow. Normally, I wouldn't have thought much about it – it's not a secret or anything. But as you too are going to spending a lot of time together, I thought it best to tell you.'

I wasn't surprised, as every second house had non-practising Micks living in it. My own parents never went to Mass, in protest at the priest telling people to vote DLP, and in fact neither did most of the other Irish parents. Mum, who came from two old Irish families, the Taggertys and the Magees, had told Dad many times that Mannix could stick his church up his arse, and Dad always nodded, which for him was saying a lot. The church was therefore always full of DLP members and New Australians, mainly Maltese and Italians, as Richmond had received a special shipment of them after the War, on the house. There were also a lot of other European types: Yugoslavs, Poles and so on, most of whom didn't really give a bugger what the priest told them, as the priests were mostly Irish. But most of the churchgoers who had the vote were DLP supporters. You also had the odd Liberal voter, of course, not that many of those went to Mass. However, my friend James's family did, though it was usually one of the later Masses, and most of the time it was just his mother, Wonder Woman, his beautiful sister, Veronica, and him.

'Wo-ho, bewdy, Mum!'

So off we went. When we arrived I plonked Raffi down the back, told him not to leave his seat, but just to do what everyone else was doing, and not to say anything. It worked; Raffi was on his way. I actually thought that Raffi was turning into a regular religious fanatic, until I saw from my vantage point up on the altar not only that the Camponis had turned up in force but the old Raff had moved from his spot down the back, and managed to join the family down near the front, and was sitting next to Tina. Somewhere during the Mass, however, Mrs Camponi spotted the situation, and managed to get in between Tina and him (God knows how – I mean it), to prevent hanky-panky, though you can take my word for it that it's pretty hard to get up to h-p inside a Catholic church – I say nothing about your Protestant outfits, which the brothers are forever going on about.

Meanwhile, down in the front row, there was Mona, as usual, looking like a million bucks, as Larry Kent would say. Mona had long ago copied out my monthly Mass schedule, and always came to my Mass and sat in the front row, so we could look at each other; and she always went to Communion, and I talked Christopher Muldoon into letting me carry the Communion tray, so I could look at her when she stuck out her tongue. We liked that. It was our secret, which no one in the universe had guessed.

Mona's Aunty Lucky usually went along to the same Mass and Communion, and seeing her was an experience in itself, as it was always distracting, not only for me but for all the other altar boys, and also for Father, who was only flesh and blood, and for all the other boys and men in the Church, and probably within a radius of half a mile. I am willing to bet that because of Lucky a lot of blokes got a smack in the ear when they got home.

The other funny thing that happened was that father said that he was offering the Mass for 'the local boy who was abducted', which made me feel very frightened, as I definitely did not want God sticking his bib in and buggering things up, which would be typical of him, according to Barney. I quickly said a little prayer to God, asking him not to pay any attention to Father, who was probably half stung, despite the early hour. My family didn't need any help from God, and he would be aware of that.

When the Mass was over I took a peek into the church, but couldn't see Raffi. When I opened the sacristy side door, he was waiting for me.

'Ready?'

'What d'ya mean ready? What about you and Tina and Mrs Camponi? Nice try, Radion. Talk about laugh.'

'I got carried away.'

'Hello, and what do we have here?' said Father Hagen. 'Another young Blayney, I see. And why didn't I see you at Communion?'

'No, he's not, Father. He's my friend.'

'Oh I see. Well then, ah …'

'Raffi.'

'Ralphie.'

'No, Father: Raffi – it's Armenian.' I was saying it, but I wasn't believing it.

'Um, Raffi. Is that a saint's name?'

'It is in Armenia, Father' said Raffi, warming up, as I had now seen him do with the kids many times. 'Saint Raffi saved the Armenians from the Devil, and then went on a trip to Rome to be made a saint by the Pope. But he was poisoned on the way home by the wicked St George – not the good one from England but another one who really the devil's son pretending. No one would touch his body, because of the poison. So they buried him right there where he died – in Turkey, I think.'

You could see Father Hagen had more than a few questions, him being a stickler for historical correctness, but also didn't want to be rude, which is rare in an Irishman. 'So, are you Armenian Orthodox?'

'Not any more: I've been vaccinated.'

Father looked at him strangely. 'Well, I hope we see you again, ah, Ralphie.' He toddled off.

'He seems like a nice enough bloke.'

'*I've been vaccinated.*' I used my Oliver Hardy voice.

'Well, I have.'

After that Raffi had to go over to his cousin's place for Sunday lunch, and I had to go home for the same reason, these big lunches being an excellent excuse for the men of the family to guzzle the amber fluid for a few hours and play darts, while the women drank sherry and tore other women to shreds behind their backs. But I had a fiendish plan: I was going to sneak out the house as soon as I could and revisit the mysterious Caravan People. I was on a mission.

Straight after lunch, I got my cousins Lewis and Brendan interested in a jigsaw puzzle (*An English Country Garden* – I slipped a piece into my pocket before I left) and defongulated through the back door. I was on my way to Merry Old Merri, the land of tents, caravans and beautiful, mysterious girls.

This was a one-man job, and besides, what the old Raff didn't know couldn't possibly hurt him – that is a very well-known kids rule that I swear by; also *Finders Keepers* – that's another one. I thought up a few more of these handy rules while I rode my bike up to Merri. I'd had a good look at the map of the town Mr Sanderson had given me last year, and I was laughing. The trip by road wasn't nearly as roundabout as the trip by secret underground railway, and there were no electrical hazards at the end.

When I got to the end of Field Street, Clifton Hill, I came to the park on top of a little hill, circled with trees. In the clearing were the caravans, all being towed by big American cars: Fords, Chevs, Dodges, the lot. They were formed up in two circles. In the middle was the large tent I had seen, and on the other side of the park was the electricity station. I walked my bike to the big tent: nothing ventured nothing gained. There was a lot of cooking going on, and a lot of talking, but as far as I could tell, no work. No one paid any attention to me. I had become the Invisible Boy. But then again, not.

'Don't I know you?'

I turned around, expecting to see a copper – perfectly reasonable in my case. It was Father Sheehan. He had first achieved fame by stopping a knife fight inside St Dom's church at a time when the police, who had put in an appearance from across the road then run out of ideas and were making bets about who was going to carve up whom, as we say in Richmond. Then he had topped it off by rescuing a man from a burning car, losing half his face and half of one hand in the process, and getting a gong for his trouble. That had been one of those days when God was so damn hot he couldn't put up with even himself, so, just to be bloody-minded, which for God is kid's stuff, he made Barney, who was as drunk as a skunk, smash his brand new second-hand Ford Consul into a tram. The general opinion – only Nanna and I disagreed – was that Father S should have let Barney fry.

But now he could only manage one Mass a day, because he couldn't easily pick things up or speak properly. I heard from Musso Taranto that he can hardly say Mass Anymore, and has the altar boys at St Dominic's running around getting him dressed and undressed and practically saying Mass for him, and that on Sundays, he only has to say one Mass in the afternoon, and does not give a sermon. His first Mass was one Sunday arvo three weeks ago and Granddad told me there were more people packed into the place than the day after Richmond won the 1920 premiership, and most of them had already been to Mass that day. He was regarded as a living saint; I could almost feel the holiness, or was that Lux soap flakes?

I doffed my cap, as we did with priests, but in the case of this bloke, meaning it. 'Hello, Father. I go to St Dom's.'

'Oh, I know: you're Mrs Blayney's grandson, aren't you? Were you at her house this morning? I didn't see you. I saw young

Barney Flanagan though – what a lovely man he is. Do you know, he insisted I bless him last.' He shook his head in disbelief.

He would have gone to Nanna's place to give her Communion – she had been excommunicated for exceeding the maximum number of husbands allowable, but it was well-known that this little Irishman made up the rules as he went along – and to have a sherbet or two.

'No, Father, I was serving Mass at St Felix's. But what are you doing here? Is somebody dying?'

'No, young Blayney, I'm here to say Mass and to perform a wedding. All these people you see around you are travelling folk, and are here to work at the circus that's coming to Richmond. That half' – he pointed – 'are Travellers, and Irish like you and me. And that other lot' – he waved his half hand at the more colourfully dressed group – 'are Roma, or what ignorant people call gypsies, though if you want to get out of here alive you won't let that word pass your lips.'

This was practically an avalanche of information. A circus! Gypsies, or rather Roma! 'Ah, yes, Father, I have a friend from Roma: Luigi Esposito. He's an altar boy too.'

'He'll be from Rome, in Italy, where the Holy Father lives. I don't think the Romani people are even European. But they're all Catholics, since it's more convenient for the Roma to join the Holy Mother Church – cuts down on the need for priests, and so on, if you catch my meaning. Also, it's easier if they want to marry Travellers, and they do of course. So I suppose I'll be doing a Nuptial Mass. How would you like to be my server? I dare say there'll be a pound or two in it for you.'

'You bet, Father. But I haven't got any altar boys clothes.'

'Ha ha. If the Almighty cared about looks, he wouldn't let me carry on being a priest, now would he?'

He had me there. 'S'pose not, Father. But I'll have to ring my parents and tell them.' I jumped on my bike. 'I'll be back shortly.'

Clifton Hill was not short of a phone. And I'd been spending my ride to the main drag dreaming up my conversation with Mum. It was going to take all my skills of bullshitting. But I felt that I had God in my corner, not that this was always a good thing, as I have explained. Dad answered the phone, which was a good sign, as I could try the bullshit out on him first.

'G'day, Dad.'

'What d'ya mean: *G'day*. Where the hell are ya? You're supposed to be up in your room.'

'It's a long story, Dad. But it turns out that I had to serve a Nuptial Mass this arvo and I clean forgot. So I rang Father and he was hoppin' mad, because none of the altar boys had turned up. So I jumped on my bike and shot over to the church, thinkin' I'd only have to hold the fort until someone else turned up. But Dad, I'm the only altar boy here; I can't leave. And besides, there'll be a quid in it for me – you know how it works. Please explain to Mum and apologise to others' – that was me at my fiendish best – 'and ask Mum not to dong me when I get home.'

'She's still gunna hit the roof. Who's getting married?'

'Dunno, but one of 'em's Irish.'

'Poor bastards.'

'Thanks, Dad. Yer blood's worth bottlin'.'

'Don't be home too late.'

Five minutes later I was surrounded by Travellers and Roma, all of whom treated Father Sheehan like the Duke of Edinburgh, and apparently knew all about him, and would not have been surprised if he had walked on the nearby river as a special treat. In the middle of all the kissing and handshaking I was grabbed by a bloke who had Roma written all over him, and practically dragged to a caravan inside one of the circles. On the way we passed a lot of ladies with babies, which made me wonder if Mick was one of them, as I'd heard from Mrs Hutchinson that your average gypsy lady is not above dipping into the odd pram when short of a quid.

'Is this the one?'

I was facing a beautiful, swarthy woman who reminded me of Jane Russell in *Hot Blood*, wearing enough jewellery to give a puny woman a hernia, and about thirty-five dresses, one over the other. Her head was wrapped in a red scarf. She was sitting at a table, staring up at me as if she'd just heard that I was the kid who pinched her dog. Standing beside her was the girl I had seen from the doorway of the secret underground railway. Her clothes were similar, though even prettier, if that was possible. She looked at me as if I was a little kid – boys get a lot of that. I liked them both straight away despite being frightened of them. Had she dobbed me in about you-know-what? Was this the end of the line for Railwayman, not to mention the Cartographer and the mighty Octopus?

'That's him,' said the girl.

The bloke shrugged and left, which was a big relief, as I had been wondering if I was about to become the first altar boy in Clifton Hill to get his throat cut by a gypsy, or rather Rom, if that's the word.

They couldn't have looked any more foreign if they'd just been poured off the *Fairstar*. Where I came from being foreign meant nothing in itself, but often told you that a good story wasn't far away, and these two looked as Australian as the inside of a delicatessen. But it turned out they were just very strange Aussies.

'Sit down, mysterious boy,' said the lady. 'I am Mrs Petulengro. Are you Shelta?'

'Um, nuh.' So far so good.

'Then what are you doing here?'

'I'm going to be the altar boy at the wedding.'

'His name is Blayney,' said the girl. I was impressed and worried at the same time. 'I heard the priest say his name. His first name shall be Devlin.'

'No, actually, my name –'

'Your name is whatever I say it is,' said the girl, in the most stuck-up way you could imagine, 'and I say it is Devlin.'

I looked from the woman to the girl, and saw that they were mother and daughter, and that both of them were a bit like Lucky, only browner and with darker eyes. The daughter was covered up like a nun who had been let loose in Dimmeys, but the mother was letting me see about as much of her chest as she could without getting arrested (I made a mental note to find out from Barney if a twelve year-old could make a citizen's arrest; not that I intended to – I'm just saying).

This seemed to settle the matter, so I nodded. I supposed it was a gypsy thing, and I for one did not want these two amazing women – I think the girl might have been a woman too, though I was unclear on this point; she was rude enough to be a girl, but beautiful enough to be a woman – to shoo me away like a chook.

'Well,' – I jumped – 'Sunny said she'd seen you somewhere before, so I consulted the Tarot, and it told me that I should do a reading for you. It is unwise to ignore the Tarot. Do you understand?'

'Yes, the cards.'

'He knows!' said Sunny, with her eyes wide, as if I knew how many yards of chintz it takes to make curtains for a caravan (sorry, wouldn't have a clue).

'Mrs Bira reads them.'

'Who is this Bira woman?'

'A Russian lady in our old street who's descended from the Romanovs' – I was on solid ground here, having got it from the horse's mouth – 'and has a set of Tarot cards – I've seen them.'

'And has she read the Tarot for you?'

'No, but she read them for Mum once, and a week later my brother died, so Mum thinks it's bad luck.'

'And what do you think?'

'I think there's no such thing as bad luck, just God having an off day.' I was feeling pretty cocky, I admit.

The mother blessed herself, and muttered a prayer in a strange language; but I know a prayer when I hear it. 'God does not kill children. What kind of altar boy are you, anyway?'

'I'm an altar boy who used to have a twin brother, that's all I know.'

'We're sorry about that, aren't we Sunny? Now, shuffle these cards.'

I knew what was going to happen, because I had not told the whole truth, that never being a good idea. Nanna Blayney spent half her day reading the Tarot, and let people think she had mystic powers. But I didn't want this woman to know our family's secrets, so I dobbed in Mrs Bira instead, though what I had said about her reading the Tarot was true.

When Mrs Petulengro (I know) turned over the first card she quickly blessed herself all over again, and said the same prayer, so that I was beginning to doubt what I had said about bad luck already. Sunny covered her face with her hands and turned around, as if a grenade was about to go off. The card showed a man hanging from a cross by his foot, not a good start. On the plus side, he had a lovely halo. I made it one-all.

'*The Hanged Man!*' She said it as if she was announcing the winner of a raffle, but without smiling. I thought I was going to pass out.

She snatched up the card and put it back in the deck, which she kept on shuffling.

'I can read no more for this boy.'

'Mama, you have to tell him. He has to know, to take the power out of the card. We don't want bad luck for the wedding.'

'All right. You will be called on to make a sacrifice. Do not be afraid, no matter what happens. I cannot say more, as you are too young.'

'Mama, let him choose another card. Maybe we can keep going.'

Mrs P held the deck out to me and fanned the cards. Sunny began to pray to herself. I thought they were doing the best with what little material they had, so I didn't laugh or anything, but I had seen Mrs Bira carry on the same way. I picked a card from the fanned deck and gave it to Mrs P, who turned it over. It was the same card, the man with the halo, looking like he was in a fix. Now I was starting to feel in the mood for a bit of a pray myself.

'There can be no reading. I'm sorry young man. Come here.'

I went around to her side of the table, and she hugged me to her chest and asked God to protect me and give me strength during my coming trial. I could have told her that she was probably wasting her breath, God being as fickle as an antsy schoolgirl. That hug, though, was definitely worth two Hanged Men. When she released me I looked at Sunny, whose face had now lost its dark glow, and seemed to me to have gone a little pale. I was more than half hoping for a hug from SP as well, but I could tell that I would be hoping till the cows came home.

'Goodbye, Devlin,' said Sunny cheekily. 'See you at the wedding.'

Back inside the marquis, while I was helping Father J put his vestments on, he said to me, 'Your grandmother told me it was your brother who was abducted. I will be offering all my Masses and prayers for his speedy and safe return.'

'Thanks, Father.' I held my tongue, not out of fear, for priests think nothing of giving an altar boy a bit of a smack, but out of respect, for what he did for Barney.

The wedding was a crazy affair, not like any I'd seen before, and took place in the marquis. The only recognisable bit was the Mass itself. I answered it from memory, which made Father a happy little Vegemite. But I had been on automatic the whole time. I was more than a little worried about the Hanged Man. He didn't strike me as someone I'd want to be.

After Mass, the bride (Rosa) and groom (Paddy Bootsy) were married all over again, gypsy style, outside. A fire was lit and a very irritating band (half cut and just getting cranked up) swung into action, and the local gypsy king cut the bride and groom with a knife and tied their hands together, so that their blood could mix, just like in the cowboy movies. I thought Paddy was going to pass out. I heard a voice behind me say, 'You must be strong.' It was Mrs Petulengro. The wedding ended with Mr and Mrs Bootsy jumping through the fire. As I said, crazy, and I could see why Father hadn't invited them over to St Dominic's for the event: the neighbours would have called the police.

Sunny came over and spoke to me afterwards, and gave me a piece of cake. The whole time she spoke to me as if I was a little kid and she was a grown-up. While I munched she dragged me around by the sleeve and introduced me to the gypsy, or Romani as she called them, families. All the women kissed me while the men ignored or just tolerated me, except Paddy Bootsy, who gave me ten quid. 'Me and Rosa loved the way you helped that poor little priest, who could barely do the Mass. I almost cried, you know, despite being terrified.' He looked at me seriously, and I saw a scrawny man who was not used to being sober at this time of day. 'What happened to him?'

'He pulled a man out of a burning car.'

'Jesus.' He patted me on the shoulder, and Rosa appeared and whisked him away.

'Put that money away, or you won't leave with it,' said Sunny. 'It's only because you're with me that they let you walk around like this, you know.'

'Suits me. I like it here.'

'Maybe you've got Traveller blood in you.'

I thought about Nanna. 'That wouldn't surprise me, you know. My nanna has had a lot of husbands, not all of them real, if you know what I mean. And she can read the cards.' I said it before I could stop myself. I had been showing off, and had let slip family information that I had planned on keeping to myself.

'So, the mysterious Russian lady was a lie.' It was Mrs Petulengro, who had suddenly appeared behind us, like a ghost who was having trouble keeping all her bits inside her wispy clothes.

'No, they can both do it. But believe me, my nanna is far more mysterious.'

'Really?' She frowned. 'Is this your Nanna Blayney?'

'Yes.'

She laughed and shook her head. 'Oh God, I don't believe it!' She kept on laughing and shaking her head.

'So what's so bad about *The Hanged Man*? And what do I have to sacrifice?'

'There's nothing wrong with it,' said Sunny. 'It just means that your life is going to be turned upside down – you know like the card – and you're going to lose control of everything. And the only way to get out of it will be to make a human sacrifice.'

She said all this sounding like a ticket inspector who'd had elocution lessons.

'What d'ya mean: *human sacrifice?* Who do I have to sacrifice?' My voice might have shot up a notch, but there was so much noise – I swear everyone in Clifton Hill who could play the accordion and who wasn't Italian must have been there – that I wouldn't have attracted any attention.

'Stop it, Sunny, he's only a boy,' said the voice of Mrs P. 'Now, you should go home, I think. Say goodbye, darling.' She evaporated into the colours and swirls, leaving me with Sunny.

'Goodbye again, Devlin. Maybe I'll see you at the Circus over in Richmond next weekend. We'll all be there.'

'How come?'

'We'll be working there.'

This was gold-plated news all right, as I hadn't been to one of those for years, and it was also my birthday in a few weeks; so the old wheels started turning, and I immediately wondered if I could combine the two. Your average twelve year-old boy is rather partial to the sight of some bloke sticking his head into a lion's mouth. I mean, until you can actually feel the old blood run cold, you've only got the doctor's word for it that it's normally ninety-eight point six. I made a mental note to check *The Sun* for information, which is what Cookie would do in *77 Sunset Strip*. Before I could say anything, she turned around and walked away.

7 The Detectives

The next day, Monday, was the Feast of the Assumption of the Blessed Virgin Mary into Heaven – I give its correct name in case God is watching, as I do not wish to be struck down and end up in hospital again – though why Mary picked the 15th of August to disappear is beyond me. Think about it. And as it was a Holy Day of Obligation, we all got the day off school, providing we went to Mass, which, like ten thousand other Catholic kids, I had no problem with.

My altar boys group was rostered on for the seven o'clock Mass, and I was serving along with the following altar boys, in order of seniority: Christopher Muldoon (certifiable holy kid), yours truly (permanently uncertifiable, I would say), Matthew Foster (pest), Valentine Popovich (famous for having more restless legs than a bucket of yabbies), Luigi Esposito (one of my best friends), and Dennis Shanahan, who was always falling asleep, and will probably end up getting run over by a tram.

The seven o'clock is a terrific Mass to serve on a day when the weather is fine and warm, and you've got a great adventure planned, like going to St Kilda Beach. But there is nothing great about it when it's winter and raining to boot, and the last thing you want to do is get out of bed in the dark and choof off with no breakfast. But I knew that Communion wouldn't take as long as the day before, as so many people would have had brekky, this being a working day for most.

After Mass, because of the rain, Christopher Muldoon's dad said he would give me a lift home so that I could change out of my Mass clothes and pick up my school uniform for the next day. I was a bit worried that the Muldoon family might want to drop in and visit the family, because Granddad was infamous and his presence tended to make people stutter. Also, I was worried that Mum might be in one of her moods. But mainly I was worried about all the bad language they might hear, because neither the Taggertys nor the Blayneys were fans of the Holy Mother Church or its founding family; neither did we have an altar in the living room. But they decided to duck into St Dominic's church, and 'pay a visit' instead, giving me half an hour to have brekky and get changed.

As we turned into Brougham Street I saw Dad catching a tram down the hill, on his way to work, and running late. When I got home, everything seemed normal, but Mum was in a rotten mood, and I could tell by the look on Aunty Daffy's dial that something had happened. Just then, Granddad appeared, took one look at their fizzogs, and waited – ours was one of those families that doesn't speak when nudges and winks will do the trick. 'The car's been stolen,' she said to Granddad. 'Bill's reported it to the police. He asked them to let Passmore know, in case there's a connection.'

Granddad just nodded as if he was some kind of wise man in a movie, and sat down at the table. Mum made him a cuppa with lemon and I watched him sip it quietly as she bustled around, threatening to cook something. Mum was thoughtful; she was in a mood I had never seen before. She had the look of a person who thinks she might have been short-changed, and is remembering the things she brought during the day, to check. Also, she was sniffling and coughing and looked like she was at death's door. I had never seen her looking so crook.

As for Granddad, he was simply looking like he wasn't thinking at all, like a horse with his nose in a feedbag. But that would have been all front. His brain would have been going flat out.

The whole way they were getting on had changed. Mum had ceased to be a raving lunatic, which was usual for her, and had become more or less normal, if slightly more preoccupied than I like my mums to be. And Granddad had become more closed up, a bit like one of those cigarette tins you're supposed to open with your fingernail, but never can.

He waited till we were alone. 'Now, what did Luca Martello want the other day?'

I knew that for some reason that had to do with politics, Granddad did not like or trust the Martello family, and neither did Uncle Seamus, with whom he was as thick as molten lava. The Martello family was run by this character called G.A. Martello, who was a bit of a wheel in the Catholic world, and would do anything within his power to rid Melbourne of the ordinary self-respecting working man and replace him with some kind of Menzies-loving sissy. All the women in the family were beautiful, and one of them had an MG, and another one liked kissing me, and her brother, Johnny, was a bit of a mate, despite being a year ahead of me at school, and at a different school. But the Martello family, or at least, those who knew me, seemed to like me. So I thought this G.A. Martello member of the platoon couldn't be all bad.

All this ran through my head as Granddad looked at me with a serious face, like the time he asked me if I knew anything about the break-ins at Dimmeys last year. (I did, and I told him so, but I also told him that I wouldn't dob in a mate, and that, in any case,

85

nothing was taken; it was just that a Melbourne football jumper was strung up on the flag pole, you know, to upset the locals, which it did, believe me). I decided to tell the truth. After all, at the end of the day I was on Granddad's team, not Lucky's.

'Nothing, really. She just wanted us to know that she knew about Mick. She told me she was going to make enquiries.'

'Why?'

'Dunno – because she likes me, I think.'

Granddad laughed and slapped his thigh. 'That's a good'n, that is.'

'No, she does, Granddad. She's like Mona.' I had said too much.

'Oh, so that's how it is, is it? Well, you just keep family matters in the family. But if she gives you any information, let me know.'

I nodded. 'How'd you know I ran into Lucky?'

'Nothin' gets past me, boy. Just remember what I said.'

'Yeah. Hey, Granddad, you know that circus that's in Richmond at the moment. Well, I heard there's a lot of gypsies working there. D'ya think one of them might have pinched Mick?'

'Where'd ya get that silly idea?'

'From Mrs Hutchinson.'

'Gypsies don't have to lift babies; they're pretty good at making their own.'

I wished he hadn't said that. 'Gotcha, Granddad. So, have ya got any clues yet?'

'Never mind what I've got. But I will get to the bottom of it, don't you worry about that.'

Someone was going to wish they'd never been born. I watched as he calmly finished his tea, and a poached egg on toast, then left, with only a wink for a goodbye. I had an idea where he might be going; I was thinking of Ryrie's Gym. It was his favourite hangout, and a place he had trained at as a youngster. The Ryrie family ran the place, and they were like a spy network. They know all and see all, but they do not tell all, no. If they know what's good for them they wait for Archie Taggerty, the Richmond Terrier, to turn up and make enquiries. Archie Taggerty was a man you wanted to stay on the right side of. And even without his offsider and business associate, Blarney Barney, he could strike fear into a man – I had seen it.

Aunty Daffy was in the living room, having a cuppa and looking through Mum's record collection. When I walked in she patted the couch beside her, which is a thing that girls often do when they want to know if you like them (Mona had once done this, and the answer was yes).

I moved over to where she was sitting.

'I just want you to know that your family's not ignoring you. It's just that Granddad thinks you'll be safer with the Sandersons for the time being. They go way back, those two.'

'What do you mean *safer*?'

'Oh, I meant *more comfortable*.' But it was too late.

The Muldoons took me down to the Sandersons' house in Kipling Street, where I dropped my uniform off; next stop was Charles's place, just around the corner from St Felix's church, where a meeting of our new club had been scheduled to take place.

Charles got out his notebook, as usual.

'Men, you know that kid who was kidnapped last week? Well, that was my brother, Mick.'

There was a silence, while they all thought about what that meant to them. Luigi Esposito, who had about a thousand brothers and sisters spoke first. 'Jesus ... oh, sorry.'

'It's okay, Luig. It's not swearing when you get a shock.' I made it up, but I realised it was true.

'Hell,' said Douggie, 'I think those bastards pinched the wrong baby this time.'

They all nodded. Charles put his hand on my shoulder for a moment, then shoved it in his pocket. But it was all right, as we had all been friends since first grade.

'So the club's new mission is to look for clues.'

'What? You want the Olympians to find the kidnapper?'

'Not the Olympians … the Detectives! And all we have to do is keep our eyes open, so I can report anything we find.'

'Who to?' asked Charles, looking up from his notebook.

'My granddad. Eventually, he'll probably mention it to the police. But that's up to him.'

They all knew what I was talking about. In Richmond, if someone harmed a child he was lucky if the police caught up with him before the locals did. Also, they all would have heard of Granddad, as he was famous for having guys beaten up (though I thought this was rot).

'This kidnapping happened in Dimmeys on a Saturday, so lots of people must have seen something. So keep your ears to the ground. Also, we've got a new problem to investigate. Last night, someone stole Dad's car. I reckon it was the same blokes we're already looking for. So keep your ear to the ground. It's a blue and white FB Holden.'

'Is it a station-wagon?'

'Nuh.'

'Is it a ute?'

'Nuh.'

'Is it a panel van?

'Nuh.'

'Can it do a hundred?'

'Nuh.'

'What's its rego number?'

'FDE 008.'

'Well,' said Charles, writing like mad. 'That narrows it down.'

Everyone looked at me, in case I had some news.

'So,' said, Johnno Johnson, 'what's on at the flicks this week?'

'Johnno!' said Luigi, softly.

'What?'

Charles broke the silence; no one else knew how. 'Any other items?'

'What about dogs?' asked Johnno, who was still cheesed off about the naming of the club. Everyone knew what he was talking about. In the Olympians, dogs could only be members if they were not little, and you couldn't even join if you had a cocker spaniel (MBF had two of them).

'Yeah,' said Douggie, whose foxie had been knocked back.

Charles looked up from his notebook; I gave him the nod.

'I move,' said he, 'that dogs can be members.'

They all nodded. 'A detective needs his dog,' said I. A good captain lets the men feel that they are making the decisions.

8 The Octopus kicks a goal

At six o'clock, when I knew James Palmer and his family would be home, as they usually attended the final Mass of the day, I rode across Church Street bridge to their house in Chapel Street. I always liked going to James's house, despite one of his parents making me slightly nervous (Wonder Woman) and the other *very* nervous (Ken, who was a bit of a bastard). This was because they both had my number. James was in love with Veronica's best friend, Barbara, but she didn't seem to have the faintest idea that he even existed.

I once asked one of my favourite people, Uncle Seamus about this, as he seemed to know a lot about what he called the Fairer Sex, and I had observed that he was not scared of walking right up to them in the middle of the street, or after Mass, and talking to them to their faces, when just thinking of walking up to a girl was for me a bit like jumping off a cliff, the exception being Mona, who usually liked it when I talked to her.

'Well, young Tommy (Uncle Seamus was always getting us mixed up, but I didn't mind, because he was very lovely for a man, when most of the men in our family, and in our town, for that matter, were so far from being lovely that I had to agree with almost of the women I had ever met who had an opinion about them – and that's all of them), your gentler sex' – I wished he would use some other word, but he never did – 'is a very, shall we say, subtle creature, not given to outrageous advertising of her charms and wiles, of which she has been well-endowed by Almighty God.'

I had no idea what he was talking about. 'I see.'

He looked at me as if he was frozen in a time warp, then carried on. 'Your friend is oblivious to all this, and carries on as if he thinks she is not observing, yet all the while his fate is sealed. He is doomed.'

'Doomed?' This wasn't going the way I'd hoped. 'Doomed? But isn't there anything he can do?'

'Nothing – read comics, watch television, play alleys, barrack for Hawthorn' – he paused. 'No, can't think of anything else. That's it. From this point on, control has reverted to this Barbara lady, and of course, God Almighty. He is a fly in a spider's web.' He smiled like one of those kids in the holy pictures who has just beheld Our Lady of Perpetual Succour and been granted three wishes. 'It's not such a bad fate.'

I could see that he was speaking from the heart, and believed what he was saying. I wondered if Barbara was having that effect on young James.

The reason I mention this is that when I got to James's place it turned out that Barbara was visiting. Barbara opened the door and said hello to me, but that was all, as she and Veronica had some secret thing to talk about that required that they go to Veronica's bedroom as soon as they saw me turn up. Veronica, on the other hand, did not go to her bedroom straight away, but remained in the hall and spoke to me.

'Looking for James?'

I turned this question around in my mind. I had learnt that girls' questions are often about something completely different from what they sound like, and that girls often do not ask questions to find out stuff, like boys. What they do is ask questions to make you feel like you are an idiot, or for some other reason that I had not yet worked out, though I was sure it would be worth the effort in the end.

Veronica had long dark hair, and big brown eyes that looked like she was taking the mickey out of me, though the rest of her face didn't. On the Blayney Scale of Beautiful Girls and Ladies, she got a nine, just like Mona. The difference was that Mona stuck out in more places. Also Mona could kiss either noisily or quietly, which is handy when there are people around, so she deserved her nine. Also, being hugged by Mona had taken away my fear of giant squids.

The reason Mona and Veronica did not get ten was that I always gave ten to Josephine Thompson, the most beautiful girl in Australia. Josephine Thompson lived in Balmain Street and was the younger sister of Leo Thompson, the Captain of the Destroyers Club, and a kid who, it was well known, would bash up any kid who so much as looked sideways at his sister, which I thought was a bit rough. But I had looked more than sideways at Josephine, and had in fact even spoken to her. But all that happened was that I got into a hell of a lot of trouble with Mona, who did not see that I was just being friendly.

All of this flashed through my mind while Veronica patiently stood there waiting for me to answer her question. When I came to my senses and it hit me that I had not answered I realised at the same time two things: that Veronica was not upset at me for not answering but had been caught in some kind of cosmic force-field that made her patient, and second, that she was holding my hand.

Now I don't know about you, but when I have just come to my senses from a mild coma and found a girl holding my hand it is usually to find that I am in the Epworth Hospital and am having my pulse taken, because I have had one of my turns. But this was entirely different, because I was pretty sure I had not had one of my turns (but a lot less sure that I was not about to have one in the near future). I was careful not to make any sudden moves, in case girls have the same instincts as jungle cats or grizzly bears, both of which are also warm, fuzzy and cute. But it was unnecessary, because she just went on smiling and holding my hand. Then there was a call from Barbara, upstairs.

'Veronica!'

Veronica kissed me on the cheek, and toddled off up the stairs, watching me as she went. I waited while my brain started itself up again, and then waited some more while my heart started itself up again – it had stopped – then went into the kitchen to say hello to Mrs Palmer, which is what I always do, because I have noticed that mothers appreciate that, and I can always use a few more points with the various mothers around the place, especially this one, with whom I once had a bad experience, one that involved me breaking into this very house back in the days before I had ever met any of the inmates, and then being nabbed by Mrs Palmer herself. Let me tell you that it was not because of my charm and wit that she learned to like – or, perhaps, tolerate – me, but because it turned out that she and the Sandersons were old friends, and also because James and I hit it off straight away; and Wonder Woman adored James above everything. I would summarise my relationship with Mrs Palmer as one of mutual suspicion.

I found her in the kitchen making herself a cuppa. I decided against the Big Blayney Hello, as it tends to put a certain type of person on guard, I have noticed, that kind of person being mothers, though it seems to give fair to good results with all other members of the human race. Opinions are divided on its advisability. Granddad once told me to use it sparingly; Uncle

Seamus, not at all; Barney, never in front of a magistrate. I gave her my polite smile. Careful Blayney, careful.

'Hello, Mrs Palmer.'

She did not answer, but just looked at me as if I was a maths problem with two solutions.

'James home?'

She sighed and reached for her Benson and Hedges and lighter. 'He's upstairs.'

There was not a lot of joy in the room. First, it crossed my mind that she might have seen what Veronica did. *Then* it crossed my mind that she might have been expecting Mr Palmer to walk in at any minute, because he was a real bastard by South Yarra standards (though not by Richmond standards). Either way, I couldn't take a trick.

As I walked past Veronica's door I thought of the way she had lightly taken my hand; I could still feel the warmth on my skin, as if she had taken her hand away only seconds before. I used my other hand to turn the knob on James's door, so as not to lose the sensation.

James was as happy as Larry to see me. He had reorganised his train set, which was huge, and was playing trains like there was no tomorrow, still dressed in his Mass clothes.

'Ha ha, just in time. You can be the diesel.'

'G'day, James Palmer.' I was always saying that. 'I see your girlfriend is here.'

'Ha ha. What're ya talkin' about, 'girlfriend'? She's not my girlfriend; she doesn't even like me; thinks I'm a dill.' He had started off being funny, but ended up being sad. I felt stupid.

'No, James, she does like you – a lot. I even think she, um, loves you, I'm sure of it. Sometimes girls don't say how they feel. They just do stuff instead, right out of the blue. And before you know it, the stuff you'd like to happen is actually happening.'

'Is that what happened with you and Mona?'

'Sort of. I didn't have the faintest idea that she liked me, and I went over to swap comics with her brother Johnny, and the next thing I know she's asking me if I wanted to kiss her.' I hadn't told this stuff to anyone before, because I was letting all the kids think that I was like Cliff Richard and Tab Hunter rolled into one. James was all ears. 'So I said yes. I didn't do anything.'

'All the Olympians think Mona's terrific. They can't see what she sees in you. They reckon she must need glasses.' He was having fun.

'They're probably right, I reckon. If she dumped me I wouldn't be surprised.' I ran out of words. The fact is, I couldn't see it either, but it was terrific.

'James, do you really like Barbara, I mean a lot?'

'I s'pose so. But what's the use?'

'Then come over here for a minute.' He came over to his desk. 'Get your spy notebook.' He did. 'Now write this down: *Dear Barbara. I love you. Yours truly, James.*'

'I can't do that.'

'Just do it.'

James was a very obedient boy, a bit like a Dalmatian in school shorts. He did it. I grabbed the page and folded it a few times. Now write this on the outside: *S.W.A.L.K.*'

'I can't do that.' But he did.

I grabbed the paper and put it in my pocket. James looked extremely worried, a bit like the time I took him down the underground tunnel in the city and he almost got killed by a little tram that was carrying stuff in bags. He was your nervy type of kid.

'What if she sees it?'

'James, James, James,' I sighed. 'Are we chickening out?'

'Yes, definitely.'

'I didn't hear that. Don't forget: you're a detective.'

'A what?'

'The Olympians have been disbanded and replaced by the Detectives.'

'Wow, the Detectives! Who else is in it?'

'Just the old Olympians. There's another thing. You know that baby that was kidnapped; that was my baby brother Mick. We don't know where he is, but Granddad's going to find him. Also, just today they kidnapped – I mean stole – Dad's new FB Holden. So we're looking for that as well. It's a blue FB, so keep your eyes peeled.'

'You bet. Did they tell the police?'

'James, my son, they told every policeman between Richmond and Woop Woop. Also, there are certain people – I can't name names – making personal enquiries. Whoever stole my brother made a big mistake.' I said that very slowly and angrily, the way Richard Widmark would have said it.

But then James said something in a kind of absent-minded way, as if he was miles away, something that I wouldn't have thought him capable of saying, but which rocked me as if he'd punched me in the guts.

'If the kidnappers know so much about your family, they must have thought of that a long time ago.'

'James –'

But he was off. 'They'd know who your granddad was, and that he used to be the Bantamweight Champion of Australia, and that he was a war hero. They'd know that your mum used to be an army officer and killed a hundred Japs with her bare hands.' I don't know *where* he got that idea. 'They'd know that your family knows a lot of people who practically live in jail, or ought to –'

'Hey, just a minute, James old son. What d'ya mean?'

'Oh, sorry, that's what Dad said.'

'Well, those people he's talking about are Irish, you know, like Ned Kelly. They can't help it, can they?' I was on the point of telling him I knew a few blokes who'd dump his old man in the river if they heard that, and not necessarily alive either, but changed my mind even though it was the truth.

'I s'pose not. I never thought of that.'

'It's okay, James. Your Irishman is a much maligned creature, though unfairly.' I heard Father O'Connor say that, and I hoped I got it right. 'The main thing is, James, we are going to get to the bottom of this before these bastards strike again.'

'What do you mean: *we?*

'The Detectives.'

'Oh. What makes you think they'll strike again? They've got what they want, haven't they?'

'They would; they left a note saying they would. And we don't like it.'

'We should leave it to the police.'

'The police will need all the help they can get. We're going to be like the Terrible Ten.'

'Ye-ah!'

'"Cept there'll be more of us, and we'll be spread out in clubs all over Richmond.'

'But how'll we do that.'

'Not *we*, James, but ... *The Octopus! Yes, the Octopus, a strange being from up on the Hill, with powers and abilities far beyond those of mortal kids. The Octopus! Who can secretly slither up lanes and down drains, and blend into the shadows. And who, disguised as an ordinary kid, infiltrates clubs and*

gangs, to fight a never-ending battle for truth, justice, and the name and address
of the bastard who nicked his baby brother.'

'Ye-ah!'

I left the door open while we messed around, because I knew that Barbara would go home before dark. As soon as she came out of Veronica's room, I put my head through the door and held the note out to her.

'Put this in your pocket and don't read it until you get home. Promise.'

'No, I will not.' Which is girl for: *Just try and stop me.*

My work was done. Outside, the Octopus turned his head towards Richmond and the Sandersons' warm house, and slid into the long, cold shadows.

9 The Mazemaster

Half-way across Church Street Bridge, standing between the lights and staring into the Yarra, was a tall, thin boy I had known all my life, but who kept to himself. This was Carmel Bus, a boy who not only had a girl's name, but a surname that was also asking for trouble. He had just come out of Turana, a prison for kids, just for borrowing a car (which he drove to Murrumbeena, where he crashed into a mechanical excavator, which he drove to Chadstone, where he was pulled over for driving without the required lights). Now he was very sad, and at school did not participate, and when the brothers hit him, felt nothing, and fell silent. I had asked Barney about Turana, and he told me that it was a place where they 'broke' kids. Well, it had worked.

I hopped off my bike, and Carmel and me looked at each other in the bad light.

'Hi, Carmo.'

'Blayno.'

We walked together down Howard Street, to where he lived. I had no reason to do that, but I did. At the gate, he nodded for me to follow. I propped the bike, and followed him down a dark passage lined on one side with a long snake of plastic toy cars, end to end, and into a room with not much furniture, that was as hot as hell. A really old bloke sat and looked at a boy who was naked except for sunglasses, and who bounced a tennis ball against a wall.

'*Czesc, Dziadek.*' Carmo kissed the old man.

I took a seat alongside Carmo and watched.

Ka-bup … ka-bup …

'That's Atilla, that's all he does,' said Carmo. 'That's my great-granddad. He looks after him. They want to lock Atilla up, but Grandpa says no.'

The dim light, the heat, the beating on the wall, made me sad.

'Can he go out?'

'He won't wear clothes. In the summer we take him out to the back yard and put the hose on him: he loves it. I will never let them lock him up.' He looked straight at me, so hard that it was hard to believe he was about my age. 'I saw you with that Eddie kid. Watch out for him.'

'Why?' I knew I was going to hear something bad before I could stop myself.

'I met him when I was … away. He's a bit crazy. His real name's not Williams, you know. His Aunty used to talk to him in Croatian when she visited him – we're Polish you know; I can understand it a bit.'

'You mean his Mum.'

No, she never came, just his aunty.'

'Why didn't they speak English?'

'So they could have secrets.'

'What kind?'

He didn't look at me. 'Doesn't matter. Just watch out.'

'Thanks. Best I be off.'

'Go home the long way, down around Fawkner Street.'

'Why?'

'Someone's following you.' Terrific. 'Wait here while I go and see if the coast is clear.'

As I sat there in Carmo's living room and watched Atilla doing his sad thing in the nuddy, my brain felt clogged up with the events of the past few days. I had met this new kid, Eddie, whom I was forced to take a shine to simply because his old man was a test pilot (which is only the hottest job on earth, that's all). But that made me feel not quite honest with myself, as I didn't really like this kid all that much. The way he acted showed a certain *carefulness* (I would say sneakiness, but I wanted to give him the benefit of the doubt, which Granddad says you should never do, but hey, that's just me). Matthew Bloody Foster had decided to form a new club to impress Eddie (who looked like a hard kid to impress, if you want to know). But that was all right, because a very clever person had countered by forming the Detectives, and actually holding its first meeting, so as not to let the grass grow under his feet.

I had also had my face kissed by the gorgeous Veronica Palmer, who would one day look like Wonder Woman, and would probably end up getting her picture on the front of *Australasian Post*, wearing midnight blue bathers.

I had met Atilla the Naked Ball Bouncer, who practically broke my heart, but who was at least loved by someone. And finally, Carmo had filled me in about Eddie Williams, who was not Australian at all. The Octopus, always a slippery customer, had extended his tentacles deeper into Richmond & Environs.

I also thought about my map, and how it looked like a maze. When I had gone to the Exhibition Building maze with Raffi, we had discovered that you can take a map of the maze in with you, in case you get lost, especially because at chucking out time they expect everyone to either be out of the maze, or be prepared to spend the night there, which I for one would not do even if you paid me. I was very interested in how a picture of a maze and a map could be the same thing.

But mainly, I remembered that just before Tom died we had gone to the Show, and went into the Mirror Maze. That place was terrific, and had mirrors on all the walls and doors. You could get lost in there, and marooned, like Benn Gunn in *Treasure Island*, and spend the rest in your life wandering around looking at yourself in the mirror, and go nuts, and die of starvation. I heard that that actually happened to a kid, and his ghost is still there and haunts you. Or am I thinking of the Ghost Train?

Anyway, when Tom and me were in there, you'd think that we'd have a very hard time finding our way out, because there were two of us, and we would have seen twice as many reflections of ourselves as ordinary kids, and gone round the bend twice as fast – you'd think. But that's not what happened, because we were used to looking at our reflection all the time, even when there were no mirrors around. So we weren't lost at all, and found our way to the exit like a couple of bloodhounds who'd smelled a dead body.

I thought the same thing would happen last year, when I went back to the Mirror Maze with Peanut on Show Day, but something strange happened, because when I looked at myself in the mirror I saw Tom looking back at me.

'Peanut, look, it's Tom,' said I.

'It's both of you,' said the Peanut, who had known us both since the day he was born, and was therefore allowed to say stuff like this. 'You look the same,' he added, in case I had forgotten that Tom and me were identical twins, because Peanut has a way of summarising the situation, whatever it is.

When we got our Herald Learn-to-Swim Certificate last summer, Peanut couldn't make his hand let go of the side of the pool, till the examiner said to him: 'No swim, no certificate.' So Peanut said: 'I think I've got it,' and off he went. That was one hundred per cent Peanut.

But the point is, I was never the same after being in the Mirror Maze, and when I came out I felt like I was two people again, like last year when I kept turning into Tom and then back into me every five minutes, and completely forgot which one I was supposed to be for a few months. It disappeared after a while, but I never forgot the weird feeling, and how lovely it was for Tom to be alive again, even if it meant that I was completely gone for a while. Peanut was dead worried when he saw the funny look on my dial in the Mirror Maze, because he had seen me have some of my seizures – like everyone and his dog – and was worried I was going to have one on the spot, because of the mirrors and the way I had said I could see Tom. He grabbed me by the arm and started to steer me out of the place like mad.

'Peanut, stop it – I still haven't had my bob's worth of mirrors!'

'I thought … you know.'

'Strike me pink,' I said, which was one of Granddad's favourites. 'If I feel like chucking a wobbly – not that I do – I'll bloody-well let you know.' I thought this was one of those times when a 'bloody' would be in order, as it was practically a rule between Peanut and me that when we were out and about we had to say bloody as much as possible, to make up for all the times we couldn't say it at home, in case our mothers murdered us. But Peanut had been genuinely worried, so I gave him a little bit of the old pretend boxing routine, ducking and weaving and throwing a few little punches to his arms to show him I was okay. 'See?'

We were still having our pretend boxing match when we came out, and a beautiful girl with red hair gave us a lovely green and gold maze medal each.

'Can I have two?' I asked.

'I'm not *made* of bloody medals,' said the beautiful girl, suddenly sounding a lot like one of the strappers at the track. 'Piss off.'

'It's for his twin brother,' said Peanut, who could read my mind like the back of a corn flakes box.

'Why can't his brother get his own medal?'

'Cos he's dead,' said Peanut, summing up the situation very neatly, if a bit on the harsh side.

The girl looked at me with just the kind of look you always want to see on a girl's face, especially if that girl is Josephine Thompson, the most beautiful girl I had ever seen, but who I was beginning to think would never take an interest in me. She dipped into the box, and gave me another medal, looking around at the spruiker as she did so.

'Don't let my dad see this, or he'll kill me. I'm sorry I said that about your brother.'

'It's all right, I'm used to it … thanks.' But that was a load of bull. I knew deep down that I would never be used to it, not if I lived to be a hundred and twenty and ended up in a freak show as the World's Wrinkliest Man. Basically, if anyone other than Granddad mentioned Tom's name, it made me hurt inside like something had busted, like one of the air hoses in your chest. Peanut, Charles, and a few of my mates were okay too, as they had liked Tom a lot. But around the house, and with the rellies, it was hard yakka putting up with a conversation about Tom without screaming at everyone to shut up. I mean it.

While all this was going on, a queue of kids had formed behind us, and one of them pushed me out of the way. 'Where's *my* medal?' said the kid.

'Here's your bloody medal. Now piss off!' That girl was dynamite.

All the way back, Peanut and me made sure that everyone on the train saw our special medals, though every kid on that flamin' train had one. But secretly, in my pocket, I had another, one that was eventually going to come to rest on Tom's grave over at the Melbourne Cemetery.

Then an idea started forming in my scone, not clearly, more like one of those ideas you get when you're on the Big Dipper, but you keep wondering instead if it's going to come off the tracks, and you're going to die.

Then I snapped out of it as I realised that Carmo was back.

'I couldn't see anyone. They could be waiting up at Church Street. Don't forget: go the long way. I left your bike down the corner.'

I did as Carmo suggested, but saw nothing unusual, and rode down all the old streets I had brought up in, until I came to Fawkner Street. As I was riding past Raffi's place, the idea I had suddenly hit me. It had been all that thinking about the Mirror Maze that had started it. It was time to adopt a new secret superhero identity – I know, I already had one or two – one which would give me the kind of secret powers I'd need to solve the puzzle.

As I pedalled, I felt myself changing into … *The Mazemaster! Yes, the Mazemaster, a strange being from up on the Hill with powers and abilities far beyond those of normal kids. The Mazemaster! Who can work out puzzles at a single try, go places no one else can go, and, with his knowledge of the streets, lanes, and drains of Richmond, gets around secretly, dodging police, De La Salle Brothers, and other bad bastards. And who, with his faithful offsiders, the Detectives, gathers the intelligence needed to avenge his dead brother* – no, I mean: *to rescue Mick.*

A gentle excitement happened inside me as I turned up Kipling Street, only to run smack into the door of a car which had opened suddenly in front of me. As I hit the ground, someone grabbed me and dragged me over to the car. Just as I was wondering what was going to happen to me something was put into my arms, and the car took off and shot down a lane. It was Mick.

I was paralysed with terror even though the danger was gone, and looked at him to see if he was okay, but he looked his usual self. I felt that I should say something.

'G'day, Mick.' But Mick was playing no talkies.

On the way to the Sandersons, I told Mick he was famous, to make him feel better, and filled him on tomorrow's news headlines: *Boy finds missing baby*. No: *Boy risks life to save brother* – much better. Or how about: *Octopus* – no – *Mazemaster, rescues baby brother*. That hit the spot.

At the Sandersons' house, I leaned my bike to their fence and took Mick in.

Mrs S put Mick on the table and unwrapped him, while Mr S watched, and I told them what happened. There was a note, which Mr S read, then put in his pocket.

'He's all right,' said Mrs S.

'I'll ring Jean,' said Mr S.

'Tell her it was a black Vanguard, Mr Sanderson.

'Did you get the number?'

'Nuh, sorry.'

'How about the people?'

'Both men – that's it.'

They made me stay behind while they drove Mick home. Mrs S reckoned Mum would like some peace and quiet over the weekend. I headed for the kitchen. The Mazemaster was still in a daze, and was feeling a bit peckish.

Next morning's newspaper headline was not as I had hoped. In fact, I didn't get a guernsey at all. It was all Michael this, and

Michael that. Fair dinkum! Mrs Sanderson watched me reading the front page as I hopped into brekky.

'It was thought best to keep you out of it,' said Mrs Sanderson, turning to Mr S.

'Still a lot of work to be done,' said Mr S. 'Still, you did a terrific job, and Mick will thank you one day.'

'What did Mum say?' I realised it was a stupid question as soon as I asked it.

'Don't worry, she'll thank you when she sees you.'

I thought I had better not hold my breath.

'And in the meantime your grandfather asked me to give you this as a little reward.'

It was a tenner.

'Mm, a brick, ta, Mr S. A bloke can always use one or two of these. I think I'll buy Mick a present – he looked a bit worried when he realised he was going back to Mum – and shout my mates to the Circus.'

'And until these people are caught, it will be better if you stay here with us.'

I could tell by the way they forgot to smile as they told me this, that they weren't offering me a holiday home, more like a hide-out.

10 The black Vanguard

Thursday night is the worst night of the week. Usually, all the good things that happened to you last weekend have worn off, and you feel like you've run out of ways to keep yourself amused. On Monday your club was probably swinging into action as the result of something exciting or disastrous that happened on the weekend, often something you couldn't possibly have tipped, owing to the inconsiderateness of the modern parent. Tuesday you realise you're behind in your homework (Brother Ambrose was kind enough to remind you) and have to get your arse into gear if you are to avoid *beaucoup* pain. By Wednesday night all you want is to kiss Mona again, especially as you saw her after school and she said hello from across The Vaucluse (because if girls or boys cross the street they can be sentenced to more pain and suffering than you would believe possible unless you were an expert on medieval torture), and passed you a note through her friend Maria Esposito, who is one of Luigi's eighty-five sisters (who *are* allowed to cross the street, if you can believe it). The note would say: *Sweetheart* (she's always calling me that) *I can hardly wait until our lips meet again. See you again tomorrow.* And on the back were the letters *S.W.A.L.K.*

But this week had been different. On Monday the Mazemaster, who had only been made up a few seconds earlier, had risked his life to rescue his brother from a truckload of bloodthirsty kidnappers (and car-nappers, don't forget), which just goes to show that this superhero thing really works, and on the same night had got a nice crisp tenner from Granddad as a reward. Also, on the Tuesday night Aunty Daffy had given me a present.

'This is for reuniting my sister and me, rescuing my nephew, who seems to have turned over a new leaf, and giving up your bedroom – and for what you did last night of course. Also, I understand it's your birthday on Sunday. Your mum tells me you want one of these, so here you are.'

It was a Kodak Starmatic, probably the greatest invention since the Chiko Roll. The first thing I did was get Mum to take a picture of Daffy and me. She had no way of knowing it, of course, but Daffy had made it possible for me to become: *The Photographer! A strange kid from the shadows with powers and abilities far greater than mortal kids. The Photographer! Who takes pictures of bad bastards (and the occasional good bastard), and sticks them on his Map of Mystery.*

Then I was packed off back to the Sandersons' place again, as it was considered that Mum and Mick needed a bit of quiet time together. Actually, I thought this was a good idea, because Mick had now spent half of his life with the kidnappers, and might have forgotten who Mum *was*.

But on that Thursday, after school and before going over to the Sandersons' place, I had a detective mission to carry out. I had discovered that the closest park to my new home up the Hill was just around the corner in Lyndhurst Street, and was always full of kids. As my old friends lived way down the hill near the river, I was tempted to go over and see what the local kids were up to, especially as the twilight was getting longer, and to look for clues about the kidnappers. My plan was to go down there, and 'introduce' myself. Little did they know that they would be meeting: *The Mazemaster!*

So after school I went home and changed into my South Melbourne football jumper and footy shorts, and took off carrying my footy boots. At the corner of Lyndhurst Street I ran into a huge mob of local kids who were not in their usual place down at the park, but on their way up the hill. They took one look at me, decided that I fully equipped for kicking a few goals, and waved at me to come with them. They had the attitude of a lynch mob who had just found out that a well-known murderer had just arrived in town and was wetting his whistle down at the local saloon.

'Where're we goin'?' I asked one particularly nasty looking kid, who I had noticed was in a position of authority, perhaps chief vigilante.

'We're having a quick match against the Bridge Road mob. Coming?'

I'd never heard of them, but where I came from any group of kids with the word 'mob' after it was usually one of those kids groups your mother didn't want you associating with, for reasons of personal safety.

'Course. I could do with a bit of kick-to-kick.'

'No, this is a real match, with goals 'n' things. It's a grudge match, for what they did to us last year.'

I swallowed. 'Well I'm not really much of a player actually.' I had noticed that adults say 'actually' on the end of things when they want to sound fair dinkum.

'Don't be silly. I know who you are. You're that Blayney kid whose as mad as a snake, and bashes up bullies 'n' stuff. Anyway, I've seen you play footy at school. You're just what we need to *smash* those kids to bits.' He suddenly brightened up and stuck out his hand. 'I'm Bruce Dees. Call me Diesel.'

I had heard of this Diesel kid, who was in Form Two at St Dom's: he had a reputation for murdering kids in a variety of sports and getting away with it, because it was, well, sports. The brothers adored him, because he had met one of their standards for being favoured: brains, sports or holiness. The way he was going he was probably going to be canonised for playing football. I also heard that no matter what position on the ground he was assigned he just ignored it and played wherever he liked. His team usually won, so it was hard to argue with him. Also, he was always the captain.

'Hi, um, Diesel.' I stuck my hand out.

'We call our team the Dakotas, because that's the name of our club; we're all in it.'

'That's a cool name for a club.'

'Yeah, we named it after the plane.' I wasn't surprised, as probably half the clubs in Australia were named after aircraft. 'So you'll be playing as a Dakota.'

'So what do the Dakotas do?'

'We play footy after school – what does it look like?'

'Well, I've got this terrific thing that my old club down near the river used to do. We used to spy on everyone we met to see if anyone said or did anything dodgy, in case it was a clue to some crime that had been committed around here.'

'Why?'

'Because the police always give a big reward to any kids who help them track down and catch criminals.'

'What criminals did you have in mind?'

'Well, a baby was kidnapped the week before last, while its mother was in Dimmeys and then, a few days ago, was returned to its home in Brougham Street. How weird it that? So how about the Dakotas listens to other people's conversations until we get a few clues as to who did this rotten thing to this baby?'

'Okay, we will.'

I could tell that this club, while having a terrific name, did not know its arse from its elbow and badly needed someone like Charles to come along and organise it – you know, have proper meetings and so on – so that it would able to get things done like a real club and take a bit of pride in itself. This is what Granddad says you need if you are going to succeed, which is exactly why the Victorian Police Force is in the sad state it's in and why no self-respecting crim wants to be arrested: because he does not want to be seen in the company of such deadbeats.

When we reached the oval behind the Town Hall we discovered that the Circus, complete with Travellers and Roma, had set up shop and taken over the whole oval. I nearly got eye strain looking for Sunny, but it was a case of no go.

'What're you doing, Blayney? We're playing over here,' said Diesel, pulling my jumper.

Alongside the main oval was a smaller one on which there was a bunch of kids playing kick-to-kick and looking like they meant business. Without any conversation at all we paired off and took whatever positions we liked. The umpire was a girl who appeared as if by magic, wearing shorts and football boots and with a real umpire's whistle around her neck. It was worth going up there just to see a girl umpire. Just before ball-up Diesel walked past me, and murmured to me, 'Now that *you're* here, Blayno, we're gunna kill these Croatian kids.'

I had heard about these Croatian kids of course, but I had always thought they took no interest in Aussie Rules footy. I like to see New Australians enjoying a game of footy as much as the next kid, but I felt that we would have an unfair advantage. I needn't have worried.

What the Croatian kids lacked in knowledge of the rules they made up for in good old-fashioned violence. You have to admire that. There were only three rays of sunshine in the whole episode. First, the game was eventually called off due to darkness. Second, I got into a fight, which I eventually won by kicking the other kid in the pills, a trick that Dad taught me. And third, the Ruckman for the Croatian Mob turned out to be a friend of mine from school, and from Cremorne, Tangles Dudek.

After the match he came up to me and shook hands. It was like being grabbed by a giant stick insect.

'Great match, Blayno. Ha ha.'

'Hi, Tangles. Yeah, who won – do you know?'

'You did, not that it matters. We'll have a rematch next year I s'pose. That's quite a nasty kick to the knackers you've got there. And they say *I've* got a temper.'

'Yeah, 'cept I didn't do me block, Tangles. I remained cool, calm and collected.'

'Yeah, an' I still believe in the Easter Bunny, Blayno, my lad.'

'But Tangles, what're *you* doing up here?'

'My uncle's opening a restaurant in Bridge Road, so the whole Croatian Club's turned up to have a party.'

'But I thought you kids only played soccer?'

'We do; that's why you won. Next year, your club has to play soccer against us. Ha ha. That's going to be great. Better watch your nuts *then*, Blayno.'

'Yeah. Hey, Tangles, Matthew Foster's forming a new club with his new next-door neighbour, a kid called Eddie Williams, whose old man's a test pilot, and I was wondering if you and your friends would be interested in being in it.'

'Yeah, sure. By the way, I heard about your little nipper from Darko Stepanovic. His said his dad's making enquiries.'

'Why isn't Darko here. His old man'd be in the Croatian Club wouldn't he?'

'His father wouldn't let him play, you know, because of the umpire. She's Debby Shineberg from the milk bar near school.'

'Yeah. I've never seen a girl umpiring a game of footy. So what?'

'She's a Jew.'

'Who gives a stuff?'

'Ha ha! That's a bewdy, Blayno: *Who gives a stuff?* You wouldn't want to say that to Darko's old man.'

'I don't get it.'

'Neither do I. I think she's pretty good-looking, but.'

'She sure is. Oh well.'

Tangles seemed to have run out of gas completely, so I caught up to the Dakotas, who were on their way down Lyndhurst Street. As I got to the corner of Brougham Lane, the lane that ran behind our house, the kid who'd been playing full forward for us and had kicked a few goals stopped me.

'Wait a sec.'

'G'day. What's up?'

'It's about that kidnapping you were talking about, the one that was on the news, on the wireless.'

'What about it?'

Well, you wanted to know if we'd seen anything unusual.'

'Yeah, it's part of my investigation.'

'Why are you investigating?'

'Because the baby was my brother, Mick. What of it?'

'Well, I did see something unusual, but I got into strife for seeing it. Look I'll show you what I mean.'

We turned into Brougham Lane and walked up it until I was outside my own back gate.

'Well?'

'That Saturday, I saw a black car park here, and a bloke get out and break into your back door and go inside for a few minutes later. When he came out again they went like hell.'

'But the lock wasn't busted, or anything; we would have noticed.'

'He did something to the lock.'

'How'd you see all this?'

'I live just here' – he pointed to the house on the other side of the lane. 'I saw them through my bedroom window. I've seen you lots of times.'

'Did you see their faces?'

'Not really.'

'What kind of car was it?'

'A black Vanguard.'

'Why didn't you tell someone?'

'I told my old man and got a smack in the ear.'

I could see that; he probably just picked a bad time. Or more likely, they didn't want to get involved. 'What else?'

'That's it. I thought there might have been a connection, because it was the same morning that baby was kidnapped.'

'How'd you know that baby was my brother?'

He looked a bit worried. 'Cos that's the day your baby stopped crying all the time. Also, we could hear your mum doing her block about it.'

'Oh, yeah. No, you did the right thing. Thanks for telling me.'

'That's all right. I'll see ya.'

'See ya.'

I could hardly wait to get over to the Sandersons' place, and mark my discovery on the map. When I got inside I found Mum organising dinner.

'Hi, Mum.'

'Get those filthy clothes off.'

'Hey, you know that circus that's up at Bridge Road?'

'What about it?'

'Well, I made a couple of quid at that wedding I served at the other day and I was thinking of taking a few of my friends to the Circus instead of having a birthday party. What d'ya reckon?'

'It's your money.'

'You little ripper, Mum.'

I took my clothes off, and found Granddad in front the heater having a cuppa.

'G'day Granddad, give 's a bit of heater.'

He moved over – you have to know how to handle him.

'G'day boy, what's new?'

'Those people who stole that stuff from your room, they were in a Black Vanguard. I reckon they got in by picking the lock – you know.'

He looked at me for a while with a straight face, then relaxed.

'Was it the same car, you know, from last Monday?'

'I think so.'

'Thanks, it's a start. Who told you that?'

'Kid over the back I was playing footy with tonight. His parents told him to mind his own business, so he did. But I asked the Dakotas – that's our club down the park – to help me, and this kid did.'

'Number plate?'

'Uh-uh. You know, I reckon they were the ones who pinched Mick.'

'We'll find it.'

'Granddad, Darko Stepanovic's old man wouldn't let him play footy because the ump' was a Jew.'

'Who told you?'

'Tangles Dudek.'

'Tall, skinny kid.'

'That's him.'

'Jesus was a Jew wasn't he?'

'Ye-ah.'

'Darko's old man's a dickhead. You like Mrs Bira, don't you?'

'Course, but she's Russian.'

'She's a Russian Jew.'

'You learn something new every day, Granddad.'

He did the big eyes, and nodded the lemon, only slowly.

11 Banned

So now it was Thursday night, and I was back at the home of Mrs and Mrs Sanderson, 32 Kipling St, Sth Richmond E.1, Vic. There was the usual homework, and on top of that I had to study for a bloody Latin test the next day. But the best thing about it being Thursday was that I got to look forward to Friday. And that was because Lucky usually took Mona and me for coffee after school in her MG.

But it was on this particular Friday that my difficult relationship with the De La Salle brothers came to a head. I was called to the Principal's office, and passed Charles coming out as I was on my way in – it's a bit like the Court system – and had just drawn breath to ask him what was up, because he was in tears, when a voice yelped: 'Blayney!' and I had to keep going.

The Principal, a nasty piece of work called Brother Timothy who had my number and had been informed by Mother Sylvester at St Felix's that I was bad to the bone and needed watching like boiling milk, was sitting upright behind his desk like some kind of magistrate about to pronounce sentence – I had been here before – and attempting to give me the evil eye (he didn't have a hope: he had not perfected it, and I could have told him for free that he was not a patch on the nuns down near the river).

As I stood in front of him I thought about something Granddad had once told me about him: that he came from the arsehole of

Melbourne, Collingwood. I was tempted to feel sorry for him, but then, not. He was still not talking. This was something I had learned about Brother Timothy, that he would sometimes keep you waiting for as long as five minutes before speaking, as a way of putting the fear of God into you. Pretty soon, you'd either piss your pants from terror, or wish you had just to break the monotony. Then, like a trapdoor spider he would strike.

But you can't put the fear of God into a kid who doesn't care anymore. In fact my whole life had become a search for God, so that I could exact my fiendish revenge, that or give the whole God thing a big miss. I mean, fuck him. I'm sorry but that's the truth. This is what I was thinking as I watched this bloke treat me like a crim. And I thought to myself that if Barney was here he'd give him a little tap and put him in hospital for six months, because Barney was a very big bloke, and took a dim view of anyone who looked sideways at me, and this bloke had gone well beyond sideways.

'How dare you look at me in that insolent manner when I'm speaking to you, Blayney.'

I attempted to adjust my look, but I knew I wasn't going to win the Looking Competition. These brothers learn twenty different looks in their training, like the Gestapo, and Smersh, the crowd who torture James Bond every five minutes – I've read the books.

'I couldn't sleep last night, Blayney. And do you know why?'

I didn't, but he was beginning to get my interest.

'Because I was seething. I was *seething*.' I was tempted to point out that he had begun to repeat himself, which Granddad told me is never a good sign, and could mean anything from poor conversational skills to a brain disorder. I decided to keep my suspicions to myself. I still didn't know why I was being interrogated. If it was to find out secret information I didn't have any just then, so I was thinking that I might have to fall back on some advice I had been given by Barney.

'So Barn,' I had recently said, 'you've been in strife a few times, haven't you?'

'But never caught red-handed, young feller, except in the course of committing a burglary, but that doesn't count, as I am what is known in the profession as semi-retired, and besides, I'm not even sure that burglary is a crime, if you see what I mean.'

I didn't. 'What I mean is, you've been in court a few times.'

'Before the beak, yes, but never fairly. Your Irishman's lot is a hard one, nipper. Look at Ned Kelly.'

'Yes, but you've never shot a copper, Barn.'

'I've wanted to, though, oh yes I have. But I never carry, you see; I prefer the old Bowie knife.' He patted his lower trouser leg, where I knew he kept a huge knife sheathed. 'Also, a bloke like me caught carrying would get a very long holiday, and let me tell you the College is a bad place for an Irishman. For one thing, jails are dry – did you know that? Dry as a nun's nasty.'

'Sounds awful.'

'Stay out of the clutches of the rozzers. It just requires a bit of the old brains, and you've got stacks of 'em. So what's happened – you in strife?'

'It's these flamin' brothers, Barn. They think that just because I'm half Blayney and half Taggerty that I must be responsible for everything that happens at school. While other kids are getting away with murder I'm getting pinched every five minutes for stuff I didn't do.'

'I get you: *stuff you didn't do*'. He winked.

'No, Barn, stuff I *really* didn't do. If I really do stuff, no one finds out; I'm very careful. I remember all the things you taught me.'

'Good lad. But it means they'll only have circumstantial evidence and you can't convict on that.'

I thought Barney had gone mad. I mean, I had watched enough Perry Mason to know that that was just not the case.

'Barn, all my friends are getting into trouble too, just for being my friends.'

'The same thing happened to Ned Kelly.'

'Barn, can we stop talking about Ned Kelly for a minute?' I knew that even though he was a lovely bloke, Ned had definitely done a few things that were frowned upon by the law, like killing rozzers, robbing banks, and the like. And I didn't think the evidence was very circumstantial. I couldn't help thinking that Ned had been a little careless, though I kept my opinions to myself.

'Okay, well, you have to stand rock-solid by your mates, don't you? I mean, lose your loyalty to them and where are you? You're not a man and you'll never be one. Not to mention that if you bump into anyone you knife later in life you better be prepared to have it done to you.'

This is what I was thinking as I stood in front of Brother Timothy who was, as far as I could tell, seething on all cylinders.

'You will stop associating with' – he picked up a sheet of paper and began reading – 'Charles Dixon, Luigi Esposito, David Johnson, and Douglas Quirk. You will not speak to them or be seen with them. They are a bad influence, especially Dixon. Do I make myself clear?'

I could hardly believe he had told Charles he was a bad influence, because Charles would not be a bad influence even if he became an axe murderer. He did not have what it takes to be a b.i. Just seeing Charles crying had made me feel very bad. Johnno and Douggie, I could understand. Their parents treated them worse than animals a lot of the time – I had seen and heard terrible things – and had even told Granddad, though he thought it was none of my business what they did to their kids. That was the way of the town. What I mean is, they were a bit rough round the edges, and that was to be expected. Still, they had no influence on me at all compared to the devil, who got right into me and gave me hell every time I turned around.

I told Father Hagen about the devil recently and he only sighed. Not just a little sigh though. It was like he was remembering what it was like to be a kid. I could feel it through the screen in the confessional box. 'You're too hard on yourself. That's not the devil, that's just pain, and we all have it. Your parents have it, too – that's not your problem, though. Now forget about that devil stuff. Just remember that Our Blessed Lord is always with you.' He had been doing well there for a minute, and then he had spoiled it.

But I hoped that Luigi would spend the evening telling his father what Brother Timothy had said, and perhaps add, whether it was true or not, that the Chief Thug had said that all dagos were bastards, because if he did, the next visit Brother Timothy'd get would be from some blokes from Vic Market, carrying wire cutters and what have you.

Brother Timothy was looking at me as if I was a picture puzzle. I thought I'd chip in with a question.

'What about Matthew Foster, Brother?'

'Do I make myself clear?' he yelled as loud as he could. The secretary in the outer office stopped typing. I could smell floor polish.

'Yes, Brother.'

'Get out.'

At the end of the day, the Banned Buddies had a lot of catching up to do, and we did, but we had to do it outside the school gate.

'Well, what they hell was *that* all about,' said Douggie Quirk.

'That bastard told me you were all bad influences on me,' said Johnno Johnson. 'I think I can be a bad influence all by myself, thank you very much.'

'Course you can,' said Luigi. 'But what if my father finds out? You don't know him. He's got a pretty bad temper.'

It was hard to imagine, as Mr Esposito was not a big man. In fact, the whole Esposito platoon was smallish, and would have been able to take a submarine trip to China without banging their heads once.

'I say let him come over and do whatever he likes to Timmo,' said Charles, in a rare burst of vengefulness. 'He said I was a bad influence. I don't mean to be. I mean, do I?'

'Charlie, that was all bullshit. He knows you're the only one of us who's *not* rotten to the core.'

'Hey, take it easy, Blayney. Who do you think you are?' said Johnno.

'Fellers, let's not fight,' said Luigi. 'That's what Timmo wants. We have to find some way of fixing him, preferably without my father finding out about this whole thing, or he'll arrange for a little accident to happen to Brother – accidents do happen, right?'

I could tell that the others thought this was just big talk, especially as the Espositos were just little guys, but I knew from what Granddad had said here and there that the local Italians could take care of their own, and the results might not be pretty.

'And why the hell wasn't Matthew Foster included in this ban, like the rest of us?' said Johnno. 'I mean, he's always hanging around us, and then there's his way of laughing at everything we

126

say as if it's the funniest thing since *Abbot and Costello meet The Mummy*. And also, he's pretty hard to take at the best of times.'

We were all looking at the Matthew Foster at this stage because he was coming towards us.

'Hi, fellers. What's up?'

'We've been banned from talking to each other at school,' said Charles, who was used to summarising club business, for the minutes.

'Well, you must admit you've been asking for it, haven't you?' said Matthew, pretty smugly.

'Brother Timothy said you were next, Foster,' said Johnno. 'He said he had a special punishment saved up for you.'

'Ha ha, special punishment, that's rich Johnson. Brother Timothy thinks I'm De La Salle material, you know – that's what he told Mum. I could end up being *Brother* Matthew one day.'

No matter what you say to Matthew Bloody Foster he bounces back like a lacker band. I gave up a long time ago, and the sooner Johnno and the others did the same the smoother their lives would be.

'Oh well, now that you're here I can tell you that Tangles Dudek told me last night that he wants to be in the Rockets, and some of his mates too.'

'Okay. That Tangles kills me.'

'Well, anyway a couple of us can visit them in the morning and see what they think. Why don't I come over to your place Matthew?'

Meanwhile, while all this was going on, there was a deep burbling noise, and Lucky's MG swung into The Vaucluse and nosed into the gateway of Vaucluse College. As the car rolled past, Lucky gave a little wave to me, but swept the group of friends with her bright, dark eyes. They in turn became silent lest they miss a moment of the scene, which was one made for a boy. I smiled and waved back and turned to my friends.

'Must be off; that'll be my ride. I'll catch you in the morning,' which I realised must have sounded odd, as I lived a hundred yards away. I crossed to the sports car, opened the door and hopped in, and said hello to Lucky, who was happy to see me.

She often turned up on Friday after school and took Mona and me to some Italian cafe or other, where she shouted us coffee and cake – as far as my parents knew, it was hot chocolate, thanks to a little tip from Lucky – and we discussed the week's adventures.

'This is a treat, Mr Blayney,' said Lucky. 'Looks like this is becoming a regular event. Tongues will begin to wag.'

I could have told her that tongues had been wagging all over the Blayney household and the precincts of St Dominic's De La Salle College, and probably a few places I hadn't even heard of yet, as there would be very few twelve year-old boys within the Melbourne metropolitan area who would ever be seen with such a beautiful woman in a sports car, except maybe in their own imaginations. As usual, I did not know what to say to this, as Lucky was a Commonwealth Games level kidder; so I just gave her a little smile and tried hard not to look at her open shirt.

'Mr Blayney, what a devastating response! Now you have *me* blushing. Ah, here is my gorgeous niece.'

'Hello Aunty Lucky; hello, um …'

'Mr Blayney,' suggested Lucky, playfully.

'Yes – *Mr* Blayney,' said Mona, imitating Lucky.

As Mona opened the door I looked around to see how the boys were taking it – the answer, to my secret delight, was badly. I chalked that up as a clear victory to … *the Secret Agent!*

Yes, the Secret Agent, a mild mannered kid from up on the Hill, who gets around with gorgeous women in very hot sports cars, tangles with evil-doers, and organises kids so that they carry out his plans to save the kids of Melbourne from the clutches of … the Kidnapper! (his evil and mysterious nemesis). And who, disguised as particularly bright kid from North Richmond, will stop at nothing to carry out his mission.

'Hello, um, Mona.' It sounded daggy.

By this time we were away, and Mona straightaway started interrogating me like mad about Mick. I answered all her questions, and threw in a bit of extra stuff about what happened in Kipling Street, which is always okay when your interrogator is a beautiful spy who is actually sitting on you.

By the time we had reached Coco's, I was all interrogated out and creased up, which is not the look your secret agent strives for. (He does not mind a smidgeon of lip-stick on his shirt, but Mona does not wear lipstick to school, she being one of those students who is keen on living to a ripe old age).

When we went in, we got the Big Hello from Mr Coco, and let me tell you that the Italians leave the Aussies in the starting gates when it comes to Big Hellos. For a start there is kissing. There is also cake, and I had come to see that, even though Lucky always offered to pay, her money was no good there. I asked her about this once.

'Lucky?'

'Yes, dear?'

'How come Mr Coco never lets you pay.'

'He's a close friend of our family. You could say that we consider him to be one of the family.'

'Yes, I see, like when you call someone uncle but they're really just old friends of your parents or your granddad.'

'Yes, except sometimes they're business friends, not family friends.'

'Oh, yes, like my Uncle Barney. He's always around at family dos but he's not really a rellie.'

'Yes, a bit. Barney would never refuse your granddad a favour, would he?'

'No fear, nor me if he thought I was in trouble.'

'That's right. Well, we have people like Barney too.'

'I see, and Mr Coco is one of them.'

'No, he's just an old friend who loves to give us coffee and cake.'

'Wow, lucky you.'

'Not just me.' She looked up. 'Mr Coco?'

Mr Coco came over and rubbed his hands together. 'Hello, everyone. Coffee and cake, she's on the way.'

'Mr Coco, Mr Blayney here would like to pay for his own coffee today.'

Mr Coco immediately closed his eyes and waved his hands as if I was a cloud of poison gas heading in his direction. 'Is impossible, you are my guest – *always*, you will be my guest.'

'Thank you, Mr Coco. Um ... *grazie signor Coco*.'

Mr Coco acts as if I have just pulled a basset hound from my blazer pocket. '*Parla italiano*?'

'He is a man of many talents, our Mr Blayney,' says Lucky.

'Yes, I can see that,' says Mr C, winking and looking at Mona, who is wondering when the cake will turn up.

Today, after saying hello Mr Coco disappeared with Mona, who wanted to supervise the supply of victuals, and Lucky gave me one of those looks which is supposed to mean that she is about to say something unimportant, for instance, about the pattern on the ceiling.

'We heard about Michael, and we are all very relieved. It's just a matter of time before we catch those people?'

'Mm.'

'What did the kidnappers say to you?'

'Not a word.'

'Ah, so it *was* you they gave Mick to.'

'How did you know?'

'I didn't. So, come on, then, what can you tell me?'

'Only that they had a black Vanguard.'

'I wonder why they returned him when they did, and no ransom demand – is that right?'

'As far as I know.'

'Mm. Oh well, onto other matters. Are they still looking for that boy who burnt your house down last Christmas?'

This was an easy question to field, and one that I had been asked by practically everyone in Victoria since the Great Fire of Yorkshire Street, last Christmas, so I wheel out my standard reply, which is to say, I start by heaving a sigh, like the whole thing is starting to get me down.

'Yep, still looking. Him and his mum have probably gone to some other state to live – I'm thinking Tasmania. I mean, the fires have stopped, haven't they?'

I hoped that would be the end of that. But Lucky had been leading up to something.

'You know, Mr Camponi thinks that the boy had nothing to do with it.'

This was news, as I thought that the only person in Australia who thought he was innocent was Mrs Foster, and her reason was simple: he had told her so.

'But he hasn't ever said that – has he?'

'Tell me,' said Lucky, 'why do you think your mum helped him to escape – *that* surprised you, didn't it?'

It did, because I thought no one knew about that. On the night Flame Boy skipped town with his mum and Aunty Daphne we had all helped. We just wanted to get rid of him and put the whole thing behind us. But how Lucky knew that was beyond me. But I thought she might have been on one of her famous fishing expeditions.

'What makes you think she'd help him. I mean, he burnt our house down.'

'I'll tell you a secret that your Granddad has known since the fire. Mr Camponi saw someone coming out of your back gate just before the fire started, and it wasn't Keith Kavanagh.'

'Then why didn't he tell the police?'

But I knew the answer before I'd finished asking.

'He did. But they wanted the boy for some other fires as well. Well, you know what the police can be like.'

'So what did he do then?'

'He told your grandfather – they've known each other for years.'

'So who did he see?'

'He only said it was a woman – he didn't know who. Please don't tell anyone I told you this, not even your family. I just didn't want you to think badly of the Kavanagh boy. And don't tell Mona. Certain people are still looking for that woman, and it's important that no one knows.'

'*Capisco.*'

'*Bravo!*'

12 The Organiser

I don't know about other kids, but I find Saturday mornings a little overwhelming at the best of times. I mean, there's just so much to do. All week you've been a prisoner in a red brick prison run by very bad bastards, a bit like Nazis only dressed in black, a cross between male witches – I don't know if there are such things, but I can imagine – and people who torture secret agents; and you've been made to do algebra, Latin and other pretty horrible things you wouldn't choose to do in a month of Sundays. On top of all that, you can't see any old friends whenever you like, because some of them go to different schools and get home at different times, and sometimes have to do stuff with their families, though that is never my problem, as Mum needs me like she needs some new disease that's doing the rounds.

On this particular Saturday morning I had ridden my bike down to the Sandersons' place, picked up Zac, and taken him for a walk over to Matthew Foster's house for the purpose of organising the Rockets for him, he being a kid who needed organising worse than ten blokes digging a road. I was also thinking that if you have to organise a new club you need someone like Charles along to make sure that everything gets done properly, so I went to his place first. Of course, to do this I had to go right past Josephine Thompson's house in Balmain Street. It turned out that she was standing at her front gate so I stopped to say hello.

But before I said anything, I had a look at the house, to see if her big brother, Leo, was watching. After all, your average kid does not want to start the weekend off with a heart attack.

She had a friendly smile on her face which was, I thought, a good start, as I had no idea what to say or do next. It was a bit like when you're visiting your cousin in Sandringham and you've just hopped over some mysterious neighbour's fence to get your ball, when you hear the very heavy pitter-patter of a large dog heading around the side to kill you: that's how your mouth goes inside. I wondered if I could possibly look any stupider … nope, not really.

She smoothed her hair. 'You're Mona De Coney's boyfriend, aren't you?'

This was not a good start, as Mona had told me – that was after she saw me staring at Josephine in Mass (the only reason I became an altar boy in the first place) – that Josephine was not interested in me at all, and did not even know who I was. Whatever I said now could well end up being spread all over Vaucluse College during French ('*Hey, filles, j'ai un secret …!*')

'Yes.'

'Oh, I know all about you.'

Great. 'Really?'

'Oh yes, Mona tells us everything.'

This was something I wouldn't in my wildest imaginings have imagined. But now I saw that, whereas your average boy does not talk to other boys about his girlfriend, for fear of being laughed at, or disbelieved, or of being reported to someone who could throw a spanner into the works, like a parent, your average girl is more like a human public address system, and once unleashed upon an unprepared public makes a beeline for fame and notoriety.

'What do you mean, *everything*?'

'About how you're good at doing movie kisses, for one thing.'

134

This was both good and bad news, as I wanted Josephine to think of me in a certain light, but then again, not with another girl. I decided to roll with the punches, which is what Granddad told me boxers do when they want to minimise injury.

'I wouldn't say that.'

'Well, Mona does. I never thought of you as a good kisser before, just one of Charles's friends.'

'Charles Dixon? You know Charles Dixon?'

She laughed, and my heart went *boom boody-boom*, like in the song. 'Of course I know him, his mum and my mum are old friends.'

Now I knew what it was like to go stark raving mad, as Charles and I were like that, and he had known for years how I felt about the lovely Josephine, after whom men name islands – I had renamed the island in the Yarra after her – yet he had not told me about this mothers club his family was signed up with. So that was it: Charles and Josephine! What other explanation could there be? I felt as though he had crept up behind me and bayoneted me in the back.

Josephine bent down to pat Zac; bringing him had been a stroke of genius.

'So, does Charles come over, 'n' stuff?' I could hardly bring myself to say the words, but someone had to. I couldn't visualise it, though.

'No, why should he?'

'Um, to mess around with Leo.' Leo was older than Charles, and I knew that Charles was scared of him, not because of Josephine, but because Leo was the captain of the Destroyers, and Charles saw him as a potentially dangerous club rival, despite their parents being buddy-buddy.

She laughed again, and I felt as though I had carked it and was up with the angels, contrary to popular predictions. 'I don't *think* so.' Mysteriouser and mysteriouser. I could see I was going to have to interrogate Charles.

Next stop was his house, which was just two streets down. If I knew Charles, he was stuck at home with his beautiful mother watching TV, and that is no way for a boy to grow up. For that you need fun, danger and mechanical things. I was so happy that I didn't take much notice of a black car that followed Zac and me along, or rather, I was so busy day-dreaming about JT that I didn't really give a bugger, and wouldn't have noticed if I was being followed by a runaway train.

We went down Dover Street and into Charles's place where we were greeted like long-lost brothers. Zac promptly went to sleep on the front porch and I went in with Charles, who warned me not to make any noise, as his mother had been up late doing a TV show, and had then come home and had a snifter or two (or three) and had then thrown the towel in. She did not expect to re-enter the atmosphere until sometime in the afternoon.

It turned out that Charles was playing trains. But a trip to some other kid's place usually beats the shit out of that. The trains would still be there when we got back. I got straight down to business. 'Charles, why didn't you tell me you knew Josephine Thompson?'

'I don't, really. My mum knows her mum, that's all.'

'Charlie, level with me. Are you in love with JT? I can take it if you are. I know you'll be a good boyfriend to her, even though you could never love her as I, um, kind of do.'

Charles went as red as you can go without turning into a salad vegetable. 'No, I'm not, and I never have been, and I never will be. Happy?'

'All right Charlie, don't get off your bike. I had to know, that's all. I know you've got a soft spot for *one* of the inmates of this town, but I am not like the rest of the kids, and will not pressure you to tell. Let's just say that whoever she is she's a lucky girl. Now, about this club business. Let's go round to Foster's place.'

We woke Zac up and left, and this time I noticed the black car further down Dover Street start off behind us, but soon began to think about my talk to JT, and completely put young Charles out my mind, as he had proved to be on the up and up in the matter of girls I was interested in.

We headed down Balmain Street. As we walked down the dark dip under the railway bridge, the black car I had noticed suddenly sped past us and tore up Balmain Street towards Church Street. This time I realised with a shock that it was a black Vanguard. I looked at Charles, but he was off with the fairies and not paying attention. I was too late to get the number and decided not to say anything to Charles so he wouldn't pass out from fright. But I kept my eyes wide open for the rest of the day.

At Matthew's place, we found him and his new neighbour, Eddie Williams, both of whom were expecting us. Eddie ignored me completely.

'G'day, Blayno. G'day, Dixie'

'G'day, Matthew. G'day, Eddie.'

'Where've y' been?'

'Pickin' up Dixie,' I said in my tough guy voice, which was practically a rule when discussing club business.

'So now what, Blayno?'

'Now we all go round to Piglet's place.'

Piglet Price's house was down the end of Cubitt Street, right near the Yarra. As we walked, Matthew Foster filled his new mate in on the inhabitants of Priceville.

'He's got a new father who's an artist – you know, he paints all day,' said Matthew. 'Piglet says he can paint like anything.'

'Yeah, but why do you call him Piglet?' asked Eddie, who was very hard to impress.

'Because his mum's a guard over at the Loony Bin – get it? His real name's Peter, but. His mum doesn't like it if you call him Piglet. Try it and you'll see,' said Matthew. 'Go on, I dare ya. We dare him, don't we Blayno?'

'Charles, you're closer, will you please give Foster a smack in the head for me?'

'Blayno's always kiddin' around, aren't you Blayno?'

'What you said interests me, Matthew. As you know, I'm a bit of a painter myself – watercolours, nothing flash.'

'Well, it's Saturday,' said the Foster,' so he should be home. I can't see a painter working on a Saturday.'

We were left mulling over – if that's the word I want – this unbelievably dumb comment until we got down the hill to the Piglet playpen.

Outside the gate, on the riverbank, Piglet's stand-in dad was painting, and had an easel set up. This bloke was actually Mr Martin from across the street from Piglet's place. I should explain. Apparently – I first heard this from Granddad, though Piglet was happy to confirm it – Mrs Price had gotten extremely cheesed off with her hubby at about the same time as he had become an attractive item to the lady across the road, a Mrs Violet Martin, who was willing to make a swap, as the last thing she wanted were two hubbies – you can see the difficulties: two blokes fighting over the footy card at the bottom of the corn flakes box and the newspaper and the television, to say nothing of one of them being covered with oil paint half the time. So Mrs Price says: 'Done!' or whatever you say, and – Bob's your uncle – Piglet has a new dad.

Though the old one hasn't gone far and he can still visit him any time he likes. Also, Mrs Martin's daughter, Sally, can come over and visit her dad any time *she* likes. Naturally, Father Hagen tells Piglet to tell his parents that until they stop doing the old swaparoony they are no longer welcome at Mass (he does not care about Violet Martin, as she is not a Catholic.)

'Geez!' I said to Piglet. What did your mum say to that?'

'She told me to tell Father to go and whatsaname himself.'

'Wow! Did you?'

'What, and miss out on all that free altar grog! You'd have to be joking. But I told her I did, and she said: fair enough. And Father asked me what she said, so I said she would pray on it. And he said: fair enough, as well. Fair dinkum, I've never seen so much leg-pulling in my life.'

Meanwhile, Piglet appeared, wearing a baseball hat, as was the fashion. Normally I would be happy to see Piglet, even though we were not best friends, but not today. That was because he was wearing the exact same tee shirt that Tom had been wearing on the day he was killed, and I straightaway got a bad feeling in my legs, which I recognised as the Dread.

'So what do you guys want?' said Piglet.

'I've formed a new club, the Rockets, and we want you to be in it.'

'Only if Freddo and Tangles can be in it too. We hang out together.'

'Course. Tangles knows about it already. Let's go 'n' get 'em,' says MBF, smirking at Eddie.

'Bewdy, I'll be back in a tick.'

And like the Flash, he was gone.

Freddo's main claim to fame was that he was some kind of genius, and was forever winning competitions: spelling, mental arithmetic, general knowledge and so on. You could ask him any question and he would either answer it, or make up an answer that was so good, you didn't know if it was right or wrong. He achieved this incredible feat by reading a lot, and by having a special kind of memory. Basically, he could remember everything he had seen or heard since the day he was born. He had been studied by special people who he said would like to remove his brain with a hacksaw and soup ladle and see how it ticked. But his parents, who were no slouches in the brains department themselves, put their feet down every time. They did not want a kid with stitch marks around his forehead, like Frankenstein.

Freddo appeared ready for an adventure, and was wearing a very funny-looking baseball hat, which he said his mother made him wear. I think that there are some parts of kids that mothers should be banned from putting clothes on, the top of the head being the main one, feet being another.

'What's up?' said Freddo, finally. 'We gunna play kick-to-kick in the rain?'

'Nah,' said Matthew, who was the kind of kid who didn't do *anything* in the rain. 'We just want you to join our new club, the Rockets – *I'm* the captain. We can have our first meeting at your place if you want to join.'

'Go on,' said Piglet. 'I joined.'

'Sure,' said Freddo. 'I could do with a fresh club. The old one I was in – the Jaguars – conked out ages ago.'

Next, Piglet choofed off to get Tangles. While we were waiting and the Octopus was congratulating himself for cleverly extending his tentacles into the world of clubs and gangs, not unlike the Mafia in, according to Granddad, the world of fruit and veg, Mr Martin came toward us and called to me.

'H'lo Mr, um, Martin. What is it?' You never know just how to address a husband who's on loan.

'I've just received this note from a man who was riding along the river on a bike. What do you think of this?'

I took the note from him. It said: *Tell the Blayney boy to go straight home.*

My insides went all cold. 'Did he say anything?'

'No, he didn't speak at all; he just kept on riding. Do you know what it means?'

'No. Have you got a phone, Mr Martin? I have to call Mum and see if she's all right.'

'Of course. I'll take you to it.'

I ignored the gawking Rockets – don't let anyone tell you boys don't gawk – and went in with Mr Martin.

'Mum? Hi, it's me. Is everything all right? Mr Martin – he's Piglet's stand-in father – just told me that a bloke on a bike gave him a note to give me, and the note said: *Please tell the Blayney boy to go straight home.* So I thought I'd better see if everything's okay.'

'Yes, everything's all right. Where are you now, exactly?'

'At Peter Price's place, down Cubitt Street. Mum, I saw that black car again, the one the kidnappers were driving when they gave me Mick. It went past me and Charles in Balmain Street.'

'Have you got your bike?'

'It's at the Sandersons'. I've got Zac win me.'

'I want you to come home straight away. Do you think Mr Martin would drive you both?'

Mr Martin was in the next room. 'Mum? He says yes. See you soon.'

Mr Martin's car turned out to be a black Austin A40, which looked a hell of a lot like a Vanguard. I took a long look at it before hopping in the back with Zac, while Mr Martin waited patiently, as if he thought I was a bit slow. Once I had shut the door, which needed about five tries, I noticed that on the inside it was nothing but an old bomb, and smelt of petrol and grease. I looked at Mr M, and he at me.

'Got it cheap – been in the wars. Hope we make up it up the Hill – just joking.'

I kept one hand on Zac, and the other on the door handle.

13 Happy Birthday from God

At home, it turned out that Dad had received a similar note from a bloke in the King Brian, and Granddad had received one from a bloke at Sanky's Gym, where he was making enquiries.

'Who gave you that, boy?' said Granddad, sounding a lot like a married policeman.

'A bloke down Cubitt Street gave it to Mr Martin to give to me.'

No one said anything, but everyone was thinking the same thing, that Taggertys and Blayneys do not like being told what to do. Also, it was plain as paper that this had something to do with the strange goings-on.

A few minutes later, a car pulled up at the front door, and Granddad watched it through the front window without speaking. Dad went over and stood beside him.

'What the hell's *he* doing here,' said Dad.

'Who is it, Dad?'

'It's that Turner bodgie. What the hell does he want?'

Now as far as I was concerned, this was both good and bad news. Gazza – I called him Gazza – was an up-and-coming bodgie who was making good money customising cars, a talent which he had once confided in Tom and me and one or two of the neighbourhood kids, was going to make him stinking rich. He had been in a lot of trouble over the years, and acquired the nickname 'Chain', because he had a tendency to use one to dong people who called him a fatherless bastard, which was true if impolite. Gazza could be found at any given time either in custody or in his car, a beautiful green and white Ford Customline, which Tom and me had been for a ride in (in the front).

Gazza had seen me do one or two things over the years that would land me in the cells so fast I would just be a kid-shaped blur, and I had seen him do a few things that would land him in an adjoining cell. The popular view was that Gazza would probably spend the rest of his life customising number plates in Pentridge. But I liked him, because he wore gorgeous bodgie clothes, had a matching gorgeous widgie girlfriend, and did whatever he liked.

Dad went to answer the door, but Granddad stepped in front of it. 'I'll handle this.' He opened the door. 'G'day, what can I do for ya?'

'I've got a message for Mrs Blayney.'

'I'll give it to her.'

'I have to give it to her myself.'

'Then you can piss off.'

'Now, now, Mr Taggerty, I'm being paid a lot of money to give her the message personally. And I'm to tell you that if you let me in, you'll be one step closer to finding the bloke you're after. That's all I know. Otherwise, I have to give the message to someone else – can't say who.'

Granddad let Gazza in. He was dressed in a pink shirt with a gold tie, and a while sports coat. He was wearing blue trousers with the cuffs turned up, and very fancy shoes. He winked at me when he saw me staring at his shoes.

'Custom-made. Hello, Mr Blayney, Mrs Blayney.'

'Well, where's this bloody message?' said Granddad, who was itching to get rid of him, when I couldn't even understand why he let him in the first place. I mean, I'd seen him tell rozzers who knocked on the door to go and whatsaname themselves.

'It's for Mrs Blayney only.' He produced an envelope and gave it to Mum. She opened it, and read it with a frown. Then she understood, the way you suddenly understand what *déjeuner* means, but it's too late because Brother has now asked the kid behind you. She looked at Gazza, and he smiled back in his smart-arse way of smiling at adults.

'Do you know what this is?' she asked him.

'Wouldn't have a clue,' said Gazza. 'And don't give a bugger, either. Well, my job's done; easiest brick a man ever made.'

Suddenly, she had a new thought, and turned to Granddad. 'You know what this *is*, don't you, Dad? Of course you bloody well do. This is what was nicked from your room. Christ, Dad, how could you?'

She gave it to Gazza to read. I thought that any tick of the clock I was going to be sent to my room for about ten years, but nothing happened. Mum looked like she'd seen a ghost. She searched Gazza's face while he looked at the paper, and tried to figure it out. Dad just stood by and watched, because he was, when all was said and done, an outsider in this house. And it was at moments like this I could sense his loneliness. No wonder he preferred to be with Mrs Bentley.

Finally, Gazza got it, but he did not look up from the paper. He lost all his bodginess. His clothes suddenly seemed to be holding *him* up, instead of the other way around. I never thought I'd see him like this, turned into an ordinary person with a brushback haircut and a pair of expensive shoes, and clothes he suddenly looked like he'd nicked.

'Sit down,' Mum said. She was tired, not smiling, but she was watching Gazza like a kid watching a fairy floss machine. It was like the day right at the start of the year when I spied on her while she told her friends down at Yorkshire Street that she was expecting. Same kind of tension, just no tears.

Everyone sat down. Dad sat down with a look on his face like he wanted a choice but knew he wasn't going to get one. I had a feeling just then that I was watching a decision set in his heart, like concrete. No one else saw it. I felt it in my own heart. I was missing him already. Mum started talking. I felt that something was wrong the whole time she spoke, as if everyone was missing the point; when you're a kid you get hit for missing the point so often that soon you learn to *smell* it in adults. But it turned out I was wrong: they were *getting* the point, whatever it was.

'When I was fourteen, no more than a kid, war broke out, and I was sent to work at the Ammunition Factory in Footscray. After a few years I met a soldier – he went overseas – and fell pregnant. I was thrown out of home.'

'It wasn't as simple as that, Jeannie,' said Granddad.

Mum ignored him. 'I ended up in a barracks at the Ammunition Factory, for pregnant girls who'd been disowned.'

Granddad made a complaining noise and shook his head, but Mum paid no attention.

'We had to give our babies up to the hospital and go straight back to work. Nobody gave a damn.'

'I made sure he was never far away,' said Granddad.

I suddenly realised what was happening. It was like when some bloke in a car stops and asks you for directions and you realise that for the first time in your life you actually know exactly what to tell him. And my feet, stomach, and chest suddenly filled with molten lava, and my head filled with ice-water, and made that noise like a diesel engine at a roadworks, and that was that.

There was a bit of a fuss, but it turned out I had just fainted for a few seconds, and hadn't really had one of my turns. Mum made me a cup of tea, and I could hear her crying in the kitchen. And still, I realised, no one knew what to do, and something wasn't right. I looked at Granddad, who was looking at Gazza with what I thought was a soft kind of look, and I realised that he seemed to be on a different wavelength to me. Dad was holding me in his arms, which was nice, I thought. Gazza was still looking at the paper, but now he was sighing and nodding. Suddenly, Mrs Blayney from up the road was really his mum – he got it, but he couldn't do anything about it. This wasn't customising cars.

When Mum came back I got my cuppa, and she got her spot on the lounge back, and Dad moved back to his chair. It wasn't one of those situations where we could all start asking each other what we'd been up to all these years, because we all knew each other. But Mum wasn't your big-hearted mum. She was no Mrs Radion, or Mrs Foster, or even Mrs Sanderson, who wasn't even a mum at all, but would have made a good one. Mum was your basic pissed-off person, and she could be pissed off at anyone regardless of race, class or creed – she was entirely fair in that regard. So I wasn't surprised when Gazza could stand life in the fridge no longer and got up to go, particularly as I happened to know that he had two terrific parents who would welcome him home with open arms when he got back from the footy later in the day, and ask him over a coldie how it went.

No one said anything, not even goodbye. Gazza gave me a wink, then let himself out. Everyone went to the door to see him leave, automatically really, as you do. I went to the window and knelt on the lounge chair. It was like watching people forget how to be people, and turn into confused toy robots. Gazza didn't turn back or wave; he'd been had wholesale, just like everyone else. I wondered if he, like me, was wondering why someone had gone to all this trouble, what had been the point.

I went back to my cuppa, and Mum watched me sipping. I was dreading a cancellation of that night's trip to the Circus. It was my special birthday treat, and I had talked Granddad into letting me shout Charles, James, Peanut, and Raffi. Finally, Mum spoke to Granddad.

'I want Barney to go with the boys tonight.'

He nodded. 'I'll give him a call.'

She turned to me. 'You're staying here for the rest of the afternoon.'

'Can I ask Raffi to come over and stay for tea?'

'All right.'

I rang Raffi and he said he would jump on a tram. Then I gave Granddad the nod, and met him in the dining room.

'Granddad, I didn't tell you this before, because you and Mum had enough on your plate, but I saw that black Vanguard again – this morning. It was following me near Charles's place, in Balmain Street.'

'Did you get the number or see the driver?'

'Nuh, one minute he was way behind me, then suddenly he was shootin' past – sorry.'

'It's all right, we'll get the bastard.'

Back in the living room, I announced that Raffi would be over on the first tram.

'Why doesn't he ride his bike?' said Mum, who had shown no interest in Raffi since he started coming over.

'He's not allowed to have one, because of his seizures.'

'What?' said Mum. I had completely forgotten that she had no idea about this. Mum and me aren't what you would call close. 'What seizures?'

'You know: epilepsy. He's always had it.'

'I didn't know. I'm sorry.'

I didn't know what she was being sorry about, or even if she was talking to me when she said it, as having babies can be a bit of a strain, I've noticed. So I thought it best to say nothing at all.

'So, how's the investigation going,' asked Raffi, once we were together again, and in the kitchen, where the family victuals were stashed.

'Still no leads on Dad's car. I think it was the same bunch.'

'It's probably been re-sprayed by now,' said Raffi, putting on his extra wise face. I was impressed, because I hadn't thought of that.

'Also, Veronica Palmer kissed me.'

'Mona'll kill you.'

'No, she won't, because nobody will blab, will they Radion?'

'What kind of kiss was it, a little peck, or a movie kiss?'

'Just on the cheek.'

'She'll still kill you.'

'Also, Carmel Bus – he goes to our school and lives down in Howard Street – told me I was being followed.'

'Jeez.'

'Also, I found out from the kid over the back that the kidnappers were driving a black Vanguard, which I saw this morning in Balmain Street.'

'Oh My God,' said Raffi, 'you've practically caught them.'

'Not me, Raffi, but … *The Mazemaster!*

Yes, the Mazemaster! A strange being from up on the Hill with powers and abilities far beyond those of mortal kids. The Mazemaster! Who can find out stuff no one else can, sneak around all over the place gathering clues, and dodge all kinds of bad bastards, until he successfully finds his way through the maze and catches the kidnappers. And avenges his brother as well.'

'Mick.'

'Him too.'

'What happened to the Octopus?'

'Oh, he's still slithering around somewhere. It's the Octopus's job to extend his tentacles into clubs 'n' stuff, while the Mazemaster actually catches the crims.'

'So does he have an offsider?'

'No Raffi, he prefers to work alone.'

'Oh.'

'Just jokin! He can often be seen with a shadowy figure from down near the Yarra, they call … *River Boy!*'

'I'll think about it.'

That night Barney took us kids to the Circus, where we had a damn good time, especially James, who had led a sheltered life over in South Yarra. I introduced Barney as Mr Flanagan, just for fun, and Barney gave me a wink, so that's what they called him, and I noticed that they were especially polite to him, so he wouldn't murder them, though Raffi seemed comfortable with him, which made me feel good, as I did not want to frighten him. Afterwards, we went to look at the animals that weren't in the show, and while the boys were getting some fairy floss I went to have a chat with an orangutan called Rufus. He seemed like a nice enough sort of bloke, though a bit on the sad side, what with being in jail and everything, and reached out to me between the bars.

'Wanna shake hands?' I grabbed his hand and gave it a shake, which turned out to be a mistake, as Rufus was in one his moods. He promptly tried to pull me into the cage with him. Now, when you're a twelve-year old boy and you're in the public eye, as I was just then, the name of the game is looking cool, like Cookie in *77 Sunset Strip*. You're torn: on the one hand you don't want to call for help, like a girl, as this would get around the whole school before Monday morning break; on the other hand, you don't want to go home with your right arm missing, like a war hero (not that there's anything wrong with that). Suddenly, some bloke grabbed my other arm and just about pulled it out of its socket, so that within seconds I had half decided that life with Rufus was starting to look pretty rosy, when Rufus suddenly let go, causing us to fall down. I have to admit, I had no idea that red-haired apes had the same sense of humour as red-haired girls, but there you are.

The bloke then picked me up and started running between the cages and wagons with me, dragging me along. It's not often you get snatched by an orangutan then immediately after by a bloke you wished *was* an orangutan; at least I knew Rufus only did these things to get a bit of fun out of life. I tried to yell for help and got a thump across the head that made me see stars. When I opened my eyes I saw in front of me the black Vanguard. The door opened and I was pushed into the back seat, where another bloke grabbed me. I saw Barney and another bloke try to grab the door, but they were too late. As the car took off, it drove within a yard of a girl with a face like a ghost. It was Sunny, looking like she was dressed in silver under the lights. She didn't say anything or move – I understood. We drove out of the parking area and down a drive, and turned right onto Church Street. The driver drove straight up Church Street, and seemed to settle into the Saturday night traffic like just another car. I had always thought that getaway cars went like hell – they do on TV – but this bloke was as cool as an Eskimo Pie, and I reckoned (and not for the first time in my life) that I was cactus for sure. I was just wondering how weird it was none of these three blokes had said a single word, when we were suddenly rammed by a car trying to cut us off. For a second we were driving along together, then the other car, which was pretty big, suddenly dropped back, and our bloke went like hell up a side street. We did a few more crazy turns, then ended up on a wide street with tram tracks. We were just tearing past a tram, when it suddenly turned left in front of us, and there was an almighty noise like a Vangard-size sardine tin being opened, and we ricocheted onto the footpath, and stopped. As the door on my side of the car was missing, I jumped out, just in time to see the car that had cut us off, a red and white 1958 Plymouth Belvedere, come up to us. I ran to it and jumped in the back. The car belonged to the Roma bloke who had collared me at the gypsy camp. With him was Barney.

We reversed back up the road and out of the way of the tram, which had torn the right side of the car clean off, and was now wearing it on its running board, and did a U-ey up what I recognised was Victoria Street, turned up a lane, and stopped.

'You okay?'

'Yeah. Thanks. But you're letting 'em get away.'

'No police,' said Barney.

'No police,' said the Roma bloke.

'Yeah, course.'

I had forgotten the code of the Flanagans, and, apparently, of the Roma. We drove around the back streets, with Barney directing, and came back to the Circus car park, where a small crowd of Roma were waiting.

As soon as I hopped out, Sunny slapped me across the face and yelled: 'You frightened me!' and ran away. That gypsy had a textbook right!

'Looks like you can't take a trick, tonight,' said Barney.

'Barn, take me back; I don't want Raffi to worry.'

'Got it.'

'Thanks, mate.' That was for the Roma bloke.

'Any time.'

152

'Don't worry about that panel, said Barney to the other bloke, and pointing to the Plymouth. I'll take care of it.'

Back at the fairy floss machine, the other kids were waiting, and trying to eat fairy floss without getting it on their faces which, as everyone knows, is a losing battle.

'Jeez, Blayno, where the hell've ya' been?' said Peanut.

'Saw someone I knew. So, fairy floss is it? Well, I think I'll live dangerously tonight.'

When the kids spotted Rufus, and went over to shake hands with him – yes, I know, but I couldn't resist – I took Barney aside for a quite word.

'Barn, I've been thinking. No need to tell to tell Mum about this, is there?'

'Are you kiddin'? I was supposed to be keeping an eye on you. She'd skin me alive.'

'And what about Granddad?'

'Have to tell him, mate; there's things to be done. Now, what did those bastards say to you?'

'Not a word. I still haven't heard them speak.'

'That's 'cos they're not game – must have accents.'

'Hell, why didn't I think of that?'

'Don't worry, you're still learning – all in good time.'

'Barn, why didn't you grab those bloke at the crash. I reckon you could've got one of 'em.'

'Cos that bloke who grabbed you was strapped – I saw it.'

'Shit.'

'Don't worry. They're locals, I can smell it. And they're drongos, too.'

'How can you tell?'

'Well, they were driving a bloody Vanguard, for a start. What kind of getaway car is that?'

14 The Lennox Street Mob

When I got up the following morning, the place was like the opening of that poem: *There was movement at the station*, and that's because Dad had just put the phone down, and now made the following announcement.

'That was Mum. She found the car parked outside her house.'

'So they know where your mother lives,' said Mum, deadpan. 'Wonderful. Anyway, first things first: Happy Birthday.'

They gave me a portable record player, so that I wouldn't have to drive them mad down in the living room. My clever plan had worked.

'You little rippers, ta.'

'Well, I'm off to get the car,' said Dad. 'Back for lunch.'

I had to serve at the nine-thirty Mass, so I couldn't go over to Nanna's with Dad, but it was going to be my first stop after Mass. This was because Nanna was known in certain circles as the Queen of Richmond, as she was famous for being a collector of information, and seemed to know everyone in town, and every few weeks, always on a Sunday morning, would invite a bunch of people over for morning tea. These people included artists and musicians, police (not bastards, but good ones – no, come to think of it, they were all bastards, but ones that looked after Nanna's friends and family), priests (but not brothers, whom she hated like the plague for the horrible things they had done to her sons and to me), sports people, like footballers, and persons of interest to the police, in other words, crims. I wasn't missing out on this.

Dad had put his coat and hat on, and slipped out the front door, before anybody could slip the leg irons on him, and I left with him. I was happy to get out of the place before Granddad got up, because it was obvious that Mum and Dad had no idea what had happened at the Circus, though I knew Barney would have told Granddad by now.

'Where d'ya think *you're* going?' said Dad.

'I'm off to Mass, where else?'

He said nothing but trudged up the hill to Church Street with me hurrying alongside with my bike, then crossed over. He was going to take my secret route to Nanna's: down The Vaucluse, past my school, around Rowena Parade, and up Lennox Street. The last time we had walked to Nanna's that way I had said. 'Hey, Dad, this is how I get to Nanna's from school.'

'Yeah? This is how I went home from school every night when I was a kid.'

'Ye-ah.' I heard what he said, but I couldn't picture him in a pair of navy blue shorts, though I kept trying all the way down to St Felix's, to pass the time, as it was a cold bastard of a day.

After Mass, I rode up to Nanna's place, and sure enough, parked outside was Dad's lovely Holden, looking as cool as ever, without a scratch. I knocked on the front door and Dad let me in.

'What're you doin' here?'

'Visiting Nanna.'

He didn't say anything, because he was just having a sherbet himself – I know how these little visits work.

'Hello, Nanna.'

'Well, here's trouble, Happy Birthday; I've got something for you.'

Nanna quickly picked up a note from the phone table and gave it to Dad, who pocketed it, but not before I noticed that it was a folded up bit of writing pad paper just like the note we found with Mick.

'What did it say, Dad?'

He didn't answer, but shoved it deeper into his pocket. But the Octopus is a patient creature, and I knew that sooner or later he would have to take his pants off, and at that moment I would strike.

We went in to the front room and my head was immediately filled with the smell of Nanna's house, which was one of those huge houses that you sometimes see in narrow streets when you're least expecting to see one. Unlike most of the houses in Richmond it had a passage up the middle and rooms on both sides, the main one being a huge living room at the front, which was where we went, because the fire was in there.

The room smelt of Uncle Mick's sweet Plumcake pipe tobacco, the fire, and a thousand other things I could probably describe given time, but don't want to, because they also remind me of all the times Tom and me had been here, and those things were like little treasures inside me. Uncle Mick and Uncle Seb, Nanna's pretend husbands, were there and they gave me a wave as I went in.

Uncle Seb was the pianist in the Hot Potatoes Jazz Band, and could play anything you liked right off the top of his head. His mates were all musicians, and mad as snakes. I never saw him without a shiny waistcoat – today's was a lovely silver colour, with stripes. I reckon if I spotted him at the baths, he'd be wearing one of those things.

Uncle Mick was a professional gambler, and according to Granddad, seldom lost except on purpose, to lengthen the odds. He was very well off, and was always dressed like an important person – like Bert Newton, for example – so I knew this was the truth, though in my family the truth is not used often, so as not to wear it out.

These two blokes were as alike as beer and brandy, but you could tell that they balanced each other out like fish and chips, which I thought would not be a coincidence, as Nanna liked to keep a civilised household, and you could see how two husbands who were both live-wires would be a pain in at the arse, and would probably end up needing a third, someone who was more like Robert Mitchum, to balance *them* out; or two husbands who were both like Robert Mitchum would need someone like Spike Jones to balance them out. But Nanna has got it right, which did not surprise me.

Aunty Betty was always saying (but not to Nanna's face) that having two husbands at once was disgraceful, and she didn't know how the family put up with the shame. Mum was another person who did not approve of Nanna having two husbands, which was one more than her at the last weigh-in. Also, Mum had never approved of the fact that Nanna enjoyed life a lot more than the average person (I got the story from Barney: the doctor once told her she had a heart condition, so she decided to spend her last few days on Earth going nuts – that was forty years ago). In fact, the only people who didn't think Nanna was disgraceful were people like Granddad, who had been around, and Dad, who's own father had been Nanna's third real husband – she had a way of going through them.

Uncle Seb was resting up, as he would be playing with the band that night, but on Sunday mornings he would usually give us a little tune while we were all having a natter, even though he would have had a late night. Being a jazz musician requires a lot of stamina, he once told me. A man who fusses too much over his

158

body is bound to be too much of a namby-pamby to stay the field. As I had decided to become a saxophone player myself one day, I took all this in.

Dex Patterson, the Hot Potatoes' sax player had once told me that the only real thing you have to remember if you want to be a good sax player is to hold your liquor, because the music just takes care of itself. I'm glad he said that because playing the sax looked about as easy as knitting, but I could already hold my liquor, as long as it was just a snifter; beyond that I would throw up all over the place. Uncle Seb was normally a bit of a comedian, but just then he was content to nod and wink a few times. Piano can take it out of a man.

Uncle Mick, who was always soft-spoken and liked to have a little think before he spoke, was reading the Herald, because he usually got home late on Saturdays. Nanna took me to the table and gave me a present, from her and Uncles Mick and Seb. It was a portable tape recorder. Now nobody in Richmond would be safe. Nanna must have read my mind.

'Don't take it out in front of this morning's mob, or the conversation will die on the spot, and we wouldn't want that.'

'Expecting a crowd, this morning?' said Dad, who did not often attend these Sunday morning parties of Nanna's, as he had been brought up on a steady diet of them, and knew that they were really just a chance for Nanna to find out the local gossip (and start some herself). But the main reason he didn't often go was because Nanna always invited a few people he could never take to, which is fair enough. I mean, I could never take to any of the Rozac kids, even though I saw a lot of them; and I couldn't stand my cousin Lewis, the *interesting* one – though his mum and dad were terrific, and always took me with them when they went golfing. Also, there was another reason Dad didn't like to go: Nanna liked to have the odd copper over, though God knows why.

It turned out that this was one of those mornings when a few visitors were going to drop in for morning tea, so I was keen on staying.

'I thought we might have a beer or two this morning,' said Nanna to Dad.

Dad nodded. 'That sounds all right, Mum. I want to see what's what, if you know what I mean.' This was one of the longest sentences I had ever heard Dad say, and I immediately wondered if he'd been bitten by some kind of rare tropical spider whose venom had gone straight to his vocal cords – it happens.

'What's the occasion, Nanna?' said I.

'Never you mind, Big Ears. I just had a whole crate of mixed soft drinks delivered for the likes of you.'

'Terrific, Nanna. Who's coming over?'

I was keen on getting names and information on these people before they arrived, as I knew that some of them would be reluctant to tell you anything they would not want repeated in front of a magistrate.

'Well now, let's see. There's that bloke from the North Melbourne footy team that Barney likes so much – though God knows what he sees in him; he's not a footballer's bootlace.' Nanna was talking about a Kangaroos player I had seen here before, and she was dead right. 'And Barney, of course, as I we haven't seen him for ages.' I could have told her that I had seen him only last night, saving my life. But really, the weird thing was that she invited him at all, as he was really Granddad's mate – and mine, of course – though I knew that wasn't why he was invited. Another mystery. 'And I wouldn't be surprised if your Granddad dropped in for a cuppa, you know, because of what's been going on.' She said that in a pleasant kind of voice, as if she was talking about how to make scones, though really I know she was speaking as the Queen of Richmond, a person who could be very serious indeed. 'He'll want to talk to a few people about this, that and the other. And Father Sheehan, because he's back on deck, and he's coming over to give me Communion.'

To me this was a very strange arrangement, because at school we were made to go to Confession every five minutes to have our sooty souls cleaned, just so we could go to Mass and Communion, whereas Nanna, who never went to Mass – which was itself a mortal sin – had been unofficially excommunicated for living in sin, as Mum said, and was therefore no longer a Catholic. However, Nanna was Irish, and so was Father Sheehan – he was fresh off the boat only last year – and his view, repeated to me by Uncle Seamus, who was an expert on everything, was that adultery was not the same as bigamy. So there you go, or as Barney would say: *Quod erat demonstrandum*. This was the same curate who had performed the marriage at the gypsy camp, and who was generally viewed as a cross between Audie Murphy and Batman.

'Also Inspector Passmore; what a lovely man he is. We like him very much.' She winked at me and wrinkled her nose. I got a shock when she did this, as I knew that ladies only wrinkled their noses when they were pretty keen on a member of the male bunch, when they were thinking of adding him to their menagerie. I looked at Uncle Mick and Uncle Seb, and wondered if they had the slightest idea that one day soon they might all be going shopping, arm in arm, for an extra pouffe for the lounge room, looking like Dorothy and her friends on the yellow brick road.

Not for the first time, it occurred to me that when God was doling out sneakiness to the female half of the human race, someone might have bumped his elbow. Passmore couldn't have been a bastard, otherwise he would not have had a ticket. But I was amazed that Nanna would want a rozzer around the house for some other reason than getting as full as a tick and letting slip some juicy titbit of police gossip. I reckoned he must be one of those fair-minded coppers who is prepared to turn a blind eye to anything that does not involve actual GBH (or kidnapping), which has got to be a good sign for all concerned.

'Then there are the boys in the band, bound to be one or two of them dropping in, plus some of the girls from the Pepper Club – that's very thirsty work they do, believe me.' I believed her. These girls, though extremely good-looking, like film stars, usually had not been home the night before coming over, so that they tended to be a bit off their game by the time the sun came up, and according to Barney, were practically running on Bennies, whatever they were. Whatever they did I know it must be hot work, as once they took off their coats they never had a lot on underneath, regardless of the weather. I also knew that if Mum ever copped an eyeful of them, my days as a Sunday visitor would be over. She was bad enough whenever Mona was around, and I prayed she never got to see her in a bathing suit.

'And lovely Mr Wilmott – you know him, who's promised to bring his daughter over – she's been in Tasmania. I'm sure that must have been very interesting for her.' Nanna made the platypus mouth when she said Tasmania, so I knew she was looking forward to hearing all about the place like a dose of shingles. But I knew she'd had her eye on Mr Wilmott ever since his wife carked it, and I wondered – there would have been a twinkle in my eye – if he knew the betting had blown out, owing to the police having their own entrant. Probably not, as most men – I include myself – are plasticine in the hands of women. This is not a secret.

Dad and I stuck around, and it wasn't long before the rest of the Hot Potatoes turned up with the girls from the club. Nanna was very generous with the grog, I noticed, and I knew why. It was because loose lips spill beans, or something. She was in her information gathering mood, like Larry Kent, because of the kidnapping, and that meant I was too.

Pretty soon all the people Nanna had invited had turned up, all except Father Sheehan carrying their share of grog and a bit for the pot. When Father turned up he was given a big hand by all those present, even though most of them had seen him out and about since the Big Fire in Church Street, last summer. He had spent the next three months in hospital, close to death, and was a national flamin' hero. The Church shouted him a trip home to Ireland to visit his family, and it was fresh back from his trip that he now was. Still, he was in high spirits, as if he had just won Tatts, and Barney gave him a big hug, amid loud cheering and clapping.

'Kevin, will you do me the honour of blessing me? I need it like beer needs bubbles, and me conscience is givin' me the kind of hell I wouldn't wish on a Presbyterian magistrate.'

So Father Sheehan blessed Barney, who asked for seconds, this time for special protection from Italian tram drivers – which brings the house down. Then Father Sheehan blessed everyone else in the place, and indeed, the house itself, because he was, as I said, in a good mood. I can tell you that there were people all over Melbourne who would have killed for one of those blessings.

'Here's my Traveller altar boy,' he shouted, when he saw me, and put his arm around my shoulder while he did the rounds; I acted as if we did this every day, in other words, cool. 'I hear it's your birthday; so I've got something in my case you might like.' He disappeared for a minute, and came back with a set of rosary beads, made of black wood, very lovely. He turned the crucifix over. Inside it was a tiny glass capsule of water. 'It's from Lourdes. You never know when you might need it.' He blessed the rosary and gave it to me. I felt honoured, because I knew it stood for something important, when really, sometimes it seemed to me that nothing did. I looked around, and noticed that the conversation had dropped a little while the crowd watched, more out of curiosity than recognition. I slipped it on like a necklace, so everyone could have a look at it.

When he let me go, I was cornered by a couple of the, um girls, from the club. They were pleased to see me, and one of them wrapped an arm around me and drew me to her practically bare chest, and kept on talking to her friend as if I wasn't even there, in such a way that I knew she was used to doing that with other people, possibly friends who weren't women. All I know is I was not going to offend her by unravelling myself; I mean, you don't want to be rude.

I slurped on my lemonade, suddenly feeling the heat, and keeping an eye on Nanna, Dad, Granddad, and Father Sheehan, who were all in different parts of the room, to make sure they were, you know, having a good time. Like everyone else in the room, these girls were mostly talking pretty loudly, but every now and then, when they wanted to talk about someone else, they turned the volume knob down to *1*. And what one of them had to say was especially interesting to me, because of a familiar name that was mentioned.

'So, Chels, d'ja have a good night in the end?'

'Yeah, in the end. Bob said I could talk to the punters. I made a few friends, but.'

'Be careful; best not to rush things when you're new. And they're not friends. The Pepper's not like the Sportsman's. It can get rough.'

164

'Sharl, men are all the same. I know what to do.'

'Look, you didn't get the job because of what you know; you got it because of those.' She nodded in the direction of where I was being clutched.

'Hey, want to hear what one bloke told me?'

'No, I want to mind me own flamin' business.'

'That Yank bloke, want to know what his name was? You'll never believe it: Brik.'

'Brick.'

'That's what I said. He said he was a film producer, said I'd go far in the Hollywood, that's what he said.'

'Don't make me laugh. They're all film producers, you bloody dill.'

'Jeez, yeah, but what if he was, eh? Wow!'

When I heard this I got that feeling in my stomach like I just got picked to be the first kid in the class to conjugate the Latin verb *to listen to*, and that was because I knew who this Brik bloke was, and I had to tell Granddad straight away.

I tried to unwind myself from Chelsea, who seemed to see me for the first time. 'Hello, you're a bit ambitious, aren't you. What's your name?' But she didn't let go. I didn't want to say Blayney, because if she knew I was Nanna's grandson, she'd drop me like a hot spud.

'Jack Sterling. I'm just visiting.'

'Well, Jack Sterling, nice try. Come back in a couple of years.'

She let go and I turned around and walked smack into Dad, who had one of those funny looks on his face, first, at Chelsea then at me. He didn't say anything – Dad always prefers to let things speak for themselves.

'Oh-oh,' said Chelsea's friend, and Chelsea made the big eyes sign at Dad, which means, 'Well, I guess that's the end of that'.

We walked over to Nanna. Nanna was talking to a bloke I took one look at and decided was a plainclothesman, though I knew I hadn't seen him talking to Detective Inspector Passmore. Still he had all the earmarks: a suit he looked like he'd pinched off a dead guy, unshaven, and a very dodgy look on his face.

Nanna piped up. 'Bill, this is —'

'I know, Mum. G'day Dutch, what brings you over this side of town?'

'G'day, Bill. Just catching up with friends. How's the bike?'

'That's the best Triumph I've ever been on, mate. Thanks again. Time we were off, Mum. I'll drop in later for a cuppa.' He meant, to find out if she'd heard anything. 'Nice to see you again, Dutch.'

Nanna looked at the Chelsea and Charlotte, who were blowing me kisses, to get me into strife, then back at me and shook her head and sighed.

15 The Queen of South Melbourne

If Nanna was the Queen of Richmond, Aunty Queenie was the Queen of South Melbourne. For a start she lived all by herself in a mansion in Dorcas Street, my favourite street, it being the home of Channel 7. She often had large parties in this mansion, though they always took place at night, and I had never been to one. Granddad, on the other hand, had been to practically all of them.

Aunty Queenie was not a real aunty, but Granddad's special friend, and they had both told me that they had known each other since they were kids. I knew a few secrets about Aunty Queenie. I knew, for example, that she was the first girl that Granddad ever kissed – she told me that herself when she was stung one day. Also, I knew – from Nanna, in fact – that both Aunty Daffy and Flame Boy's mum were her sisters. I knew a few other things too, but I never told anyone, not even them. I just pretended to be a dumb kid, because that is what adults love to see, and they will do anything to avoid facing the truth, which is that some of us kids are real people and have feelings and know stuff, and miss people. That's all I want to say about that.

So as soon as I left Nanna's place I knew that I had to go and see Aunty Queenie, because of what I had heard. But first I had to put up with Dad giving me an ear-bashing about the girls from the Pepper Club. Talk about rotten luck.

'I want you to stay away from those three.'

'I only spoke to Chelsea and Charlotte.'

That got me a clip over the ear that stung like hell.

'Don't back-chat. You looked like a bloody nong.'

'Sorry.' I knew what he meant: he meant that *he* looked like a bloody nong.

'If you want to be part of this family you have to grow up. I hear you're practically living over at that dago's place.'

I wondered which dago he was talking about, as I had lately turned myself in to the local branch of the United Nations, and was giving all the countries in town an equal vote about then, not to mention embracing some of them with open arms, as Mr Calwell would say.

I neatly dodged this jab. 'Dad, half the kids at school are New Australians. They invite me over to their houses. It's what they do.'

Dad knew that he was on shaky ground here, because half the workers at his and Mum's factories were also New Australians. He changed his approach. 'And what about this girlfriend of yours? You're too young for girls. And who is she anyway? I seem to be the only bastard in the place who hasn't met her.'

'Her name's Mona; she goes to Vaucluse.' I didn't know what to say, how much, or how little, because when it came to girlfriends Dad was still fresh from being forced by Granddad to leave his girlfriend, who we both liked a lot. I could see in his eyes that he was still hurting as if he'd been burned, even though it was a few months ago. He had lost his get up and go and had been reminded by seeing me talking to Chels and Sharl, who were just having a bit of a laugh with me. He missed his girlfriend. And I realised that I was on his side, and always had been.

'Dad, who's Dutch? I haven't seen him before.'

'Dutch Holland. He's a private detective – used to be in the Force. Sells second-hand motorbikes on the side.'

'Is that where you got yours, Dad?'

'Yeah.'

'What kind of stuff does he investigate? Is it like *77 Sunset Strip*?'

'No,' said Dad, who'd seen this show, because I always forced everyone to watch it. 'He mainly just spies on people who hate their husbands and wives.'

I had to try so hard not to say something I got a face-ache. Dad seemed to read my mind, an adult talent I hoped to have myself one day. He said nothing; he didn't even start the car.

'Dad.' I was whispering. 'Let's go and visit Mrs B.'

He looked at me and his face went red. I thought for sure I was going to cop another thick ear. Dad had become a bit of an Olympic class ear thickener since he came home, and this was something he had never done before, being content in the old days to leave the violence to Mum, who was a natural. But he started the car and we slowly drove up to Victoria Street and turned right.

I loved the sound of the indicators. It's one of the things about the FB Holden I love. I can take or leave the sound of the engine – just give me the indicators, and the little lights that come on when they tick. Dad gave it a few extra seconds in first, then a few extra seconds in second, then indicated another right turn. Tick-tick, tick-tick. Up the hill we went, still in second at our street, where he changed into top and went past St Dominic's at what I thought was a beautiful speed for that model: not too fast and not too slow, a speed the car itself enjoyed. Then down the hill a little way to Elm Grove. Tick-tick, tick-tick. Left. Half-way down, we stopped. I had never been here in a car before. It was very peaceful. I was peckish. I wondered if Dad would remember to bring me back a bikky.

Mum was edgy. She wanted to know if anyone at Nanna's had said anything. She wasn't interested in the usual stuff: *Did we realise what time it was? Did we think lunch made itself? Why the hell does she even put up with us?* and so on. All she wanted was what we in the detective business call information. Dad kissed her on the mouth with a little noise. I was fascinated – it was like kissing a crocodile. Then he handed her the note, which she read, folded up and gave back to him. She talked while she organised lunch.

'They'll never find this bloke.'

'He's just a bloke with a grudge of some kind. He'll give himself away.'

'Bill, they'll never find this bloke. I can smell it. I've met blokes like him.'

Dad was all ears. Mum had never sounded like this – soft and firm, a little scary. He was wondering when and where, but he was waiting; that was Dad's style.

Mum sat down and sighed. 'I can't tell you want you want to know. But I've met blokes like this. He's got a plan. He wants to cause as much trouble as he can, short of –'

They both looked at me. They were wondering if they should talk about it in front of me. Kids aren't supposed to hear things. Why the hell did God bother giving us ears?

'Okay, so how can you be sure he isn't dangerous?'

'I think he wants us to worry. He wants us to feel pain.'

'But we're just ordinary people. Why us?'

'We're not *all* ordinary.'

'Mm.' Dad was quiet. 'But hurting Arch would be sheer bloody suicide. No one would do that.'

I had heard conversations like this one before, usually when Granddad came home with an injury of some kind – it had happened a couple of times – a cut face or a cut hand. But problem always went away – always. The point is, they didn't think it necessary to hide it from me.

'He'll act again. And when he does, we'll have the information we need.'

After lunch I said: 'See ya later, alligator' to one and all, and headed off out the front door. But before leaving I went next door to visit Mrs Morgan.

'Hello Aunty Vera.' I had stopped calling her Mrs Morgan – one day, 'Aunty Vera' had just slipped out, and it seemed to fit better.

'Well speak of the devil. Come in. I was just talking to Arch on the phone over at your Nanna's place, to find out if he was going to drop in for a drink later. Now that your Mum's staying with you we don't see as much of each other as we'd like. Jean's a little bit, well, touchy about that, though God knows why. It's been a few years since Ruth passed away, and we've all got to get on with lives.'

This was Mrs Morgan's special way of speaking to me, not as if I was a complete dill but as a friend, which is just what I was. Also, I knew what she had meant about getting on with life, as her husband had been killed in the War when his fighter ran out petrol in New Guinea and he disappeared in the jungle; she doesn't like to talk about it. She didn't know it but it stung a little to hear her say this, because I knew Mum expected me to somehow get on with life without Tom.

But Mrs Morgan herself was a terrific lady, and had what is known as an obsession for anything that was electrical, something I have never seen in any other lady, though I think that by the time Mrs Palmer is her age she will probably have so many electrical appliances in her kitchen that if a burglar gets in there and trips over in the dark, he will probably end up being totally unidentifiable. And many's the time I had put my feet up in Mrs Morgan's living room with her and Granddad, among the leafy plants in their tubs and flower-pots, with my hand wrapped around a cool glass of Marchant's best lemonade, and wondered what the poor people were doing.

But all that had come to an end with the Invasion of Poland, as I thought of Mum's arrival in Brougham Street. And Granddad and me had to sneak around to accomplish our mission, which was as always to remain loyal to our old friends.

Granddad had it, and I know I had inherited it, and I think my friends would have known it, too. I don't know if Mum had it, because she didn't have many friends, though there was Aunty Daffy, and those two loved each other like Heckle and Jeckle.

'So young man, to what do I owe this pleasure?'

'I just thought I'd say hello and tell you what's been happening.'

'Yes, I know about Michael – and about what you did, too. Well done. I'm sure your granddad will get to the bottom of it all. Whoever did it will soon find out that they pinched the wrong baby.'

'See, that's just it, Aunty Vera, they didn't make a mistake, just like they didn't make a mistake when they pinched Dad's car. And they'll strike again, too.'

'You've been watching too much TV.'

'You can't watch too much TV, Aunty Vera; that's not possible.'

'Well, I don't think your granddad would want you getting involved in this. These people could be dangerous.'

'Too late for that. I've already found out one piece of valuable information just by joining a club up here, the Dakotas.'

'I can only repeat what I said.'

'Aunty Vera, I just wanted to ask you to keep your eyes and ears open in case anything unusual happens around here. I mean, nothing gets by you, and Mum's flat out changing nappies all day.'

'All right, then. But no promises. I don't want to meddle.'

'Then you would have made a rotten boy, Aunty Vera.'

And the Mazemaster's work was done.

Next stop was the Sandersons'. I wanted to tell Mr S about the note. But I couldn't get a look at it because Dad had it in his pocket. In the end I decided it would just contain another threat of nothing in particular.

The Sandersons were inside, hiding from the winter weather like all the other sensible people in town. While I was waiting for the door to open I thought for a second of the derros who camped under the railway bridge, and hoped they were all right. It was funny: I hardly ever thought of them, but I knew they were there, because I had seen them, or sometimes just their deserted sleeping spots, while on my explorations. Some of them wore old army clothes. Mum once told me that some of them were old soldiers who couldn't get work, who'd taken to the grog, who were sick from the War. All of this crossed my mind as I waited for the door to open. I heard Mr Sanderson's footsteps. He would never sleep under a bridge.

The door opened and there he was, in his tartan slippers, looking about as stupid as you can look from the ankles down, but from the neck up looking as sharp as a sabre.

'Hello, it's Kimball O'Hara, late of South Richmond.' He was talking about the book, *Kim*, about a boy in India who was a spy, which was strange, because the Sandersons lived in Kipling Street. Mr Sanderson would have called that a coincidence. But I knew it was a just God pulling the levers and pushing the buttons, and being the Big Connector of all the things that happened. Well, I had his bloody number. He could kill my brother, but he would never wear me down.

In the living room we ran into Mrs S, who had been watching something on TV, but turned it off when I came in.

She piped up straight away. 'You've saved me from a fate worse than death, young man: Sunday television. I mean, who cares who won yesterday? We all know Melbourne did, so that's all we need to know, isn't it? I won't ask you how *your* team went.' She suddenly raised her voice, while looking at her husband. But I knew she was really looking at both of us. The Swans and the Hawks had gone down again, as she well knew. The Sandersons were one of those rare couples – I had only met one or two – who were nuts about each other; but on this one point, footy, they were just like everyone else in Richmond. The fact is that Richmond people are seriously buggered in the head when it comes to the old footy. I don't blame them: a game invented by Irishmen for Irishmen. I mean, how can you miss?

'H'lo, Mrs Sanderson. Just dropped in to bring you and Mr Sanderson up to date on the car situation. It turned up outside Nanna's – no damage.'

'Lennox Street, if I remember correctly,' said Mr S.

'You know my Nanna?'

'Not personally. And the note?'

'I couldn't get my hands on it. But Mum and Dad didn't think it was very funny, whatever it said.'

I decided not to tell Mr Sanderson about what had happened to me at the Circus, or about Mr Camponi saying he was going to make enquiries, on the off-chance that he was up to no good. Granddad had sold him his TV last year and it had fallen off the back of a truck, apparently. Also, the way Mr C had said *enquiries*

174

had made me think of the way Granddad says it. As far as I was concerned Mr Sanderson could make his own enquiries.

'Also, I have formed a new club, and we'll be meeting here, like the Olympians used to, if that's all right. We could use the old stable down the back.'

'To investigate these recent events regarding your family,' said Mr Sanderson.

'That's right. We call ourselves the Detectives.' We have decided to get together with one or two other clubs in the area and keep our ears to the ground.'

'You're going to discuss family business with strangers?' said Mr S.

'No, I thought of that. We'll just be poking around generally.'

'If I know your Grandfather, a lot of people are doing that already. It would be better if you didn't get in the way.'

'You know me, Mr Sanderson.'

'Yes, hence my advice. Now, how's life at St Dom's?'

Mr Sanderson was always interested in life at St Dominic's, because he had talked me into going there at the end of last year, when I was thinking of going to City Boys High, over in South Yarra, because of the fees – I didn't want to put Mum and Dad under any more pressure. I mean they were still very unhappy about Tom dying, and Dad had shot through to Mrs Bentley's place. In the end St Dom's got its greasy hands on me and I was immediately declared a known felon by an assortment of De La Salle brothers, due to my record of evil-doing at St Felix's Primary School. To be fair – to me – half of the crimes I had been accused of had actually been the work of Tom, who had a way of getting into strife that you had to see to believe.

I had pinned my hopes on the sadistic bastards who taught me coming to *love, love, love me*, like that Teddy Bears song, but that had not happened, with the result that, not only was I the number one suspect whenever anything went wrong but often so were my friends, who occasionally got hauled in for questioning on the off-chance that they might turn out to be, if not accomplices then accessories after the fact, and dob me in. In this they had failed time and time again. The fact was that most of my friends, especially Johnno Johnson, who was known far and wide to be a bit of hard case, wouldn't dob in a mass murderer, as his family had had its fill of the Bloody Authorities. But I reckon Charles was the only one who wouldn't dob me in out of pure friendship.

'St Dom's? Right now it's about nought out of ten. My best friends and me have been banned from talking to each other, or even hanging out together.'

'Are these boys in your club, the Detectives?'

'Yeah. Thank God we can still catch up after school.'

'Yes, indeed. You must be thankful for small mercies. But I don't think Brother Timothy knows you very well,' said Mrs Sanderson. 'You are a resourceful young man, and I'm sure you will cope.'

'Mm, I think I'll have a word with Granddad. He knows Brother Timothy, you know.'

Mr and Mrs S said nothing, just exchanged glances, the kind that mean: *I don't know why we bother, really.*

'Back in a tick.' I went upstairs to our study, and updated the map with my adventures of the past few days, and doing special drawings of Rufus, who almost tore me limb from limb, and the black Vanguard, and marked the spot where I thought we'd collected the tram.

'Can I use the phone, please?'

'Of course, you know you don't have to ask. Just help yourself.'

I'd remembered that I had a mission.

'Hello, Queenie Brennan speaking.'

'H'lo Aunty Queenie. I was wondering if you could stand a visit.' The young lad knows how to talk to gorgeous women, because that's what Aunty Queenie was, if I've got the right word.

'What, just you?' She had said that because I nearly always turned up on her doorstep with Granddad, who was her best friend in the world, bar none, and vice versa.

'Yep, it's important. I have to see you.'

'God, where have I heard *that* before? But isn't this pretty rotten weather to be travelling around?'

'Not for what I have to tell you.' Really, I had no idea what I was talking about, as usual, but I had a strong feeling about what I had to do.

'Is this something you should be telling your granddad? Perhaps it would be better if –'

'No, Aunty Queenie, I have to tell you as soon as possible. It's private.'

'Well, okay. But I don't think Arch would –'

'But you told me once I could always go to your place.'

'And I haven't changed my mind. Oh all right, come over then.'

I went back into the lounge room, where Mrs S had turned on the TV, to be polite.

'I've remembered that I have to see someone. I'll just say hello to Zac and I'll be off. I'll come back later and pick up my stuff before I go home.'

I found Zac out the back having a nap on the back porch with Abbotsford the cat lounging nearby. Zac was happy to see me, and he knew that later today or perhaps tomorrow I'd be back and take him for a trip somewhere, perhaps even to South Yarra, as Mona had a pet Dalmatian called Dotty and they seemed to get on well.

Then the Octopus – that's who I was just then – shot off, leaving only his outline behind in the air.

16 The Epworth Kid

The Mazemaster knows all about getting from place to place, and is comfortable on trains, buses, and trams, but mostly trams. Soon I was rocking along the tracks to the city, and looking forward to seeing Aunty Queenie again. To tell the truth, the main reason I rang first was to make sure Granddad wasn't there, because I know that sometimes when they are hanging out together they don't like to be disturbed.

Aunty Queenie is Granddad's best friend, and since Nanna Taggerty died a few years ago, he has needed one of those. There's Mrs Morgan next door in Brougham Street, of course – those two are like the flamin' Bobbsey Twins – but that was pretty much on hold. I was betting that Granddad had a plan where Mrs M was concerned, because he always has a plan for everything. He's always flush, for one thing, so I'm guessing the plan involves buying Mum and Dad another house. It's just an idea I have, but as far as I can tell he thinks as I do about Mum, that she's a pain in the bum and would be better off in her own place, sort of like Raffi and his mum. I would go too of course, and that would leave Granddad and Aunty Vera free to get on with putting their feet up and watching TV together. And where's the harm in that?

At Dorcas Street I got off the tram with my special getting-off-the-tram jump that I'm hoping will one day be named after me, giving the tram driver, the clippie and a bloke driving alongside the tram a heart attack in the process, and headed down to Aunty Queenie's.

Aunty Queenie's place was not so much a house as a palace and was, as far as I could tell, about the same size as Buckingham Palace. As I said, Aunty Queenie was not a real aunty but she was called Queenie, like the Queen. However, she did not look like the Queen who, it must be said, needs a horse and a uniform to make her look anything like terrific and looks like she'd be happier munching on a carrot. No, Aunty Queenie really does look like a queen, as she has blonde hair like Diana Dors and a, um, figure most ladies would kill for. What I'm trying to say is that Aunty Queenie is no ordinary lady. Also, like Granddad she has oodles of the stuff and owns this huge house all by herself.

On the inside her house looks like a cross between the foyer of the Gala Picture Theatre in Church Street, which is one of my favourite places, and a museum. It has huge red carpets all over the place, more lounges than a furniture shop, and more statues and pictures than an art gallery. It also has a complete bar, like a little pub, complete with fridges and everything. Granddad told me last December that Aunty Queenie had made a packet by the clever use of her natural assets, and had retired sitting pretty.

Aunty Queenie opened the door, looked around the street, and hauled me in with a hug and kiss that probably would have killed a smaller kid. It was only because I was ready for it that I survived. These kisses of Aunty Queenie's were much more powerful than a real aunty's, and could land anywhere, depending on how much Gilbeys she'd had that day. But whereas real aunties tended to kiss on the lips – I don't know why – pretend one's tended to kiss on the cheek. But they did not hug like Aunty Queenie, who nearly always had most of her chest exposed, no matter what time of the year it was. The best thing about this form of the Big Hello was that it always made me feel very special.

'Well, this is a lovely surprise. Here's me thinking I could use a visit from an old friend, and blow me down, one of the best turns up on my doorstep. I must still have it. Still, you are a shade on the young side, and – no offence – not my first preference, that being your Granddad, as everyone in South Melbourne knows, owing to me having a reputation, as you know.'

'No Aunty Queenie, I didn't know that.'

'Well I have, and I'm telling you now before you hear it from others. But I love Archie as if he was mine, and that means I love you the same.'

Aunty Queenie had been hitting the top shelf again, and I didn't blame her, the quality of daytime telly being what it was, and the weather outside being bloody lousy.

'Come and sit down beside me and tell me what's happened, and I'll get you something to drink. I know just the thing for you.'

And she got up and made me a raspberry vinegar and lemonade, but not in a lady's waist, like in the pub, but in a lemonade glass. My God, do I love that stuff!

'Get those shoes off and hop up on the sofa with me.'

I did as she suggested, and immediately felt much warmer, especially as I was now so close to her that there was what you would call overlap.

'Thanks, Aunty Queenie. Now, I was over at Nanna's place this morning –'

'Had one of her knees-ups, did she?'

'Yes, and there were a couple of, um, girls, from the Pepper Club there –'

'Oh yes?'

'One of them wouldn't let go of me –'

'So you kicked her and bit her until she let go —'

'I wouldn't go that far.'

'No, I didn't think Archie Taggerty's grandson would. Go on.'

'She was talking to another, um, one of the girls about what they did last night at the club.'

'Who were these girls?'

'Chelsea and Charlotte, 'cept they said Chels and Sharl.'

'You remembered *that* pretty well.'

'Yes, and Chelsea said that she met a man at the club who told her that he was an American film producer, and that his name was Brik.'

'Shit.'

'So I remembered that you told me that was your husband's name when you lived in America, and —'

'Bloody hell.'

'I thought I better tell you.'

'*Now* what do you want?' But I knew from her eyes that she wasn't talking to me, but to Mr Brik, if you know what I mean.

There was a long silence, while she breathed in and out, and, finally seemed to complete her thought, which was one of those large thoughts, like a big cloud over her head. Then she seemed to see me again, and hugged me and gave me another kiss.

'You and Archie, God, I love you both. Who else would have given a bugger? Now, think, what else did Chelsea say?'

'Nothing, but she thought it was a terrific opportunity.'

'And what did her friend say?'

'She didn't say anything, just that he was probably pulling her leg.'

'And what did Archie say?'

'I couldn't find him. He shot through, to make enquiries, about Mick, I think.' I had decided to adopt that word. It was the kind of word your superhero likes. 'So I decided to tell you, in case it's a problem.' I knew that when old hubbies turn up it's nearly always a major headache for the female half of the outfit, and a blind man could see that Aunty Queenie wasn't overjoyed at the news.

'Is it him?'

'Yes, love, it's him all right. But what the hell's he doing over here? That's the question. I mean, it's been so long. Still, he hates me, and he hates Arch even more.'

'I'll stay here with you, if you like.' I couldn't think of anything else to say. I had known Aunty Queenie for years. She was Granddad's deadly secret. I felt safer with her than I ever had with any other woman, even though she was not a rellie. I think the reason was that Granddad trusted her completely, and also, that she always told me the truth. I knew that Nanna knew who she was, and that Mum did too. But her name had never been mentioned at home. I also knew that Granddad had a picture of her when she was young, with her son, and that he put it on his bedside table after Nanna Taggerty died. I also noticed that when Mum moved in after our house burnt down, he put the picture away.

'No, love. The best thing would be if you told Archie.'

I had a lot of questions about the past, so I thought I'd try my luck and ask a few. But I could sense that she was worried.

'Aunty Queenie, do you think he's here because of you?'

'I s'pose so. He's going to do something bad; that's what he always does.'

'I'll ring home and see if Granddad's there, okay?'

'All right, give it a try. But you best not tell your mum where you're calling from. She wouldn't like that at all.'

'Okay.'

I rang home and got Mum, and it turned out Granddad hadn't been home. I said I was at Charles's place and that I would be home soon.

'I have to go, Aunty Queenie.'

'It's okay, off you go. We'll get to the bottom of this.'

At home, Mum and Dad were happy to see me, and told me not to go out. Something had worried them, or they wouldn't have given a continental about what I did. When the phone rang it was Granddad.

'Hello, boy. How've you been? I hear you got friendly with Chelsea this morning. What the hell was that all about?'

'Granddad, Chelsea told Charlotte that last night at the Pepper Club she met an American film producer called Brik.'

There was silence on the other end. I thought Granddad might have passed out or something.

'Granddad?'

'What else did she say?'

'Nothing – that's all. Granddad, I couldn't find you, so I went over to Aunty Queenie's place and told her.'

'How did you know who he was?'

'Aunty Queenie told me last year that when you and her went to America she married a film producer called Brik, and I remembered. I wouldn't forget a name like that.'

'I see. What did she say?'

'She was surprised that he was back – um, shocked, really. She wanted me to tell you straight away. Granddad, she was scared. She said he was going to do something bad.'

'Don't you worry. I'll take care of that bastard. Thanks for the tip. Tell your mother I'll be home late – business. Don't say anything about this.'

'Okay, daddy-o.'

'What?'

'You know, *77 Sunset Strip* ... the TV show?'

'Oh, yeah. Just remember.'

He didn't even say goodbye. The Mazemaster always says goodbye.

That night, I was woken up by an explosion, muffled but still loud enough to wake me up, not close, just big, I thought to myself. A few minutes later the Eastern Hills Fire Brigade tore down Church Street.

Granddad came home at breakfast time.

'Christ, Dad, where the hell have you been?' said Mum.

He didn't answer. He said nothing at all, no matter what was said to him. Finally, he made himself a cup of tea with lemon, the way he did every morning. The news was on the radio, and the newsreader said a car had been bombed in Saunders Street, Richmond, and the driver killed. The car had been parked at the home of Mr and Mrs Turner, and was a green and white Ford Customline. Police were interested talking to anyone who may have seen a red and white Holden in the lane yesterday.

Mum closed her eyes and gritted her teeth. 'Damn you, Dad.' That was all she said. She started crying, but without making much noise, and without moving. Her tears just fell down all over the place. I know adults: there's old tears and young tears; the old one's are bigger.

For some strange reason that I couldn't put my finger on, it finally made sense to me. Granddad was paralysed; I don't think he knew what to do. 'Who did it, and why, for God's sake?'

'I know who – I think – but why, I'm not sure.'

'Will they get the bastard?'

'No love, they won't want to. But I will. We can take care of our own.'

'Jesus, Dad, not in front of the boy.'

Suddenly, I was 'the boy': the dog, the cat, the boy.

She wasn't talking about what he said, but the way he said it. Granddad had gone hard and grey, like a statue. It was like Tom all over again. Somebody close was suddenly and violently dead, and there was not enough caring. Then I thought of the photograph in Granddad's room, the one of Aunty Queenie and Brik's son, Murphy, the copper.

When Granddad spoke again, he was mumbling, to himself more than to Mum, as if he'd been reading my mind. 'He bashed Queenie – *my* Queenie.'

I felt an electric shock all over my skin, and swallowed hard. Something seemed to snap inside me, I think for the first time in my life. I looked at Granddad and nodded gently and he did the same to me. Brik was never going to see America again, and I didn't give a shit.

'Don't do that to him,' said Mum suddenly to Granddad. 'Don't let him see that side of you. Dad!'

'Shut up, girlie!' I had never heard him call Mum that before. I realised for the first time that they had a long history before I was even born, and I'd just seen a splinter of it. You want stuff from the old days when it makes you laugh, but not when it frightens you. It was like being in Douggie's house, and gave me a funny taste in the nose. I also realised that the family, if that's what we had, was twisting and changing shape right in front of me.

A breeze seemed to pass over Granddad's face, and he suddenly became strangely cheerful, a bit like an evil scientist in a 'Captain Video' serial.

'I think I'll have another cuppa, Jeannie, then I have to see a man about a dog.'

'You, off to school!'

'Mum, it's too early.'

'Do as you're told!' In her head, Mum was back in the army fighting the Japs, or whatever she did.

Instead of going to school, which was just at the end of the street, I went to St Dom's church, right beside it, where there was a morning Mass going on. I was exhausted from dragging my body up the hill, and from the conversation at home. I had been with Queenie just hours ago, and I had not protected her. I felt as sick as a waiting room, and my brain was flickering off and on like a light switch that's buggered.

I sat down the back and watched the altar boys in their black cassocks – we wore red ones down at St Felix's – and then, because I hadn't had breakfast and was as far as I could tell free of mortal sin that day, I decided to go to Communion. Or rather my feet decided to go; I just went with them. It wasn't until I knelt at the altar rail that I suddenly realised that in my heart I had just had a silent conversation with Granddad in which I had told him that as far as I was concerned it was all right with me if he made certain enquiries about Brik, tracked him down like a rat, and crushed him. I had given him the nod, and I had felt a cold surge of vengeance.

But it was too late, and I was given Communion. I half expected to be struck down in the church. I stood up and turned around and saw Brother Timothy put his arms around me, which was strange, and saw that the huge interior of the church, which was always a grey, dingy colour (which the Mazemaster normally likes) now seemed full of flowers and grass and beautiful scents and soft bright light. I was happy.

I woke up in the Epworth Hospital, which I recognised from all my visits. In fact, I was one of their better known patients, edging out a number of injury-prone footballers – I won't embarrass them by saying who – and kids who always had tubes stuck in various parts of their bodies. You could say I was famous. That is the benefit of having epilepsy. Imagine my surprise, therefore, when a beautiful nurse came over to me and smoothed my hair – it had no effect – and said: 'Hello Raffi, been in the wars again have we?' I realised straight away that I wasn't as famous as I thought, and probably neither was Raffi, and I laughed a little, though straight away a lot of bits of my body hurt like hell.

'What happened?' I asked, innocently because the truth hadn't sunk in, and I honestly didn't have a clue. All I knew was that I had got out of school and was probably going to be inducted into the Epworth Hospital Hall of Fame – I knew without being able to put my finger on it that I deserved it. Then, in big jumps of clarity things happened: loud sounds, stinging smells, swishing nurses, and Brother Timothy, sitting by my beside and holding my hand – I made a mental note to count my fingers before he left. He was telling the rosary with his other hand, and had his eyes closed. When he opened them, he had been crying.

'Hello Brother.'

'Mr Blayney, thank God you're back with us. I thought I'd lost one of my children.'

'No, Brother, I come here all the time. I've been crook since my brother Tom died. He was my twin. There's nothing they can do.' The Mazemaster likes to give a full account of events, though economically.

'Yes, I heard about that. You know, I've got twin nieces; they can't bear to be separated. Mr Blayney, I've been too harsh. What

I said the last time we spoke … about your friends … I want you to go on speaking to them. I had forgotten what you must be going through. I had no idea you were so devoted to the Blessed Sacrament, that you come to school without breakfast to receive the gift of God's grace, when to do so places you in danger.'

'That's all that's keeping me going, Brother: Holy Communion, and fasting is the only way I can go to Communion.' I was taking a risk. I reckoned this bloke had probably heard every excuse and bit of bull under the sun in his day. The Mazemaster needed all his skill and talent. I added the word 'Holy', even though we never used it. There are those in the family – I am too modest to name names – who consider that I have a gift.

'No, it's not. From now on, make sure you have your breakfast before you go to Mass. As long as you fast from the beginning of the Mass you will be welcome at Communion. You are not well. God asks nothing more of you.' He looked suddenly cross. 'You should have been told this.'

I was moved by this speech, not because I wanted to pal up with God, who will always be, as far as I am concerned, a certifiable lunatic, but because I saw a side of Brother Timothy that I had never seen in any nun or brother, and I was slightly stunned, so that I thought I might still be in la-la land. This bloke then patted my hand, got up and left.

Next, a nurse came in and tucked me in all over again, so that I was practically welded into bed – how do they do that? – and took my pulse and temperature. I could have told her that my pulse and temperature would be normal, as it was my brain that was stuffed, not my wrist or whatever was under my tongue, but they do this. Then along comes a doctor to tell you that you gave 'us' quite a fright (young man). And you can tell that this doctor – I've met them all, I think – not only doesn't give a stuff about what state you're in, but, judging by the nasty look in his eyes, has never had a fright in his life. Then – my favourite part – in comes a nurse that you've met lots of times, and seems to like you.

'Master Blayney, hello again. We'll have to get a bed with your name on it.'

'Hello' – I read her badge – 'Nurse McLintock. I think that's not a bad idea. Could you put it over there, near the door?'

'But that's the noisy part of the ward.'

'Yes, but I would get dinner first.'

'Ah yes, what a clever boy. Now, do you think you could stand a visitor for a minute?'

I hoped it might be Mum, because I was (sort of) worried about her, but it turned out to be Charles, who was fresh from school. He had his walking-in-church walk going, as if he was on his way down to Communion, and I thought he looked a bit funny, because his shoes were squeaking on the linoleum. He came and sat beside me, and a nurse came and drew the curtain of the bed next to me, so that we were suddenly alone. Charles looked at my face and I could tell by his expression that I had hurt myself, which is the risk you run when you chuck wobblies near immovable objects. He leaned over me and kissed my face, so gently I could hardly feel it, but very warmly. His eyes watched mine from only an inch away, as a teardrop fell on my cheek. He sniffled and sat by my side holding my hand. Charles had seen me have seizures before – they all had – and I could tell that it was finally beginning to get him down.

'It's all right, Charlie, I'm not gunna die or anything.'

'Don't tell the others.'

'Don't worry, I won't.'

'Is it all right if I hold your hand?'

'Course it is.'

'Now you'll hate me.'

'No, Charlie, you're the only one who came. Even my mum didn't come. From now on we're blood brothers.'

He nodded.

'Does it hurt, you know, when it happens? It looks like you're going to die.'

'No, it doesn't hurt because I'm not even there – I sort of disappear. Sometimes I have a lovely vision that I'm in Heaven, and there's flowers and stuff – it's beautiful. It's the waking up part that's bad.'

'Please don't tell.'

'Come here, Charlie.' I pulled him towards me, and he leaned over. I kissed his face, the way he kissed me, and more tears fell on me. 'Now we're even.'

17 Escape from Colditz

Charles had no sooner left than Mum turned up. Apparently she had already come in during the day, taken one look at me and left. She'd seen me out cold before, and had other things to do. Being a mum doesn't do much for your outlook.

This time she had a small stack of my comics with her, and a couple of new ones. I saw that she had been crying too, and I didn't blame her

'H'lo Mum, how's Granddad?'

'Never you mind.' Mum didn't know that I had known Aunty Queenie for years, and would be worried about how Granddad was going with this Brik customer.

'Where's Mick?'

'Your grandfather's looking after him.'

'How's he going?'

'His usual cantankerous self.'

I knew what cantankerous meant, and I thought that was a bit unfair, as he was just a baby, and couldn't be expected to be happy about the rotten world he had been born into. Tom and me only coped because we had each other. I think I was feeling a bit cantankerous myself just then.

'What have *you* been crying about? Feeling sorry for yourself won't help.' Mum was always quick with a soothing word or two, you will notice. I couldn't tell her they were Charles's tears, and I planned on leaving them there till they evaporated, out of respect for his feelings. But she reached over and wiped them off, automatically, as mothers do.

'Sometimes it just happens without me feeling anything at all,' I said.

This was partly true, and had been happening a lot since Tom left. Sometimes he and I used to cry at the same time, like the time we went to see *Tammy and the Bachelor*. We couldn't see anything wrong with it at all, and neither could anyone else, because they thought it was a twins thing, like barking is a dog thing. But if I tried to do it by myself I was a sissy or a dill. I reckoned I would kill to have him back. I must have let my guard down, because Mum had read my mind.

'Yes, I know. I know exactly how you feel – you don't think I do, but I do. You feel that Tom was a part of you, don't you?'

I nodded as if I was held in some evil professor's Paralysis Ray: this was the first time I had heard her say Tom's name since he died.

'Well, he *was* a part of me, you both were. Do you know that I can't look at you without seeing the two of you? Can you imagine how that feels?'

I had a think. 'I think so.'

'And now this. And on top of …' She started crying. I had never seen her so bad, not even when Tom died. It was like she'd reached the end of the road.

'I can try and stop having seizures, Mum. I can take the medicine again, if you like.' I had tried medicine, but it had only made me vomit blood, and Mum had nearly gone around and murdered Dr Dunnett, so that was the end of that. Dunnett had then wanted me to have electric shocks to the brain, like Flame Boy, because he thought I was mad. Mum thought that was the stupidest suggestion she'd ever heard, and so did I, but it was a close call. It was only then that I realised that, contrary to appearances she was probably on my side. Suddenly I thought I might have said too much, and she might have changed her mind about the electric shocks.

'No, I'm not talking about the fit, I'm talking about this other business. Look, if any stranger talks to you for any reason you must come and tell me, do you understand?'

'Or Granddad.'

'No, not your grandfather. It would be better if he didn't find this person first. Better if the police do it.'

I knew what she was talking about. She wasn't worried about the crims; Granddad and Barney wouldn't put their own safety first.

'How did this happen to you?' she suddenly asked.

'I don't know. I was in Mass at the time, you know, having a bit of a pray for you and Granddad and Mick. And the next thing I know, I'm in here and Brother Timothy is saying the rosary over me. For a second I thought I was dead.'

'You were praying.' Mum didn't believe me.

'I'm always praying, mostly to Tom, but. I call it praying. I don't really pray to God much, not since he took Tom away.'

'What did Brother Timothy have to say?'

'He said I didn't have to fast before Mass. He said I could keep talking to my friends at school. He said he was sorry.'

'What's all this about your friends?'

'We were banned from being friends. He said they were a bad influence on me, especially Charles.'

'Charles Dixon?' Mum had known Charles since kinder.

'Yeah.'

'What's wrong with these blokes, for Christ's sake? Has the whole bloody world gone mad?'

I shrugged, and my head and shoulder filled with pain. I closed my eyes and sucked in hospital air.

'And you aren't going anywhere for a few days. You have concussion. And there are family matters to take care of – best you don't get involved.' She took my hand, finally, and kissed me. It was not a Charles kiss, which said: *I hate to see you like this*. It was a mum kiss which said: *Looks like I'm going to be stuck with him all week*. I reckoned that at the current rate I would get the next kiss around Christmas.

'What's this?' she said, grabbing an envelope off the side cabinet.

'Dunno. I haven't seen it.' I was lying. I didn't want to be the one who told her what was in it. The note said: *I'm just getting warmed up*.

She opened it and unfolded a familiar sheet of writing pad paper, and read it. Then she folded it and put it in her bag, with a sigh.

'What was it, Mum?'

'Never mind. And don't worry, we'll make sure you don't have to worry about anything. Just try to get better.'

I had a lot of questions, especially about Gazza, but I wasn't sure if I'd ever get to ask them. I already knew that Mum had wanted me to know who he was in the end, so perhaps I'd have to be content with that.

After Mum left there was a break during which I tried to read, but found my headache kept getting in the way. I decided therefore that the Phantom would just have to stop the smugglers without me. At night I had an unexpected visit from Mona De Coney, who was still wearing her school uniform. I heard her rushing in, in a way that disciplined nurses and tired parents never did, and knew before she even got in the door that it was if not her then some other Italian girl – I can tell these things. I quickly closed my eyes and pretended to be asleep. Mona came to the bed and bent over me so that her hair fell on my face, and kissed my lips. I tasted lolly bananas. I gave it a four, because she wasn't really trying.

All the boys in the ward – there were about a million of them – started making noises when this happened, so she jumped up and drew the curtain around my bed. I opened my eyes to see.

'Sweetheart, what happened to you? Were you in a car accident?'

'Oh, you know, the usual.'

'Oh dearest, your face is hurt. Are you in pain? Oh, you must be.'

She took off her blazer and put it on the chair. 'I brought you some comics – they're from Aunty Lucky. She drove me over; she's waiting outside. She wanted to come in but I said the shock of seeing two beautiful Italian ladies at the same time might give you a relapse.'

She was dead right about that. I tried to nod, but my head was splitting, and all I could do was close my eyes for a second and hold my breath.

'Oh sweetheart, am I making you worse?'

'I've got a headache, that's all. Thanks for the comics. I have to stay here for a few days; I've got concussion. How did you know I was here?' I didn't think Charles would have told her, as I knew he wasn't one hundred percent keen on my having a girlfriend in the first place.

'You didn't meet me after school the way you usually do, so I asked a couple of your friends where you were, you know, that horrible David Johnson, and he said you didn't come to school. So when I got home I rang your house, and your father said you were in hospital and that he was going to visit you later, and I said: "What time?", and he said: "Seven o'clock", so I thought I'd just get in before him. Wasn't that lucky? I think it was.'

'What time is it?'

She looked at her watch. 'Seven o'clock. Oh dearest, we only have time for one last kiss.' She said this using her movie voice – girls do voices too.

She leaned over to kiss me, but was suddenly grabbed and jerked away from me by a nurse shaped like a professional wrestler. I could see that the nurse was actually trying her best not to hurt Mona, because of the Hippocratic Oath, and anyway, Mona wasn't objecting, because she was busy breathing like a racehorse on the way back to the weighing-in area.

'Oh no you don't, you two,' says the hefty nurse. 'He's supposed to be resting, young lady. And who are you, anyway?'

'I'm his girlfriend,' says, Mona. 'So I'm sure it's all right.'

'Oh to be young again,' says the nurse. 'I think it's lucky I came in, don't you?'

Mona ignored this remark, which in any case was all very mysterious to me. The nurse gave me a look that said: *The things girls get up to.* I tried to give her a similar look back. My look said: *What can a bloke do?*

Just then, Dad came in and gave me a polite smile, which for him was practically hilarious laughter. He gave Mona the once-over without being rude, and raised his eyebrows to me, a secret signal that meant: *My God!* He had not met Mona before.

'G'day, Dad. This is Mona De Coney.'

'H'lo Mr Blayney.'

'G'day.'

'Mona came over to see if I was okay,' I said, in case Dad's brain had conked out.

'Yeah.'

But the nurse hadn't finished. 'One visitor at a time. You'll have to leave, young lady.'

Mona frowned and stuck out her lower lip. 'I'll be off, then. Goodnight, Mr Blayney,' said Mona. She never called me anything but sweetheart or dearest, or one of those types of names, as she seemed to think that life was like in the movies. She left, and so did the muscly nurse.

Dad pulled up a chair. He looked at me and with his eyes wide, and stuck out his lower lip as Mona had done, except that for him it meant something completely different. 'Granddad won't be over tonight. He's got a lot on his plate just now.'

'Yeah, I know: he's helping Aunty Queenie.' It was a slip of the tongue, but it was too late.

'What do you mean: *Aunty*'?

'I know her – Granddad took us over.' Another slip – it was the concussion.

'*Us* – you mean you and Tom? Well, he shouldn't have done that.'

'It was after Nanna died. I've been going over there every now and then. Please don't let on to Mum that you know; Granddad said not to tell her. Aunty Queenie liked me and Tom a lot. She told me that I could go there any time I'm in trouble, and as you know, that has happened once or twice.'

'Yeah, I'm sorry I haven't been around more. I don't know what's going to happen. But whatever I do, don't forget that I love you.'

I got a hell of a fright when he said that, for two reasons: first, because the blokes around our part of the world had a habit of running off to work on the Snowy, or joining the Navy – I made that up, but the Navy had terrific uniforms, and I heard that the grub was good – or going to Tasmania, like Uncle Maury after Dad bashed him up for doing something with Mum – sorry, that's all I know. Also, he had never said he loved me before – it's not a dad thing, unless of course you're Italian, in which case you slip the word 'love' into every second sentence. I half expected God to appear and announce that the world had come to an end, and tomorrow would be Judgment Day.

'Dad, you're not thinking of shooting through to some place where I'll never see you again, are you?'

'No fear, I'll never be far away, you know that.'

'So you and Mrs B are still friends?'

'That's none of your business, understand?'

Yes! 'Yeah.' I tapped the side of my nose, which is secret sign language for *what Mum doesn't know won't hurt her*. I understood all right: we all need friends, and Dad was no different.

'Dad, will Aunty Queenie be all right. It's just that I heard what Brik did to her.'

'Who's Brik?'

'He was her husband – that's who bashed her up.'

'I don't know anything about that. Anyway, it's none of your business.'

'Okay, Dad.' No wonder kids have fits.

Later that night I had a visitor who turned up after visiting hours. I was asleep when he came in, and heard him search my cupboard and drawer. It was the metallic sound that woke me. My first thought that one of the other boys was helping himself to my comics, as a sleeping boy is considered to be fair game, but no, it was a bloke. The sister was just standing there, letting him do whatever he liked and looking pleased with herself, too. Though I was now awake and looking at the bloke, he spoke as if that didn't matter, and when he did, my blood turned to widdle.

'What's wrong with him?' He was American.

'Concussion. He's under observation for a few days.'

'How'd it happen?'

'He had a fit and banged his head.'

'So when do you think he'll be released?'

'I would say the day after tomorrow, probably about lunch time.'

'So you're awake, are you? Can he speak?'

'Oh, yes, he can speak all right.'

'I see. Well, he is not to be released unless there is a policeman present. Not under any circumstances. He is involved in a murder.'

'I'll see to it.'

They left, and I was amazed that they had that conversation right in front of me, completely unaware, of course that they had been overheard by ... *The Mazemaster!* The Mazemaster immediately decided in his quiet but determined way that there were exactly two chances that he was going allow himself to be involved in a murder: Buckley's and none. And anyway, what bloody murder? He must have been talking about Gazza Turner. But what did I have to do with that? It didn't matter, as I wasn't waiting around to be his next victim. I had to get out of there lickety-split. It was Colditz Castle all over again.

I waited until all the boys had gone to sleep and no one was crying – some kids can't do hospital time, and crack under the strain – and got my clothes out of the cabinet. After lots of pauses, during which I was paralysed with pain, I got dressed and put my comics in my school bag, which was still with me. I knew how to get out of the hospital – I wasn't born yesterday – and this wasn't the first time I'd had to sneak out of this place, just the first time anyone would give a bugger about it. I waited until the night nurse started her rounds – we were never first – and slid out onto the linoleum glacier.

The one exit that was always unattended was the ambulance bay. It was cold and swirly down there, but it led to freedom. I realised as I walked down the long ramp that I had come up there many times, though not in a conscious state. It was like walking through my own ghost. I realised also that this was where they would have brought Tom, as it would have been the closest. It made me stop and look around for a few seconds, out of respect, because he would have liked that. Then I turned towards Lennox Street. I was going to the nearest person I could trust not to dob me into the Texas Rangers. Sick as a sausage dog, I dragged my body up the hill to Bridge Road, crossed, and staggered the short distance to Nanna's house.

18 Laying low

Nanna was happy to see me, but not happy to see me crook. She was still up, because she couldn't sleep, but normally the household would have turned in, minus Uncle Seb who usually got home a bit late.

'Oh My God, what's happened to you?' She rushed me into the smaller lounge and I lay on the couch.

I wasn't sure how to begin. On the one hand, she was the Queen of Richmond, and was entitled to all the intelligence I could give her. But on the other hand, I didn't want her worrying herself sick. She wasn't as young as she used to be.

'Nanna, I've got a stinkin' headache. Could I have some water, please?'

She went to get me water, and Uncle Mick came in wearing a dressing gown and a pair of slippers I wouldn't be seen dead in.

'G'day, Uncle Mick. What happened, did you lose a bet? Ooh!' My head hurt too much to speak.

'Never mind me, who did this to you?'

'God did it, Uncle Mick. He has a funny sense of humour.'

Nanna came back with the water and some Disprins; I guzzled them down. 'You better sit down.'

They did as they were told. Basically, old people aren't much different than cocker spaniels.

'First of all, I had one of my turns and ended up in the Epworth. Then tonight this really bad bastard, I mean bloke, turned up and scared the life out of me – I think it was Brik; he's Aunty Queenie's old husband from America – so I shot through. He bashed up Aunty Queenie yesterday, you know.'

'Yes, I heard about it. You knew her, didn't you?'

'Yeah, Tom and me've known her since Nanna Taggerty died. Granddad took us around and introduced us. She's been terrific to me, you know.'

'Oh, I know, all right. I've known Queenie most of my life. She was very keen on Archie in the old days, but it wasn't to be. But she stuck to him through thick and thin.'

'Well, when I was here last Sunday –'

'Yesterday –'

'Was it yesterday? I haven't been well. Anyway, I heard one of those girls, the one with, um …'

'Chelsea – saw her talking to you. I had a word to her about that; she was far too friendly. What did you hear?'

'I heard her tell the other girl –'

Nanna nodded at Uncle Mick and made the frog mouth. 'Charlotte.'

'That she met an American film producer called Brik at the Club.' I paused, but the name meant nothing to Nanna. 'Aunty Queenie once told me that she was married to this bloke in America. She told me he was no good. So I went around to her place to warn her. We had a chat, and she was very worried about it. I offered to stay but she said no. When I told Granddad he wasn't very happy either, but it was too late because Brik went round to her place and bashed her up, and it was my fault for not staying with her. Then, this morning at Mass I had a, um, seizure.'

'Is that how you hurt yourself?'

'Yeah, I hit my head. They said I have concussion and I have to stay in hospital for a couple of days, but I thought: *Yeah, over my dead body*. And also' – I wasn't sure if I should mention Gazza, as I still didn't understand it all myself – 'I think he might have killed someone, someone called Gary Turner, or at least that he was involved.'

'We heard about that – your father's been here – bad, bad business. How a person can hate that much, and for so long. Poor Jean, not to mention the Turners.'

Suddenly I got a very bad feeling. 'Nanna, I think I'm gunna throw up.'

After all the drama was over, Nanna put me to bed. She wasn't exactly Florence Nightingale – more like Ma Baker – but she got the job done. If I was in danger, she'd protect me.

'Let's see who rings first, shall we?' she said over toast the next morning. Watching Nanna eat breakfast was like watching a magic act: you could hardly believe your eyes. She didn't just eat the stuff, she waved it around dramatically while she talked, and licked her fingers, and did swishes and figures in the air. Fair dinkum, you never saw toast disappear like that. She could do it with tea and bikkies too – I've seen it.

Pretty soon we got a call from Mum, who'd had a panic call from the Epworth demanding to know where their prisoner was, as escape is punishable by shooting in Colditz. Mum would have told them to find her baby before she came over there and murdered someone. Then she would have got in touch with Nanna for the same reason that I did.

Nanna went away to talk to Mum, then came back and told me Mum said I was not to worry, and also that she had to tell Mum the whole story about Aunty Queenie, but it was better this way, because at least I was safe. But I had to be sure.

'Thanks, Nanna, but that bloke at the hospital, what if he's Brik?'

'Don't worry, he won't find you here, simple as that. Right, Mick?'

'Right, and if you get worse, we'll get the doctor, okay?'

'Ripper, Uncle Mick. What's the story with the marmalade, Nanna?'

Later that day, Mum turned up with my winter pyjamas and a few things I liked to read.

'I rang Charles,' she said. 'I told him you came home but you wouldn't be able to have visitors for a few days, probably not until the weekend. I asked him to tell your friends at school. Granddad explained this Brik business to me, and a few people are looking for him. But that's got nothing to do with you, as far as I can see. You just stay here and rest.'

'Thanks Mum, Charles tends to worry about me. Mum, I had to shoot through. A bloke came to the hospital in the middle of the night and searched my things, and told the nurse I was involved in a murder and I wasn't allowed to leave; I think he was Brik – *Mr* Brik. I didn't feel safe there. And I had to go to Aunty Queenie's place on Sunday, Mum, you know, to warn her.'

Mum didn't know what to say to that. She had gone beyond upset. 'Nanna told me all about it. I want you to stay out of this. I don't want anything to happen to you.'

'Mum, that Brik bloke, did he leave another note?'

'I don't think what happened to Mick and the car had anything to do with the Turner boy – just coincidence.'

Coincidence! That's what adults wheel out for everything that happens, as if nothing's connected. But I've noticed that everything that happens to me is connected: to *me*. So I wasn't listening to that rubbish. And everything that happens to

Granddad's connected to Mum. And Mum's connected to me, and so on. I once asked Mr and Mrs Sanderson about this and they told me I'd have no chance at all at putting a stop to the coincidences that were making my life a misery. And Raffi's mum said the same thing, and she above all people should know. No, there was a connection all right, and the Mazemaster would find it. If only I had Tom to talk to, as he would always help me work stuff out. Granddad always said that he was as bold as brass, while I was as sharp as a tack, but I was at my sharpest when I was with Tom, and he was always boldest when he was with me.

'No, Mum, I don't believe in coincidence anymore. There are all these connections everywhere. Remember that time Nanna came over for lunch and said that the Brennan girls were related to Keith Kavanagh's mother. Remember? Did you know that? I didn't. And you had that big connection with Keith's Aunty Daphne in the War, didn't you. So that means you had a big connection with Aunty Queenie, without, even knowing it.'

'Don't call her that, she's Mrs Brennan.'

It was on the tip of my tongue to say: 'Actually, Mum, it's Mrs Brik,' but that would have got me another dose of concussion. But Mum had said it quietly so I knew she wasn't telling me to shut up, though millions would have.

'Sorry. Anyway, I'm not so sure about all these things being just coincidences anymore. And anyway, I hate coincidences. I'd much rather know how all these things happen.'

'Believe me, I wouldn't mind knowing how these things happen myself.'

'And what about that Brik bloke coming over to the hospital? What would he have against *me*? He didn't even know me.'

'I think your granddad might have met him once or twice. I've found that people who have run-ins with your grandfather tend not to forget easily.' She looked at me as if she was inviting me to ask more questions, and this was something she'd never done before. Since Tom had died I had become just another mouth to feed, someone who took up space in the house, a pest, a bit like a spider. Mum had stopped loving me a long time ago. But it was all right. I understood; she'd never wanted us in the first place. It would have been better if we'd both died, instead of one hanging around to remind her of what happened all day and all night. I wasn't sad about me and Mum though; it was Tom I was sad about. I thought I might try one more question.

'Mum, what happens when Mona goes to the Epworth to visit me, and I'm not there?'

'Mona can live without you for a while. You're too young to be seeing girls like her, anyway.'

I knew what Mum meant, but Mona had a lot going for her. For one thing, none of my friends, except Raffi, had a girl-friend, and I didn't even know if Tina and Raffi kissed (though I don't even know why I said that, as she was Italian). The way I looked at it, if you're going to be the captain of a club you need a girlfriend, so the men can look up to you. When I thought about it, Mum probably didn't know what she was talking about, because when you've got girlfriend like Mona nothing could possibly go wrong.

'What d'ya mean, girls like her, Mum?'

'I mean girls who are developing a lot faster than usual.'

'She's just Italian, that's all. You should see Raffi's girlfriend, Tina Camponi. She's developin' like there's no tomorrow.'

Mum said nothing, just reached for a Stuyvesant. I was glad we'd had this conversation; I had learned a new word.

As soon as Mum left I rang Mona's place. Mona answered the phone.

'H'lo?'

'G'day, Mona. It's me.'

Mona was practically in tears. 'Sweetheart you rang me. How much you must care for me. Are you all right? Of course you're not, yet you dragged yourself to the phone.' I wondered which movie she got that out of; it sounded damn good, and she was half right about the dragging.

'I left the hospital and I'll be staying at my Nanna's place for the rest of the week: she lives in Lennox Street, not far from school.'

'Oh sweetheart, as long as you're all right. I went to the hospital after school but they told me you'd gone home. I rang your mum but she told me you weren't having visitors until the weekend and couldn't come to the phone. I was sorry we couldn't spend more time together last night. That nurse was horrible, wasn't she? And her shoes, did you notice? You'd think nurses would take better care of themselves, wouldn't you? I know you would. I'm never going to become a nurse. I was thinking of becoming an actress, like Sophia Loren − *she's* Italian − or a singer. I hope your nanna is feeding you properly. Would you like to me to visit you? I could come over for a little while before tea. Would you get into trouble?'

Most of this was said at a new world record rate for talking, as Mona had a tendency to worry out loud, which is what Italian girls and ladies do. With Australian girls and ladies it's mostly complaining that they do out loud, which is not the same thing.

'I think I better ask Nanna about that. Hang on a sec.' I stuck my head around the corner. 'Hey, Nanna, can Mona De Coney come and visit for a few minutes? You'd like her − she's Italian.'

'Is she the one your mother said visited you in hospital?'

'Yes, she's very worried about me.'

'I think your mother's overreacting a bit, don't you? Tell Mona it's all right. She can have tea with you, if you like. We'll keep it to ourselves.' There's no doubt about it, Mum was definitely not Nanna's favourite person, and this was working in my favour.

Nanna treated Mona like one of the family, even though she'd never seen her before, and said she could have tea with me in the bedroom, as if she was a hospital visitor who was allowed to eat the hospital food. While we were waiting for tea Mona insisted on kissing me, and climbed up on the bed, the way she had done in hospital. She was wearing her school uniform, as usual, and a school dress that I was sure was probably not long enough, as I had heard from Judy Pickle that girls could be chucked out of a school if their dress did not come within a hand's breadth of the ground when they were kneeling. I reckoned that Mona would have to be sitting on her heels to qualify. When she hopped on top of me, to give me a kiss, I looked at her in the wardrobe door mirror. I could see this was going to be a tough week.

After a while, Nanna yelled out at the top of her lungs, 'Dinner's ready. I'm coming down.'

Mona jumped off and pulled down her dress and did up her shirt button, which was always coming undone, and sat on my bedside chair as if she was at Mass. That was how she was when Nanna came in carrying a tray with soup on it. Her hair was messed up and her face was red, and she was breathing like a deep sea diver, but Nanna did not notice. Oldies can be a pushover.

I couldn't eat much, but Mona could put it away like a wild hyena. Nanna stayed for a minute and watched, then asked a funny question.

'Mona, what a lovely name. Are you any relation to Tony De Coney, from Carlton?'

'He's my uncle.'

210

'Please tell him Mrs Blayney says hello to the family next time you meet him. He'll know who you mean.'

'Okay, Mrs Blayney.'

Mona thought this was terrific, as Italians are better at passing on social information than ants. But Nanna wasn't just being pleasant; she was being the Queen of Richmond. Then Nanna looked at her watch and said: 'Time for telly,' and left.

'I like your nanna,' said Mona. 'Fancy her knowing Uncle Tony. I wonder how.'

'Don't forget the message,' I said. 'I think it's important.'

'Don't worry, sweetheart, I won't. Does your nanna go to bed early?'

'No, Mona. I don't think so. Something tells me she'll stay up till you leave.'

She looked at me as she slurped her soup. No matter how much soup she put away she still looked hungry.

When Mona had gone, Nanna came and tucked me in. I was tired, and needed to sleep. The Mazemaster was beat.

'Mona is a lovely girl,' said Nanna. 'She can come back any time, provided I'm here, of course. We don't want her parents worrying about her.'

'That's great Nanna. She won't be any trouble.'

'Well, I wouldn't go that far,' said Nanna. 'Let's see how it goes.'

'So, Nanna, how come you know her Uncle Tony in Carlton. You don't get over there, do you?'

Nanna settled in for the duration. 'Well, when the De Coneys came to Australia, the War hadn't begun, but when it did all the Italians were rounded up and interned in a camp in Rowville. My family had a big farm in the area, and we employed a lot of the Italian men, including the De Coneys. My cousin Audrey married one of them.'

'She married Tony De Coney?'

'That's right. And now she owns half the Vic Market and a fair slice of Lygon Street.'

'Wow!'

'That's right.'

'But Nanna, my head.'

'Time for you to sleep.'

'No, I mean, my head is just about exploding with the connections. They won't stop.'

'Oh, I see what you mean. I suppose I should have told you about the family, but the Blayneys tend to keep to themselves, and the Taggertys, well, they're even more Irish than we are. Tell you what, if you're interested, we could have a look at the family tree while you're here.

'I know what that is, Nanna. Sounds great. All I know about your family is that you're in it. And of course I know about some of the uncles and aunties, and some of the cousins.'

'Oh, there's a lot more to it than you think, and it's time I passed on some of the truth to someone. But finding out where you stand is like finding your way through a maze. Let's start tomorrow.'

19 The Mazemaster connects some dots

On Wednesday morning, during crumpets and jam, Granddad
turned up.

'Have a cuppa and a crumpet, Granddad.'

'Don't mind if I do. So, what's new?'

'First things first Granddad: how's Aunty Queenie?'

'Don't you worry about her. It's Brik who should be worried.'

'Oh hell, I should have stayed with her.'

'Then you would've copped it too. No, you did the right thing.
So what's happenin'?'

'Well, let's see, an American bloke – did'ja hear that? – came to
see me in hospital, and searched my things, and told the nurses not
to let me go because I was involved in a murder, so I escaped over
here. Mum came over yesterday and visited. Mona De Coney
came over for dinner last night – wasn't that nice? And I've got
this theory (fair dinkum, that word is a ball-tearer).'

'Since when do you have theories?'

'Since we started doing science. Anyway, remember that
bastard Murphy, who shot Biscuit?'

'Hey, hey –'

'Yeah, well he was, wasn't he? Anyway, I remembered you
telling me that he was Aunty Queenie's son, but according to
rumours I'd heard –'

'What did I tell you about –?'

'Just a sec, Granddad – he hated her guts all his life, even though she was his mum. Then I realised that you told me that he had known that his father was this Brik bloke, Rollo Brik the film producer. *Then* I realised that Murphy hated *you* like hell – I haven't worked out why, mind you – which means that these two might be in cahoots.'

'What?'

'You know, mates, like in the cowboys.'

'Oh, yeah.'

'Which means that Brik might be at Murphy's place.'

'He's not.'

'What? But –'

'That's the first place I looked. Look, I think you should forget all about that bloke Brik; just leave him to me – but you didn't hear me say that. Okay?'

'Okay.'

But I still liked my theory. Good theories are hard to come by.

'I heard all about Saturday night. Best you don't tell your mother. I've asked Barn to keep an eye on you.'

'Thanks, Granddad. But who's gunna keep an eye on Barn?' I gave him the Octopus Wink, but he wasn't biting. 'I s'pose those blokes who grabbed me got away.'

'Don't worry, we'll get the bastards.'

'Well, at least now you've got a car to trace.'

'Stolen. You finished with that marmalade?'

'So now what?'

Granddad settled in with a crumpet and marmalade. 'I'll tell Queenie you asked after her.'

'Granddad, you can do better than that: give her my love.' I'd never said that in my life, but I felt grown up enough to start.

The Mazemaster and his nanna had a fascinating few days together. It turned out that what people had been telling me about connections was dead right, and what I had been thinking of for years as coincidence was complete bullshit. It was as if there was a Great Big Signals Box in the Sky and someone up there could see everything that was going on and was pulling levers and stuff. I knew that this was what the brothers called God, but I also knew that God could be a sick bastard. I felt like a complete fool when I realised this, and wondered what was the point of it all. After all, this was the same God that took Tom away. He must have laughed himself silly that day.

'Nanna, we're all connected.'

Nanna thought this was a wonderful discovery.

'Yes, we are. Isn't it wonderful? We *are* all connected.'

'But it means I'm connected to that Brik bastard that hurt Aunty Queenie.'

'No dear, no! You mustn't think that. He's American, for a start. You can't be connected to people from the other side of the world.'

'But you're connected to the De Coneys – hell, that means I'm connected to the De Coneys too – and they're from the other side of the world, aren't they?'

'Well, not from America.'

'But Brik's connected to Aunty Queenie, and she's connected to Granddad –'

'Not legally connected, not family.'

I thought Nanna didn't get what I was saying. 'Nanna, to God it doesn't matter how people are connected. He doesn't give a stuff how it happens, as long as the bits of track are connected up in the right way.'

'Now, now – language. What bits of track?'

'The tracks that people run on till we smash into each other.'

'Yes, but only a few of us are connected, not all of us.'

'No, Nanna, it's *all* of us, and not just the people but the stuff that happens to them.'

'What stuff?' Nanna was getting worried and I could see that she was beginning to think what everyone thought once they stopped seeing me as a loveable half of a pair of twins: a nut who's brain badly needed zapping. Nothing scares an adult more than seeing a kid think.

'Like … like when I first met my friend James Palmer, who isn't even a relative; it turned out that his mother had met me once.'

'That's just coincidence; they happen to everyone.'

'No, Nanna, that's not coincidence because there isn't any such thing as coincidence. It just means there's another connection.'

'But of course there's coincidence. Take Uncle Seb and Uncle Mick. Both their fathers are called Patrick, but that's nothing, because they're both Irish, and half the Irishman in town are called Patrick. I wouldn't call that much of a connection.'

'But Nanna, the *real* connection with Uncle Mick and Uncle Seb is *you*: *you're* the connection.' I had a think. 'And these people who nicked my brother, they're connected to me and Mum and Dad and Granddad and you – all of us.' I had a little thought. 'We'll catch 'em because of that, you know.'

'No, dear, we'll catch them by waiting till they slip up; crims always do.'

'Yes, I know, everyone's making *enquiries* aren't they: Mr Camponi, Granddad, Inspector Passmore, all of them, making enquiries.'

'It's the way it's always been done.'

'Well I've invented a different way, Nanna: connections. These blokes're in a sort of giant maze and so am I, and I'm going to find them because I know my way around.'

'What maze? What are you talking about?'

'Richmond.'

Then Nanna saw what I meant. And it was true: I knew my way around like a beauty.

'Nanna?'

'Still here.'

'I need information.'

'Of course you do.'

'It's about connections. You know a lot about the people around here, don't you?'

'Enough to blackmail half the men in Richmond, and half the women, and make the rest open a special savings account for when their turn comes. But you didn't hear me say that.'

'That's what I thought. Nanna, I'm going to give you a list of names, and I want you to tell me if any of them hates Granddad or Mum and Dad.'

'I don't think this is a good –'

'Murphy the copper.'

'Mmm, well as a matter of fact Murphy has never liked Archie, but I don't think I should mention the reason – it's an old and complicated story.'

'Murphy is Aunty Queenie's son, isn't he?'

'How did you know that?' Nanna was so surprised I thought for a second she was going to have a stroke.

'I'm sorry Nanna. Granddad told me, when I discovered he had a picture of Aunty Queenie and Murphy when he was a kid.'

'Yes, and Murphy has always been bitter about his mum and Archie being old friends; in fact, a lot of people have over the years. In her youth Queenie was what is known as a rare beauty.'

'Like Mona.'

Nanna didn't reply, but looked at me sideways, to see if I was having her on. She was sharp as a hatpin.

'Also, Murphy and Archie have had the odd run-in over the years, because Murphy has always been keen on Jean.'

'Mum?'

'Yes, but it hasn't worked.'

'But Nanna, that's our connection! Murphy stole Mick!'

'Can you see Murphy sneaking into Dimmeys and stealing a baby, then looking after him for the best part of two weeks? Have you seen that bloke?'

'Yeah, I see what you mean. I had a bit of a run-in with Murphy myself once, when he sprung me burglarising his house in Stephenson Street. Granddad talked him out of pressing charges, though God knows how.'

'Yes, I heard about that. Unfortunate business.'

'I didn't know it was his house, Nanna.'

'A common beginner's mistake.'

'Who told you – Granddad?'

'No, Barney. He watches you like a hawk. You don't know the things he's done for you.'

'Mum says Barney's bad news. So do the Sandersons. So do a lot of other people.'

'He's got a heart of gold, young Barney.'

'Nanna, how come he sometimes comes over on Sunday mornings? I didn't even know you knew him until a few months ago.'

Nanna had a sip of her cuppa – she liked to stick her little finger out. 'Barney's mother was my bridesmaid – Mary Finn. She was older than me, and lovely as an angel, though plain. Neither of us thought she'd ever get married, so she became my bridesmaid, more for luck that anything. Anyway, it worked, because she met a rough diamond called Barry Flanagan at my wedding, and next thing you know there's little Barneys running round all over the place. They disowned him when he went to prison for the first time – haven't spoken to him since, even though they only live around the corner.' She sighed. 'Have a bikky, love. You need to build up your strength. Where was I?'

'They wouldn't talk to him.'

'Yes, well that's none of my business, but I've known Barney since he was a kid, and he knows he can come over any time. And I'm afraid other people will just have to like it or lump it.' She raised her eyebrows and made the duck face at the same time, just as Dad had when he saw Mona at the hospital. So that's where he got it from! 'Barney's not exactly a rocket scientist, as I'm sure you've noticed, but he'd do anything for you. He fought the Japs in New Guinea, you know. I bet those Japs wished they'd joined the flamin' Navy. He's as tough as old boots. When he came home he wasn't the same – became a drinker – you've seen it.'

'Is that why Dad ...?'

'Probably. God knows. I suspect it's in the Blayney blood. Take my advice and stay away from the bottle – I mean it, love.'

'Who else, Nanna?'

'Well, there's Mr Radion, of course, though I'm sure he doesn't know who Raffi's father is, or I think he would have done something a long time ago.'

'But that was a long time ago when Dad and, um ...' I hadn't really thought about it before, I mean the details, if there were any.

I had made the connection months ago but without thinking how it might have happened.

'It was a long time ago, but time means nothing to a person bent on revenge.'

'Do you think he's come back and done a bit of detective work?'

'He wouldn't have to do any of that if Val Radion told him, would he?'

'She wouldn't cause trouble, Nanna. She's a nice person.'

'She's nice to you, but I don't think she'd be nice to your dad.'

'But she wouldn't take Mick, and anyway, she didn't even know Aunty Queenie. Who else?'

'Well, there's the whole Magee family. They hate the Taggertys, and they've never had anything to do with Jean. It's a very old and horrible story, and one that I can't tell you, as it would only poison your mind, and I would never do that. But they hate Archie and they've made sure from time to time that he remembered. I can't say more than that, love, so you mustn't ask me.'

'It's because Granddad was once put in prison, wasn't it?'

'How did you know that? Oh, Barney, I suppose. Well, no, that wasn't the reason, as a matter of fact, thought you'd think that'd do it, wouldn't you?'

'But Granddad was a war hero.'

'What happened wiped all that out in the eyes of the Magees. One day you'll find out the whole story, but best you don't hear it from me, I think.'

I knew, of course, that Nanna Taggerty was a Magee, and that her family weren't keen on her marrying Granddad, but the rest was going to have to stay a mystery for a while. But Nanna was right: they wouldn't have waited so long to get their revenge.

'Nanna, do you think Mrs Bentley could have taken Mick? She was pretty angry about Dad going back to Mum. I was there the day he told her Mum was, you know ...'

'No, dear, of course not. She has her own children. And besides, she doesn't hate Jean. I know all about Lorna Bentley. She knew Molly Kavanagh, you know. She would have been happy that Molly and her son went to live up at Wodonga.' This was an information avalanche; I'd had no idea that Nanna even knew who Mrs Bentley was, let alone know her history and her family. The connections were starting to crush me; they were soft, but heavy, like it was raining giant pandas.

'Nanna, you know everyone, and you seem to already know all the people who didn't do it. Who do you think *did* do it?'

Nanna swirled her tea around in the teacup, and suddenly upended the cup in a saucer, then looked into it. Reading the tea leaves was one of her well-known dramatic acts, and someone – it might have been Nanna herself – had once told Tom and me that she had real magic powers.

'Well, working on the theory that it was not someone who wanted to hurt your dad – no enemies that I know of, and I think I'd know – I'd say someone from Jean's past, because she has a past, you know.'

'What do you mean?'

'I mean the War. She won't talk about what she did, and neither will your grandfather, who knows. See, it's because she can't. People like that have enemies.' Nanna looked at me sideways, as if we were characters in a movie starring Humphrey Bogart and Lauren Bacall. 'That's where I'd put my money. And if I'm right, no amount of nosing around Richmond's going to turn anybody up. If the bloke who Jean upset is one of her crowd from the War, he'll be as closed-mouth as she is.' So much for your connections.

He won't be in any maze waiting for you or anyone else to come along.'

'I bet I know who might know something: Mr Sanderson. He knows what Mum did in the War, you know.'

'He'll never tell you. I know his type. I asked about him through some friends. He doesn't exist; he's just a bloke in a house in Kipling Street. Jean was an officer during the War and he worked with her, but he never went to any officer school. He wasn't a cop either, I checked. He was something entirely different. But you tell me he works for COMPOL –'

'That's what he told me.'

'Yes, that's what he says. And anything else he tells you will be untrue, a porky; it's his job. I'll bet he couldn't lie straight in bed.'

I tried to think of Mr and Mrs Sanderson lying in bed – nothing happened.

'Did you tell him about Mick getting pinched?'

'Yeah, straight away.'

'What did he say?'

'Nothing.'

'There you go. I'd bet my bottom dollar he's got a short list already. Jean might have one too, and they might even be the same. But they'll keep it to themselves.'

I thought about this for a long time.

'Nanna, when Mick was first pinched I thought it might have been a gypsy.'

'Oh? Why?'

'Because there are a bunch of 'em working over at the Circus, and Mrs Hutchinson told me once they pinch babies.'

'What would that woman know about gypsies – or babies, for that matter? Gypsies are very decent people – I can't speak for the Irish variety, mind, who are a bit on the wild side.'

'Nanna, can I tell you a secret?'

'Does it have anything to do with you visiting the gypsy camp a few weeks ago, and getting pretty friendly with Sunny Petulengro?'

'Nanna, how the heck – oh, I know, it was Father Sheehan, wasn't it?'

'He mentioned it last Sunday, but I already knew all about it.' She got a faraway look in her eyes. 'My second husband, Joe Williams, was a Traveller – that was a Travellers wedding you went to – and I lived with them for a while, till he came to a sticky end – those were wild days – then I settled down with your grandfather and became a respectable woman again. I've known Lela Petulengro all her life. I visited her as soon as I heard they were in Richmond, and she told me about the boy she read the cards for.'

'Jeez, Nanna, I mean hell.' I thought my brain had had about all it could take.

'I know, I'm like you in many ways: I haven't let the grass grown under my feet, and neither will you.'

'Did she tell you about that Tarot card that kept coming up?'

'*The Hanged Man.*' Nanna looked into my head through my eyes. 'I can't help you with that. What's in the cards is in the cards.'

Wonderful. Why the hell did I ask?

'But Nanna, you *always* know what to do.'

'And so do you, my darling.' She tried to smooth my hair.

20 A bloke like Barney

The next day was one of those days you dream about if you live in Melbourne. The rain had stopped and the sun was out, the birds were pretending they were in Hawaii, and I didn't have to go to school. Nanna had gone shopping and the uncles were absent, no doubt pursuing their chosen professions, both of which were prone to the odd ups and downs. I was wandering around in my pyjamas, wondering whether I should organise some morning tea — a second go at toast was looking good — or turn on the wireless. The fact was, I was only just able to stand up, my head still hurting like mad — don't ever get epilepsy.

All of this was spoiled by the sight of someone at the back door. Nanna's was an enormous house and had entrances at the front, side and back, via the lane, so that itself wasn't weird. But people tend to turn up at the front of big houses, you know, because it feels so good. So I went down to the back door to see who it was, but I was only two yards away when I realised it was a burglar having a go at the lock, but no ordinary burglar. For one thing he was not dressed like an Aussie but like a New Australian. He didn't have a bloke's hat, for a start, but a cap. And he was wearing a funny looking jumper. But the thing that struck me was the way he worked, quietly. I knew from watching Barney, who had given me the odd lesson, that you tend to make a bit of noise on heavier locks. This bloke was doing it like a brain surgeon.

I backed out of the room and headed for the stairs. This bloke was going to get what he came for – it was written all over him. If it was me he would know where to look. I went up the stairs quietly, knowing he was probably already inside, and went into Nanna's room. When I got to the window I opened it, climbed out, and closed it behind me. Then I edged sideways a few feet and waited. Half an hour later I heard the back gate close – he wasn't worried about making a noise any more – and a car start. I watched as it appeared at end of the lane and turned. It was a white FE Holden with a red roof.

Inside, everything was as normal. The place had not been turned over. Burglars usually turn over certain things, looking for valuables, whereas police just wreck the place. But this was neither. Only one thing had been touched, my room. I left a note for Nanna. Then I got dressed, threw my things into a pillowslip, and left. I had just reached the front gate when Barney turned up in his new second-hand Ford Zephyr.

'G'day, Barn, can ya give 's a lift home, please?'

'Stone the crows, what're you doin' out here. And what happened to yer face?'

'Chucked a wobbly last Mond'y, Barn – you should see the look on your face.'

'Ah hell, I'm sorry to hear that, nipper. A bloke shoulda been told.'

'Not to worry. I've been staying at Nanna's. Hey, remember that bloke from the Circus, the one who grabbed me? Well, he just broke in through the back door and searched the house for me, so I reckoned it was time I moved.'

'Ah shit, and I wasn't here. Your granddad'll have me guts for gaiters.'

'He was no amateur, Barn, he was like you. Anyway, he's well away, in a white FE Holden with a red roof – there was a woman driving. Barn, this was the same car that was seen at the back of Gary Turner's place, well, you know –'

'I know.'

Barney took me home, but he cursed himself all the way; I never saw him take anything so hard. I thought it best to have a word with him. 'Barn, I don't think Granddad told Mum what happened at the Circus, so best we keep it that way. I'll tell her just what she needs to know about what just happened.'

Inside, we ran into Mum and Mick, listening to the wireless.

'Hello, Mum, what's new?'

'What the bloody hell do you think *you're* doing? G'day Barn, what happened?'

'Some bloke broke into the house while I was parked out front, cheeky bugger.'

'He broke in the back way, Mum, but I hid from him. He had a look around, then he left.'

'Did you see him?'

'Not his face. But I got a look at his clothes. He was dressed like a New Australian.'

'How would you know?'

'I dunno. They dress different, that's all. I left a note for Nanna. I don't think he pinched anything.'

'Your grandfather will know what to do. How's your head?'

I was tempted to fib about this, in case Mum wanted to keep me in the house for the next few weeks, like a prisoner of war, because I couldn't think of anything worse. Even school would be better. But we had a problem, and I knew that when Mum was in her lieutenant mode, as she was now, she was capable of pulling off superhero-type stunts.

'It's as sore as hell. By the time we got to St Dom's I half felt like dropping in and doing a French test or two to relieve the pain.'

Mum didn't laugh. She was hard to get a chuckle out of at the best of times. I often wondered why Dad married her, or even how they managed to bump into each other in the first place. It was a mystery, like the loaves and the fishes.

She got me a couple of Disprins and a glass of water, and watched me drink it.

'You'll stay here for the rest of the day, and later I'll get Barney to take you over to the Sandersons for the rest of the week. Okay?'

Barn nodded. 'I'll find Arch. Back in a few hours.'

While Mum got on the blower to Mrs Sanderson, I climbed out of my clothes and back into my pyjamas and dressing gown, and hopped up on the couch. It would be hours until TV came on, and I didn't feel like trying to read a comic or a book.

'Mum, what do you know about our family tree?'

The Mazemaster thought that he might catch his mother unawares, as he had so many times before – I made that bit up: it never happened.

'What do you want to know?'

'Everything, bar none. The truth, the whole truth, and nothing but the truth.'

'All right, but I'm only going to say this once, so are you going to write it down or what?'

'Can Johnny Ray sing?' I got out my explorer's Spirax notebook and a pen. 'Off you go, Mum.'

'Your dad's mother is Nanna Blayney and his father was Granddad Blayney. Nanna Blayney's mother was Minnie White and her father was Patrick Ryan.'

'Didn't take long for us to run into a Ryan, did it, Mum?'
'Are you interested in hearing this or not?'
'Sorry, Mum. You were saying?'

'Granddad Blayney was Nanna Blayney's third husband – third *official* husband.'

I winked. 'Gotcha, Mum. So what happened to the others?'

'She married Eb Conway in 1916 and he was killed in France. Then she married Joe Williams in 1919, and he was murdered, don't ask me how.'

'Oh-oh.'

'But before he married Nanna he married Lilian Wood, who had three children, then died. Those children are your Aunty Dot and your Uncles Clive and Bert –'

'The one who lights fires.'

'No, the one who steals money boxes.'

'Oh, yeah. Mum, how can you remember all this stuff?'

'I have a special memory.'

'Jeez, you mean like spies have?'

'Nanna Blayney and Granddad Blayney had three kids apart from your father –'

'I know, Uncle Frank, Uncle Nick, and Uncle Ivor.'

'Yes, but she also had three kids by her first marriage: the Conways.'

I waited.

'Aunty Mazie –'

'I like her –'

'Uncle Maury.'

I said nothing, as his name was a bit of a swear word around the family. He had done something to Mum, or maybe *with* Mum – I was unclear on the facts – and Dad had cleaned his clock for him. Don't ever get on the wrong side of a Blayney. I glanced at her secretly, but she didn't bat an eyelash.

'Uncle Pat, and Uncle Bert –'

'The one who lights fires.'

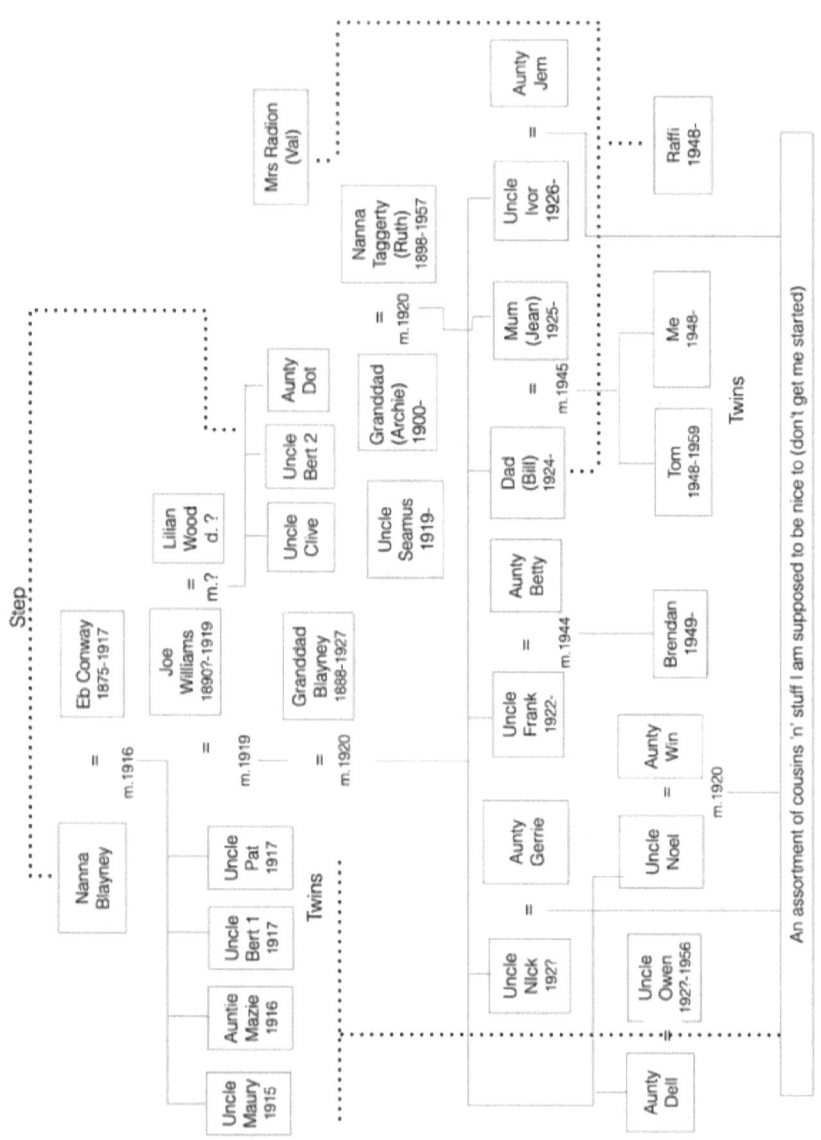

An assortment of cousins 'n' stuff I am supposed to be nice to (don't get me started)

Step

Nanna Blayney = m.1916 Eb Conway 1875-1917

= m.1919 Joe Williams 1890?-1919 = m.? Lilian Wood d. ?

= m.1920 Granddad Blayney 1888-1927

Uncle Maury 1915

Auntie Mazie 1916

Uncle Bert 1 1917

Uncle Pat 1917

Twins

Uncle Clive

Uncle Bert 2

Aunty Dot

Uncle Seamus 1919-

Granddad (Archie) 1900- = m.1920 Nanna Taggerty (Ruth) 1898-1957

Mrs Radion (Val)

Aunty Jem

Uncle Nick 1927 = Aunty Gerrie

Uncle Frank 1922- = m.1944 Aunty Betty

Dad (Bill) 1924- = m.1945 Mum (Jean) 1925-

Uncle Ivor 1926- = Aunty Jem

Uncle Owen 1927-1956 = m.1920 Uncle Noel = Aunty Win

Aunty Dell

Brendan 1949-

Tom 1948-1959

Me 1948-

Twins

Raffi 1948-

Mum said nothing but pushed on. 'You can fill in your cousins, Brendan and the rest.'

'What about the Taggertys?'

'Some other time. I just want to tell you one thing, because I know you're having a hard time working things out just now, and I know you and Raffi have a special relationship, so I think you're old enough to have the facts, but I don't want you to write this down, and I don't want you to tell anyone about this. I'm just trying to help you. Do you understand what I'm saying?'

'Sure, Mum.' This was all as clear as Marmite.

'Raffi's mother's great-grandfather was a Blayney.'

'I had no idea there were so many Blayneys.'

'Your great-great-grandfather was Raffi's great-great-grandfather, too.'

'Wow! Mum, does that mean we're rellies?'

Mum sighed. 'It just means you're relatives in more ways than one, that's all. Third cousins never look as alike as you two do. Now you know the reason.'

'Hell, Mum, third cousins. That's close, isn't it?'

'No, not really. Being half-brothers is much closer.'

'Gee, it's lucky we live in Richmond, isn't it, Mum?'

'Yes, I thank God every day.'

I didn't say anything; I thought Mum didn't really mean that.

I was dying to ask just the one more question, but I thought I might get a smack in the head for my trouble, and Mum had given me a couple of them this year, and all in connection with what I was going to ask now. But I was dead curious.

'Mum, does that mean that Raffi's mum is my aunty.'

Mum had a hard think about that. I could just about hear the wheels turning; it was an ugly sound.

'No, more like some kind of distant cousin, I think. Now, that's enough of that subject. And don't go pestering your Nanna about it, because she doesn't remember it as well as I do, and she's likely to tell you any old thing. And the same goes for Raffi's mother. Is that clear?'

'You bet, Mum.' I tapped the side of my nose.

Mum just shook her head. For some reason I wasn't all that shocked about Raffi being my third cousin. I mean, I didn't really understand all that third cousin stuff anyway, but I could see that if you went back far enough in time, Captain Flamin' Cook could be your third cousin.

But although it had been about six months since I had found out I was related to Raffi, I still hadn't got over the surprise at finding out. I mean, how many kids in the world have a half-brother? Practically none, really. I didn't want to think about it. It was bad enough that married people had kids, but that was entirely normal and didn't need any thinking about – at least, I had no intention of doing that. It was ten times worse when I wondered how it all worked with people who weren't married. As I say, best not to think about some things.

The main thing was that after all this I could see that the connections I had been thinking about were not wispy little things like the bits of a spider web, but great thick things, like the cables that held up the Sidney Myer Music Bowl. They were heavy and scary, and meant that your chances of escaping to a connection-free world, like Heaven (where there were none of the buggers, and everything really *was* a wonderful coincidence) were zip-a-dee-doo-dah.

One thing that was apparent from this whole episode – I think you could call it an episode – was that this break-in seemed to have nothing to do with Gazza, but a lot to do with what had happened to Mick. This was going to get the Mum memory going like mad, I reckoned, because I was still sure this was some bastard she had pissed off wholesale, and I said as much in my careful way.

'Mum, I've been thinking about all these things, and I reckon this bloke might be someone you really irritated like hell during the War. I mean, let's face it, you weren't being paid to please people, were you? Now, I've looked up the population of Japan, and done a few calculations —'

'Tell me, just how many Japanese people have you ever seen around Richmond?' said Mum.

'That would be about, in round figures, taking into account comings and goings —'

'Yes?'

'None.'

'This has nothing to do with the Japanese. This is closer to home.'

'So someone who knows you, you reckon, Mum?'

'I think you should stop asking questions about this. We'll take care of it. I don't want you worrying yourself sick. That's my job.'

'Okay Mum.'

Mum had begun to feed Mick. Mum thought nothing of doing this around the house when we were there, but wouldn't be seen dead doing it outside. In fact, I'd never seen any ladies feeding their babies outside, and there were a million babies floating around just then. I was used to it, but, and I thought Mick seemed to enjoy it too.

'Look, while you're at the Sandersons' place I don't want you to call here. If you need to talk to me I want you to tell the Sandersons instead, do you understand?'

Mum had been asking me if I understood a lot lately, but the way I looked at it, at least she was talking to me.

'Ten-four, Mum.'

Mum didn't say anything when I left. I gave Mick a kiss, and looked at her; but she didn't insist on one for herself, so I gave her one anyway. It was like kissing a dead person, or maybe it was just the weather. She had built a little invisible fort around herself and bunged herself and Mick inside it. At least Mick was still warm to kiss.

Barney was waiting outside, and drove me down to Kipling Street.

Mrs Sanderson got a rude shock when she copped an eyeful of my fizzog. 'Oh My God, what happened to your face?'

'Seizure, Mrs Sanderson.'

I told her everything, how I had a seizure, and ended up in hospital, and escaped, and how a bloke broke into Nanna's house while I was there.

'It was me he was after. He came into my room and messed it up. I hid by climbing out of an upstairs window onto the roof until he left. Then I went home.'

'Yes, so I heard.'

'Well, Mrs Sanderson, looks like you're stuck with me for a couple of days. I'm a bit of a hot spud just at the moment.'

'Nonsense. As far as Russell and I are concerned you can stay for ever; you'll always have a home here.'

'Thanks, Mrs Sanderson. I know a lot of people who'd rather have rabies.'

Saying that turned out to be a mistake, as it caused Mrs S to wrap me up in one of her all-day hugs, which is a hug that doesn't wear off until you get to relax in a hot bath for about an hour.

'Hey, I'm only two hundred yards from Raffi's place. Mind if I go over there for a while?'

'Just for a short visit, then straight back before it gets dark, or I'll be worried sick.'

'Okeydokey, Mrs S.'

Raffi's mum had just got home from the Match Factory, and yelled at me to come in when I knocked, but went all quiet when she saw my face.

'Hello, you've been in the wars.'

'I had a seizure.'

'When? Are you all right?'

'Yes, thanks. Last Monday morning, when I was in Mass. They took me to the Epworth'

I was dying to tell her about my adventures, but I still wasn't sure if I was allowed to. She gave me a hug, and kissed me on the head. I realised that there are kisses that hurt, and kisses that don't.

'Are you all right now?'

'I hit my head, and I've still got a headache.'

'You should be in bed.'

'I've been getting better, but I can't go back to school till next week. I'm staying with the Sandersons for a few days.'

'Do you think they'd mind if you had tea with us?'

'No, course not.'

'Then I'll give them a ring.'

Mrs Radion rang Mrs Sanderson, and introduced herself. I got the impression that Mrs Sanderson wasn't surprised at all, as there was a lot of friendly chuckling. Fair dinkum, I reckon if two women rang each other up to discuss the outbreak of nuclear war, they'd spend most of the time chuckling.

Remembering my conversation with Mum, I took the opportunity to study Mrs Radion, now that I knew we were cousins, to see if we looked alike in any way, but I couldn't see it. Mrs R finished her call and gave me the nod.

'What're you staring at? Have I got my wig on crooked?'

I was shocked when she said that, because I had no idea that she was wearing a wig, and in fact, had never seen anyone wearing a wig. It was the biggest embarrassment of the day – of the year, probably. But it turned out to be a leg-pull, which Mrs Radion was famous for, and a second later I realised it.

'No, I was just looking at your, um, to see if you looked like, um …'

'Oh I see, someone's been letting the cat out of the bag, has she?' I didn't know what to say, because I had been told not to blab. 'Don't worry, I won't talk about it if you don't want to. But you have to admit, it's a bloody small world, isn't it? Come here.'

She put her arm out, and I went to her and she gave me a kiss and a hug. 'I think the less we say about all this the better right now. I mean, there's a lot of stuff going on, and you kids are under a lot of pressure, right? So let's just be happy that we're all together in the kitchen –' she turned toward the door: 'Ra-ffi! – and enjoying each other's company.' I heard Raffi coming down the hall.

'Aha, and here's Raffi fresh from the shower and wearing his wonderful new pyjamas.'

'Oh My God,' says I. 'Space ships!'

'Yeah, why, what've *you* got – Walt Disney stuff?'

It was true.

Raffi was happy to see me as usual, but worried about my face, I think because he suspected the truth.

'It's all right, I just chucked a wobbly. Hey, you know what? Some of the nurses at the Epworth thought I was you.'

'Yeah, they all know me over there.'

'Yeah, how often do you go over there?'

'I used to go all the time, didn't I, Mum? But this year, not much at all. I think it's wearing off.'

'I think it is too,' said his mum. 'Fingers crossed, eh?'

'Yeah. Wow, maybe mine'll wear off too.'

'I think it will eventually.'

'Hey, Mona came to see me in hospital, and got heaved out by that huge nurse who's shaped like a wrestler.'

'Yeah, I know that nurse. But why'd she chuck Mona out?'

'Dunno.'

'Oh, I think I can guess,' said Mrs R.

Raffi looked at me nervously. We had just crossed into No Man's Land.

21 The Group

I had come to see Raffi, but ended up seeing his mum as well, as they are both friends, and by the time I left I had formed the opinion that Dad had shot through to the wrong person, and that Mrs Bentley, though a nice enough lady, and one who undoubtedly had a lot in common with Dad, was not a patch on Mrs Radion, who was prettier, funnier, and nowhere near as angry, in spite of pretending she was cheesed off about Dad for some reason. I would have told her this, but when it comes to ladies, I have a sixth sense (I wish I had it for girls as well, but I'm sure that nine out of ten housewives would agree that that they are not the same thing).

I had discovered that Raffi had no secrets from his mum at all, which is something I often wondered about. At my place, survival depended on not telling anyone anything, not even under torture. This was Granddad's way, and he swore by it. Also, if Dad had told Mum half the stuff he got up to he would have been dead a long time ago. As for Barney, his whole modus operandi – detective talk for his way of doing stuff – was dependent on total silence and secrecy, that and carrying a big knife to scare the bejesus out of punters.

After tea Mrs Radion walked with me back to the Sandersons' place, and as we walked we talked of this and that. I have noticed that ladies and girls generally talk a lot more when it's dark, probably because the sunlight does something to their vocal cords and stops them talking, at least that's what I've been thinking for a little while. Now that I'm doing science at school I'm doing these experiments in my mind, and working out the results without any apparatus and chemicals and stuff – it's like mental arithmetic, only there are more explosions, giant aliens, space ships, and other planets. But it's a good way to work out how things probably work, like with the sun and girls talking. I had already decided that I could use this *method* (one of our scientific words) to work out how the evil-doer I was after was finding his way around the maze. I don't mean the real maze, which is how I thought of the town, but the maze of our connections. I mean, he wouldn't be hiding right out in the open for everyone to see. If he knew Mum, and possibly Mr Sanderson, he wouldn't be able to show his face outside, or he'd be spotted like a beauty.

No, he was laying low. But still, if he'd been planning this for a while, since the War, he'd have to go out for victuals and supplies every now and then. He'd have to go out – yes, he *would* have to go out: to the grocers and the milk bar and the newsagent's, and maybe to get the odd new pair of socks and undies. No matter how bad a person is, they still need socks and undies. I mean, what if you get hit by a car – you need clean undies, right?

The Sandersons were happy to see me again, and even happier to meet Mrs Radion. I was beginning to understand why: it was the connections. Adults crave them like alkies crave the demon drink. They have to connect or they'll die, whereas kids just do it without thinking. But adults have to shake hands like there's no tomorrow when a polite little grab is all that's required to get the point across. And it's all: '*Oh, you would know Mrs What's-her-name from across the street*' or '*Not the Mrs Bloggs who plays with our little Freddie?*' and so on. It's the connection they want. It's a regular disease. And while I stood there I noticed that the Sandersons weren't playing the connections game with Mrs Radion, because they didn't need it, they were coppers – or at least Mr S was – and they could get the connections any time they liked just by making enquiries. But Mrs R *was* playing the game, and very smoothly too, I thought.

'Do you know, we've never met, but I've known your next-door neighbours, the Crawleys, for donkey's years. We used to live over in Cremorne, you know, and my parents knew them. We haven't been over here very long; I must look in on them, see how they're going.

'Ah yes, lovely people,' said Mrs Sanderson.

They can't help it, I thought. *The connection game has them by the throat.*

'So you're Raffi's mother. Lovely boy,' said Mrs S. 'We're always happy to see him.'

And so on, until you thought the connectionometer couldn't stand any more.

But finally, Mrs R ruffled my hair – I don't know why she bothered, as it just springs back into its preferred shape (it's birth shape, I think) straight away – and choofed off home.

The Sandersons took me inside and started settling in for the night.

Mr S wanted to talk, not to be sociable, but to extract valuable intelligence from me – there's a difference. But I was prepared, as I knew him well enough to know that at the Sanderson place there's no such thing as a free feed; it's always tit for tat.

'So, young man, there has been a bit of excitement while my back has been turned. Tell me about this man you saw at your grandmother's house – if you're up to it that is.'

Mr S knew that I had a one of those special memories, like my mum, only different. With mum if was more like she could remember everything that happened within a mile of her since the day she was born, as if it was just five minutes ago, and with me it was like once something got my attention I never forgot it. Mr S knew this about me, and had, in fact spotted it soon after he met me. It was because of my memory that he sometimes called me Kim.

'He was a New Australian. He had on one of those caps like Andy Capp wears, but his hair was sticking out from under it — black and straight, I think. I couldn't see his face — he was bending over, picking the lock.'

'I see.'

'He was wearing a beige jumper with a round neck, and no shirt underneath.'

'Mm.'

'And brown corduroy pants.'

'Wh—?'

'Clean. And a gold bracelet on his right hand, like a lady. His car was a white FE Holden with a red roof. I couldn't see the number. It had a radio.'

'How —?'

'It had an aerial. But he wasn't the driver: the driver was a woman. She was wearing a black scarf on her head. That's it.'

He looked at me for a while. 'Remarkable. What do you think he was looking for in your room?'

'He probably started off looking for me, but when he couldn't find me, he just wanted me to know he'd been there, so he turned the place over, like a copper, I mean policeman. That was his calling card.' That's what Larry Kent would have said.

'What do you mean, like a policeman?'

'Burglars know exactly where to look for things. They haven't got time to mess around. Cops — police — often haven't got a clue what they're looking for, so they just wreck the place in the hope that something will turn up.'

'I see. And where were you while all this was going on?'

'On the roof. I slipped out of Nanna's bedroom window upstairs, and waited till he'd gone. That's how I saw the car leaving.'

'And when the car got to the end of the lane, which way did it go?'

'Right, into Lennox Street.'

'Anything else?'

There was, of course: everything that happened the previous Saturday night. But Granddad was on top of that.

'Nuh, that's it.'

'You've done well, my lad, very well.'

'This Holden, it looked almost new.'

'One of the most common makes, probably stolen. Not a lot of women driving cars in Richmond, though; not a lot of need for them to do that. You see that more in the new outer suburbs.' He was thinking out loud; I've seen a lot of old people do that.

'I've been thinking that this person we're looking for is someone Mum upset during the War. Mr Sanderson, what did Mum do?'

He looked at me for so long I thought he might have dropped off, but then he suddenly spoke, like an Egyptian mummy who's had electricity passed through him and come back to life.

'She was an officer in the AWAS, that's the Australian Women's Army Service. She spent the best part of the War in the Australian Intelligence Corp in various places, but mainly here in Melbourne. She worked for a secret organisation called the Group, which is where I met her. Their job was to help track down people in this country who were assisting the enemy. She was very good at her job. And it's just possible she might have made one or two enemies herself while she was doing it. That's something we're looking into. I can't tell you more than that. What I've told you isn't really a secret, but the details of her work are, so I think it would be better if you didn't talk about it at all, no matter how close to you they are.'

'Is that what she won that special medal for?'

'No. Did she tell you about it?'

'No, Nanna did. But I know it's got something to do with Aunty Daphne.'

'Who?'

'Mrs Honeysett, Keith Kavanagh's aunty – was she in the Group too?'

'No, she was a nurse. But yes, it had a lot to do with her, in fact – you'll find out in good time.'

'Okay. Does Granddad know about Mum's, um, secret job?'

'Yes, but no one else in your family does, though as I said, the small amount of information I've just given you is not in itself a secret. A lot of seemingly ordinary people did wartime work that they'd prefer not to discuss. That's how *we* met, didn't we Lottie?'

'Gee, that's an old connection.'

'Well, we prefer not to use that word.'

I reddened suddenly. 'Sorry. Mr Sanderson, I got the impression that time you drove me home a few months ago that you and Granddad were old friends. Is that right?'

'I wouldn't say friends, more like comrades, another wartime term. You see, we're all connected in some way.'

'I don't like this connection business, Mr Sanderson. It's like everything's worked out for me before I even get started.'

'Actually, for most people that might be the case. But only because they don't make their own choices as they go through life.

244

For others, like you, life is what you make it, and everyone had better get out of the way. Does that sound about right?'

'Funny but it does in a way. I mean, when I want something I usually find a way of getting it. Usually, I find someone who can help me.'

'It's that Tom Sawyer side of you I've often commented on. He knew how to marshal his resources, and so do you, doesn't he Lottie?'

'I've never seen a boy as good at organising his friends as you – never. First you built up the Commandos, then talked them into dissolving themselves when that Foster boy joined, then reformed the club with a new name, the Olympians, which is a perfectly good name for a club, we think, and now you're reforming the club into the Detectives. And you've told Matthew Foster about it, which seems to me to breaking your personal rule against letting him join your club.'

'He's up to something, Lottie. What is it?'

'Well, Matthew Foster has a new friend whose father is a test pilot, and he has formed a new club with his kid. But we want him too, so I've arranged for us to form new, joint clubs that don't meet together.

'But why not just let him have his own club?'

'Mrs Sanderson, we're talking about a test pilot. We want to be able to say that we have an arrangement with this kid. What if his dad invites the Rockets to see his Canberra Bomber? We need to know about stuff like this. Also, they can help me – us – with our enquiries.'

'I thought you were going to let the authorities take care of this.'

'The authorities are you and Mum, and Mum's got her hands full with Mick, and you need all the help you can get.'

'I hardly –'

''Scuse me, Mr Sanderson, kids hear and see things. Also, no one pays any attention to them. We're bound to hear something sooner or later: it's the Law of Averages, isn't it?'

'Is it?'

'Course.'

'No interfering,' said Mr Sanderson, sternly.

I would have laughed, but then there was always the chance that he wasn't kidding.

But after dinner I got a sheet of paper and started to draw the things I knew with connecting lines. This is how the Mazemaster works: he follows the maze on the puzzle page with his pencil, so that he knows which paths are right and which ones aren't. I was making a maze that had no walls, just streets, tunnels and drains. One of these streets contained the bad bastard's house. I put a label for him in the legend: 'BB' in red.

22 The road to Eddie's place

By late Friday arvo I'd had enough of hiding out, so as the week was at an end I decided that what was called for was a bit of nosing around. The first place I went to was Peanut's house, because he had been practically inseparable from Tom and me in the old days, and I wanted to catch up with him. When it came to trouble no one in the world could hold a candle to Peanut, and it was a pretty safe bet around the traps that he would be the first kid in Richmond to break the world record for something that didn't count as Olympic. His mother, on the other hand, was not one of my best friends, and had always thought that I was a bad influence on her little boy. Talk about laugh. Even Peanut thought this was the funniest thing he'd ever heard.

So I rapped on the door to see what would happen, and the peanut himself opened it. He looked at my face for a long while, then realised that there was nothing to be said.

'G'day.'

'G'day.'

'Wanna do something?'

'Sure. I'll just put on my shoes. See ya, Mum!'

'Be home before dark!'

'Okeydokey!' The truth was, Mrs Hobson didn't care what time he came home. But 'before dark' was the standard thing with kids. 'So where're we off to?'

'Well, you know how I'm trying to work out who kidnapped Mick?'

'Who the hell is Mick?'

'My baby brother.'

'Oh yeah, I knew that; he's a nice kid. How's he goin'?'

'Oh, he's alright – you know babies. Anyway, I have to go round to Judy's place for a sec, and I was wondering if you wanted to come.'

Now this was just pure evil on my part, as everyone and his dog knew that Peanut Hobson was in love with Judy Pickle, and someone had even written it on the wall down at the corner – it was not me – so it was a moral that both lots of parents knew this, and were having a secret chuckle about this in bed at night. But where JP was concerned, Peanut, who was in every other way a bit of a daredevil, was a coward. I knew the feeling, because I was exactly the same when it came to Josephine Thompson. But the way I looked at it, Peanut was not going to get anywhere unless he had lots of practice at being with Judy, who would get used to seeing him, the way you get used to having a wart, and finally decide to be his girlfriend. It was like in science: you put the right chemicals together and you get a reaction, then you can write down your observations and conclusion, even if it turns out to be a bit of a fizzer.

'Do I what!' said Peanut, looking suddenly hungry, like a lion stalking an antelope.

'Thought you'd say that. Come on.'

It was a short walk to the Pickles' place, as it was just across the road, which is really a bit rough on Peanut, when you think about it. I mean, he would sit at his front window and stake out her house, which he told me he had done a hundred times, but had hardly ever seen her coming and going. I didn't have the heart to tell him that Judy knew all about the famous Hobson stake-out, and made a point of coming and going by her back gate in Yarra Street. Judy always told me everything, and this was for a very good reason: she was in love with me. I'm sorry, but it's true. Before Tom died she looked on us both as a pair of pests, but lately she had changed. Don't let anyone tell you that girls are predictable, because in my experience, they are about as predictable as earthquakes.

Judy came to the door, wearing her school uniform. She gasped when she saw my face, and I could see she was genuinely shocked, though she knew the story of the Blayney brain. 'Oh no!'

'It's all right, Judy. I'll live.'

She gave PH the kind of look you give to a door-to-door salesman.

'I see you brought a friend,' she said to me.

'Peanut and me are on our way over to Matthew Foster's place, and I thought I'd drop in on the way. There's something I wanted to ask you.'

'In front of him?'

'Peanut's all right.'

'All right, come in then.'

Peanut was struck dumb by all of this, and was happy just be in the presence of the Vegetable's radiant beauty.

'You know how you and your dad are in this model aircraft club?'

'Yes, so what?'

'Wow, are you really?' asked the incredibly dumb Peanut, who had only known Judy since she was born, and had failed to notice the one thing about her that probably everyone in Australasia knew – not a good start.

'Of course I am,' said Judy, giving him a look that would slice Kraft cheddar cheese with the cardboard still on.

'Well, you know what happened to Mick, don't you?'

'No, what? Is he all right?'

'He was the baby who was kidnapped. But the kidnappers brought him back, because they realised he was too hot to handle.'

'Oh no!'

'Yes, and now I'm looking for the bastards who did it.' I paused to see if Judy was put off by the strong language, but she was strangely interested – I couldn't take a trick. 'And I need your help … please.'

'Anything! What a horrible thing to do. Who are these people?'

'That's just the thing, Judith Pickle, nobody knows. But that's where you come in. It just happens that I am the captain of a secret club.'

'The Detectives, yes I know all about it.'

'How did you know? I didn't think anyone knew.'

'Tina told me, and Raffi told her.'

'I can see I'll have to have a word with young Raffi. Anyway, I was wondering if *you* were in a club.'

'Girls don't have silly clubs. We just do stuff together, like Morag and me. We do everything together. She's my best friend. She'll probably be my bridesmaid, after I come back from my record-breaking flight – that's if I'm still alive.'

'What flight?'

'I'm going to be a pilot – it's my destiny.'

'I see. So do you have any other friends that you hang around with all the time?'

'Girls don't *hang around*. We have activities. And the answer is no, only Rosie O'Shea, and she lives over in Burnley, but she goes

250

to my school. At school we are inseparable. You know what the teachers call us? The Terrible Trio.'

I was amazed at all this brand new girl-type information. To think that I would probably know all this backwards if I had a sister.

'Well, Judy,' – I was sticking to Granddad's Rules of Conversation: *First, mention their name* – 'about this aeroplane club –'

'*Model aircraft* club –'

'Model aircraft club, what I'd like you to do is keep your ears open when you're at their meetings, and report anything strange to me, secretly of course. You could tell Peanut too, of course, as he's dying to help find these' – I decided to try a bit of rough language again, in the hope that Judy would swing from the uncouth Blayney to the rather shy and ready-to-help Hobson – rotten bastards.'

The Green Veggie blushed when I said this, and Peanut looked very excited indeed, so I thought the desired effect had been achieved.

'You can count on me. Nothing gets past Judy Pickle. I'm a very good listener, in fact; you'd be surprised. I've heard a lot about you, for example, an *awful* lot, though I don't believe half of it.'

'Oh, it's all true, Judy, isn't it Peanut?'

'Sure, is Blayno. You've done a lot of things, all right. How about that time –'

'Can I go with you on your adventure to that other boy's place?' said Judy, paying no attention to him.

'Matthew Foster. He's not exactly my best friend, or anything, but he's got a new next door neighbour whose father is a jet pilot – did you hear that, Judy, a *jet pilot*?'

'I'm not deaf or anything. What kind of jet?'

'A Canberra bomber!'

'I said I'm not deaf.'

'I bet you haven't met one of those before. Maybe he could show you some pictures of his jet bomber.'

'Yes, p'raps he will.'

'Okay then, you can come.' I was now hoping, of course, that the Pickle would fall in love with this Williams kid and that they would live happily ever after, and have lots of little kids who went around with pilot's goggles on.

All the way over to Matthew Foster's house Judy talked her head off, while Peanut tagged along with her like a sheep. Judy covered, in the ten minutes it took to get to Munro Street: current affairs as they related to aviation, the state of Australian politics from the point of view of the working pilot, the different grades of balsa wood and their uses in the various parts of a model aircraft, confetti – its many little-known uses, the state of the Yarra River, why Morag Munster knew less than her about certain things (which we never learnt), and the lost art of puppetry. It turns out there was a lot of stuff going on in the Pickle scone, and we got a fair cross-section of it. The result was that for the first time in history I was glad when I arrived at Matthew Foster's house. Peanut arrived with mixed feeling, if that's the word, as he got his hand smacked – unnecessarily hard, I thought – by the Pickle when she thought he had made a grab for her, but I could have told her that, despite being a daredevil, the day when the Peanut had that much guts would probably be the same day that Fitzroy won the premiership. Peanut got a hell of a fright, of course. Nevertheless, I think it was better that she saw him as someone who was more prepared to show his love than not.

Just as we walked through the front gate I saw Barney's car turn into Munro Street from Balmain Street, and realised for the first time that he'd probably been following me for days. I gave him a little wave as I closed the gate.

Guess who opened the door. 'Wow, Blayno, and Hobbo! G'day, fellers. Come in and have a look at my Spitfire – I'm just putting the dope on.' This was in case we were the only kids within a mile of Munro Street who couldn't smell the aeroplane dope (which by the way gets a nine on the Blayney Scale of Smells and Pongs).

'G'day, Matthew. Yeah, we could smell it a mile off.'

'Ha, ha. Blayney, you kill me.' Matthew Foster was the happiest kid in Australia. He was a moral to die laughing, probably while someone was murdering him.

'Don't call me Hobbo,' said Peanut, already irritated by this kid who he had known for a long time, though not all that well, and mainly through his over-the-back mate, Shane Purvis.

'Sorry Hobbo, ha ha – I mean, Peanut.'

'This is our friend Judy. She wanted to meet Eddie, so we thought we'd bring her over.'

'Yeah, bewdy, Blayno. G'day.' Matthew didn't take more than a glance at the Pickle, what I would call a five out of ten look, which was fair enough.

We went into his room, which was your typical boy's room, except that half the floor was taken up with a model Spitfire, and the whole place was full of bits of balsa, and all the smelly things you need to build a model plane. Judy immediately went over to it and started pushing the control line linkages in and out.

'It needs an aileron balance,' she said to Matthew, in one of those irritating voices that has made girls so unpopular all over the world for so many years.

'Yeah, but how do you do that?' asked Matthew, genuinely mystified.

'I'll show you.' She started fooling around with the plane, while Peanut watched her from his position on the bed.

'Judy can do anything,' he said to me.

I thought of Mona. 'Not everything, Peanut my son.'

I decided that this would be a good time to get the lay of the land. 'Think I'll go and say hello to the Mrs Foster half of the outfit. Back shortly.'

I went down to the kitchen, where I found Mrs Foster, probably the world's loveliest mother, making something. She had known me for a year or so, and had rescued me on more than one occasion when life was trampling all over me, like the time Keith Kavanagh, who was a bob short of a quid, locked me inside the altar at St Felix's church, and she rescued me; and the time she saved my bacon when I had gone to her place to escape a bloke who was giving me a hard time – I think Peanut and me blew up his letter-box – (this is the way a lot of kids get to meet parents who they would otherwise not meet even if they lived to be forty).

'Hi Mrs Foster.'

'Well, well, speak of the devil. I was just saying to Matthew that we hadn't had a visit from you lately, and here you are. I heard about what happened in the church. Come here.' She gave me a hug and a kiss as if I was the prodigal son, and I could tell she really cared about me. I had been on the receiving end of this lady's hugs and kisses before, and while I was just as embarrassed as always, I found them different to the hugs and kisses of any other lady. This was because she was ten out of ten in the softness department (I only knew one other lady who gave those kinds of hugs, and that was Aunty Queenie, a certain absence of bony bits being required, though with Aunty Queenie there was often the risk that you would get stabbed by a piece of jewellery). Of course I knew why I felt this way; it was because of me losing Tom. She seemed to understand that I needed extra hugs to make up for it. She now spoke while still hugging me closely to her soft – but not soft enough to be lollopy – body. 'Don't forget, you're always to come over any time, if you'd like to talk. You don't need any other reason. Now, how's your mother? She must be just about due.'

'She had a boy. His name's Michael, but I call him Mick.' I like to issue all the news economically.

'Course you do. Brothers know best, don't they?' She gave me a wink. 'Well, that is wonderful news; please give my congratulations to your parents.'

I mentioned this opening bit of the conversation to give you an idea of how lovely Mrs F was, as any other lady in Richmond would have told me to call him what my parents called him (though I hadn't heard what Dad would have called him, and wasn't holding my breath), or they would personally call my mother and tell her to feel free to give me a lift under the ear when I got home, just in case I had gotten up to any mischief on the way.

I thought to myself for about the two-hundredth time that if it wasn't for Matthew Bloody Foster being a paid-up member of the Foster Platoon, I would ask Helen and Wasley (yes, I swear) to adopt me.

I also knew for a fact that when that psycho Kavanagh kid – to me, Flame Boy, a fellow superhero driven by mighty, if flawed, ambitions – had nowhere to run to and was within an ace of being arrested for arson, put in the local loony bin, and having his brain electrocuted (and not for the first time), it was Mrs Foster who helped him out by secretly cleaning him up and feeding him (I caught her red-handed, and a more guilty parent I have yet to see). For two bob I reckon she would have changed that kid's name to Keith Foster. That was the day she told me that she did not believe it was him who burnt down our house at the end of last year.

The Mr half of the Foster tag-team I could take or leave. He was bald, and it was hard for me to warm to bald men. I'm sorry, but it's true. It's wrong, I know: it's not their fault. Bald women, now that's another story. I hadn't met any, so I was open-minded on the subject. Mr F was a baked bean tester, which I am embarrassed to tell you, so I don't know how Matthew Foster can bear it. I know if my old man came home and told me he'd decided to make a living testing canned foods, I'd probably stick my head in the oven.

In summary, Matthew Foster had something I had not seen in any house in Richmond, a mother and a father who not only loved him as if he had nothing wrong with him, in other words, as if they were blind, deaf and stupid, but also were prepared to love any other kid who got within range. Not for the first time, I actually envied him, though I'd rather be smeared with treacle and tied down over a bull-ants nest than admit it.

'I'm so glad you came over; Matthew's been a bit lonely lately.' This was solid gold news, as I'd always thought of MBF as being one of those kids who was too irritating to be lonely, but there you are. *Good on you, God,* I thought, *for making him feel the same way the rest of us feel every now and then. Maybe one day, Foster will learn the true meaning of unhappiness.* But no sooner did I have this thought than I realised that there was nothing bad about Matthew, and that the reason he was lonely was simply because he was a pain in the arse, which his lovely mother and better than average father would have known all about since the day they brought him home from hospital and noticed that he laughed at everything that moved, and liked stuff that was boring, and barracked for Footscray (can you believe it?). But once you bring your baby home you're stuck with it, which is why nine out of ten kids recommend road-testing them first (my brother Mick being the exception that proves the rule, as Mr Sanderson would say).

'But what about his new friend, Eddie Williams, next door?'

'Well, Eddie's a nice enough boy in his way, but all the signs are there of a boy who's been … well, who's had a rough time, I'm sure you know what I mean.'

I knew what she meant all right. Half the kids in Richmond had experienced or seen some pretty horrible things in their short lives, and I was one of them. I had friends who'd had all kinds of attacks: fits, asthma, black-outs, fainting, nightmares, and who knew a dozen different ways of panicking. One of Jimmy Carson's brothers had drowned in the Yarra and though everyone had said it was an accident no one was really sure. And then there was the hurting. It went on all the time, in homes I knew and had been in – strange things you couldn't mention at home. You knew that that was the reason why some kids couldn't learn at school, or ever be serious. You couldn't try to tell the Brothers, or they'd give you a taste of the old torture yourself. It was, 'You mustn't blame him; it's the War that that made him that way', or 'It's just the drink; he really loves him, you know.' That one killed me. So Eddie had had a hard time, had he? *Well welcome to South Richmond, Eddie; it's no better in the South than it is in the North, mate.*

As soon as I thought this I felt bad, because I remembered what Carmo had told me about him, and that, like Carmo, he'd been 'broken'.

'Yes, Mrs Foster, I know what you mean, all right. I'd like to go and visit him, but I don't know him as well as Matthew. I've only met him a few times.'

Just then Matthew burst into the room, laughing and shaking his head. 'Fair dinkum, Blayney. What the hell are you doing down here?'

'Just telling your mum about my new baby brother.' The young feller always has a quick comeback.

'You didn't tell me.'

'He's being polite, Matthew, like a gentleman.'

'Wow, what's his name?'

'Mick.' I winked at Mrs Foster.

'My God, Blayney, that's a ripper – *Mick*, ha ha.'

'It really *is* Mick.'

'Oh.' He shrugged, and ran back to his bedroom.

'I brought my friend Judy over to meet Eddie because she likes aeroplanes. She wants to be a pilot when she grows up.'

'Well, why didn't you say she was here? She'll be bored stiff down there with the boys.'

We went down to MBF's room, where the scene was as follows: Peanut was lying on the bed reading a *Sad Sack* comic; while the Pickle and Matthew were down on the floor with their heads together doing something tricky to the wing of an aeroplane, with Judy bending over so far you could practically read the label on her undies – it made my day. Mrs Foster and me looked at the scene – it was definitely a scene – then at each other, then Mrs Foster spoke, not too loud, so as not to mess up the delicate work that was going on.

'Hello, everyone. Well, and who do we have here?'

'This is Judy Pickle, Mrs Foster. She loves aeroplanes – model aeroplane, real aeroplanes … any kind of aeroplanes.'

'Pleased to meet you, Mrs Foster. Matthew's ailerons needed adjustment.'

'I see. Well, it's lucky you came along then. Hello, Robin.'

If a train hadn't gone by just outside the back fence at that moment, there would have been complete silence.

'Hello, Mrs Foster.'

'How are your parents?'

'They're terrific, um, I think.'

The fact is, they weren't all that terrific at all, but this is what you said.

'Well, I hear you're all going next door to say hello to Eddie. So I'll get back to work. Lovely to meet you, Judy.'

When we got outside the door, Matthew Foster said: 'Ha ha, what a bewdy: *Robin*! God, talk about funny, Hobbo.'

'That's enough,' said I. 'We never call him that – you oughta know by now.'

'That's right,' said Peanut. 'I'm Peanut. Only my mum and dad and nanna and uncles and aunties call me that. Anyone else who calls me that gets a knuckle sandwich. Get it?'

'Ha ha, take it easy, Hobbo. Can't you take a joke?'

'No, I can't,' said Peanut.

Judy gave my hand a squeeze as we went up the steps to Eddie place and whispered in my ear: 'Good on you for sticking up for your friend, dear.'

This was not a good sign. I should have taken the piss out Peanut like a beauty. When will I learn?

23 The test pilot's wife

Eddie's place was not, I thought, your typical test pilot's house. For a start, it contained Eddie, who was not your typical test pilot's kid, but one who seemed to have a few problems of his own. He opened the door himself, took one look at Judy Pickle, and said: 'What's *she* doin' here?'

'This is Judy. She's with us,' said Peanut, in case this Eddie thought she was collecting for the Lost Cats Home.

'And who are you?'

'He's Peanut Hobson,' said Matthew, as if he was introducing a champion racing driver.

'Oh, and who're *you* again?' he said to me.

'Eddie, this is *Blayno*, ha ha,' said Matthew Bloody Foster, rolling his eyes all over the place.

'Oh yeah, Blayney. Oh well, are ya comin' in, or what?'

As we followed Eddie up the stairs, Matthew continued to give me the 'what's wrong with Eddie?' look, but I seemed to be the only one who realised that Eddie had been pulling Matthew's leg, though if you'd asked me I would have said that something was definitely eating old Eddie, and that that something was probably the appearance of the Green Vegetable.

Eddie's bedroom overlooked the street, and he lost no time pointing out a feature of his house that made me feel a bit weird: you could see right down Balmain Street, across Church Street and down Kipling Street, all the way to Fawkner Street, just around the corner from Raffi's place. And in the window was a telescope.

'Can I've a look?' said I, and not out of curiosity, either. I mean, why look down Kipling Street? I could see most of the west side of the Sandersons' house, as it was one of the biggest houses in the street, and down at the end the exact spot in Rooney Park where Tom had died when the monkey bars accidentally fell on his throat. In fact the monkey bars had been replaced with a new set, which now looked at me up in my grey tower in Cremorne.

When I turned around Eddie was looking at me in an odd way, as if I had done something funny, or as if he was embarrassed at something he had said. He had a way of smiling and frowning at the same time that told me that he'd had a hard time. I'd seen that look on kids who'd been forced to grow up too fast, often around hard cases. I knew this because he hadn't learnt to keep his face straight all the time, which is how you want your face to be in front of punters. But he had a dad and a mum, so I couldn't see the problem. I mean, he had one of everything, just not what we in the detective business call a cool look.

I felt sorry for Eddie. I didn't want to like him, but he seemed kind of lame, like a horse, except he didn't limp. Instead he sort of leant his scone to one side a fraction whenever he spoke, as if he wasn't sure how you'd take it. As for Judy, she was totally rapt in the pictures of planes, which were all over the place: Macchis, Sabres, Vampires, and the Mighty Canberra Bomber. The Mazemaster made a mental note to shift her interest in me over to Eddie, Son of Test Pilot.

But I had been worried about what I saw through Eddie's telescope.

'What's the telescope for?'

'Dunno, it's Mum's. She like to look at the stars 'n' stuff.'

I looked at the sky when he said this. I couldn't remember the last time I'd seen a star. I mean, this was Melbourne: most of the time you were lucky if you saw the sun.

'What stars?'

She has a special filter for looking through the clouds.

'Oh yeah, course.' I felt like a real nong.

Suddenly Mrs Williams appeared, like a ghost. This was definitely a new way for a mother to appear, as most of them preferred to carry on as if they owned the place, tramping and shouting. I had a theory that my own mother had actually invented tramping. As I say, just a theory.

Mrs Williams had a very sad body, as if she'd been in a car accident that didn't leave any marks, or as if she'd been in hospital for a long time. I wondered if she'd been in the War herself, like Mum; she looked it, or I don't know my war heroes.

Unlike the younger Williams, the elder neither smiled nor frowned, but kept a straight face, much like a railway station attendant. She also did something that a lot of mothers do whenever I'm around, and that is study me, as I am what is known as a troubled child, and someone you must keep an eye on – I guessed that the Foster contingent would already have warned them about me. But in the world of the Mazemaster, it's all tit for tat, and I did a bit of detecting of my own.

'Hello Mrs Williams. Hmm, *Williams*, that's an unusual name. It's not Irish, is it?

'So you think Williams is an unusual name, do you? And what do you make of *Edward*, then?'

'Well to be honest, I've never met one before, but it's a nice enough name.'

'It's his father's name; he was killed in the War. Mr Williams is his step-father.'

I felt as I was being given information I was supposed to remember, as if there was going to be a test tomorrow. I needed more information, but as we were studying each other I didn't want to be too obvious – that's one of Granddad's rules.

'There are a lot of stepfathers around the place, but I've never met one who was a test pilot.'

'Well, he's not home yet, so I'll have to do, won't I?'

'Yes. And that's a nice telescope. Eddie said you like to look at the stars.' I know it was pretty shameless fishing, but what the hell, nothing ventured, and so on.

'I do when it's not cloudy.'

I could sense that the family astronomer was reluctant to discuss her latest discoveries, as astronomers often are. Still, I felt that she was not being on the level about this thing, because of the Tom connection, and for another reason that was completely different: the telescope was not focussed on the stars, but on the street, and there's a big difference. You could say I was an expert in these matters, because I had two pairs of binoculars. In fact, I had two of just about everything I owned.

Peanut and Judy were being polite, and just nodding and smiling, which is what you're supposed to do when you meet a new adult – though Peanut was mainly nodding and smiling at the Pickle, which made him look like a half-wit.

This suited me down to the ground, because it gave me a bit of room to do some hard detecting. This Mrs W interested me greatly, because I had seen her somewhere before, but just where I couldn't remember, though I strained the brain more than a bit. Mrs W also had an accent, though I couldn't place that either; on the whole not a terrific start. Still, it reminded me of something.

When I stopped thinking I found myself rudely staring at Mrs Williams, and she not liking it a bit, and pulled my eyes away.

'Tell you what, as we haven't met any of Eddie's other new friends, apart from Matthew, why don't you stay for tea – do you think your parents would agree to that?'

Now, down in our neck of the woods, dinner invitations were not exactly unheard of, because there was a fair chance that a kid who showed up at your door was not going to get fed that night anyway, though I knew that that was not the case with any of us, as families that did not have a man about the house who guzzled and gambled the family pay packet away tended to live happily ever after.

Peanut, who is basically your yes kind of kid, said yes, and so did I as I wanted to do a bit of detecting. Judy, who was just waiting to see which way I would go, also said yes to the invitation, though we all had to ring our parents or, in my case, the Sandersons. Actually, I had clean forgotten about the Sandersons, and realised that I couldn't go over to their place for a visit and not stay for dinner, so I had to change my mind, and then so did Judy, who I knew had been thinking that with a bit of luck she could get me to walk her home. Peanut, of course, then changed his mind, too, so that he could stick to Judy, as this is the kind of silly muck that falling in love makes you do.

Meanwhile I could see that, while Eddie took no notice at all of proceedings, his mother was watching this nonsense like a mountain lion watching a baby rabbit with a sore foot. And I realised that, while she was getting as full as a goog on the ridiculous childish behaviour going on right in front of her, it was really me she was watching, and giving me the odd nudge and wink too as if we old mates and understood the poor helpless sods all around us. Of course, she had my number, and knew that I was above all of this and beyond the reach of the Pickle, no matter what, and had to go for an entirely different reason, which was quite grown-up and understandable. But I decided to hang around until darkness was closing in, so that I could complete my observations of the family.

However, though Eddie liked aeroplanes like mad, he had no interest in actually building them, so Judy did not warm to him as a future co-pilot and husband. But she did warm to him for a completely different reason: he was mysterious.

It is standard kid procedure on meeting new kids to give them the third degree about their backgrounds, not so much because you give a stuff about all that as to show who's the boss, and we all do this. It was obvious from the way MBF liked this kid that he had not shown him who was in charge, so Peanut proceeded to do this very necessary thing now. Naturally, the Pickle was intrigued by all this, for two reasons: first, it was a secret boy thing that she would not have been familiar with (her own brother, Lex being more interested in *kissing* boys than bossing them around – don't ask for details, because the whole thing is just too embarrassing to think about) and second, girls are natural-born nosy parkers.

Well, I'll leave you to chat,' said Mrs W. 'Please come and say good-bye before you go.' But she was looking at me.

'Yes, Mrs Williams.' I thought I took to being the preferred child, though I was new to the experience.

'So,' said Peanut, 'were you in a club where you used to live?'

'Course. Everyone's in a club.'

'Yeah, well *our* club –'

'Peanut, you aren't in any clubs – *are you*?' He was about to blab about the Cobras, our deadly secret.

'Sorry, I meant *Blayno's club* is looking for a kidnapper.'

'What kidnapper?' said Eddie.

'The bloke who kidnapped his baby brother. And we're going to get the rotten, um' – he looked at Judy – 'swine, too. It's just a matter of time, isn't it Blayno?'

'Sure is. You know,' – I looked at Judy as if to say: *Better get ready, because this is going to knock your socks off* – 'the Rockets could look for the kidnapper too.'

'Yeah, wow!' said the Foster Pain, 'we could, you know. We should have a meeting first thing tomorrow.'

'Well you've got lots of members now,' I reminded him. I was being my usual self, you know, summarising the problem – normally Peanut would have chipped in and done this, but he was distracted – and then coming up with the solution. 'You've got Eddie here, Piglet –'

'Piglet!' said the Vegetable, who I thought had a lot of nerve making fun of someone's name. 'What kind of name is that?'

'His mother's a guard at the Looney Bin, so we call him Piglet. He's a friend of mine. If you must know, his real name's Peter.'

'Ooh, that's a lovely name.'

'And now you've got Freddo Fogg –'

'Like the chocolate frog, ha ha!' I was pretty sure she was getting right up Eddie's nose, because he gave me that look that said: *Does she have to be here?*'

'His real name's, um, what *is* his real name?'

'Henry,' said Peanut. 'That's what his mum calls him.'

'And don't forget, you've got Tangles Dudek, too.' I gave Judy one of those looks, and she slapped her hands over her mouth, which must have been a first.

Except for Judy not exactly getting all over Eddie like a fresh coat of dope (and Peanut not even waking up to my clever plan, and stepping in to save her), the meeting visit had gone as planned, and the Rockets were off to a *flying* start – a little Mazemaster joke.

24 The nightmare

That night I had a nightmare. I was in a field of flowers, and I thought I knew my way but I didn't. I was confused. There was badness in the flowers, there was threat. Still, I walked right into them, and they began to bite me, as I knew they would. I made a loud noise, but it didn't make any difference. My hands swelled up like pink boxing gloves and went all tingly. They were swollen from the effort of trying to save Tom from dying, and I was ashamed. To hide the shame I screamed. Then I woke up. There had been no Intermission, or Coming Attractions, like at the flicks. There was just the left-over buzzing of this rotten nightmare, which I'd been having for a long time. Worst of all it left me with the taste of The Dread, which had got right into my head, and which I couldn't shake off just by waking up properly.

The last time I'd had that nightmare was the previous week. When I told Granddad all he could say was that I better get used to it, because he had been having dreams like that for fifty years, and they never seemed to get better, except on the odd occasion when Nanna was in them.

In the end I thought I would try Mum, because she had recently decided to be my friend, I think because having a baby had done something to her brain. But it turned out I was wrong.

'Mum, I've been having nightmares again.'

'I know – everyone in Richmond knows.'

'How come?' But I knew.

She made a face like old cardboard. 'I can't believe you said that. Listen, I can't help you with the nightmares – nobody can. They'll wear off eventually.'

'Eventually' was, I had noticed, one of the favourite words of almost any adult I asked for help.

Granddad had told me that my new friend Raffi Radion would 'eventually' work out that his real dad was my dad, and that was why we looked alike. I had been dying to see the look on his face when he found out, but Granddad had told me to keep it to myself, so I did. But I didn't like what happened to Raffi when he 'eventually' did find out.

However, eventually doesn't always mean that something *will* happen. Mr Sanderson said that the police would eventually catch Keith Kavanagh, for instance, for burning down half of South Richmond, yet it had not happened.

Meanwhile, I knew why I was having the nightmares. It was because the park where Tom died had been full of those flowers, and soon they would be back, because he had died in the spring, though no one should die in the spring.

Also, our family was falling to bits. Dad had had all he could take, and I didn't blame him. He wasn't a member of the Taggerty family, and Granddad and Mum let him know it all the time. He would be happier with Mrs Bentley, who really gave a stuff about him. And when I was with them it was usually very peaceful, except whenever Mum was mentioned.

Then Gazza had come along and changed Mum into a bit of a zombie, and then straight away had gotten blown up. I hadn't had time to turn into a zombie; to me he was still Gazza Turner. But to them he was someone else. It was all connected. The only member of the family that hadn't had a disaster – not counting Tom – was me, though it had been touch and go.

I was thinking about these things as I went down for brekky with the Sandersons.

'Hello, sorry about the nightmare.'

'It's quite all right, dear. You're probably entitled to the odd bad dream, isn't he, Russell?'

'He certainly is. What do your parents think of them?'

'Mum thinks they'll eventually go away, but I'm not so sure. It's all Tom stuff, I think.'

'Has anyone ever taken you to the cemetery to visit Tom's grave?'

'No, but I took myself over there a few months ago.'

'And have you ever been back to the park, you know, where it all happened?'

'No, Mrs Sanderson. I'd like to, but whenever I think about it, I feel a bit funny.'

'How about this afternoon the three of us go over there together? Would you like that?'

'Yes, I would, Mrs Sanderson – a lot. Thanks.'

Mrs S leaned over and gave me a kiss, and Mr S looked up from *The Age* and gave me a wink, and I wondered if my archnemesis, God, knew that I had these two lovely people in my life, and if he was planning on doing something horrible to them. What can you do?

It occurred to me that Raffi might be having nightmares too, not because of Tom, of course, because he had only met him once and that had only been for an hour or so, but just because he was so like me. For all I knew, something terrible had happened to him as well. If not he was the luckiest kid in Richmond. So after brekky, I went down to his house. I went by the usual route: down Kipling

Street, then up Dress Circle Lane, and then through their back gate, which was my secret entrance. I opened the gate slowly, making it squeak more, so the residents wouldn't drop dead from fright or anything. After knocking I walked straight in without waiting to be asked who it was. Mrs Radion was in the kitchen doing something with food that I could tell Mum wouldn't dream of tackling, unless it was for a bet.

'Hello, here's trouble,' said Mrs Radion, getting the ball rolling.

'Hello, Mrs Radion. Nice shoes.' I nodded at her feet.

She made a sleepy face. 'No need to overdo it, young Blayney. You know you're always welcome to stay for a feed, though you've missed out on brekky.'

I felt my face go red. 'Thanks, Mrs Radion.'

Raffi burst in and nodded for me to follow him down to his room, so we could discuss secret kid's stuff. I always enjoyed the trip down to Raffi's room, because I got to walk along the long, skinny rug that was on the passage floor. It had red roses on it, and whenever I saw it I always thought that I could actually smell those roses, which was a very strange thing. The only reason I didn't tell Raffi was because I didn't want him to laugh at me, then tell all the Detectives.

'What's up?' he said.

'What d'ya mean: *what's up?* I thought you wanted to tell *me* something.'

'I thought you wanted to tell *me* something.'

He was turning into *The Raffi From Planet X*.

'Are you having nightmares?'

'Am I what!' said Raffi, without the embarrassment you'd expect to see.

'What're they about?'

'The usual: monsters 'n' stuff chasing me. What about yours?'

'Flowers that bite.'

'What, you mean snapdragons?'

'I don't know.' I didn't; it was a good question.

'Let's ask Mum if she has any.'

I was always amazed at the way Raffi and his mum would talk about anything that wasn't nailed down. When I told Mrs Radion about my nightmares she said she wasn't surprised.

'A few scary things have happened to me, I s'pose. And last weekend' – I decided to face the fact – 'a man who was, um, part of our family died; everyone's very upset; I liked him a lot. Also' – I was saving this news for last, as I was worried about the effect it might have on the assembled mob – 'I didn't feel safe in hospital.' I didn't want to tell them that I was being hunted by a film producer who'd gone nuts (one thing at a time, Blayney). 'So I escaped and went to my nanna's in Lennox Street – you know her, Raffi – and then, because a bloke broke into Nanna's house and tried to get me, I escaped all over again and went back home. Then Mum sent me over to the Sandersons' to lay low. The doctor at the hospital said I needed a week off because I had concussion. I reckon as long as I stay on the move I should be okay.'

'But why didn't you feel safe in hospital?'

I decided to tell them the truth.

'Because one of the kids told me that the ward I was in was haunted.'

'Funny looking kid.'

'That's him.'

'He told me that too.'

Raffi was the complete genius of bullshit; it was like he invented the stuff. I was very grateful that he did not hesitate to support me, on the off-chance that I was raving on. I didn't want to upset them, so I decided to put an end to this part of the conversation. 'I'd rather not talk about it: it gives me the shivers.'

'All right, we won't. Just tell me you're all right now.'

'Yes, I'm all right again.'

'Is that why you came over in this soggy weather, to tell us about the nightmares, and your adventures as an escapee?'

'Mainly, I've got no one to tell anymore, except Nanna of course, but it's not the same. And anyway, I don't want her to worry. You and Raffi let me tell you things.'

Mrs Radion gave us both a hug at the same time, which is something she did quite a lot. 'So what have you got planned for the rest of the day?'

'Well, I was thinking of going over to James Palmer's place for a while. He's got an enormous train set. Wanna come?'

'Do I what!'

'Where does he live?' said Mrs R. Women want to know everything.

'Toorak Road, just across the bridge, Mrs Radion. Look, I'll write down the address and phone number for you, just in case.' And I did, very happy to get a chance to show off my exceptional spy memory.

'Come on,' said Raffi. 'Let's get Zac.' Raffi had become quite fond of the old Zac. A quick hello to Mrs Sanderson through the kitchen window, and we were off through the back gate into Kipling Lane, with Zac laughing all over his face. As we reached Church Street, I looked back down the lane, and saw Barney's new second-hand Zephyr slowly following.

Mrs Palmer was very pleased to meet Raffi, though puzzled (I felt like saying: *Welcome to the club*), but she was far too polite to ask questions. I thought she softened a little when she saw the condition of my face, but she said nothing, and I guessed she had learned the truth from the Sandersons. When James came down he was very happy to see us, too, because he had a new train to show off, but when he saw my face he froze.

'It's all right, James. I'll tell you all about it one day. Let's go upstairs.'

I could hear Veronica and her friend Barbara playing in the other bedroom, and wondered if Veronica knew who was visiting James.

'So James, how did the note go? Did it work?'

James blushed, he being one of your politer kids. 'She sent me a note back.'

'Well, Jimmy Palmer, do we have to torture you to find out what was in it?'

'It just said: *Me too,* And it had *S.W.A.L.K.* on the back. What do I do now?'

'Nothing, James my son, absolutely nothing.' I said this because I didn't have a clue what he was supposed to do next. All my experience of girls was the result of them doing something first.

'He doesn't know,' said Raffi, looking up from his *Spirit of Progress* scale model. 'Mona kissed him first.'

'But you've got a girlfriend too.'

'Tina kissed me first, too.'

I could see the problem, and I'm sure Raffi could, too. James wasn't going to go first in a million years – no boy was. Still, it was a start.

'I've had this,' said James suddenly. Let's go over to Charles's for a while.'

We went to Charles's place, and Charles appeared at the door all ready to go, as he had seen us coming from his bedroom window.

'Shh! Mum's asleep,' he said before even saying hello. This did not surprise us, as his mum, being a TV star, had a very delicate constitution. I knew because my Uncle Frank had one, according to Aunty Betty, and as a result had to be careful what he ate (but the closest he ever got to being a TV star was when he watched *In Melbourne Tonight*). With Mrs Dixon, it was all about piling up Zs. 'Let's go over to your place and play trains,' said Charles, who knew all about the Palmer obsession with the HO scale.

'We just came from there,' said Raffi. 'He's in love with Veronica's friend Barbara, and you'll never guess what she did.'

'Couldn't care less, I just want to play trains, and we can't play at my place.'

'Okay,' said James, who would do anything for a friend. 'Let's go back to my place, then.'

And we headed up Dover Street to Balmain Street. You'd think that in light of recent events I'd be very interested in a red and white car that followed us, but you'd be wrong. People were always doing strange things in Richmond. Also, it was drizzling rain, not enough to put us off, but just enough to make us look down. I had Zac on his leash, which he seemed to like, and he trotted alongside me like a member of the club, which is what he was, having been made an honorary member. Also, my mind was occupied with all the things that had happened, and with the fact that my family was starting to disintegrate like a bikky in a cup of tea. Besides, Zac had not detected any danger, and if there had been any he would have. Double besides, I knew that Barney was around somewhere, even if I couldn't see him just then.

We walked past the lovely JT's house, and I looked hard to see if she was sitting in the front room gazing out into the street on the off chance of catching a glimpse of Yours Truly, but that was not the case, and I had to content myself with a sigh. Charles did not look at the house but at me, as if to say, *I don't know why you're doing this to yourself when you already have one perfectly good girlfriend, practically brand new.* We walked past the Orange Tree pub, down between the Rosella factories, and under the railway bridge into the gloomy dip that was part of our world. The footpath was narrow just there, so I was walking in front with Zac beside me, and the others were following.

As we got to the lowest point, the red and white car suddenly rushed past and came to a loud sliding stop in front of us. It was the FE Holden. The back doors opened, blocking the narrow footpath, and a two blokes jumped out, ran behind me and grabbed Raffi. Ignoring me completely, they dragged him to the car and tried to push him in. Then they took a second look at him and threw him onto the ground, just as Zac went for the nearest leg. The blokes then turned to me, because it was me they had meant to grab, but they couldn't get past Zac, who was going crazy, and Raffi, who was under their feet. When James and Charles grabbed Raffi, and pulled him free, I started yelling.

'Get help from the pub.' I slid around the car door, and turned around to see both men trying to deal with Zac. I backed away from the front of the car, up Balmain Street, and yelled to them as I went. 'Run! Run!

As I reached the end of the underpass, I turned and saw Barney's Ford skid to a halt behind the Holden, and Barney jump out without even properly stopping it, so that it rolled hard into the back of the crims' car. I saw one bloke – I call him Bloke A, though it was the bloke who grabbed me at the Circus – pull a gun, and take two shots at Barney, who had just dealt the other bloke (Bloke B) a mighty blow, and was hauling off for a second when he went down like a sack of spuds. Bloke B then grabbed hold of Zac's collar, which is the only known way to stop a revenge-bent

Labrador. And suddenly, the scene cleared, and the blokes (both A and B, if you follow me) dived into their car and headed for me. I immediately cleared the underpass and turned up the lane beside the railway line, knowing that the car couldn't follow me up there. On the lane's left a fence separated it from the back yards of the houses in the nearest street, Green Street, which ran down to the back of the brewery, and I now ran down this lane for all I was worth, in the direction of the one place I knew it would be hard for the FE Gang to follow me, the gasometer.

As I ran I could hear the car tearing up Green Street. Then it stopped. I had only a few choices. If I climbed up the railway embankment and crossed the lines, I might not be able to get out on the other side. I decided to push on, and ran past the old loco sheds and the water tower, and into Electric Street, past the old power station. As I reached Hargreaves Street, I saw the car turn at the top of the street, going flat out. I turned right and skirted the cyclone wire fence of the gasometer until it reached the river, then I clung to it like hell as it leaned out over the steep embankment under my weight. I figured the blokes would never be able to pull off this stunt.

As I clambered under the wire, and headed for the old buildings, I heard the car ram the gate. The gate held. I was inside, where only days before I had introduced Peanut to the Cobras. Outside, the car sounded as if it was bogged. I looked in the little rooms to the side, then ducked into the back room. It sloped down at the back and disappeared into the dark.

As I closed the door behind me I heard a muffled bang somewhere that told me the Holden had burst through the gate, and that I had only seconds to get away.

I got my torch out of my detective bag and slid down the steep slope, and came to a set of stairs that took me to a low concrete area, under the gasometer. There were huge pipes all over the place and one that went down a steep tunnel towards the river. I ran down the tunnel's steps, about ninety percent sure that the tunnel would go under the river. After all, these were old gas mains. The steps got colder and damper as they went, and then it seemed that I was running on moss, and I slipped and fell hard on my bum, hurting myself.

I followed the tunnel down and under the river and after a long while, during which I started to think that I'd made a horrible mistake, and my theory about where this tunnel was going to come out was wrong, the tunnel suddenly ended in a fork. The big pipe went to the right, which I knew was along the south bank of the river, and the tunnel I was in turned to the left, then to the right, then came out in the most peculiar place I had ever been in, yet one I had been in before. It was the underground railway yard beneath City Boys High.

I was pretty sure the blokes who were after me would have given up by now, as they probably wouldn't have a torch. But I was wrong, and I heard them in the tunnel behind me. It was my archnemesis, God, up to his old tricks.

The railway yard was completely lit, so I turned my torch off. I'd been hiding and exploring these tunnels for the best part of a year, so I knew exactly where I was and where to run to. They, on the other hand, would be confused by the whole scene – I know I was when I first came down here – giving me the time I needed to save the Blayney skin.

25 The oldest trick in the book

I'm not one of your daredevils, like Peanut. Your Peanut sees an extremely dangerous situation, one involving the possibility of getting killed, and thinks: *Hello, I'd be mad not to give this a whirl,* and does. I on the other hand see danger lurking and remember that I have to be home early for tea. The big exception had been these little underground railroad tunnels. I had only just told Raffi that this part of the world was out of bounds for us for the foreseeable future, and suddenly here I was. But I was not on a planned visit. No, I was breaking my promise. I was sure that when I *eventually* faced an angry Mr Sanderson (unless I was dead) he would understand. Or not. To Mr Sanderson, rules were rules. He was a bit like the De La Salle Brothers in that regard, only not violent. But he was the man I least wanted to break my promise to.

Normally this would have been my kingdom, because I knew the lay of the land. Had the lights been off I would have had an extra advantage, the Blayney Factor: I had absolutely no fear of the dark. Tom had been the same, and over the years we'd played lots of tricks on terrified cousins and neighbourhood kids by using this clever talent. In fact, down here, some folks call me: The Ferret!

Yes, The Ferret, a strange being from Richmond Hill who runs around under the ground, and can see in the dark. The Ferret, who thwarts – I'm sure it's 'thwarts' *– the plans of kidnappers and murderers.*

281

However, the lights were on, and that was going to make thwarting all the more difficult.

Only three other living humans knew all the secrets of the underground railway tunnels: Raffi, alias the Fireman, Keith Kavanagh, a.k.a. Flame Boy, who was wanted in a number of states by whole teams of brain electrocutors, and Flame Boy's old man, who ran away to Russia last February, and had once used the tunnels as his Secret Spy's Maze (he himself was a spy, I think, though I'm still not clear on that point, only that Mr Sanderson hated him, and Granddad didn't, so you can guess whose side I was on). The Ferret was fiendishly clever, knowing three exits from those tunnels in Richmond alone, which these guys wouldn't have known. Also, I have noticed that terror makes you much more creative.

The nearest of the little trains was still parked where Raffi and me had left it, a fortnight earlier, and now it was begging to be my getaway train. But no: what if the other guys grabbed a train, too? I couldn't see that being pretty. So I made for the Josephine Island side-tunnel, which had no overhead lights. I had become … *The Ferret!*

The blokes followed me down the railway tunnel, probably reasoning that if I could safely run down there then so could they. I made next to no noise as I ran down the tunnel, and stuck to the wall as I edged along the side-tunnel back under the river until I felt the lift at the bottom of the fort. Then I climbed up the stairs to the top, and waited for a while to see if I could hear footsteps. There was nothing, and I guessed that was because they gave up trying to work out where I'd gone.

After about ten minutes, I raised the trap door and climbed into the basement of the fort, then went up to the ground floor. My exit to the outside was through a little window near the ground just high enough for a person to crawl though. Outside, I looked around. I knew there was at least one tunnel leading to South Richmond, the one near the bottom of Fawkner Street, and even though that one has been locked up, I didn't want to pop up right next to an exit I hadn't known about. The Ferret would find that embarrassing, not to mention the Mazemaster and the Octopus, neither of whom like being made to look like dickheads.

But from my vantage point in the long grass and shrubs of Josephine Island I saw no evil activity, though I could not see the bottom of the Gasometer, which was down around the bend.

After I began to feel a little safer I went down through the power cable tunnel, back under the river to the cliff beside the power station pool. This was one of my most secret places that I had only ever shared with Raffi and James. When I emerged from the tunnel at the pool, I looked around carefully, then climbed up the cliff. It was a short climb, but a dangerous one. From there it was a quick walk through the old Bethstone Cemetery to Fawkner Street. My destination was the Sandersons' house. I didn't want to go to Raffi's, even though it was just across the road, in case they spotted me, followed me in, and killed the lot of us.

I shot around a few corners, and into Kipling Lane, which took me to the Sandersons' ancient back gate, which had two halves, so that you could open the top or the bottom half. I opened the bottom half and shot in, after taking a quick look around to see if the coast was clear. Normally, I'd expect to be met by Zac the Wonder Dog, who could smell me a mile off, but the last time I saw him he had had his paws full saving the young master, and copping a boot or two for his trouble. But they'd keep. I would have a word in the proper quarter about that. I walked up to the back of the house and knocked on the door.

Mrs S came to the door wearing her lilac floral dress and a hat. She had either just come back, or was going out.

'Hello, what's happened to you? You're covered in dirt – have you had an accident?'

'SomeblokesinawhiteFEtriedtokidnapmeoutsidetheOrangeTre eandshotBarneybuttheotherkidsgotawayandtheychasedmeallover theplace!'

'Oh My God! Russell! Quick! Come in, dear and I'll make you a cuppa.'

Mr S came down from his study upstairs and looked at me over his reading glasses, like Mr Badger.

'What happened?'

'It was the people in the white Holden, two blokes and a woman. They tried to grab me under the railway bridge in Balmain Street. They grabbed Raffi first but let him go when they realised he wasn't me. Then Zac attacked one of the blokes and I got away. Then Barney turned up and donged one of them, but the main bloke had a gun, and shot Barney and maybe Zac, too – I dunno. The others – I was with Charles, James and Raffi – ran back up Balmain Street towards the pub, to get help. Then they chased me in the car, but I got away by running down along the railway and hiding under the gasometer. They followed me, but I discovered that one of the big gas pipes went through a tunnel under the river. I took the tunnel and ended up in the old underground railway yard. From there it was easy for me to find another way out – you know. I came here through the lanes.'

'You didn't take any of the trains, did you?'

Mr S has a very suspicious mind, you will notice.

'No. I thought it would make too much noise. And I didn't want them to see how easy it was to drive them. Also, I didn't want to get trapped at wherever I ended up.'

'Mm, well done for using your brains. Did you see their faces?'

'Not really. They were wearing sunglasses and hats.'

'Did they say anything?'

'Not a word – that's strange, isn't it. I mean, there was a lot going on, and Barney and Zac gave the bloke hell.'

'Mm. Did you get the number of the car?'

'Sorry. But the bloke had a gun, an automatic.'

'How do you know what an automatic looks like?'

'*77 Sunset Strip.*'

'What's that?'

'You know, the TV show; anyway, I heard the cartridge cases bounce. But what about Barney, and the other kids? I have to find out what happened to them.'

'Yes,' said Mrs S. 'Of course you must. Call them while I'm making the tea. Russell, you might have to speak to their parents.'

I called Charles, because he would have gotten home first, and the others were with him.

'Hello, Charles. It's me. Did you get away all right?'

'I thought they got you! Yes, we all did. We went to the pub, to get help, but by the time we got back to the underpass, everyone had gone, even Barney and Zac. The people from the pub called the police. I didn't know what to do, so we just ran here, because it was closest.'

'But I thought Barney and Zac were shot.'

'I don't think so. They must have missed. I'm sorry I left you.'

'No, Charlie, you did the right thing. I mean, you're still alive, and that's all that matters. Did you mention Barney's name at the pub?'

'No.'

'Good on ya. Did the police find you in the end?'

'No, I don't think they've got a clue who we were, any of us. But they'll find out when you report what happened, I s'pose.'

'Don't worry, Charlie. I won't mention your names. No sense in you getting mixed up with it. One of us being worried sick is enough.'

'But how did you get away?'

'I hid under the gasometer, Charlie. It's the oldest trick in the world.'

'Ye-ah.'

'Hang on a sec, Charlie, while I see if Mr Sanderson wants to talk to you – that's where I am.'

Mr Sanderson had been in a little side room, talking on his secret COMPOL police radio, and now reappeared and took the phone, while I listened in. 'Charles, this is Mr Sanderson. I need to speak to your mother.'

'It turns out she's not home at all. She must have spent the night over at her boyfriend's place.'

'Well, I don't want you boys to be alone in your house, so I'm going to come over and get you all and bring you over here. You'll be safe here until your mother gets home. I'll be there in just a few minutes. Do you know my car? It's a black Humber Super Snipe. I'll give you a toot when I arrive.'

'All right, Mr Sanderson. I'll tell the others.'

Mr Sanderson turned to me. 'Your grandfather's associate was apparently not injured, and left the scene … with your dog.' He rang another number, one that I knew by heart, but which I wasn't aware he knew. 'Archie? The boys are safe. What I need to know is whether your bloke was shot – that's all. If he was, I can have him looked after off the record – this incident is not going to become public … I see … Good. Tell Jean everything is under control at this end – no need to worry.' He hung up and turned to me. 'Flanagan was shot in the leg; the round was stopped by a large knife he was carrying. Your grandfather thought you would find that amusing – I don't. As for Zac, he is unhurt. I just want you to know that for reasons of my own I am not bringing in the local police at this time – I will take care of it myself, and how I do that is my business, do you understand?'

I nodded. 'Got it.' I was tempted to wink as well, but the Mazemaster knows just how far he can go.

Five minutes later, the Fortunate Four were all together again. Mr Sanderson rang Mrs Palmer, who was an old friend of his, and said that the boys had 'had a scare from some local troublemaker in a car', and he was bringing James home after he'd had a cup of hot chocolate to calm his nerves. Then he repeated the story with Raffi's mum. This seemed to do the trick. There were a lot of lunatics in Richmond, and all of us (except James, who was from South Yarra) had been chased and terrorised by blokes in cars at some stage. Then he sat us all down and told us that we were not to tell our parents any more than he had already told them, and not to mention the shooting, because he wanted the people responsible to think the police knew nothing about them, whereas they actually did, but had to keep it under their hats. They all nodded, seriously.

When Mr Sanderson left with James, and Raffi had gone, I was left alone with Charles. I could tell he had been crying; but he still had a way to go, and leaned his head on my shoulder. Mrs Sanderson came in and put her arms around us both, like a giant chook.

'I thought you were dead.'

'So did I, Charlie.'

'I mean *really* dead.'

'Me too.'

'Charles, you told us your mum was asleep, and she wasn't even there, and you knew all the time.'

'I know, I just wanted to play with James's trains.' I thought Charles would probably make a first-class spy if he wasn't so reluctant to kill people, etc. He seemed to have the lying part all worked out.

Mrs S forced us to knock off a cup of hot chocky and a stack of cream bikkies, and it hit the spot like nobody's business.

But I was still worried. Mr Sanderson's call to Granddad had helped, of course, but I could see that he was really just being a special rozzer, and had not really been thinking about the effect all of this would have on Mum.

'Mrs Sanderson, I'm worried about Mum.'

'Yes, dear?'

'It's just that she's got a lot on her plate just now. You know that bloke who was blown up last Sunday? Well, he was someone we all knew – he was my mother's ... son, you know, from the War, but she just found out the night before his car blew up. And those people today, who tried to grab me, they were the same people who kidnapped Mick and then tried to get me at the Circus, and at my nanna's place. And there are other things as well. No one at home is very happy at the moment. Mum's not her usual self. I don't know what will happen to her. Could you ring her, please, and tell her you'll take care of me for a few days, just until my head's better?'

'Oh God, of course, dear.'

Mrs Sanderson rang my place, and got Dad.

'Mr Blayney? Hello, this is Charlotte Sanderson, over in Kipling Street. The reason I'm ringing is because your son isn't feeling well from everything that's happened, and he still has a headache from that concussion of his – nothing serious – no, no need for that. So I've talked him into spending the weekend over here. He's curled up on the couch with a cup of cocoa right now. No need to worry; we love having him. And Russell will bring him home.'

'Mrs Sanderson, you'll end up like Pinocchio, if you're not careful.'

'I'll take my chances.'

As I was damp all over, and filthy to boot, I was ordered to take a bath, even though it was the middle of the day. I took Charles with me, so we could make plans and discuss clues and things. I relaxed in the bath and had a think, which is what the Mazemaster does when something has gone wrong, and just then I had my pick of somethings.

I was glad that it had been left to other people to explain to Mum what had happened, as her version of her life was that everything was fine and dandy until Tom and me turned up; then everything was like old porridge. As for the police, the less they knew the better, of course, and I knew from past experience that when Mr Sanderson tells them to jump, that's what they do. But then I realised that Mr S probably didn't want me to be interviewed by the police because it was a well-known fact that half the cops in town were bent, and it might only place me in more danger.

As for Granddad, I knew he would be very keen on making the acquaintance of these FE Holden bastards, and that if Barney got to them first, he would carve each of them a new belly button with the old (now slightly dented) Bowie knife. I didn't want him to go to prison or get strung up for murder. So I asked my old archnemesis, God, to arrange for the Holden run into a brick wall, or maybe take a swan dive into the river, with all its crew members buying the farm – I wasn't all that fussy.

Charles was normally one of those kids who wouldn't say boo to a grasshopper, but sitting there in the hot bath, observing the secretary of the Detectives through the perfumed steam, I saw a side to Charles that was distinctly decisive, and would, if he ever got his hands on certain people, be lacking in mercy.

'We need more information,' said Charles. 'If only we could find this car of theirs – without getting killed in the process, of course.'

'Charlie, I don't think you realise what's going to happen when I get home. My parents are going to put the absolute kibosh on my club activities, kick-to-kick down the park, going to the flicks, coffee with Mona and her aunty, and probably even going to Mass. The next time you see me, I'll probably be shaving and have a deep voice. It's a safe bet that until these ratbags are locked up, it's me who will be locked up. My granddad will go spare. He'll visit every house in Richmond and turn it upside down and shake it until the kidnappers fall out. Then he will squash them like bugs. Like bugs, Charlie!' I smashed my fist down on my hand, spraying soapy water all over the place. *Comprenez-vous?*'

'*Oui, je comprend.*'

'Very good, Charlie my son, ten out of ten. *Maintenant, s'il vous plait, passez-moi le, um, loofah.*'

'Okeydokey. Do you think they'll let you keep going to school?'

'Oh yes, there's no way I would be *that* lucky. Anyway, I don't think Mum would want to play their little game. I think she would want to do things *her* way. And I reckon Granddad would agree. No, they will definitely want me to keep going to school. Course, how to get there – and back – without ending up in the boot of a hot Holden, that's a different question, *n'est-ce pas?*'

'Mm, yes, I mean *oui*, it is. I reckon we'll have to do as much organising as we can while we're at school, pass notes 'n' stuff. If you like I'll act as secretary.'

Charles was always volunteering to be secretary, so I wasn't exactly speechless or anything.

'School may well be the only place we'll see each other after this, Charlie. Raffi and James are never going to be allowed to hang out with us again. If any of the other parents find out what happened they'll go troppo as well. I might have to give the Detectives a miss and go it alone, like the Lone Ranger.'

'He had Tonto.'

'All right, then, Superman.'

'Supergirl.'

'Are you sure?'

'And Superdog.'

'The Phantom, then. And don't tell me he had Devil.'

'Your mum'll be the same as the other parents.'

'I won't tell her.'

The door opened, and Mrs S stuck her head in.

'You boys all right? Need anything?'

'No thanks, Mrs Sanderson,' we both said, like two-thirds of Huey, Dewey and Louie.

'I'm making lunch for you when you come down. And don't you worry about your mother, Charles. I know how close you two are.'

'See, Charlie? Don't worry about Mrs S. She never interrupts club stuff.'

'What if she was listening?' said Charles.

'She can listen to me all day and all night as far as I'm concerned. But that school idea of yours is a little ripper – I'll let you take care of it. But there's something else, Charlie: that bloke had a gun, and I don't want you to end up getting killed. So I'm thinking that you and me shouldn't hang around in the street together. We can always organise it so that we can meet at one of the other kid's houses, if that's going to be possible. With a bit of luck, we'll be able to have meetings of the Detectives right here, just like we used to do with the Olympians – that is, if there *is* a Detectives. I mean, Mr S is some kind of cop, so no one's gunna come *here* and tangle with us; he'd have 'em for breakfast. It's just till we catch these bastards – and we will. Ten-four?'

'Ten-four.'

26 The Mazemaster exercises the coconut

Next morning Mrs Sanderson was not keen on me going anywhere, let alone to Mass, but I stuck to my guns as I didn't want MBF taking my place as second in command. She made sure that I had one of those breakfasts you have before setting out to find a short cut across Australia. Luckily, Brother Timothy, whom I was beginning to think more fondly of since the friends pardon and the fasting dispensation, had not set any limits on what I could eat, not that I thought there might be any, but I figured there must have been a catch somewhere. Mrs S also treated me as if I was a nervous wreck which, funnily enough, I was not. I rang Charles, who was also an altar boy at St Felix's, to find out what had happened when his mum got home.

'Nothing,' said Charles. 'Mr Sanderson tried to explain that we had been terrorised by some bloke in the street, but she was too tired to care, really. She's been having a hard enough time with her boyfriend, I think.'

I wasn't surprised, as Charles's mum was always dumping some boyfriend or other and getting a new one who had more money and bought her better presents, at least that's what Charles told me.

'She sure is using up those boyfriends, Charlie. She must be up to 'M' by now, d'ya reckon?' That was our little joke.

'Is your head, you know, okay?'

Charles was practically whispering, so I knew he was actually asking me if my brain (not my most reliable internal organ, you will notice) was firing on all cylinders. I swear Charles was more worried about me than an aunty.

'Charles, when things are looking pretty crook in Tallarook, and when the chips are down, this is a brain you can bet your undies on, thanks for asking.'

'Oh I know. I was just a bit worried, that's all.'

'Charlie, what would I do without you?'

'Yeah, ha ha. Hey, what Mass are you serving at this morning?'

'Eleven.'

'I'm on at nine-thirty. I'll wait for you in the vestry.'

'Bewdy. See ya.'

Mass turned out to very interesting, because for only the second time in history I saw Josephine Thompson in the church, while I was sitting up the front during Father's sermon, which was dead boring. The only reason I had become an altar boy in the first place was so that I could look at her in Mass, but in the last two years I had only seen her once before, and that had been a disaster, because Mona had been sitting right beside her – there ought to be a law against that. But today, she looked, I thought, a bit cheesed off. It was all beyond me.

It was also an interesting Mass for another reason: I spotted Darko's family, and with them, or so it seemed, Eddie's family, which was strange because Eddie hadn't mentioned that he knew them. But then, why should he? More than half the residents of South Richmond and environs were micks, even if they weren't all Irish. But Darko and Co. were Croatians, and I remembered what Carmo had told me. And to top it all off, I spotted Wonder Woman – that's James Palmer's mum – complete with James,

Veronica and Barbara, with V sitting between J and B. Girls can be cruel.

When I spotted them with my eagle eye, I couldn't help noticing the following arrangement of eyes: Barbara was eying off James (Blayney, you're a genius), Veronica was eyeing off Yours Truly (I tried to read her mind, but my super powers were on the blink), and Wonder Woman was eyeing me off as well, though not in the same tender, loving way. It was more like: *Has my son's life taken a turn for the worst during the past year because of you, young B, or is it just my imagination?* Something like that. I could have told her: *Leslie, boys will be boys*, and so on, but I don't think she and Ken sent James to St Kevin's so that he could be a boy. But that's what he was. Or had Veronica told her mother that I had kissed her – I don't think she would say that it had been her who had kissed *me* – and was I shortly to be murdered by Ken, her bastard of a father? Suddenly, I felt bushed.

It was as if all the girls and ladies I knew and who had played some part in my life had received an invitation from my archnemesis, God, to come along and gawk at the freak, the kid who had stood idly by while his brother died, humming a merry happy tune (which in those days probably would have been 'The Happy Wanderer', then my favourite song; however since meeting Mona it has become 'Boom Boom Baby'); the kid who has fits and get his face all smashed up (it was still a little scratched from the week before, which made me look a bit like Tarzan after accidentally swinging into a blackberry bush); the kid whose friends usually wind up getting blown up, kidnapped or shot.

The only one missing was Judy Pickle, who also went to St Felix's for Mass. Her parents, like a lot of Melburnians, were boycotting Mass, because of Mannix's view on the ALP, a view that the Italians were backing, which, if the truth be known, was part of the reason Granddad was no friend of Lucky Martello's wider family. But he had other reasons, which I did not understand, that had to do with the 'war that was coming' as Granddad had referred to it. He meant the war between the workers and the Nazis, who were pouring into Australia and making bombs like there was no tomorrow with, the support of the Government, the DLP, the Church, and the police. This was the view I had formed when Gazza was blown up: that it was the work of someone who knew all about bombs.

It also fitted in with the views of Uncle Seamus, who had turned up with Aunty Daffy when she visited.

'Uncle Seamus.'

'Hello.'

'What's all this I hear about Nazis coming to Australia and causing trouble?'

'This'd be the Yugoslav Nazis, the Ustasha, I'm guessing.'

'Why doesn't someone stop them?'

'Because they hate Communists, that's why, and Pig-Iron Bob hate's them too, so it's quite handy to have a bunch of Nazis just laying around to get his hands on, don't you think?'

'But still, Uncle Seamus, if they blow people up, surely that's illegal?'

'Not if the government does it, young man. That's where your mate Sanderson comes in, see.'

'Nuh?'

'Well, he works for ASIO, doesn't he?'

'He said he works for COMPOL.'

'He'll tell you what you want to hear, that's what. How do you think all these bomb-crazy Nazis get over here into the country, and then get the run of the place?'

'But Mr Sanderson's not a Nazi, Uncle Seamus; he's a nice bloke.'

'Archie knows him of old, you know, and only trusts him with you because Sanderson knows what would happen to him if you came to any harm. You're as safe as eggs at Sanderson's, that I do know. And why do you think he likes you so much? I mean look at you: you're Irish, a Catholic, a child, a boy who, but for the roll of the dice, might have come to a sticky end with the law a long time ago, and the grandson of an ex-boxer and felon, who makes a living by, well I won't go into that. Haven't you noticed, young man, that you have nothing in common with the Sandersons? Haven't you wondered why they like having you around – not that you aren't a lovely kid to have around, don't get me wrong – mmm?'

I was amazed at this outburst of Uncle Seamus's, which was delivered in a clearer, more ringing voice than I was used to hearing, though still booming like a tuba in a furniture van.

'As a matter of fact I've wondered that lots of times.'

'Well, I'll tell you and I don't mean to put you off the Sandersons, because I know that in their way, and particularly from where you're standing, they're fine people – I know they'll always be friends to you for one thing, and I don't mean just as long as you're useful, either, as Russell Sanderson is old school.

No, the reason he has adopted you as a kind of relative is because your mother was in the Intelligence during the War, and so was he, and he likes to keep in touch with his old colleagues. That's all I'm going to tell you about Jean, and she won't tell you any more so don't ask her. And then there's Archie, a man who would give you the shirt off his back, but a man who hates Nazis like the plague. He was even closer to Sanderson during the War, and knows him well. Sanderson likes to know where he is all the time.

Look, Sanderson works for the Government and they've been busy importing Yugoslav murderers since the War ended. These people hate everyone and they have long memories, but they have their uses. And they'll never get had up, no matter what they do, you can take it from me. Yugoslavs, Croats, Nazis: same thing.'

'But the Archbishop —'

'What does he care if a few workers get killed?'

'But he lets you live at his house, doesn't he?'

'That's an old debt, and one that's going to expire with him, then I'll be out on me ear.'

Then a couple of things dawned on me at once, which is what happens when you brain is sort of idling at the lights. First of all, I realised who Mrs Williams reminded me of: it was Darko, the Keeper of the Deadly Snakebite. She had that same edged kind of accent, though you could hardly hear it. I only heard it because I had ears like a sheepdog and because of what Carmo had said. But Eddie didn't sound like her at all, but just like the rest of us (not counting James and Charles, of course). And Darko was a member of the Croatian Club footy team, except that his old man hadn't let him play. Oh well, another mystery for the Mazemaster to fathom (and for the Octopus to get his tentacles around).

And the other thing that dawned on me was that Judy Pickle was also there in the church — though parentless — and studying me as if I was an aileron that badly needed adjusting. When she saw me looking at her from my special pew up on the altar, in my red cassock and white lacy surplus, her face lit up, and she said the word 'hello' soundlessly. That Judy sure was a strange person, but we had been friends for long time and I realised, sitting there while Father droned on like a sick seal, that if she had not been born a girl she would be in my club. And then I wondered if the other club members would be interested in having a girl in the club. And then I wondered what Mona would think of that idea. And then I started thinking about Mount Vesuvius.

By the end of Mass I had collected a lot of thoughts to take away with me, which is the most useful thing about Mass if you don't count the holiness, and I don't, as I was still no longer speaking to God.

But there was something else about that Mass that was very strange, I mean apart from all these people I knew being there: all the people I looked at had already been looking at me when I spotted them, which is a bad sign, and made me look down and see if my fly was open, because I had completely forgotten about my vestments. Then I thought I might have a giant spider crawling on me, like in some in some kind of movie where a flying saucer crashes, and it turns out that the aliens inside it are spiders and want to melt into the locals' bodies and turn them into spider people who have to be blown up with bazookas. So I went out into the vestry and looked in the mirror, then took off my vestments and checked them and put them back on again. Naturally, the congregation were all looking at me when I returned, because in Mass you'll look at anything out of the ordinary, just to keep from dying of boredom.

After the final blessing I turned to the left with the other five boys and we all filed out into the vestry, and started getting our vestments off.

'Mr Blayney, I hope the Holy Mass wasn't too boring for you. Or did you feel the need to duck out for a smoke?'

'No, father, I thought I had a spider on me.'

This got a loud laugh from some of the other boys, especially Valentine Popovich, who copped a big smack in the ear from Christopher Muldoon.

'Thank you, Muldoon,' said Father Hagen.

The door opened and in walked Charles giving the Big Hello to one and all, he being a fellow altar boy. Father Hagen immediately became very chatty.

'Blayney, Dixon, I heard something nasty happened to you yesterday right outside this church. I'm glad you weren't hurt.'

'No Father, but they shot at my dog.' What good is a parish priest if you can't get a bit of sympathy out of him, I always say.

'No!'

'Yes, Father: twice, and nearly killed him.' I thought it best not to name names.

'But why, in God's name?'

'Because he tried to save me, Father. Actually, he *did* save me. I think he saved both of us, Father.'

'Well, I hope they catch them; jail's too good for 'em.' He was getting right off his bike, the old Father.

'Hey Father,' said Dennis Shanahan.

'Yes, Shanahan?'

'If those horrible people who shot at Blayney's dog told you what they did in Confession, you'd know all about it, wouldn't you?'

'Well, I wouldn't know who they were, would I?'

'But you know who *we* are when *we* go to Confession, Father.'

'Yes, but I've known you since you made your First Communion.'

'But you could have known these guys even longer.'

'Yes, but you are forgetting the seal of Confession, Shanahan. It is absolutely inviolable.'

'Yes, Father, but it was his dog, and he was a Catholic dog, too.'
I nodded. 'He'd been baptised, Father.'

'Dennis, you must understand, mustn't he, Father?' said Christopher Muldoon, suddenly turning into *Father* Muldoon.

'Well, I wish somebody would.'

'Wow, Dixie, is it true?' said Valentine Popovich.

'I'd rather not talk about it,' said Charles. 'His dog was scared to death. We don't want to talk about it, do we?' he said to me.

'No, Zac is a terrific dog. He deserves better.' As I said it I remembered that my previous dog, Biscuit, who was Zac's nephew, had in fact died by being shot, by that rotten copper Murphy, who was probably, according to my Rollo Brik Theory, in cahoots with Brik.

Suddenly I had another theory, because one theory leads to another – we learnt that in science too. I had to make a phone call.

'Father I've just realised that I have to make a phone call. Can I use your phone, please?'

'Course you can – you know where it is?'

'Yes, Father. Meet me at the presbytery, Charles.'

I shot off to the presbytery and called home. Aunty Daffy answered the phone.

'Hello. Taggerty residence, Daphne Honeysett speaking.'

'Hello Aunty Daphne, you're back – that's good. How's Keith and Mrs K?'

'Haven't got a clue what you mean.'

'Fair enough, mum's the word. I'm staying over at the Sandersons' for the weekend. When are you going back?' Your young detective likes to collect information while it's still ripe for the picking.

'Don't know yet – no rush. Are you all right?'

'If I was feelin' any better it'd be illegal.' I got that from Spider Murphy's old man. 'Is Granddad there?'

'No, he's over at your nanna's, I think. Is there any message?'

'No thanks. I'll call him there. Tell Mum I said hello. See ya, Aunty Daphne.'

I called Nanna's next. 'Nanna, it's me. Is Granddad there?'

'Yes, love. Are you all right? Where are you?'

'I'm calling from St Felix's presbytery, but I'm staying with the Sandersons for the weekend.'

'Good-oh. Just remember what I told you about that mob.'

'Okay Nanna, see ya Nanna. Granddad? Hi. How's Barney? He saved my life, you know.'

'Oh he's all right. That Barney's got more lives than a cat, boy.'

'And how's Zac? You should have seen him Granddad: he went crazy, like a mountain lion.'

'He's fightin' fit. Labradors are descended from wolves, you know.'

'Fair dinkum?'

'Oh yes. So, is that it then?'

'No, I just had another theory. I'm not sure if it means anything, but Eddie Williams' mum knows Darko's mum, and she even sounds like Darko.'

'What the hell are you talking about? Who's Eddie Williams?'

'He's Matthew Foster's new friend, and his family have moved into the house next door to Matthew — he used to live in North Richmond, up your way. Anyway, his mum — Mrs Williams (I realised that I was beginning to sound like a twelve-year old) — sounds like Darko, and I was thinking that she might —'

'Who the hell is Darko?'

'Darko Stepanovic, this Croatian kid who's in our club. Remember? I told you about his old man hating Jews. Anyway Uncle Seamus told me they're keen on bombs, and —'

'Look, there's a lot of Yugoslavs in Melbourne, boy. And I for one would very reluctant to upset 'em.'

'I'm just sayin' that maybe Eddie's mum might be one of the people that Mum upset in her travels — you never know.'

'So you want me to ask your mother if she might have upset anyone in the past, do you? Think about it.'

'I see what you mean, Granddad. But I still think she might know the person who's doing all this. Carmel Bus told me that Eddie's last name's not really Williams, and that he can speak Croatian, and that when Carmo was in ... um, you know, Turana, Eddie was too.'

'Listen, I want you to stay away from those Buses, d'ya understand?' I wanted to tell him that I'd put my money on Carmo over Eddie any day, but held my tongue. 'Now, are you okay over there with the Sandersons?'

'Yeah. Uncle Seamus doesn't like them, you know.'

'Don't you worry, they'll never let anything happen to you. Anything else?'

'Um, Granddad, that red and white FE —'

'What about it?'

'They said on the news that it was seen near Gazza's place just before, um ...'

'So what?'

'It was the same car — you know, from yesterday.'

'Not surprised. Now, how're you getting back to Sanderson's from the church?'

'Mr Sanderson is picking me up shortly. See you tonight.'

Later that day I got Raffi to come over to the Sandersons' place and help me with the map, and when he was finished take it over to his place. I reckoned Mr Sanderson would have copped a fair eyeful of it by now, and wouldn't get any more information from it. And anyway, it would be just as safe over at Raffi's. My whole life story, at least the bits that mattered, were on that map.

27 Touched by God

Word gets around. There had been six other kids from school in the church the day I chucked my wobbly: the altar boys, who would normally take no notice of anything that went on in the stalls and dress circle – not even if it involved the use of machine guns – their territory being the Holy Land up front. As I say, *normally*. But the sight (and sound – God likes to smite dramatically) of one of their fellow students receiving into his heart the Light of God simply by going to Communion was too much for mere flesh and blood to contain. Besides, your average altar boy – make that your average boy – is about as restrained as a race caller at a factory potato sack race.

That's the way it is at a boys school: it's like a little town in which, no matter where you turn, you are knee deep in rozzers, Gestapo, pimps, pricks and gossips. The only way to survive at St Dom's if you weren't one of these was to be a holy kid, a terrific football player, or brainy. So, thanks to those altar boys, and to the gossip of sundry working class eye-witnesses who had never seen anyone chuck a wobbly before, but mainly thanks to Brother Timothy being in the church at the same time as me and being right behind me in the Communion line, I was now officially holy. You wouldn't read about it.

The downside of being holy was that I had to keep going to Mass every morning that I was not serving on the altar at St Felix's, which was one week in every four. I also had to lead the class in the weekly rosary, which would have got my face rearranged if were it not for the fact that early in the year I had bashed up the class bully, Oby O'Brien, who had then decided to be my friend and bodyguard. Let's face it, you don't want to bash up a saint who can beat the shit out of you, do you? There was more downside, believe it or not. I was made the class representative of the Archconfraternity of the Divine Child Jesus, which is a club for kids who are saints. I had to organise prayer meetings and so on for kids I wouldn't normally be caught dead with, and wear a special medal that marked me out as a teacher's pet, like the Doris Day song.

The upside was that it was known far and wide that I had been touched by God (before, I was just touched), was probably going to become a priest (I did not deny this, as you can imagine), and was told that I could knock off early on Fridays to go to Benediction which, though dead boring, was chockers with your holier parishioners, whom the Octopus likes to keep an eye on, it being well known that such people are having themselves on, and are more often than not secret dipsos, wife beaters and child molesters. I could easily see one of these holier-than-thou types nicking a baby from its pram, or a car from its street. There was a rumour (I heard it from Sister Valerian) – that there were people – Aborigines – who sneaked into Melbourne at night to steal babies, whom they later sold to other Aborigines in the bush. I was therefore on the lookout for Aborigines at the Friday afternoon Benedictions, but I don't think I ever saw any, (though I was never sure what to look for, in any case).

At school, kids looked at me funny whenever I turned up, to see if I had grown a halo, or if I was going to work a miracle, because someone – I have no idea how these rumours get started – had said that he had seen me perform one. Again, I did not deny this, and had in fact taken to blessing my classmates, just in case a miracle did occur. But nothing happened that I could put my finger on, though Tubby Maculitis did pass a Latin test after I blessed him, which was taken to be my first public miracle.

Needless to say, Brother Gabriel, who was one of your more religious types, and would have been better at window dressing than hurting kids, took me aside after the Latin test to have a nervous word in my shell-like, expert to expert, as you might say.

'Mr Blayney.'

'Hello, Brother.'

'It's about this blessing business.'

'I wouldn't call it a business just yet Brother, as I still haven't fixed my scale of rates, though I think thruppence a throw would be fair.'

'You can't charge for blessings.'

'Father gets paid for weddings.'

'Those are tips, gratuities.'

'I'm with you, Brother' – I gave him a wink – '*tips*'. Now he was talking my language, because Granddad was always giving punters tips, usually on how to save their hard-earned.

'Look, I appreciate that you come from a business family' – he winced – 'but you can't take money for blessings.'

'It's all right, Brother. I'm going into the prayer business, anyway. I'll throw in the blessings for free.'

'You can't charge for prayers either.'

'Try telling Tubby Maculitis that, Brother. He gave me a zac to pray that he would get five out of ten for the Latin test – let's face it, he didn't have a hope – and that's what he got. That's the power of prayer. Hey, that's not a bad slogan: *The Power of Prayer.*'

'I must admit, that was pretty unexpected.'

'More like a miracle, Brother. *Dear Lord —*'

'What?'

'*Please give Tubby Maculitis, who's got diabetes, five out of ten for Latin. He can't help it if he's hopeless.*'

'Is that what you said to God?'

'*Thanking you in advance —*'

'Mr Blayney, I don't think —'

'*Yours sincerely —*'

'Stop it!'

'Sorry, Brother. I thought I might put a penny in the poor box for every prayer – you know, give God a cut – that way, everybody's happy.'

Brother Gabriel stared at me for a long time. He was not a natural. 'You may pray and bless, but not charge.'

'You make it hard for a bloke to earn an honest quid, Brother. How about Fee-for-Prayers only?'

'Okay, but no payment in advance – and only if God grants your prayer. Half to the poor-box.' Brother Gabriel had missed his vocation.

'Done. Um, Brother, why did you become a brother?'

'I heard a calling.'

'Was there anyone standing next to you at the time?'

Brother Gabe had a good laugh at that. I hadn't missed *my* vocation.

The week that followed was one of the strangest of my life, and that's saying a mouthful. Now that I was a saint, or at least well on the way to becoming one – it turns out that practically any divine response to the Blessed Sacrament lumps you in with such holy favourites as the Children of Lourdes, and Padre Pio – I found myself blessing not only my classmates, but kids from other Forms.

Musso Taranto bought his dog, Dingo, to school to be blessed – the dog had a nasty cough and bad breath, but I turned him not away. My best friends, whose parents still allowed them to hang out with me – another miracle! – were kind enough to act as my assistants when we were in the playground, listening attentively and devoutly to requests for blessings and prayers, which, after Monday, they only accepted on paper, to separate the deserving from the undeserving, you might say (but really, the rich from the poor).

Word spread, and on Tuesday night the girls from Vaucluse were excused their rule of not crossing the road after school, and crowded around St Dom's side entrance to wait for me. They all had their heads covered with white lace scarves and hankies as if they were in church – a condition of their visit set by their boss, Mother Joseph. As I came to the side gate with my friends – I do not call them disciples – the girls all knelt for my blessing and bowed their heads.

'*In nomine Patris, et Filii, et Spiritus Sancti. Amen.*'

I said it in a loud voice, giving myself a fright into the bargain – I was still not used to doing it; heavy lies the beretta, and so on. They all blessed themselves and said 'Amen' and looked up. Most, if not all of them, were crying. In the front row was Mona. She had tears running down her cheeks. I fell in love with her *statim*, as we say in Latin class. I also saw, just a few along, Josephine Thompson. She was watching me looking at Mona, and had an expression on her face like she'd caught her lips in a sewing machine – not her best look. I saw in that moment a side of Josephine – of the girl and lady species, in fact – that I decided I did not care for. I had seen it in my mum, in all my aunties, and in a lot of ladies around our part of town who were married. But I realised in that moment that I had never seen it in Mona, not even when she was stamping her foot.

I gestured like Jesus beckoning to John the Baptist to get off his knees, as he was not worthy of this adoration. And the crowd arose and went away to attest to what they had seen. But Mona stayed.

Just a few yards away on the other side of the street Aunty Lucky was waiting in her MG, which I realised would have been accidentally caught up in the blessing. I hopped in first as usual, and Mona hopped in on top of me, the way she always did.

'Well,' said Lucky. 'After meeting Gregory Peck I thought I'd never be impressed by another man, but how wrong was I.'

'Hello, Lucky.'

'Hello yourself. I had to see if the rumours were true.'

'Your car should run a bit better now, if any of that blessing hit it.'

'No doubt. I have to say Mr Blayney, I've seen some blessings in my time – and I have been blessed by the *Papa* himself, and let me tell you that's not a blessing you forget in a hurry – but that blessing of yours hit the spot: I feel like a new woman. Mona, do you feel like a new woman?'

Mona couldn't hold back the tears. 'Just get going Aunty Lucky, quick.'

We tore up The Vaucluse, scattering freshly blessed schoolgirls, and turned left at Church Street, in the opposite direction to home.

All the way to Carlton I paid no attention to the trip, though normally I paid as much attention as I could to the car, which I coveted sinfully, and to Lucky's shirt, which always interested me greatly. And normally Lucky insisted on rambling gayly in a loud voice as she threw the car around like Jack Brabham, who I had begun to think must have had a touch of the Italian in him. But today she turned the radio on loud, and paid no attention to me.

In Carlton, I met some new people, all Italian. When the other person's English was poor Mona spoke Italian, to be polite. She happily introduced me all round, and I said: '*Piacere di conoscerla*', which seemed to do the trick.

'So,' said Lucky, once Mona had gone off to organise the victuals and coffee, 'I hear you've been in the wars.'

'It's no picnic being me, Lucky.'

'You know, you talk pretty tough for a twelve-year old. And I know why too, don't think I don't. But Mona and me know that beneath that rugged exterior lies a very sensitive boy. Otherwise, I wouldn't let Mona have anything to do with you, *capisci?*'

'*Capisco.* And I'm not twelve anymore.'

'Since when?'

'Since last week.'

'Well then, Happy Birthday. Mona, you didn't tell me.'

'It was a secret. I gave him Johnny's Phantom ring, the one with eyes that sparkle; Johnny didn't want it anymore.'

'Now, tell me the truth: is this person who tried to grab you yesterday the same person who abducted your baby brother?'

'Yes, but how did you know about that?'

'Tell him Mona.'

'Because it happened practically outside Josephine Thompson's front gate, that's how, and your friends were shouting it out to the whole neighbourhood. Jo rang Tina and told her that she saw Raffi at the Orange Tree, and Tina rang me, and I told Aunty Lucky.'

I had no idea that that girls were such efficient communicators, though I'd heard rumours, of course – boys do. I wondered, not for the first time, if we'd still be using semaphore flags and smoke signals had girls not cottoned on to the telephone.

'Are you listening?'

'Like a border collie. But how did you know they didn't get me?'

'Because Tina rang Raffi afterwards, then rang me, of course.'

Of course is girl for *you idiot*. 'I see. That will help with our enquiries.'

'Whose enquiries?'

'Uncle Vinnie's,' said Lucky. 'Don't worry, it's all taken care of. Have you any idea why this is happening? Has anyone threatened you?'

'No, but I think it might have something to do with Mum, with something she did in the War. It's hush-hush – um, *secreto*?' I rolled the 'r' in case it was right.

'No: *segreto*,' said Lucky, 'but nice try, eh, Mona? Now listen, I know your grandfather doesn't see eye to eye with my family on a lot of things, but this is different. Did you know that a man died in a car … ah … accident, not far from where you used to live, last week?'

'Um, yes.'

'Did your family know that man?'

'Yes, but I don't know how.' I figured that was family business.

'And did you know that the car those people were in yesterday in Balmain Street was somehow involved?'

'No,' I lied. 'What does it mean?'

'It means you have to make sure you have someone with you all the time, until those people are caught. Now apparently, you have a friend who looks a lot like you.'

'Yes, Raffi Radion.'

'He's Tina's boyfriend,' said Mona.

'We're –' I stopped.

'What? What are you?'

'Best friends, but he doesn't go to St Dom's, he goes to City Boys High.'

'Raffi Radion. That's an unusual name.'

Lucky was fishing again, always fishing. When Granddad found out that I knew her, he told me not to trust her, but it was because of someone in her family, her Uncle George. But it was all right.

'It's Armenian.'

'Is Raffi an Armenian, do you think?'

'No, it's just his name that's Armenian.'

'I don't get it,' said Mona. 'I mean, my name's Italian, and so am I.'

I shrugged, as I was in the same boat.

'Do you think you might have been mistaken for him?' asked Lucky.

'Actually, they grabbed him first, then realised he wasn't me, and threw him on the ground.'

'Well, they knew what they were doing, by the look of it. Still, I don't think they're interested in you personally. It's the family they're trying to hurt.'

'Well, it's working.'

'Don't worry. If I know your grandfather, they won't get a chance to try that again.'

'How can you be so sure?'

'Look across the road. Do you know that man?'

I looked through the big window across the street, and saw Barney sitting in his car, doing a rotten job of blending in with the scenery, with his mop of red curly hair.

'Yes, he works for my grandfather.'

'Well, I'm willing to bet he's not the only person keeping an eye on you. See?'

'Yeah, I see what you mean.'

'He was parked down The Vaucluse waiting for you to come out of school.'

'I hope he didn't cop any of that blessing.'

'Why not?'

'I saw him get blessed just last week. I don't think he's ready for another one just yet.'

When Lucky left us alone for a minute so that she could talk to Mr Coco Mona sipped her drink and looked at me with red eyes. She didn't try to talk for a while.

'Sweetheart, are you sure it's okay for you to go back to school? You've been hurt.' She jumped off her chair with a little bounce, and leant over and kissed my face despite the presence of other customers, who took no notice. I'm guessing that if you're an Italian and you haven't seen at least half a dozen beautiful girls kissing their boyfriends in cafes by four p.m. then you're probably in a coma.

'Do you like that?'

I made a mental note to file that question away under Dumbest Questions I Will Probably Ever Hear, along with: *Is Superman the strongest person on Earth? Do black jellybeans taste better than white ones?* and *Is Buddy Holly cool?* When I tried to answer I discovered that my tongue had seized up. I took a sip of my cappuccino. I wanted to make sure that I would be understood.

'Yes, sweetheart, I love it.' I had noticed that the Mona of the species likes to be called sweetheart, and while I would normally vomit rather than call a girl that, I found that the results were always worth the effort.

'I'm so glad. I thought that when you became, you know, holy, that you might have lost your love for me and started to love God instead.'

I wanted to tell her that as far as I was concerned God was a first class bastard who could rot in hell, but I had the feeling that saying that in a room full of Italians, with a picture of the Pope right there on the wall, would probably get me dragged out into Lygon Street and lynched, Barney or no bloody Barney. Time to marshal all my resources, all my thirteen years of experience, and knock Mona's socks off, throwing caution to the wind, which was definitely never my personal policy – that was always Tom's department.

'Sweetheart, all this holy stuff, I don't really deserve it you know. I just happened to be in the church at the same time that God turned up and decided to fill someone up with his grace – not that I don't appreciate what he did, of course. But when you think about, I'm lucky I wasn't killed. So please don't treat me as any different.'

I was tempted to add an 'amen', but decided not to. I was definitely hot, and I wondered idly if any of this stuff was a confessable sin.

She suddenly went very teary and gave me a little kiss on the lips. I was very touched. I wanted Tom to be alive again so I could get Mona to kiss him too. They would have liked each other.

28 The Murphy Caper

On Thursday I was allowed to go down to Raffi's place after school, and I knew why, too: it was because Barney was following me around like a hungry guinea pig. And I guessed that he wasn't the only one, because that is what Lucky had said, and she had always struck me as a lady who knew a bit about this and that. But even though I had a look around every now and then, I couldn't spot anyone else following me. Still, I was sure. Your average thirteen-year old kid knows these things from years of personal experience at being sneaky and suspicious, not to mention evil (though I had the evil part of it licked, now that I was holy).

But things had seemed to be all in order when I rang on Wednesday night to check if this was all right, except that Raffi had heard about the holiness business.

'Hey, I heard all about you being holy.'

'Strike me pink,' says I. 'Can't a man be holy in peace?'

'I heard that you've been blessing people and performing miracles and everything.'

'I wouldn't go that far, young Raffi.'

'Well, Tina would. She suddenly thinks you're shit-hot. Can you please tell her that it's all a mistake, you know, do something horrible?'

'I will, Raffi young feller. You know me, anything to please a friend, not to mention relative.'

'Not to mention brother.'

'That too.' I still wasn't one hundred per-cent used to the idea.

'I'll stop over at the Camponis' on the way over and tell them it was all a mistake.'

'Thanks. I'll be waiting for you. Mum's going to cook something special for tea, just because you're coming over. Terrific, eh?'

'Bewdy.'

So the next night I decided to go down to the Camponis' place, which was in the same street as our old house, and put the inmates' minds at ease. The ride down was smooth and uneventful, apart from a whole tram-load of kids from our school announcing to a largish bunch of Tech School boys, Secondary School girls, and assorted local passengers that the tram was carrying none other than the Holy Boy, as I had become known. The conductor, a tired (but not completely unattractive) lady with hairy legs, called Lorna (I heard Granddad call her that once), who had known me for years, thought this was worth a trip up the tram to see for herself.

'Aren't you Archie Taggerty's grandson?'

'The same, Lorna (First Rule). It's nice to meet you again.'

She shook her head. 'Like grandfather, like grandson, I see.'

'He's been touched by God,' said a little kid from St Dom's primary outfit, with wide eyes.

'I see,' see Lorna. 'That'll be fourpence, please Your Holiness.'

'I don't think he has to pay,' said the little kid, pointing at me as if I was in a pram.

'Well, I've yet to meet a holy schoolboy,' said Lorna.

I got to my feet and gave Lorna eight pence.

'It's all right, my son. You have my seat and I'll pay your fare.'

There was a general murmur of approval from the St Dom's kids, and a big laugh from the Tech School kids, some of whom were much bigger than us.

'Are you looking for trouble?' asked one of the older St Dom's kids, loudly.

'It's all right, boys. I'll give him one of my special blessings. Hold my bag.'

I went right up close to a big Tech School kid, who I suddenly realised was a few years older than me, and raised my hand as if to begin a blessing. He followed my hand up to where it came to a stop in front of his face. Then I gave him my Sunday Kick in the Pills, taught to me by Granddad, and a move that is as reliable in delivering the goods as any of Rudy Nureyev's or Ron Barrassi's. The trick is to kick your opponent so hard that he will fold up like a deck chair, and be reluctant to retaliate within a fortnight.

Then I pulled the tram cord, collected my bag, and bid the applauding and cheering throng good afternoon. I may have bowed – I don't remember. As I stood on Church Street and the tram rumbled away, I gave it my final blessing: *'Dominus vobiscum, my friends, have a safe journey.'* I was bound to be expelled for that little caper, but the way I looked at it, I had been holy for four days, which would have to be a world record for a Richmond kid.

When I arrived at the Camponis' house I knocked on the door, and a very small kid opened the door.

'What d'*you* want?' said the little Camponi.

'I came to see Tina.'

'Hey, Tina!'

The kid ran away, and Tina came to the door.

'It's you! Come in!'

'I just came over to –'

'Mama, it's him! We were just talking about you and you appeared. It's like one of your miracles!' She was dragging me down to the lounge room.

'Yes, well, that's what I wanted to … um, hello, Mrs Camponi, g'day Sal, g'day Mario, g'day, um …'

'Ha ha, he doesn't know my name!'

The little Camponi kid got a rap round the earhole from his mother.

'I know you come to talk to our Tina, but would you please bless us before you do anything else,' said Mrs Camponi, shifting nicely into top gear.

'I don't think … it's just that … I mean, I'm not a priest or anything.'

'We heard about the mentally retarded boy who came top of the class after you blessed him.'

'Well, I don't think Tubby was mentally —'

'And the girl who walked again —'

This was one I hadn't heard of, though I was happy for her. I must have looked puzzled at Tina.

'Petronella Schroeder,' said Tina with a steady glow in her eyes that I was beginning to recognise. 'One of the primary kids at Vaucluse; she had callipers.'

The whole family folded at the knees and bowed their heads. If there was one thing I'd learnt about Italians, it's that depriving them of their blessings is like depriving a crocodile of its dead chooks – best not to. I decided to give them my Sunday best.

'*Benedicat vos omnipotens Deus, Pater, et Filius, et Spiritus Sanctus. Amen.*'

'*Amen,*' they responded.

They got up and quietly returned to their various action stations. Tina dragged me into her bedroom.

'Tina, don't let them think I'm holy. I'm not. I'm just a kid. Look five minutes ago I kicked a kid on the tram in the knackers.'

'I'm sure he deserved it.'

'No, Tina, no.'

'I hope you can stay for tea – you could say grace – we would be honoured.' She came within an ace of curtseying.

'No, Tina, thanks anyway. Look, I'm on my way to Raffi's place. Raffi is upset. He thinks you like me more than him.'

'So what if I do?'

It was time to push the emergency ejector seat button. I took one of those noisy breaths. I was about to do what Boy A never does to another boy unless he wants to drop Boy B into the soup. The fact was, I didn't know how close these two were.

'But Raffi loves you.'

'Did he say that?'

'Yes.'

'And what do *you* think?'

I had my finger on the button. 'I like Mona better.'

Two seconds later I was alone, and realised that I had better get out the front door before Mario came down and thumped me. Five minutes later, I was at Raffi's back door.

'Hell-o!'

'Come in if you're good-looking,' said Mrs Radion. 'Oh, it's you. I was expecting William Holden.'

'Hello Mrs Radion.'

'How's the holiness business?'

'It's all over,' Mrs Radion. 'It's way too risky.'

'Oh, in what way?'

'People think I can work miracles. People are making stuff up about me, things I'm supposed to have done. On the tram I got into a fight –'

'Yes, I heard you kicked a Tech School kid in the family jewels.'

'How'd you find out?'

'Tony Capra from next door was on the tram. He just left. In his version you were defending every Catholic's God-given right to beat up anyone who takes the micky out of him.'

'No, I was just upset because they laughed when I tried to pay a little kid's fare for him, that's all. I'll probably get expelled tomorrow. They don't like boys fighting in uniform.'

Just then Raffi appeared.

'G'day.'

'G'day. I did what you asked; I went over to Tina's and fixed things up, um, I think. Her mum made me bless the whole family, but – I couldn't get out of it.'

'What the hell'd you do that for?'

'Look, you saw all those Catholics at Mass; well, half of them were Italians. You only have to threaten to bless 'em and they're down on their knees begging for it. I blessed a kid at school last Monday, and he passed a Latin test – and there was no way he was going to pass that test. And Mrs Camponi told me that some little crippled girl at Vaucluse started walking again. I tell you, if the Archbishop finds out about this he'll probably excommunicate me. And wait till the brothers wake up that the President of the Archconfraternity of the Divine Child Jesus is some kind of religious crook. I'll probably end up in a dungeon in the Vatican or something, and that's if I'm lucky. Don't worry, Tina was pretty dark on me when I left. I reckon you'll be laughing.'

'I better be.'

'Oh well, to business Raffi my son. I have a bit of serious investigating to do.'

'Bewdy. What?'

'I'm going to have a bit of a snoop around Murphy's house, to see if my suspicions are correct.'

'Who's Murphy?'

'He's a copper who lives next door to the Orange Tree. I think he's got something to do with Mick's kidnapping.'

'Why?'

'Because he hates Granddad, for one thing, and because he loves Mum, but she told him to get whatsanamed.'

'Why?'

'Because he's a prick.'

'But you aren't allowed to go wandering around, are you?'

'Not me, young Raffi, but … the *Mazemaster! Yes, the Mazemaster, who, in his never-ending hunt for clues, snoops around rozzers' houses while they're getting pissed out of their brains at the six o'clock swill, who tells his best friend's —*'

'*Brother's* —'

'"Scuse me — *brother's girlfriend that she's not as good as* his *girlfriend. Who kicks proddies in the nuts. And so on.*'

'What clues do you think you'll find?'

'Dunno, but I know they're there. I told Granddad that I thought Murphy was behind it, but he said he wasn't. I have to go right now, before Murphy gets home. I'll go out the front door. If your mum asks, tell her I had to tell the Sandersons something important.'

'You want me to lie to Mum?'

'Fib, Raffi, fib, not lie. Just look on it as bullshit, which you excel at.'

'I do, don't I?'

'Raff, you make crap sound good.'

Five minutes later I was in Gwynne Street, Cremorne, around the back of Murphy's place, and trying to blend in, which is what you do when you're up to no good. This was also Luigi's street, so I had to act quickly, before any of the several thousand Espositos spotted me and reeled me in, in which case I'd be up to my armpits in pasta and *Benedicat*s.

Murphy's back gate was always unlocked – I knew because in the days before I became a saint I had done a bit of the old B&E at this very address (and got caught for my trouble – so I can't claim to be an expert in the same class as Barney).

The truth is that I wanted Barney for this job, but I wasn't sure that he would agree, and was half sure that he would dob me in to Granddad – not that he was a dobber – but he would have done it while acting under starter's orders. So after satisfying myself that I was not being watched, I stuck my hand through the gate hole and opened the gate. It wasn't the gate I had to worry about, but the back door. It was locked, as expected, but I had come prepared, and got out my trusty lock-pick set, which had been a Christmas present from Barney last year. Half a mo later I was standing in the policemanly coolness of Murphy's lair.

I didn't know exactly what I was looking for, but I didn't want to wreck the place either – best to be careful and methodical, so he would never know it had been turned over.

Now the last thing a policeman expects at any time in his miserable God-forsaken life is to get his house done over by a scallywag, whether young or old. So I knew that if did find clues there was a good chance they would not be hidden too well, if at all. And sure enough, on the table I found a list of names, twelve of them. And those names had something very strange about them: they were all Yugoslav-sounding names, names ending in '-ic', for the most part. And the last one was definitely a woman: Irene Vukovic.

Quick as a cat, I whipped out my faithful Spirax notebook and copied down the names. Then I put the list back exactly as I had found it, and went for a quick look around. I knew which bedroom was Murphy's, and I knew he wouldn't be in it, so I checked the other one as quietly as possible, in case there was a houseguest – I had Brik in mind. The door to the second bedroom was open, and it was plain as day that someone was staying in it. On the dresser was a briefcase with the initials *RB* on it. I tried to open it, but it was locked. Time for the Mazemaster to make tracks.

But before I could take a step, I heard voices just outside the front door. Could anything possibly go wronger? No, not really. I tiptoed down the passage like a ballerina who'd had a sniff of something to keep her on her toes – sorry, I only know what they give to horses, not ballerinas – and turned the corner into the living room just as they opened the front door. I tried to make it out the back door, but for some reason it wouldn't unlock, which probably had something to do with the way I'd let myself in. I returned to the living room just in time to dive behind the lounge.

'All right, Holland, so why couldn't you give me the list in the pub, for Christ's sake?'

'Because you were being watched, that's why – your lot's my guess – and this is serious business – ASIO business.'

'Being watched! No wonder they gave you the boot: I think you're losin' it. Just give it to me now, then and piss off. I don't know why I'm paying for the whole list when all I want is one name and address.'

'If that woman you're looking for, Vukovic, is on that list, all her details will be there too. But first let's see the do-re-mi.'

'Here it is, now hand it over and disappear, if you're worried.'

'Here. Disappearin's what I do best these days. I'm The Invisible Bloody Man.'

There was the sound of an envelope being opened.

'I don't believe it: she just lives around the corner.'

'I don't want to know. But Murph, why didn't you just ask Brik?'

'I did, but our Yank mate is under orders to keep his mouth shut.'

'He's no mate of mine. Well, it's my shout, I think?'

'Never say no, that's my motto.'

'Fair enough. Where *is* Brik, by the way?'

'Who gives a shit?'

They went out the way they came, and I stayed there for a minute, getting my breath, then I carefully unlocked the back door, which just needed a little jiggle, and slipped out.

I had now burgled the same house twice, the first time being last year, when I scored a photo of a lady with a little kid – Aunt Queenie and Murphy – which Granddad now owns, and nearly died of fright in the process when I was spotted by Murphy. Being thirteen has its ups and downs, and being sprung during burglary is not one of the ups, ranking somewhere between getting kissed by an aunty with a moustache who has been hitting the old top shelf, and tripping over your cassock while you're serving on the altar and tipping wine all over Father. You can see how God would piss himself laughing while he was dreaming up these little pranks.

I went back to Raffi's by going the wrong way down Gwynne Street to Kelso Street and making my way across the railway line to the old tannery, then back to Balmain Street. It was the only way to get past the Orange Tree without risking being spotted.

Back at Raffi's, I discovered I hadn't been missed, which was, I think, another one of those weird miracles.

I decided that the only thing to do was to tell Barney that the lady on the list was my number one suspect – she being the only lady – and that Murphy seemed to know what she was calling herself and where she lived. It was an open and shut case. I couldn't tell Granddad, because he had made me promise never to burgle Murphy's house again, and he wasn't kidding. I wasn't sure what to do with the rest of the list, so I decided to hang onto it. But when I tried to call Barney at his place, he was out.

29 The debriefing

Later that night Barney turned up to take me home. I introduced him to Mrs Radion and Raffi, and Mrs R invited him in for a beer, which I thought was very nice.

'Barney,' I said, 'this is the second time I've seen you today.'

'Well, I'm not surprised, young feller, as I've been appointed your private body guard. So where did you spot me?'

'I didn't spot you: Lucky did, over in Lygon Street. You stuck out like dog's balls, with that mop of red hair of yours.'

'I've been meanin' to get down to the barber's.'

'Anyway, Barn, I don't think you've been watching me *everywhere* I went.'

'Oh, yes I have, *everywhere*, if you catch my meanin'.' He gave me a wink.

'I'll tell you about my adventures on the way home, Barn. No need to bore Mrs Radion.'

'Believe me, Barney,' said Mrs Radion, 'I'm never bored when these two get together. You should have heard what happened at the Camponis' place a bit earlier.'

'I always hear everything sooner or later – it's my job. Besides, I've known the nipper since he was born. Only one person knows him better, and that's his granddad. Not that his parents don't – maybe I've said too much. Well, this has been a wonderful visit if only for meeting Raffi – you see, I've only heard his name mentioned about every five minutes. I suppose the secret's out; is it all right to say that?'

Barney was not used to talking to women as attractive as Mrs Radion, I could tell. And he was worried that he was putting his foot in it, as he usually does.

'Look, Barney, I've heard about you too, and I know you're like one of the family. So you can say whatever you like when you're around here; we're all pretty straight with each other, aren't we boys?'

'Well, Mrs –'

'Val –'

'Val, I've heard that you're practically one of the family too, though I wouldn't say that in front of Jean – not game enough.'

'As a matter of fact, Barney, I *am* one of the family. My great grandfather or something like that, was a Blayney. So I'm pretty sure the two families are distantly related – though I could be wrong. But just look at the boys.'

Barney drained his beer.

'It's all beyond me, Val. But I will say that to the best of my knowledge – and I know what I'm talking about, believe me – one half of Richmond's related to the other half, which means that this is a much smaller town than it looks. Thanks for the beer; I was as dry as an Itie tank driver's crotch.'

'It's funny you should mention them. We were just discussing out Italian friends a bit earlier, weren't we boys?'

'No disrespect meant,' said Barney. 'I know the young feller's girlfriend is a De Coney.'

'They've both been smitten by the Italian female, Barney, like a lot of other men in the world, and I'm sure they won't be the last.'

Barney had a good chuckle at this, and waited for me to collect my bag, then took me home.

'Barn,' I said as we drove up Church Street, 'I couldn't say anything in front of Mrs Radion, because she doesn't know the whole story, but I want to say thanks for saving us the other day. I thought for a second there I'd had it.'

'Any time, nipper.' There was a loud, leathery *zip!*, and he flashed a large blade in front of my face. Just below the handle was a neat dent. 'What'd' ya think of the old Bowie knife now?'

'Wow, Barn, it looks terrific, much better, I'd say.'

'Yeah, that's what I think, too. Course, me leg's giving me hell, but I keep that to meself.'

'Barn, there's something you have to know. I can't tell anyone else, but I want you to know I did it for a good reason.'

'You did a bit of the old B&E over at Murphy's place. See? You don't even have to tell me. Now, does that feel better?'

'Barn, I had to, because Granddad wouldn't believe the Yugoslavs are connected with what happened to Mick and me and Gazza. He thinks I'm imagining things. I told him Brik – you know who Brik is? Okay, then – I reckon this Brik bloke is staying with Murphy. But he said he's not. But he is, Barn. I saw his briefcase in the spare bedroom.'

'D'ja see him?'

'Nuh. But just after I found it I heard Dutch Holland and Murphy come in, and – here's the bit I wanted to tell you – Murphy had a list of names and addresses, and there was a woman on it, but Murphy reckoned she'd changed her name, and Dutch gave him the woman's new name and address – Murphy paid him for it.'

'And did he say what it is?'

'Nuh, he didn't say, only that she just lived around the corner from him.'

'Did you see any of the other names on that list?'

I dug into my blazer pocket bag and found the list. 'Here's the whole list. I copied the names before they came home.'

'Strewth! Now listen. No matter what happens, you weren't there, okay? I'll tell Archie I rolled the place meself, on a tip.'

'Ten-four, Barn, Mum's the word. Hey Barn, where're we goin'?'

Barney had gone up to Brougham Street, but then turned left into The Vaucluse.

'Have to make a brief stop before takin' you home – on the q.t., if you know what I mean.'

'Suits me, Barn. I wasn't in a hurry to go home anyway. So, I'm guessing we're going to Nanna's place.'

Barney just chuckled to himself.

We parked behind a Ford Fairlane 500 and went in. Nanna had visitors, and among them was Mrs Petulengro, who kissed me on the forehead, and Sunny, who threaded her arm through mine and guided me into the other living room, the small one, and closed the door behind us. It was dark but for the moonlight coming through the curtains, which Sunny drew back, making her coloured clothes look like a grey jigsaw puzzle. She sat on the couch with me without talking, and kept her arm through mine. As with the day I met her, I was both excited and frightened. She took her scarf off and put her hair and her face against mine and I smelt – what? – a wood fire, Rinso, faint perfume, and something else I couldn't place: biting but beautiful. I sniffed.

'It's patchouli oil.'

I knew that I would never forget that smell if I lived to be sixty (though that is not something I would put money on). But I had nothing to say; you will be astonished to hear that the cat had got the young superhero's tongue.

Sunny kissed what was left of the scratches, and the touch of her eyelashes on my cheek made me think of the black butterflies. 'My poor Devlin, did that guy at the Circus do that to you? Lucky Uncle Timbo turned up, eh?'

I was ashamed to tell her I had chucked a wobbly, because it would have made me look like a loony, and that my own mother had done the rest, because I had seen how close she was to her own mum.

'So, you're one of those boys that's short on words but long on actions, eh? Mama says men like you are like *gold*.' And she whispered the word into my ear: 'You're probably wondering why I haven't let you kiss me, aren't you, Devlin?' As matter of fact, I wasn't, as I had decided weeks ago that Sunny was one of those girls who wouldn't let anyone do anything, and there are quite a few of those around, I had noticed. I tried to speak, but she put a finger on my lips. 'Well I'll tell you: it's because you haven't proved yourself worthy. But when you have, I will know, and I will expect you to find me, no matter where I am, because we're moving on.'

'How will you know?' I expected her to say that the cards would tell her.

'It'll be in the paper.'

'Oh yeah, course.'

'Now, this is for you; don't go anywhere without it. It has special powers to protect you through your coming ordeal.' She showed me the Hanged Man card, kissed it, and slipped it onto my shirt pocket. 'I painted that one myself, from the one in Mum's deck.'

I swallowed. It was all starting to get to me: her warm body, the patchouli stuff, her actress voice – I thinking she was doing Ingrid Bergman, one of my favourites – the way she treated me like a boy (it gets you down when you're now officially a teenager, but only just). And just when I thought I'd figured girls out – there was the Mona type, who you just wanted to kiss, and the Judy type, who you wished would kiss somebody else – along came a third type, the Sunny Petulengro type, who just wanted you to feel like you'd lost control of your super powers, and turned to plasticine.

'Now, are your lips clean?'

'I s'pose so.'

She stood up in front of me and shoved her hand out. 'Then you may kiss my hand.'

I did this, and she put her scarf on and led me back out into the other living room, arm in arm, then went over and started talking to Uncle Mick, as if I didn't exist.

Nanna kissed me and said quietly: 'Now then, wasn't that a nice surprise?'

'One of the nicest, Nanna, coming in just a short half-head behind my first hot jam doughnut. But Nanna, she keeps calling me Devlin.'

Nanna shrugged. 'Who cares?'

I thought about it for a moment. Nanna knew everything.

'Ye-ah, Nanna, who cares?'

That night I slept like a dog. Okay, so I had come within an ace of having two beautiful girls (who were cousins) falling in love with me at the same time, thereby causing two Italian families to come after me with knives (your Italian's preferred weapon). I had also kicked a big kid on the tram in the cods while wearing the uniform of a De La Salle college student, and would probably be expelled and sent to the Vatican to explain how I could possibly be a worse Catholic. I had broken into a bent policeman's house, and stolen valuable information he was in possession of that had to do with my baby brother's kidnapping. And I had blessed a whole family of Italians, who were probably now going to tell Archbishop Mannix, who was going to excommunicate me for pretending to be a priest. The best – and strangest – thing to come out of the week was that I got to sit in the moonlight with Sunny and listen to her do her Ingrid Bergman, and smell her hair.

Next morning, after my cruelly honest stocktake, I awoke feeling refreshed and keen to go to Mass, at which our altar boys group had to serve. I felt that the only way to get clear of all this confusion and of all the strange connections, which were getting me down wholesale, was to make a clean breast of everything to everybody all the time, like Abraham Lincoln. Or was it Jesus? No more deception. My new middle name would be Honesty. I was in uncharted territory, but that's the way the Mazemaster likes it.

I had a quick bite to eat, in accordance with Brother Timothy's instructions, but not enough to make myself feel that I had committed a sin. Then I was off on my bike. God was very kind to me on the way down by making the rain stop, probably because it was the second day of spring; still, it was a very strange thing to happen to Melbourne. But just as I reached Amsterdam Street it suddenly came down like bats and frogs, as Tom used to say, and made me wonder if it was the end of the world, because Father had said many times that Judgement Day would have abominable weather (as if it wouldn't be enough that it was Judgement Day, for god's sake).

As usual at weekday Masses only the three main altar boys turned up, no 'dummies' being required to make the Mass into the big production Sunday Mass was, as the only people who ever turned up were a smallish contingent of your Maltese and Italian mothers, all dressed in black (except Mona's family, who dressed as if it was Moomba).

So, there was: Christopher Muldoon (water and wine), Matthew Bloody Foster (bells), and yours truly (book). Matthew Foster's constant prayer was that Christopher or me would be run over by a brewery truck, so that he could be promoted to the centre spot, and get to go up onto the altar with the priest, but Christopher said that God was not that stupid, which made MBF laugh his head off. I ask you, how can you like a kid like that?

The book kid is the one who opens the sacristy door, and begins the procession out onto the altar, and he is followed by the priest, then the water and wine boy, and finally the kid who rings the bells, who closes the door behind him.

At seven on the dot I opened the door to the sanctuary and stepped out. It was like an episode of Captain Video, where the evil scientist makes two whole days disappear, and instead of it being Friday it's actually Sunday. The church was chock-a-block with devoted micks, all ogling Yours Truly as if I was Graham Kennedy, Charlton Heston and Pope John XXIII all rolled into one. In fact, at the back, there was a huge crowd standing up, and I could see people on the steps outside, hoping to get a glimpse of the young saint.

I guessed that it was the visit to the Camponis that had done it, because the earlier Masses in the week had been low key and pretty poorly attended, as is usually the case in bad weather. But add one or more Italian ladies to one or more telephones and stir briskly, and what you will get is what we in the communication business call a nuclear reaction – that's a scientific fact. And that's what must have happened. Goodbye plans; goodbye resolution.

There was a polite murmur as we walked out to the bottom of the altar steps to begin Mass. Father turned to his left and gave me a quick glance – I couldn't read it – then began the Mass. At Communion there were so many people in the queue that Father

Hagen had to go back into the vestry to get the spare ciborium full of hosts. Meanwhile, I had been told by Christopher Muldoon, who was the Communion assistant that day, to take his place.

'Why – are you sick?' That was the usual reason for any sudden change of function on the altar.

'No, I just think the people would like to see you, that's all.'

So I grabbed the little silver tray off him went over to the altar rails with Father, and the people looked at me adoringly as they received the host. At any tick of the clock I was expecting Dr Mannix to come and tap me on the shoulder.

At the end of Mass, Father came over to us as we were disrobing. 'Well, Mr Blayney, your reputation has finally reached our humble little church. I don't know if I was dreading or looking forward to this day. Are you aware that the Archbishop knows about you?'

'What, all the way over in Kew?'

'He may live in Kew, but his office is in East Melbourne, and that's just a drop-punt from Italian territory.'

'I didn't know he had an office.'

'It's called St Patrick's Cathedral.'

'Oh, yeah.'

'Is it true about the Girl Who Walked Again?'

'Haven't got a clue, Father.'

'How about the Mental Retarded Boy?'

'Diabetes, Father.'

'What do you mean?'

'Tubby Maculitis, he had diabetes.'

'Has he still got it?'

'Don't know, Father. I hope so, I mean not.'

'I heard he was speaking in tongues.'

'What's that?'

'And then there's Mrs Price.'

'What about –'

'Well you may ask, Mr Blayney. She has sent that heathen man she was living with in sin back to his wife across the road, and embraced her husband again, so to speak. And from what I heard about the abandon of those two to their filthy and depraved practices in those houses, I think we can safely call their reconciliation another miracle.'

'But Father, I know that family, and they do that every –'

'Blayney, think. Did you bless that Price boy during the week – oh, it's all right, I know all about your visitation from the Lord; you were only doing God's work – well?'

I swallowed. Mum's suspicion was coming true: the whole world *was* going mad. 'As a matter of fact, Father –'

'I knew it! The Lord's grace is spreading by proxy.'

'What?'

'You know, like the flu. But it's all right, my son. We're all with you, aren't we boys.'

'Yes, Father,' said Christopher, putting his arm around my shoulder.

'You betcha, Father,' said MBF. 'We're with you, Blayno. Ha ha.'

'What's wrong with you, boy?' said Father to Matthew. 'Are you sick in the head?'

'His parents are taking him to a doctor, Father – we're all praying for him,' said I, sadly. 'Father, before we leave, will you bless us please?'

We knelt in front of Father Hagen and he blessed just the three of us, and I for one felt much better for it. I peeked around the vestry door and saw that the church was empty again. When I went to the external door and opened it a little I could hear nothing outside.

'Okay, let's go. See you tomorrow, Father.'

We opened the door. Nobody had left. They were standing outside, waiting silently, hundreds of them. I got my bike and the crowd parted for me. At the gate, a man with a big camera stepped out and took my picture. He tried to ask me something, but I was dazed, and just kept going. I wondered as I pedalled up Church Street if Mannix got the *Herald*.

At home things were tense. I wondered as soon as I walked through the door whether news of the Second Coming had reached Mum and Dad, because they were having a hard enough time getting used to the messiah who bought the farm two thousand years ago, let alone one who had taken up residence in the spare bedroom that overlooked Brougham Lane. I gave the inmates the Big Hello, to see what would they would do, and their response told me that, while something had happened to plunge the family into the kind of hypnotic trance, it wasn't anything I had done. And when you're thirteen that's all you need to know.

'What happened?'

'A bloke was found dead under the Church Street bridge – it was on the News – and they think Barney might have been involved,' said Granddad.

'Dad!' said Mum, angrily. 'What're you telling him that for?'

'Because he knows something about it, and I want to hear it straightaway.'

'Granddad, Barn was at Raffi's last night.'

'Sit down for a minute, boy. I want to ask you something.'

Mum was just a shade below explosion point. She'd had the luxury of living in her own house since she had been married, and probably not had a close-up look at Granddad in action since she was a kid, but I had – many times – and I knew something serious had happened, and that I had to help.

'Now, this is important, so I need to hear exactly what happened last night, not something Barney might have told you to say. Okay?'

I nodded, and looked at Mum, who was looking at Granddad as if she had just swallowed an ice-cream and it had gone straight to her forehead.

'I might have ducked out of Raffi's house for a few minutes.'

Granddad gave Mum the *What did I tell you?* look.

'I want all the details – don't miss anything. I've already heard Barney's bullshit version.'

'I got into Murphy's house –'

'How?' asked Mum.

'Picked the back door lock.'

Mum smacked her forehead like in the funny movies, except no one was laughing. 'Je-sus wept!'

Granddad looked at Mum, then back at me, and nodded for me to go on.

'And I found a list of names on the table. I copied the list into my notebook – there were twelve Yugoslav-sounding names – and put it back on the table. Granddad, I only did it because you didn't believe my theory about the person who kidnapped Mick.'

'Look, it's true that we're still looking for that person, but it turns out this is a much bigger issue for a lot of people, your Mr Sanderson being one of them. Those Yugoslavs on that list –'

'You can't tell him, Dad. If he knew who they were, it would put his life in danger.'

'One of them might have blown up … that car … the Turner boy.'

'That's enough, Dad!' Mum had raised her voice. I wondered if she was going to hit him – I'd never seen that before.

'I just want you to know that those people are bad, and Sanderson has known about them for a long time, so it's essential not to tell him anything about our family. Understand?'

'Yes, Granddad. But I thought Mr Sanderson –'

'I told you, he will always keep you safe, but it's best not to get in the way of those Yugoslav blokes. And I don't want anything to do with their squabbles. It's not our business. It's old bad blood left over from the War, that's what it is. Eventually, it will work itself out. Now, is that all that happened at Murphy's place? I need to know everything if I'm going to help Barney.'

'There was someone else staying in the house, in the spare bedroom. He had a briefcase with the initials *RB*. Murphy –'

'*Constable* Murphy,' said Mum, who was busting a gut trying to bring me up properly.

'Constable Murphy and Dutch Holland –'

'*Mister* Holland.'

'Mr Holland – came in suddenly and started talking. I hid behind the lounge, and heard Constable Murphy buy something from Mr Holland – it was a list of names and addresses. He said he was only interested in one name.'

'What was the name?'

'A lady called Irene Vukovic.'

'What?' Mum finally blew up like a land mine. 'Irene Vukovic? Are you sure that was the name?'

'Yes, Mum. I'm sure, because she was the only lady on the list – at least on the list I saw on the table – Constable Murphy was very interested in finding out what she was calling herself now – because she must have changed it – and where she lived. What he found out was that she just lived around the corner from him. Mum, you know what I reckon?'

'Shit!' said Mum with her teeth closed, which is what you do when what you mean is: 'I could just scream.' She was off with the fairies, the *bad* fairies.

30 Irene Vukovic

'Now there's a name from the past,' said Mum. 'She should still be in prison, Dad. What would her name be doing on any list, unless it was a list of traitors?'

'Vukovic's a pretty common name.'

'I'm calling Sanderson.'

'He won't tell you anything.'

'We'll see.'

Mum went to the phone and rang the Sandersons without even looking up their number on our phone index.

'Russell, Jean. What can you tell me about Irene Vukovic? I see, pardoned. And when did all this happen? And when were you going to tell me? Well, I'm concerned now, aren't I? Why hasn't she been picked up? I see. Well, as usual, I'm going to have to do everything myself, and I can, believe me. Just do me this one favour, tell me her alias and where I can find her. Oh really? I find that hard to believe.'

She put the phone down without saying goodbye. She had turned back into: *The Grey Statue!* I don't know who she was, just that she was no longer my mother.

And Granddad wasn't doing much better. He sat down and picked up Mick, who was getting restless, having sensed the tension, which you would only *not* sense if you were encased in concrete. I have noticed that men only pick up babies for one of two reasons: either they think it will earn them a few points with the little woman, or they think the little woman will not attack them as long as they are using the baby as a shield. A or B?

Suddenly Mum looked up at Granddad – she had been staring at me, as people had been doing a lot lately – and seemed to come to life with a bang.

'You knew about that woman!'

It was B.

'I've known since she got out: got a tip from a mate in the Force. They get informed of all the releases, and they pass 'em on to me. A man in my position has to know who's back on the street, and who's still tucked away cosily. I didn't think you needed to be bothered with it; I knew you'd get like this.'

'I'm not upset because she's out, Dad, even though I put her there – I read the papers. I know a lot of those traitors have been released – gutless bloody Menzies. I'm upset because she kidnapped my child, that's why. Now, what does she call herself – Sanderson says he doesn't know?'

'Maybe he's telling the truth.'

'I know he's telling the truth. If he knew, he'd have pulled her in by now, as a favour to me. He's lost her, but we'll find her.'

'Mum, I reckon –'

Mum copped me a backhander across the face that knocked me senseless for a second. I came to just as I hit the floor. It had been the break and enter that did it, I reckon – that'll do it every time. Still, I should have seen it coming.

'You were told not go near that bastard's house.'

I stayed lying on the floor. I was afraid of Mum's left, which was developing nicely from the fighting point of view.

'I know, but Brik was there, I know it.'

Mum looked at Granddad as if she was looking for blackheads. 'Dad, the truth now, is this the bloke they found under the bridge?'

'I think so.'

'Who the hell is he?'

'His name's Rollo Brik. He's Queenie's ex-husband, from the States.'

'And how does *he* – Get up from there and wash your face! – know who Brik is?'

I wiped my face and got a hand full of blood. I wasn't missing any of this. I went to the bathroom and splashed my face, and looked in the mirror. Mum's engagement ring had slashed me across the right cheek bone – it looked really cool. I would tell the kids at school I was attacked by some proddies for refusing to renounce my faith. We were always giving the protestants a hard time, and they were always giving us a hard time back – so it worked out about even.

As far as the *Mum versus Granddad* fight went, I hadn't missed a beat.

'He's known about Brik for ages – Queenie told him.'

'So what the hell does this Brik character have to do with *me*?'

'Not a thing, love, he's CIA. I heard a whisper that he was brought here to organise the Yugoslavs, you know, to hit the Commos.'

'You mean he works for Sanderson?'

'God knows. He probably decided to include Queenie in his Australian itinerary – you know, for old time's sake.'

'Dad, did you sic Barney onto this Brik bloke?'

'Didn't have to. A few of the local Painters and Dockers knew he was in town – you know, Commos – and I know one or two of them were soft on Queenie. Barney won't have to worry, but he's laying low for a little while, up at Seamus's place.'

The conversation ran out of petrol, as conversations about things that should not be talked about too loud tend to, and Granddad walked me up to the school, in silence.

At school, the crowd in the quadrangle was quiet and watchful, as if I might turn the water in the taps into wine at any tick of the clock. I found my mates in their usual spot, and they at least were friendly enough.

'Jeez, what's going on?'

'They've heard about the new miracles,' said Christopher Muldoon.

'What flamin' miracles? I don't know about any miracles.'

'One you do,' said CM. 'You know: Piglet's parents getting back together again. Father said that was a miracle.'

They all nodded. I looked over at the crowd Piglet always hung around with and he gave me a really big wave, as if he was trying to become airborne, and gave me his two-bob smile.

'Piglet seems happy; I wonder how long that'll last. But you said *miracles*. What was the other one?'

'When Mr Camponi woke up this morning, his piles were gone,' said Luigi. 'Mrs Camponi told Mum at Mass this morning.'

I groaned as loudly as I thought was seemly in a saint.

'Fellers, this is crazy. Look, you all know me, and I'm no more capable of working miracles than the rest of you – less capable, probably. Look at Muldoon here. How many billycarts has he smashed up? Thousands of the buggers. And not a scratch! *There's* your miracle. And how about Matthew? How he can get through a single day without getting thumped is a miracle, isn't it? Which reminds me –' And I fetched MBF a nice whack in the side of the head. 'Sorry, couldn't resist.'

'Ha ha, Blayney, what a killer,' said the laughing idiot.

'Look, this stuff just happens all the time. Next week, Piglet will have a new dad, and Mr Camponi will have a sore arse, Petronella Whatshername will be fishing through the bin looking for her callipers, and Tubby'll wish he'd gone to the Tech School.'

'Are you saying God can't work miracles?' said Christopher Muldoon.

I was unsure what to say to this. On the one hand, CM was slightly larger than me, and might dong me if I said that God was a fraud. On the other hand, if I said that God liked nothing better than a couple of miracles before brekky, I might be seen as a hard-core party member, which would only strengthen the case of the tub-thumpers. Then I had a brilliant idea.

'That's right, Christopher, my son, it's all just tricks, like Mandrake the Magician. I'm sorry to break it to you like this, but there it is. Now, if you want to hit me, I'm ready. Go ahead.'

'Gee Blayno, I'm not going to hit you. Looks like someone already did.'

And before I could stop myself I blurted out, 'Yeah, some bloody proddy crowd, trying to get me to renounce me faith – fat chance.'

'You, boy!'

It was Father Guinane, a particularly nasty specimen of Jesuit, a cross between an SS interrogator and a Doberman. He had materialised right behind me using his supernatural powers, as they do.

'Hello, Father.'

'Catholic boys do not say "proddy": they say "protestant". It's Blayney, isn't it?'

'Yes, Father – sorry Father.'

'Well, I hope you got in at least one good kick in the nuts for our side.'

'No, Father, they were holding me down.'

'I heard about what you did on the tram.'

'He rubbished Our Lord, Father.'

'Well done, young man. If St Ignatius had been on that tram he would have done the same thing. Now, go and see the nurse about that cut.'

When I got to class a Latin test was about to begin. I hadn't studied for it, so I got that horrible feeling like when you have to go to the toilet, only up in my stomach instead. This was going to be bad. Brother Gabriel's rule was: for every error you got one cut on the hand with a cane, sometimes on the legs and sometimes on the knuckles, which usually meant you couldn't write for the rest of the day. For some reason, Tubby Maculitis was always caned on the back of the head. Brother always reminded Tubby that it was going to hurt him more than it was going to hurt Tubby, which was hard to see, given that Tubby was always sick.

Brother Gabriel wrote the questions on the board as we watched in horror. While he was doing this, Freddo Fogg, who was sitting right behind me, passed me the answers. When Brother turned around and gave us the *Begin* command, I started writing like mad.

One by one we had to go up and hand in our paper and get our cuts. Only three people had a perfect score: Freddo Fogg, who always did, Christopher Muldoon, because he was practising for the seminary, and Yours Truly. When I went up, Brother Gabriel checked my paper, and looked over his glasses at the hushed crowd.

'*Vere miraculum!*'

Everybody took this as permission to laugh themselves silly. I kept my mouth shut. Later, I asked Freddo how he managed to know the answers before the questions were even on the board.

'I saw them on Brother's desk when I came in.' Freddo had a photographic memory. 'I guessed you hadn't studied for the test – you've got a lot on your plate, just now.'

This was a side to the holiness game I had not seen.

After school I went to the gate in The Vaucluse, as usual, to meet Mona, and there was a crowd of girls waiting for me. For the past few days, I had been avoiding the blessing-starved by sneaking across to the St Dominic's vestry and from there down the church aisle to the front entrance. This had worked quite well until Friday afternoon when, as we went to our lockers, I heard a whisper from Bow-wow Tunney, a very holy big kid who knew the church precincts like most kids know their comic collection, that some of my more hard-bitten fans from Vaucluse College For The Weaker Sex – that's what Barney calls them (it's a joke, I think) – had worked out my little game, and sealed off all the exits, like some kind of commando company. I therefore found myself face to face with them, stronger sex to weaker sex, as you might say.

It turned out that a lot of the girls were carrying small bunches of flowers, which they put at my feet, in silence. One or two of them thrust creamy-paged autograph books at me, so I signed, *God bless you. TB*. At the back of this huge throng was a dark blue MG with two beautiful Italian girls in it, both waving, like a couple of Gina Lollabrigidas. Behind them, standing along the outer wall of the College stood a line of nuns with their hands hidden up their sleeves. I hoped they weren't armed – nuns can strike viciously when provoked.

I turned around and discovered that I had about two hundred black and red boys behind me, looking like half an Essendon vs Richmond footy crowd. Behind them were some of the brothers. They looked relaxed, and were chatting among themselves. It's hard to surprise a De La Salle brother. They must make them watch a lot of AO movies during their training.

As I stood there I wondered where it all was heading. I couldn't see anything good coming out of it, especially as none of the members of my family had ever been holy types. For the second time that week I prepared to give the crowd my special blessing. At that moment a little girl pushed her way through the crowd holding a couple of leg braces aloft, like the Olympic bloody torch. This was the Petronella creature I had been warned about. She stopped in front of me and showed them to the dumbfounded mob, then placed them at my feet with the flowers. She was crying quite openly – I knew how she felt.

The crowd, including the boys behind me, started clapping and cheering, as if they'd lost their minds. I had to get across the road and into Lucky's passenger seat, and underneath Mona's warm bottom as soon as possible. God help me, I wasn't asking for much.

'In nomine Patris, et Filii, et Spiritus Sancti. Amen.'

You'd think the girls would make a path for me, like in the movies, but no. And as I pushed through the warm, stirring throng I made a mental note to scratch the priesthood off my career fixture, which left only the saxophone.

Mona, who appeared not to have noticed anything unusual, smoothly hopped out while I inserted myself into the sports car, and we were off. I had often wondered what it would be like to be a circus performer; now I knew.

Once we were under way Mona wanted to have a private conversation with me, which isn't all that easy in a sports car, but she managed.

'Why did you go to Tina's house yesterday?'

'To tell Tina that Raffi was in love with her, because Raffi was worried that with all this holiness stuff, Tina might start liking me.'

'And did you tell her?'

'Yes'

'Good.'

And that was that.

We went back to Carlton for coffee and cake, and when Mona went to have a close-up look at the cake display, I scanned the street for Barney, though I couldn't see him.

'Looking for your minder?' said Lucky.

'Yes.'

I knew that Barn was laying low, but I also knew that he would willingly give that up if he had to keep an eye out for me.

'It's my turn tonight, that's if you don't mind having a female bodyguard.'

'Course not.'

'So, how did all this miracle business start?'

'A kid at school passed a Latin test after I prayed for him. Now they're saying I cured a mentally retarded kid.'

'Why did you pray for him?'

'He paid me sixpence – that was the going rate that day.'

'Mr Blayney!'

'I put half in the poor-box – Brother Gabriel thought that was fair.'

'How do you feel about all of this?'

'Well, I was much better off when I could get around secretly, if you know what I mean.'

'Oh, I know exactly what you mean.'

'Holiness is hard yakka.'

'Of course it is, Mr Blayney. That's why so few of us are holy.'

'Mona seems to be all right about it, though.'

'Mr Blayney, that is the most naive statement I have ever heard. Of course, she's all right about it. The girls in her class see her sitting on the Chosen One's lap in a top-down sports car, and they think: *What's she got that I haven't got?* But I suspect you already know the answer to that, don't you?'

I nodded, wondering where the hell the coffee had got to.

'Well, don't worry, it'll all wear off as soon as the miracles dry up. A saint's only as hot as his last miracle.' She winked. 'Then you can get back to being just plain old Mr Blayney, except I don't think you'll ever be plain, and neither does Mona.'

When they dropped me off, I found that there was nobody home. And just seconds later, the phone rang. It was Mrs Williams.

'Your friend Raffi is worried about you. I told him that if you come straight over, I'll ring the people who are looking after him for me, and tell them to take him home. How does that sound?'

'I don't believe you.'

'Then hang up the phone and wait.'

In just seconds it rang again. This time it was Raffi.

'They were waiting for me at my place. They took me to a house somewhere, but I don't know where. They —'

The call was cut off. The phone rang again.

'Come to my house straight away, alone. If anyone follows you, your friend will never go home. And no phone calls.' She hung up.

This time the Dread got right into my bladder, and I almost pissed myself. I tried to call Barney, but the phone was dead. I chucked a quick pee, then came back and got a red pencil out of my bag and wrote on the wall where it couldn't be missed: *IV is Mrs Williams, 59 Munro St, Cremorne, next door to the Fosters. She has Raffi. I am going to save him.* Underneath, I wrote the time.

I rode down to Church Motors, looking for Barney, but he wasn't there, and neither was his car. So I rode down to Elm Grove to see if Dad was at Mrs Bentley's place, but he wasn't. I kept going

352

to the far end, then took a long and twisted route down a lot of lanes and side streets to the Sandersons' place, arriving at their back door via Kipling Lane. Mrs Sanderson was home.

'I need to speak to Mr Sanderson on the phone. It's an emergency.'

'Why don't you —'

'I can't explain. It's an *emergency*.'

'What shall I say to him?'

'Mr S, I'm trying to save Raffi's life.'

She rang her husband's office.

'Hello, Russell?'

I grabbed the phone from her. 'Raffi Radion has been kidnapped by Irene Vukovic. She says if I don't go to her house right now, she'll have him killed. She is living at 59 Munro Street under the name Williams, but I think you know that already. I'm going there now. Please come.'

Mrs Sanderson grabbed hold of me and tried to stop me leaving, but I tore myself free, having had the benefit of a daily helping of Kellogg's Corn Flakes and Vegemite on toast (thick-sliced). She grabbed at the phone, but Mr S was gone. I didn't know how this was going to work, only that it was me who was going to do what had to be done.

I decided to walk to Munro Street, to stall for time. I was hoping my brain would come up with the goods. But my brain had gone on holidays.

31 Kansas

At the Williams house I was met at the door by Mrs Williams, who opened the door and pulled me in. At the same time, someone grabbed me from behind and put something over my face. I heard a loud ringing sound, and I could have sworn I was having my nightmare all over again.

As I began to wake up, a lot of odd thoughts went through my mind, meaningless waves, sounds and ideas that I couldn't have cared less about. There was a bright light in front of me. It came and went. Finally it came and stayed. My body was freezing, and I was shivering. Somebody wrapped me in a blanket. I suddenly vomited a few times, and felt better. Somewhere someone was crying. It sounded like me. I made a little moan, to check. No, it was someone else.

After a while I was completely awake. I was lying on the cold ground in a dark place, wrapped in a blanket, and near me was a hurricane lamp. Beside the lamp Mrs Williams was sitting, and behind her, in the greyness, was a man. There was movement beside me, and I turned to see Raffi, staring at me. He was wrapped in a blanket, and seemed to be petrified.

'Hello, boys. I want you to appreciate your position, and what's going to happen to you, because I want you to be very frightened for as long as you're alive, which I hope will be for a fair while.

Raffi, I don't really know you, so all I can say is thank you for being so helpful. Now, Blayney, my name is Irene Vukovic. I've been planning ways to hurt your family for a few years now – I thought the house fire was a nice touch, didn't you? – and this will be the end of it, because all I wanted was revenge, plus a little bit of satisfaction for my family's trouble: small price for years of prison, rape and torture. When I'm finished, your mother will no longer be your mother. She will wish it was her who was dead. And yet she will continue to live. Can't say fairer than that now, can I?

So, here's what's going to happen. You two are going to die of starvation – I know, it's horrible isn't it? There's lots water down here. See? Over there, a big pond. And there are rats too, I've seen a few. So you might have a go at eating them when you get hungry. Or maybe they'll eat you – who knows? And if you want to yell for help, go ahead. I know how far we are below the ground. What a wonderful place, and marked so clearly on your map, too. I'm going to leave the lamp for you, so that you can have a good look around, and see just what kind of place you're going to die in. I have nothing personal against you two – just your mother, Blayney. Bye-bye.'

She left, taking the man with her, and they disappeared down a tunnel, using a torch to light their way.

For a few seconds there was a rumbling sound, then a distinct breeze. I was afraid that we were in a water drain, and that water was coming. The I realised that it was the sound of a train nearby, and that we were near an underground railway station, and that station was Eden Park.

I tried to sit up, but it wasn't easy, as the Dread had got me by the balls, and my guts were full of molten lead. Also, I discovered that I was tethered by a long chain to some object off in the dark somewhere.

'Sorry,' said Raffi. 'Are you all right? I thought you were dead when they brought you down here.' He sounded as though he was an inch from crying like a baby. 'What happened to you, did you have a seizure?'

'Hi, Raffi. What a couple of nutsos, eh? No, I'm all right. We'll get out, don't worry. This is my world down here. Then they'll be laughing on the other side of their faces.' I had a sudden thought. 'You know, down here folks call me: *The Ferret! Yes, the Ferret, who gets kidnapped by crazy Yugoslavs, and imprisoned in their underground lair, and who, with his faithful companion, Rabbit Boy –*'

'Be serious.'

'Sorry. Didn't you like the 'Rabbit Boy' touch?'

'No.'

'How did *you* get down here?'

'They were waiting for me in our house when I got home from school. They grabbed me and asked me about the drains and tunnels. They said they'd kill Mum if I didn't tell them, so I did. I told them everything you told me. They found the map and had a look at it. Then they took me down to our underground hideout, and they asked me where the big drain went. And I remembered what you told me about Keith Kavanagh, that his old man and him were hiding up the end of the tunnel, under the station. So they brought me up the big drain to this place. Is this the place you were talking about last summer?'

'Yeah, it's actually near an old abandoned wartime station called Kansas. It's where all the yanks used to get off, instead of Flinders Street – Mum told me. It's underneath Eden Hill Station. That's what she meant when she said it was a long way below the ground. It is.' I felt the chain on my leg.

'I'm sorry. They didn't say what they were going to do. They didn't say anything about kidnapping anyone.'

'Nothing to be sorry about; people can be bastards.'

'So how did they get *you*?'

'They told me they'd let you go if I handed myself over, and I couldn't see why they'd want to keep you, so I did.'

'They kept me so I wouldn't tell, I s'pose.'

'Yeah, s'pose. I told Mr Sanderson on the phone that I was going over to their house, you know, to save you. I reckon he would have gone over there, but missed them.'

'As if they'd wait for him to turn up.'

'Yes, your average kidnapper is a restless creature, Radion, and likes to keep on the move. My guess is they got out of there as soon as they grabbed me.'

'So, who knows where we are, then?'

'No one. But don't worry, Mr Sanderson'll be chuckin' a wobbly right about now, 'n' so will Granddad when he finds out, you watch. This Vukovic woman hasn't got a chance. Hey, this is a pretty long chain.'

'Yeah, I've got one, too; it'll reach that big pond over there. That's what she meant when she said we'd have lots of water. How long will it take us to die of starvation?'

'If we don't eat any rats, probably a couple of weeks. Or, if the rats taste yummy, prob'ly years.'

'Terrific.'

'Or, if the rats eat *us*, I'm thinkin' a couple of days.'

'Well, as long as we have the light, let's see if we can find anything to break these chains.'

'While they were waiting for you to wake up, they moved a lot of bits and pieces of junk away from us.'

Raffi was right: there was nothing, and we were chained to a big steel wheel on a large piece of machinery. We tried to turn the wheel, but it was too old.

'What happens when the lamp goes out?'

'Well, I've never been down here in pitch dark; but at least we know where everything is.'

'I'm hungry.'

'You know, the last time I was down here, Keith Kavanagh was down here with his old man, hiding out. We had eggs and bacon together. Mmm, eggs and bacon.'

'Shut up!'

'It's all right, Raff; I can flip your eggs over, if you like.'

'You can stick your eggs up your arse.'

'Got it: no eggs; but you'll be sorry.'

Raffi was crying. 'What if I have a seizure?'

'You would have to say that.'

'I'm frightened. Mum will be crying, and I can't stand that. And I'm scared.'

'No need to be scared, Raff. My Mum's going to turn into a space monster when she finds out. And then there's Barney; he thinks I'm the bee's knees. Once he gets to work, he'll be like Audie Murphy. I reckon he's probably making enquiries all over Richmond right now, while we sit here enjoying ourselves. And how about Mona's Aunty Lucky? She'll tell her Cousin Vinnie, and he'll get all the Italians in Richmond on the job. Nothin' gets past them, you know: we're talking Mafia.'

'How long do you think it'll take them?'

'I'd give it a few hours. By tomorrow, we'll be home and hosed. In the meantime, how's your chain – comfy, is it? I don't like to show off, but mine's a lovely fit.'

'What happened?'

'You fell asleep.'

'The light's out.' Raffi's voice was shaky and he was starting to groan for no reason. I had seen it before, in the movies: battle fatigue. In just a matter of minutes we'd have nothing but rats to talk to.

'I'm frightened of the dark.'

'Then this is your lucky day, as I was born unafraid of the dark. That's right, that's what I said: unafraid. I'll give you lessons. It won't be long before you're laughing. My God, Radion, I can't believe how bloody lucky you are.'

'What everyone says about you's right: you're sick in the head.'

'I used to be healthy in the head – once.'

'Hell, I'm sorry – you're not –'

'Yes, I am, Raffi my son, we both are. But it's okay, we understand each other, even if no one else does.'

The rats walked all over us. I swear they were as big as Volkswagens. We discovered that if we stayed still they just walked on us gently – I think they liked us because we were warm. Some of them stayed, and we tried to talk to them, as if they were puppies. You could stroke them and pat them. My favourite was called Matthew. He was one of your happier rats. Raffi's favourite was called Dazza because that's what the kid's called the local bully, who was real bastard, and deserved to have a rat named after him, though I thought it was a bit rough on the rat. But if you moved suddenly, they nipped, and that hurt like hell. And you couldn't help moving suddenly every now and then, because there were bugs down there that liked to bite, whether you moved or not.

At first we talked a lot, then the silences got longer. Most of the time, we let each other sleep, but sometimes we didn't give a stuff.

'Why'd you take Judy Pickle around to Matthew's and Eddie's houses?'

'I was trying to get rid of her. I was hoping she might like one of them.'

'She acts like one of us, but really, she's just like all the other girls, 'cept she doesn't like pink.'

'No, but I think you'll find her brother, Lex, is partial to the stuff.'

'But just a minute, if you love her, why were you trying to get rid of her?'

'I don't love her, but Peanut does, but he won't do anything about it. Mum's got a photo of me and Judy and Peanut in a playpen together when we were babies. Judy is looking at Peanut very hungrily.'

'She kissed me.'

This was news, *big* news. 'What, you mean a little peck on the cheek?'

'No, on the gob. She just grabbed me and kissed me.'

'Did she taste like medicine?'

'Ye-ah!'

'She always tastes like that. You know, I call her *The Green Vegetable!*'

'Hey, you've got Dazza the Rat, haven't you? You lucky bugger. D'ya wanna swap for Matthew? He's such a lovely little feller. Come on, ya know ya wanna.'

'All right, here y'are.'

'Tricked ya, Radion! Matthew the Rat's been nothin' but a pain in the arse since we got here. Ha ha.'

'Hey, can you go blind from being in the dark for a long time, because I think I've gone blind?'

'No, Raffi, you can't … I think.'

'You think. Great.'

'Hey Raff, are you bored?'

'I'm only bored to tears. How about you?'

'Same. Why don't we have a chain rattling contest. Winner shouts the other to the pictures.'

'Why don't we have a bullshit contest?'

'Oh no you don't, Radion. I didn't just get off the boat.'

'They should call me Bullshit Boy.'

'Believe me, young Raffi, they do.'

'I was really looking forward to kissing Josephine Thompson, you know; I hadn't got around to that.' A thought struck me. 'Hey, I could do it in Heaven.'

'So you *are* going to Heaven, then.'

'We both are.'

'Ye-ah. But, hey, by the time she gets there she'll be an old bat.'

'Thanks for buggering up my day, Radion.'

'Sorry. Hey, maybe she'll get hit by a bus on the way home from school, and meet us up there.'

'What d'ya mean *us*'?

'I mean, you never know your luck.'

'With my luck, Mona would get hit by the same flamin' bus.'

'Yeah, with your luck.'

'September.' My mind had started up suddenly, and made my mouth talk.

'What?'

'It's September. That's when Tom died.'

'I didn't know that.'

'It was spring. There were lots of flowers everywhere, you know, in the park.' Raffi waited. 'Last Spring I wanted to go to the place where he died, and say ... I dunno, something ... but I couldn't do it. I couldn't even look at it. I still can't. You can see the spot where he died from Eddie's window, you know.'

'Fair dinkum?'

'Yeah. Did y'see that telescope, the one Eddie said was his mum's? It was pointing to the exact spot. She knew, she always knew.'

'How would she know?'

'I dunno, but everyone knew. Maybe she found out from Mrs Foster.' There was no response. In the dense blackness, as if it was the inside of a picture theatre, I saw Mrs Foster. 'I like Mrs Foster.'

'Why?'

I thought about it; everything we said was important.

'She was a rebel.'

'Do you think Eddie did this to us?'

'Knock, knock.'

'Who there?'

'What d'ya bloody mean: *Who's there?*'

I couldn't stop moaning, and Raffi couldn't stop crying. I got up close to him and hugged him, and felt him hug me back.

'Don't be frightened, dear', I said to him the way his mother talked to him. 'It's all right, Raffi. There, there, Raffi dear.'

Raffi tried to soothe me too, though I have to say that he was no Olympic-class soother. I think that could be because he had never seen anyone talk to me nicely, except Mrs Sanderson, and I didn't blame him for not being able to do a Mrs Sanderson imitation. He didn't have what it takes.

When we got thirsty, we had stormwater to burn, though it tasted awful. When we had to go the toilet, we got as far our chains would let us in opposite directions.

'Jesus Christ, what in God's name have you been eating?'

We were always saying that.

We thought we'd count the days by counting our sleeps, but we kept napping, instead of sleeping, so in the end, we didn't really know how long it was. We reckoned a week, but fair dinkum, we didn't have a clue. Finally, we just settled down to doing what boys do when they're trapped underground and their lives are at an end: we spilled our guts.

'Lucky Martello.'

'Nine.'

'Nine!'

'All right, ten.'

'That's better.'

'I loved being holy: it felt real. I didn't want it to stop, though I told everyone I did. I've never been holy before. I've actually been pretty bad, as you know.'

'Yeah, I know what you mean. I loved going to Mass. One time I went to Communion. I know you told me not to, but I wanted to see if I could get away with it. It stuck to the roof of my mouth. I don't know what you see in it. Hey, got any miracles left?'

'Sorry: ran out. I can do you a blessing cheap, but.'

'You'd charge your own flesh and blood.'

'Just joking. Hey, how about this –' I reached into my pocket and pulled out the rosary beads Father Sheehan had given me, and which I'd been carrying every day, out of respect for him. I handed it to Raffi. I heard him feeling it in the dark.

'What is it?'

'Rosary beads. They have magical properties. In the back of the crucifix is a little capsule of Lourdes water. Whoever possesses it will survive this ordeal.'

'And you want me to have it?'

I made my mind up. 'Yes, Raff. I'm protected by another man on a cross – at least I hope I am.'

'Who?'

'He hasn't got a name. Folks down here call him: the Hanged Man!'

'You made that up.'

'I wish I had, Raffi, old son, but I didn't.'

'Thanks for the beads; I'll never let go of them; and if I die first, take them back. Ten-four?'

'Ten-four.'

'Hey, you know James's sister, Veronica? She kissed me, on the gob.'

'Last time you told this story it was on the cheek.'

'She kissed me again.'

'Bull.'

'No, true dinks. It happened that day we went over to James's place.'

'Oh my God, and I thought you wanted to play trains.'

'It wasn't planned. It was an ambush.'

'Yeah, that's what Judy Pickle did to me. But Mona'll still kill you.'

'Not unless you tell her.'

'What's it worth?'

'What? That's it, you can talk to yourself from now on.'

'I wanted to see Tina's boobs, that's all I wanted. That's not asking too much is it?'

'Yes.'

'Hey, you know when that orangutan grabbed you at the Circus?'

'Yeah, what about it?' I didn't like where this was going.

'I bet you were packin' death.'

'Yes I was, if you want to know. Rufus has quite a manly grip.'

'*Rufus has quite a manly grip*! I'll give you *quite a manly grip* in a minute, Blayney.'

'I wanted to save you. She said she'd let you go if I handed myself over.'

'And you believed her.'

'No, but I knew I had to do it.'

'Why?'

'Because it was you.'

'Thanks, but I don't get it: now we're both down here.'

'It was on the cards.'

'What was Tom like?'

'He was bold as brass, that's what Granddad always said.'

'I remember that time I met you at the Baths, Tom was acting pretty tough.'

'He was just havin' a lend of you. He wasn't tough at all, he was like me, only sillier. He was as silly as a two-bob watch.' I laughed, and immediately regretted it. Something was wrong with me.

'I wish I knew him.'

'Soon you will, I s'pose. You know, we knew all the little things that made us different, and we could pretend that we were each other, and no one could tell we were doing it, not even Mum. After he died, I pretended to be him, so that he'd be back again. And one day, I even forgot I was me completely.'

'Then how do I know you're not really Tom.'

I had to think about that for a few minutes, because my brain had slowed down.

'You don't. You'll have to take my word for it.'

'No way. You're the biggest bullshit artist I've ever met.'

'The real Tom had a secret tattoo that he got in the Bengali jungle, when he was living with the Bandar pygmy people. I haven't got it.'

'Fair enough.'

'How does Superman fly, d'ya reckon?'

'Fuck knows.'

Eventually, we got *trés, trés* crook, as the Froggies say.

32 The living dead

I felt light that looked like nothing in my eyes, and hands all around me. I felt words that meant nothing to me. I heard the chains grate and rattle, as usual. Next to my chest Matthew nestled. All I had left was the wish to die, and stop the sickness.

I slowly got my senses back and found that I was in bed, and a nurse was stroking my hair. We smiled at each other, and she held my hand. Then I realised with a bang that I was not in Heaven, and I was not going to get to be with Tom. I didn't know whether I'd been short-changed or what.

'Look,' said the nurse, and pointed to the next bed.

It was Raffi, and he was looking at me with hollowed out, dark eyes, like the kind of Raffi you would see in a horror movie about a bloke who wanders around in the fog, eating people. When he smiled I almost cried, he looked so sick. But he kept on smiling. And after a while, when I realised that I probably looked the same, I smiled back. He reached out his hand to me, the way he did in the darkness, and I did the same, automatically, because that's the way we had lived – us and the rats. I saw that our skinny arms were full of tubes and needles, and bottles of stuff, and I guessed that they were replacing all the dirty water we drank with clean water.

Our skin was covered with Band-Aids and patches and spots, as though we'd stepped on a Band-Aid mine.

'What happened to our skin?' The whispered words choked in my throat.

'Doctor will look in on you shortly. Would you like some water?'

I had a drink, and felt better straight away.

'You've lost a lot of fluids and we're just making them up.'

Raffi's mother came in and saw that I was awake. She came to me and kissed me and gave me a hug.

'I'm glad you're back in the land of the living. How do you feel?'

'Wouldn't be dead for quids, Mrs Radion.'

'Good boy. Nurse, why don't we get these two beds closer together for a while?'

'It's not allowed.'

'They're brothers.'

'Not according to our records.'

'Tell you what, you go out for a minute and I'll do it, then you come back after a few minutes and tell me off, how's that, eh?'

The nurse went out, and Mrs R quickly pushed my bed over to Raffi's, allowing us to join hands. Neither of us spoke, because we had said everything to each other that two thirteen-year old boys can possibly say when they know no one is ever going to hear them speak again. We would have to wait until something new happened to us, so that we could talk about it.

After a while a couple of doctors came in and looked at their notes. A matron also came in, and chucked a seven on the spot.

'Nurse, why are these beds together?'

'So the boys can touch each other, Matron.'

'Get them back the way they were immediately! Patients do not touch each other.'

Mrs Radion whispered something in the matron's ear, and she turned three different colours at once.

'You're disgusting!' she spat.

The head doctor came to life like a ventriloquist dummy. 'Your boys are severely malnourished and have typhus, though they'll recover,' he said, without even looking at Mrs Radion. 'The proper authorities will want to know how they got into this state, but that's not my domain. Good day.' Then he looked up for the first time. 'Oh, Matron, please push these two closer to each other. They obviously want to be together.' He waited until it had been done.

Mum came in and went straight up to me and kissed me and tried to brush my hair back.

'Oh God, I'm sorry I didn't take better care you.'

I tried to whisper but my throat still wouldn't work.

'He just needs a sip of water, Mrs Blayney.'

Mum helped me sit up a bit, and gave me some water. While I was sipping, Mum spoke to Raffi's mum.

'Hello, Val.'

'Hello, Jean.'

They weren't giving much away.

'Hello, Mum, how's Mick?'

'His usual self.'

'And Dad and Granddad?'

'They're all right.'

I had another sip. 'Did you catch 'em, Mum?'

'They're behind bars.'

'She said she was gunna starve us to death. We had a good old laugh at that, didn't we Raff?'

'Yeah, we laughed ourselves silly, Mrs Blayney,' said Raffi, getting back up to speed like Stirling Moss, but with a very frightening smile on his face. I took one look at him trying to laugh, and started crying straight away.

'That's enough,' said the nurse.

Raffi and I grabbed each other's held hands as hard as we could.

'No!' he rasped.

We all fell silent. I don't know about the others, but Raffi and I were prepared to stay that way for good.

I had spent all my energy fighting the guards, and nodded off. When I woke up, Mum and Mrs Radion had gone and Dad was there, holding my hand. His hand was warm and soft, though I knew he was very strong and had been a tankie in the War.

'G'day.'

'G'day, Dad. Can I have some water? Ta. Are you still living at home?'

'Today I am.'

'Like that, is it?'

He nodded.

'Dad, how did you find us?'

'After a week we got a letter from that mad bitch telling us how she'd buried you two alive where we wouldn't find you until it was too late. Sanderson had a few ideas that we weren't allowed to know about, but they turned out to be fizzers. Then Daphne remembered the stories Keith had told her about staying in the tunnels with his father before he shot thought to Russia. Apparently you knew all about it. So she had him brought down from Wodonga. The police looked through miles of drains and tunnels, and eventually, there you were. They reckon they must have looked in that old station a dozen times before Keith remembered how to get to the old branch line tunnel.'

'He's not too bright, the old Flame Boy.'

'Flame Boy, is that what you call him?'

'Yeah. Dad, Keith didn't burn our house down – that Vukovic woman did it, she said so. Is Keith safe?'

'Yes, he's back home in Wodonga. He risked his life to come back, and then to go down there with the police. The police thought they were looking for bodies, but he wouldn't have a bar of it.'

Suddenly, the nurse who had been taking our temperatures and pulses decided that we'd had enough, and Dad was told to leave.

'Just be a minute,' said Dad. He went around to Raffi's bed and sat down between us.

'Raffi, I understand you know who I am.'

'You're my real dad.'

'Yeah. I'm sorry for everything. We'll see a lot more of each other from now on, if that's okay with you.'

'Yeah, that'd be terrific, wouldn't it?' he said to me.

'Yeah, bewdy, Dad.'

'Okay, then. These comics are for you both.'

He had brought in a stack of comics, which we ended up having to read in short bursts, because our eyes were hurting, but we didn't mind.

'Thanks, Mr, um, Dad.'

Dad ruffled his hair, and it seemed to spring back into place, though not as quickly as usual.

Next day they let Granddad and Raffi's nanna come in. Raffi's nanna turned out to be his mum's mum, if you see what I mean, and I took a good hard look at her, to see if she looked like a Blayney, but she didn't. She came over to say hello and pat my hand, though, which I thought was very nice, considering that her daughter had gone off my Dad. Granddad paid no attention to her, as he was a man of few words, like Robert Mitchum.

'Granddad, what happened to the Will – the Vukovics?'

'Put away, this time for good

'Sorry, time's up,' said the nurse. 'We have another visitor. It'll be better tomorrow.'

The oldies were bundled out, with Granddad pretending that he was the kind of person you could bundle, and a replacement relay runner came in, like with the Olympic torch. I was expecting Mona, or one of the boys, maybe Charlie, who was always worrying about me. But I nearly fell over backwards when I saw who it was.

Veronica Palmer walked in very nervously, like a black and white cat, and looked at Raffi and me very hard, as if she was confused – she had never seen the old Raff before – it's always a shock for new players – then slowly came over and sat down beside my bed. She looked like the angel I had hoped to meet in Heaven, and on the Blayney Scale of Beautiful Girls and Women, I thought I might promote her to ten. She smiled at me – sadly, I thought – and I smiled back, just a bit; I didn't want to overdo the famous Blayney charm, as it's dangerous in the wrong hands. Also, I still didn't know where I stood with her. Then I realised that she might be with her mum, alias Wonder Woman, or worse, her dad, and had a quick look at the door. There I saw James, waving at us both, and gave him a little smile.

I waited for a long time. Finally, Veronica seemed to remember something.

'Hello.'

'Hello.'

She held my hand, and ran her fingers over the Band-Aids and spots, because they were all over the place. Then she seemed to notice that they were all over all the rest of me as well, even my face.

'What happened to you?'

'Rats.'

She pressed her eyes shut and shook her head. She sat for a few minutes in silence, while her hands slowly warmed up.

'I prayed for you – well, everyone did – but I prayed for you out loud, at night when I was alone in my room, on my knees. I didn't know your friend, but I prayed for him, too.' She glanced at Raffi, who was straining to catch every word, you know, so he could take the piss out of me later. 'You didn't tell me you were famous; it was in the paper – you know, about the miracles. Father Hagen offered a Mass for you every day.' She looked down – she was beautiful just then, more beautiful than JT and Tuesday Weld – then looked up at me. 'I told God that if he saved you I would become a nun. Then, when they found you I went straight to Confession and told Father I had lied to God to get you back.' She blushed and put a hand to her face for a second. I couldn't have been more fascinated if she had produced a clarinet and taken a deep breath. 'But Father said you couldn't lie to God, so it was all right. But it's a handy thing to know, isn't it?'

While the lovely VP was unburdening her soul, not unlike Audrey Hepburn in *The Nun's Story*, I kept my mouth shut, as this is something which, I had learned from my adventures with Mona and Sunny, tends to grease the wheels with the so-called weaker sex. And I saw for the first time that the Veronica's heart was pure and simple, especially simple, which is how the Mazemaster likes his girls' hearts to be.

When James gave her a loud whisper from the door, she looked at Raffi, nervously, then got up and leaned over me, and kissed me on the cheek, just as she had at her house the very first time. I smelled musk stick.

'We have to go, but I'll come back.'

I noticed she wasn't in her school uniform, which allowed her to be shaped more like a girl.

'Is it the weekend?'

'No, it's the holidays.' She put a sealed envelope in my hand. 'This for you to read later.'

Suddenly she seemed to decide, and kissed me again, only this time on the lips, like a butterfly landing on a leaf, and resting. Then she gave Raffi a polite wave, and left. I looked at the envelope. On the front it said: *Terry Blayney*, and on the back: *S.W.A.L.K.*

Acknowledgements

Many thanks to the following for their help during the writing of this novel.

My fabulous sister, Kate Twohig, for illustrating and designing the cover and for drawing the Mazemaster's Map of Mystery.

Ann Parry for her reading of the book and editorial work and for her helpful comments.

The amazing Gary 'Gazza' Searson, for help with software problems.

My wonderful agent, Lyn Tranter, and to all at Australian Literary Management for their reading and feedback.

Also by Peter Twohig

THE

CARTOGRAPHER

If … you enjoyed Safran Foer's *Extremely Loud and Incredibly Close*, you are going to want to read this book.'
Bookseller + Publisher

Melbourne, 1959. An eleven-year old boy watches as a murder is committed in a strange house. Just one year before, he had looked on helplessly as his identical twin, Tom, suffered a violent death. God, who he no longer counts as a friend, has a pretty sick sense of humour.

Having been seen by the murderer, he is now a kid on the run, and takes refuge in the dark drains and dangerous drains tunnels beneath the city, recreating himself as a series of superheroes and creating a remarkable map to help him avoid the bad bastard he has locked eyes with. His only protectors are his very shady grandfather, a professional standover man, and an incongruous neighbourhood couple who intervene in a very unexpected way.

A captivating novel bristling with outrageous wit about a tragic figure in a rotten place who refuses to give in, and the crowd of shifty, dodgy and downright malicious bastards he has to match wits with on his extraordinary journey. *The Cartographer* is a fresh, poignant and deeply touching novel that you will never forget.

The second book in the Richmond trilogy

THE

TORCH

Not since *The Curious Incident of the Dog in the Night-time* has there been such a compelling child narrator'
Herald Sun

Melbourne, 1960. Mrs Blayney and her twelve year old son, aka 'the kid', live in Richmond. At least, they did, until their house burnt down. The prime suspect – one Keith Aloysius Gonzaga Kavanagh, also aged 12 – has mysteriously disappeared. Our narrator, the kid, sets off on a covert mission to find young Keith, who he privately dubs 'Flame Boy', to save him from the small army of irate locals – not to mention Mrs Blayney – who want to see him put away.

Flame Boy has not only made himself scarce, but he's disappeared with a very important brief case of secrets, which the kid is keen to get hold of for his grandfather, a shady character, who's got some secrets of his own. But the kid has got a lot going on: he's also organising a new gang of kids; coping with the ups and downs of having a girl-friend; trying to avoid Keith's dangerous prison-escapee father, Fergus Kavanagh, also an arsonist, who is suspected of selling secrets to the Russians; and all the while dreaming of the most covetable item in the world: the Melbourne Olympic Torch.

A madcap and irresistibly fun novel about loss, discovery and living life to the full, The Torch is a little ripper of a ride.

www.ingramcontent.com/pod-product-compliance
Lightning Source LLC
Chambersburg PA
CBHW022243020726
47496CB00004B/1033